★ THE SONS OF ★
LIBERTY
DEATH AND TAXES

★ THE SONS OF ★
LIBERTY
DEATH AND TAXES

CREATED AND WRITTEN BY **ALEXANDER LAGOS** AND **JOSEPH LAGOS**

ART BY **STEVE WALKER**   COLOR BY **OREN KRAMEK**

LETTERS BY **CHRIS DICKEY**

Random House 🏠 New York

This is a work of fiction. All incidents and dialogue, and all characters with the exception of some well-known historical and public figures, are products of the authors' imagination and are not to be construed as real. Where real-life historical or public figures appear, the situations, incidents, and dialogues concerning those persons are fictional and are not intended to depict actual events or to change the fictional nature of the work. In all other respects, any resemblance to persons living or dead is entirely coincidental.

Cover illustration by Steve Walker and Oren Kramek

 Published in the United States by Random House Children's Books, a division of Random House, Inc., New York.

Random House and the colophon are registered trademarks of Random House, Inc.

Visit us on the Web! www.randomhouse.com/teens
thesonsoflibertybooks.com

Educators and librarians, for a variety of teaching tools, visit us at
www.randomhouse.com/teachers

Library of Congress Cataloging-in-Publication Data is available upon request.
ISBN 978-0-375-85671-6 (trade hardcover)
ISBN 978-0-375-85668-6 (trade pbk.)
ISBN 978-0-375-95668-3 (lib. bdg.)

MANUFACTURED IN CHINA
10 9 8 7 6 5 4 3 2 1
First Edition

Random House Children's Books supports the First Amendment
and celebrates the right to read.

This book is dedicated to Mr. Cal Hunter . . .
and the Grand Design.

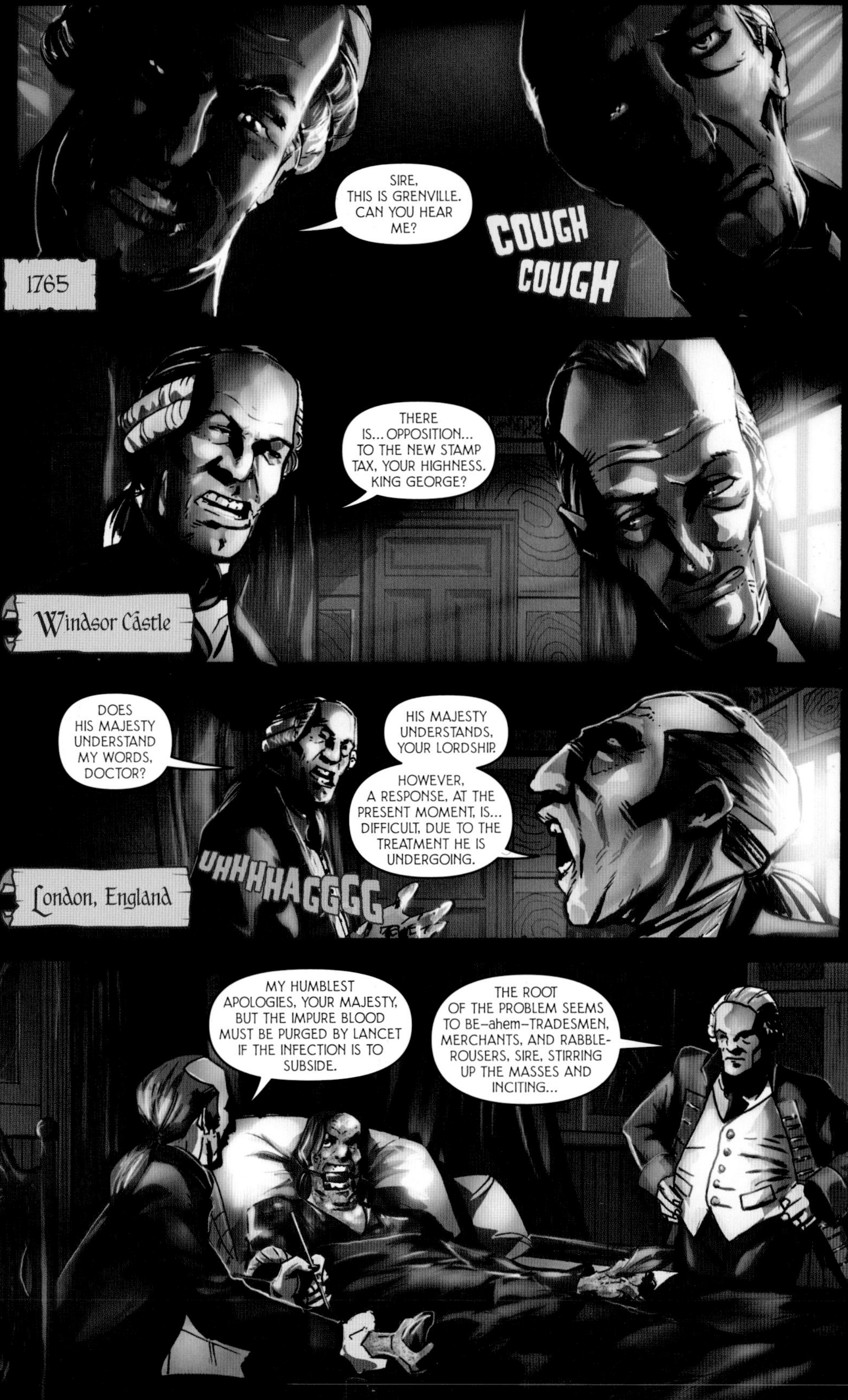
1765
SIRE, THIS IS GRENVILLE. CAN YOU HEAR ME?
COUGH COUGH
Windsor Castle
THERE IS... OPPOSITION... TO THE NEW STAMP TAX, YOUR HIGHNESS. KING GEORGE?
London, England
DOES HIS MAJESTY UNDERSTAND MY WORDS, DOCTOR?
HIS MAJESTY UNDERSTANDS, YOUR LORDSHIP.
HOWEVER, A RESPONSE, AT THE PRESENT MOMENT, IS... DIFFICULT, DUE TO THE TREATMENT HE IS UNDERGOING.
UHHHHAGGGG
MY HUMBLEST APOLOGIES, YOUR MAJESTY, BUT THE IMPURE BLOOD MUST BE PURGED BY LANCET IF THE INFECTION IS TO SUBSIDE.
THE ROOT OF THE PROBLEM SEEMS TO BE—ahem—TRADESMEN, MERCHANTS, AND RABBLE-ROUSERS, SIRE, STIRRING UP THE MASSES AND INCITING...

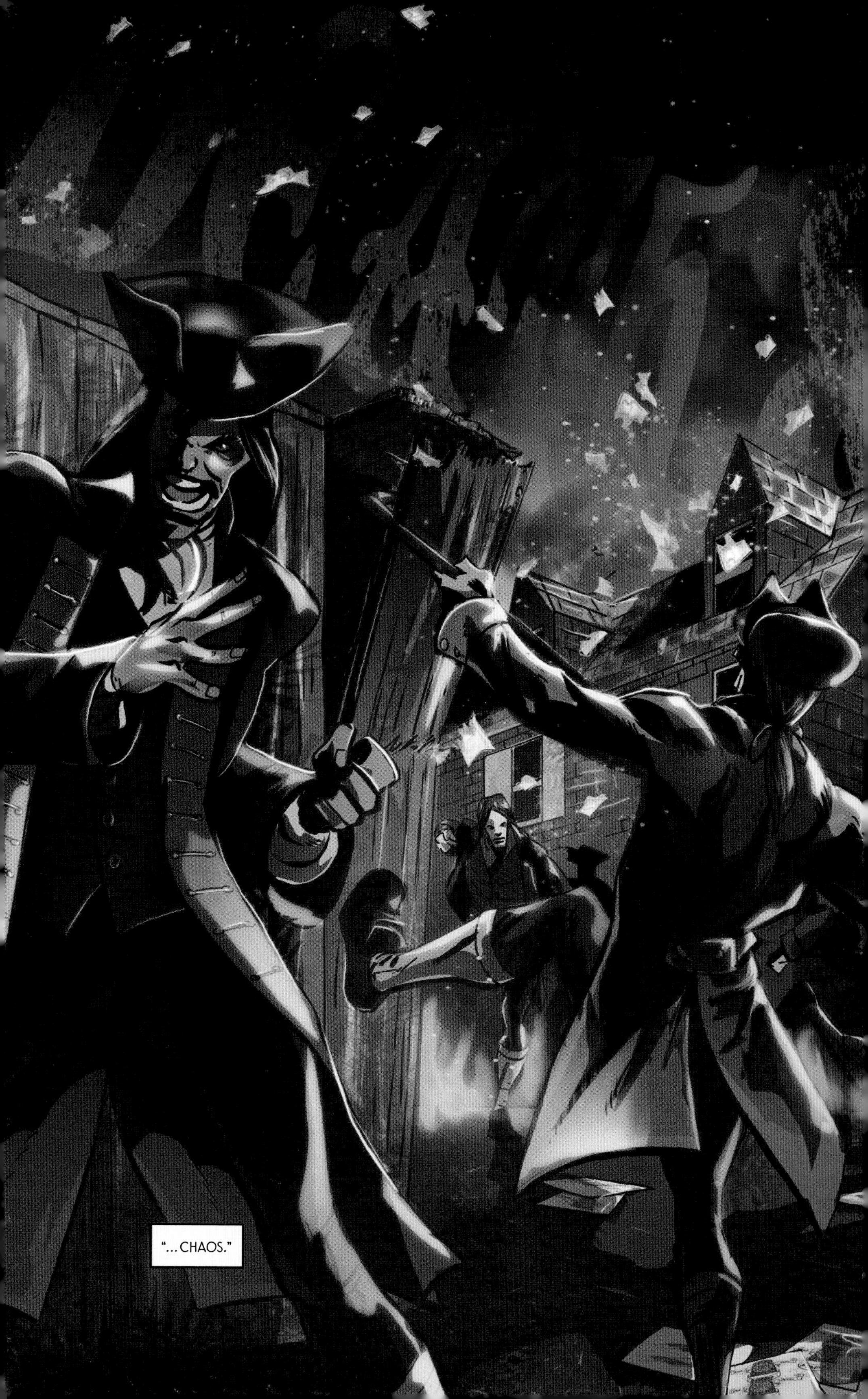
"...CHAOS."

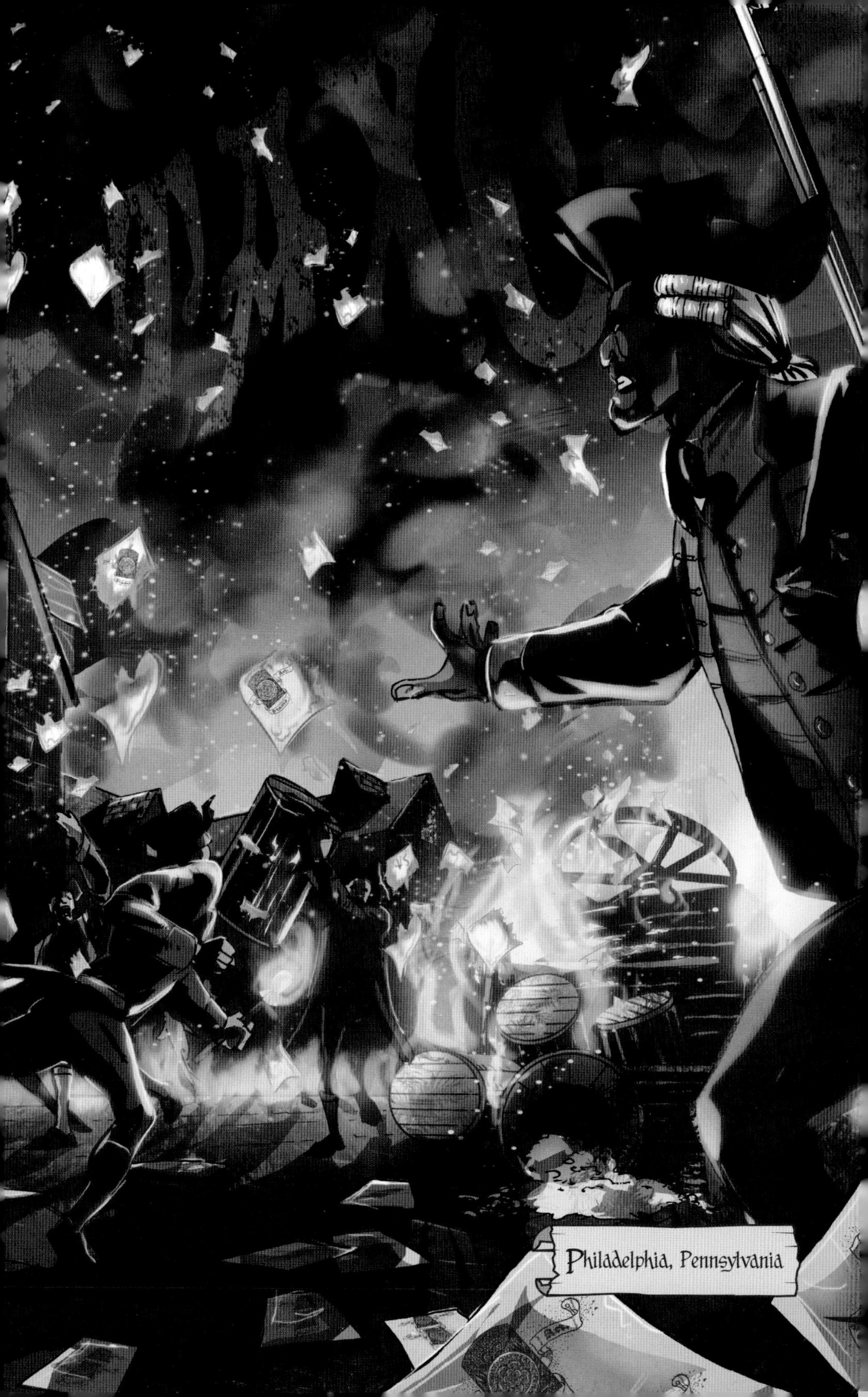
Philadelphia, Pennsylvania

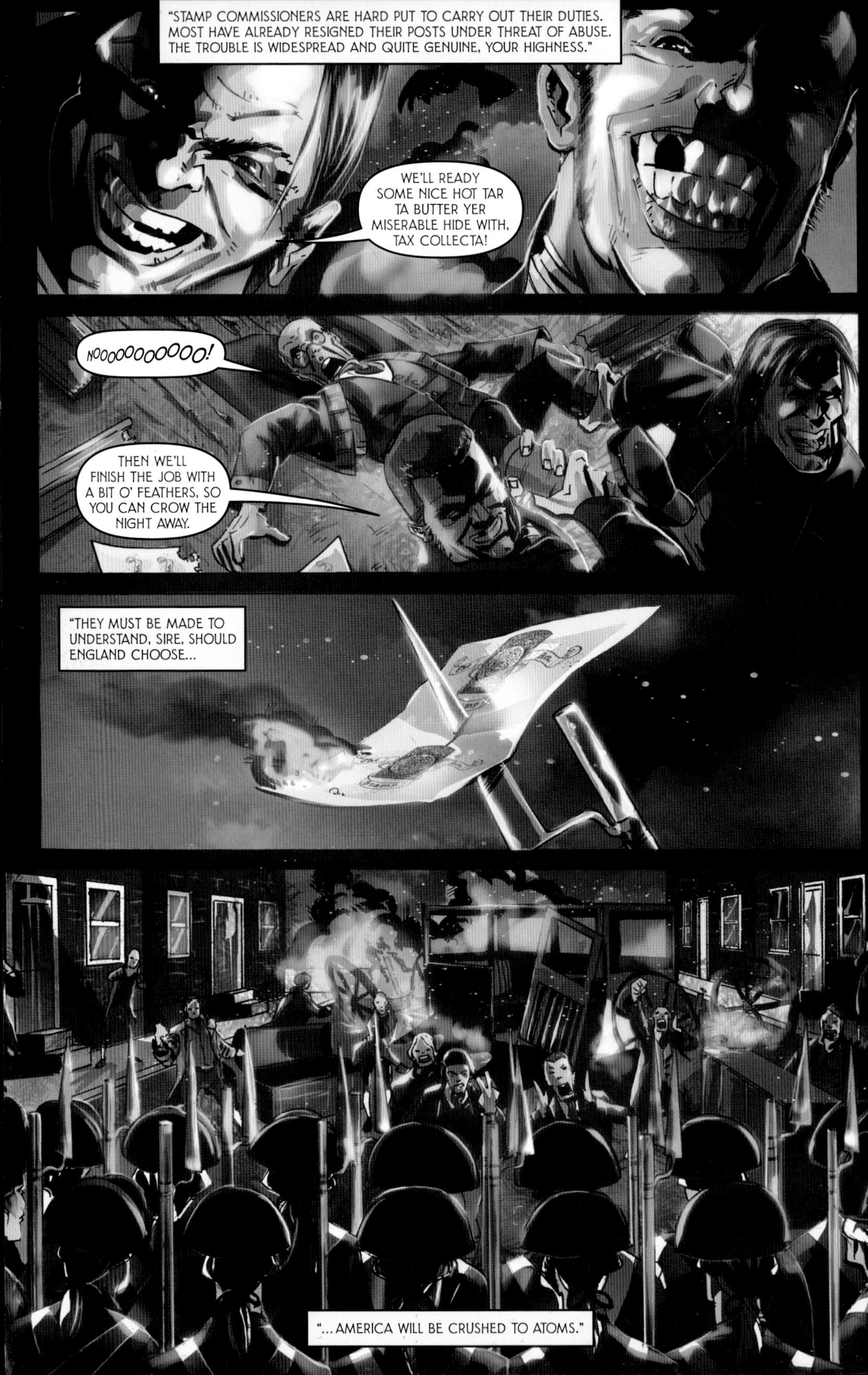
"STAMP COMMISSIONERS ARE HARD PUT TO CARRY OUT THEIR DUTIES. MOST HAVE ALREADY RESIGNED THEIR POSTS UNDER THREAT OF ABUSE. THE TROUBLE IS WIDESPREAD AND QUITE GENUINE, YOUR HIGHNESS."
WE'LL READY SOME NICE HOT TAR TA BUTTER YER MISERABLE HIDE WITH, TAX COLLECTA!
NOOOOOOOOOOO!
THEN WE'LL FINISH THE JOB WITH A BIT O' FEATHERS, SO YOU CAN CROW THE NIGHT AWAY.
"THEY MUST BE MADE TO UNDERSTAND, SIRE, SHOULD ENGLAND CHOOSE...
"...AMERICA WILL BE CRUSHED TO ATOMS."

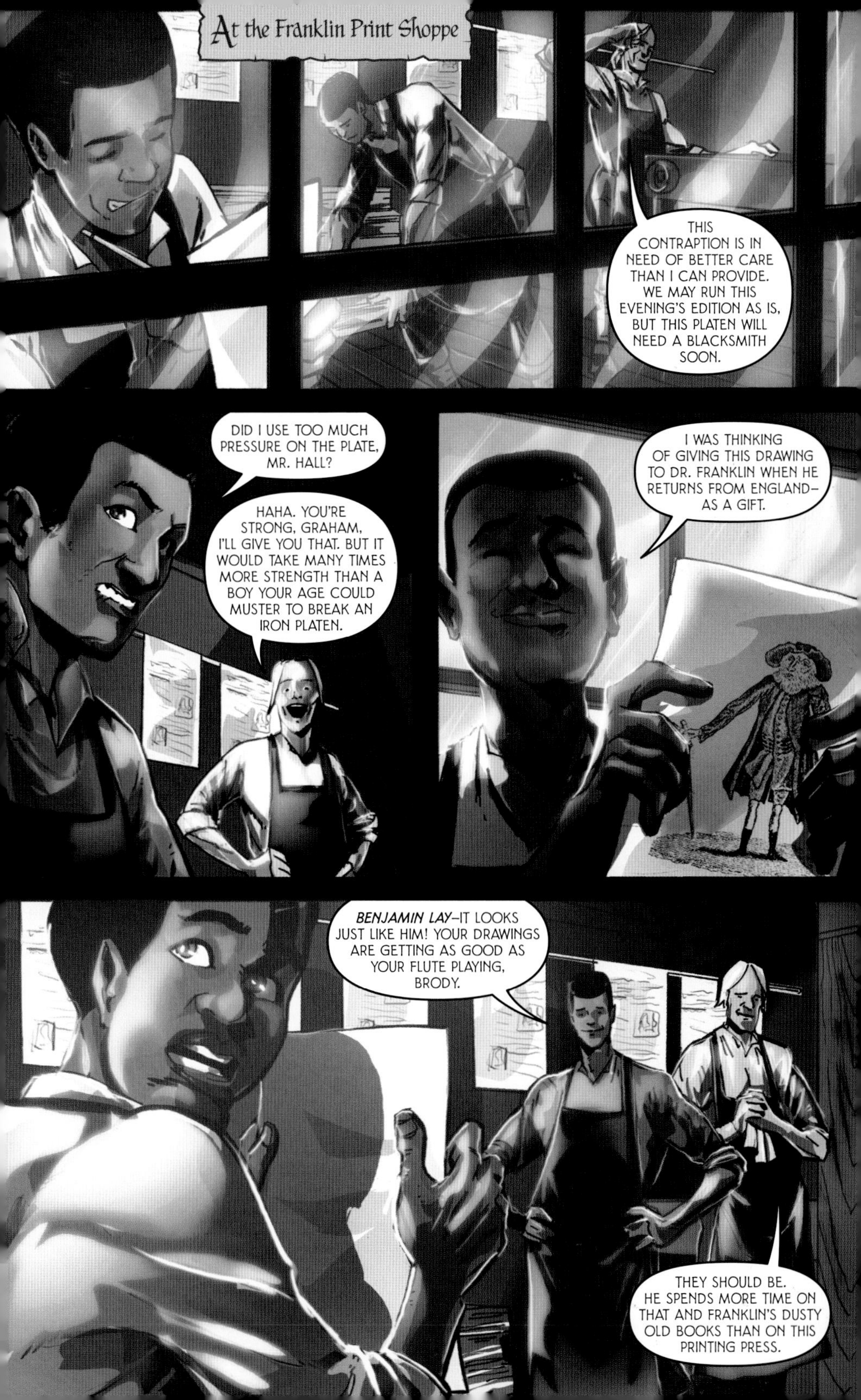
At the Franklin Print Shoppe
THIS CONTRAPTION IS IN NEED OF BETTER CARE THAN I CAN PROVIDE. WE MAY RUN THIS EVENING'S EDITION AS IS, BUT THIS PLATEN WILL NEED A BLACKSMITH SOON.
DID I USE TOO MUCH PRESSURE ON THE PLATE, MR. HALL?
HAHA. YOU'RE STRONG, GRAHAM, I'LL GIVE YOU THAT. BUT IT WOULD TAKE MANY TIMES MORE STRENGTH THAN A BOY YOUR AGE COULD MUSTER TO BREAK AN IRON PLATEN.
I WAS THINKING OF GIVING THIS DRAWING TO DR. FRANKLIN WHEN HE RETURNS FROM ENGLAND—AS A GIFT.
BENJAMIN LAY—IT LOOKS JUST LIKE HIM! YOUR DRAWINGS ARE GETTING AS GOOD AS YOUR FLUTE PLAYING, BRODY.
THEY SHOULD BE. HE SPENDS MORE TIME ON THAT AND FRANKLIN'S DUSTY OLD BOOKS THAN ON THIS PRINTING PRESS.

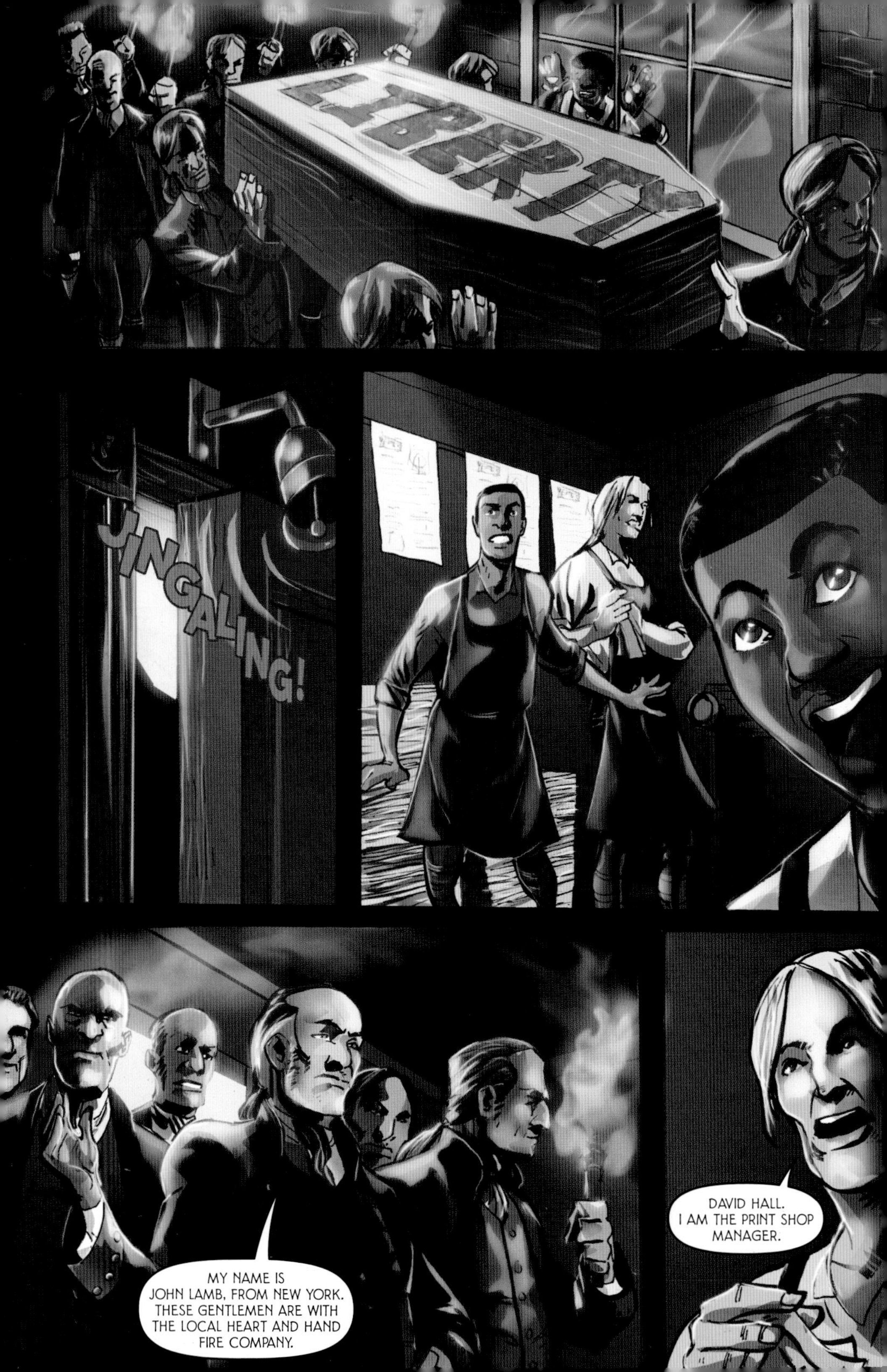
LIBERTY
JINGALING!
MY NAME IS JOHN LAMB, FROM NEW YORK. THESE GENTLEMEN ARE WITH THE LOCAL HEART AND HAND FIRE COMPANY.
DAVID HALL. I AM THE PRINT SHOP MANAGER.

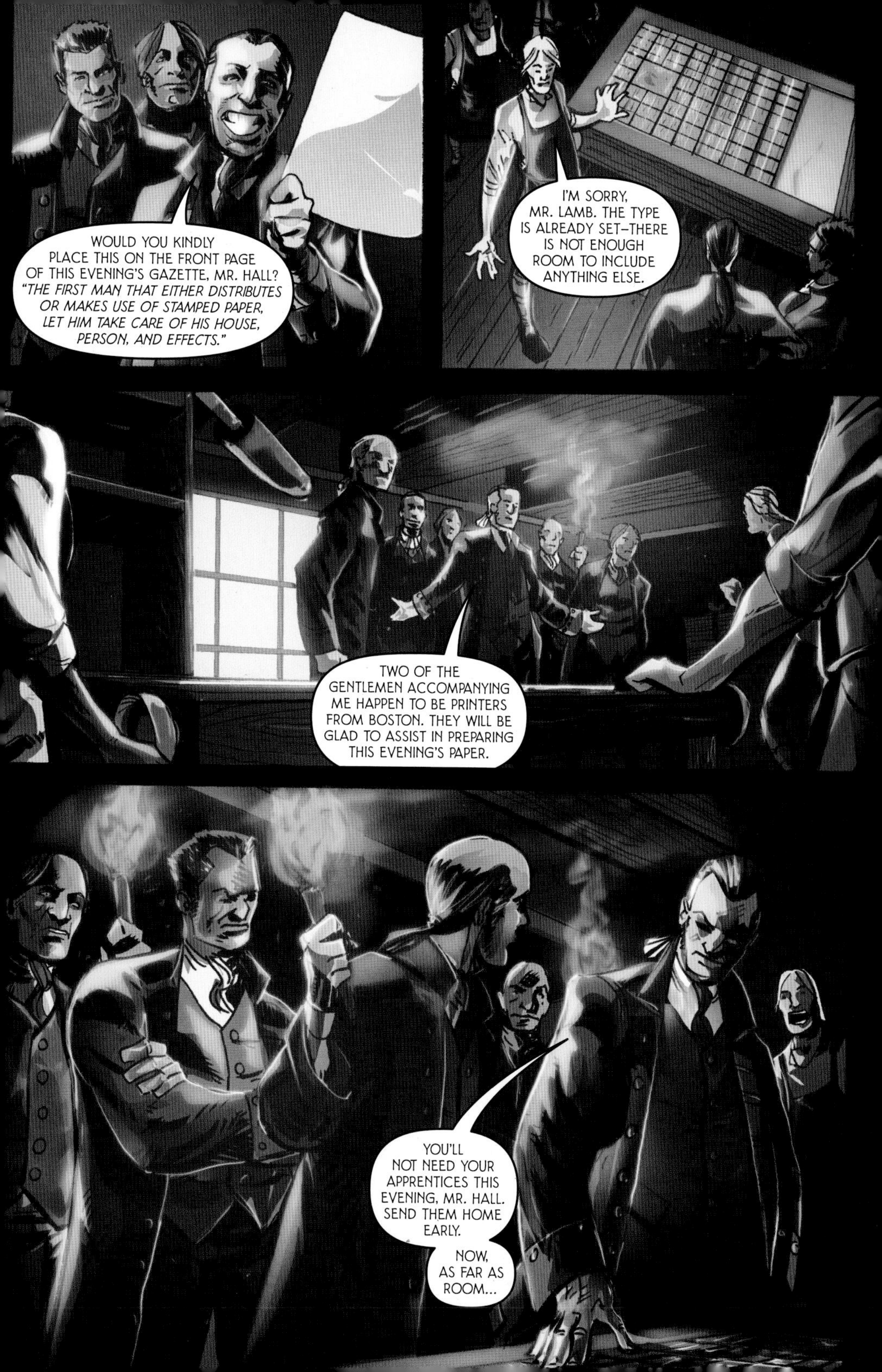
WOULD YOU KINDLY PLACE THIS ON THE FRONT PAGE OF THIS EVENING'S GAZETTE, MR. HALL? *"THE FIRST MAN THAT EITHER DISTRIBUTES OR MAKES USE OF STAMPED PAPER, LET HIM TAKE CARE OF HIS HOUSE, PERSON, AND EFFECTS."*
I'M SORRY, MR. LAMB. THE TYPE IS ALREADY SET—THERE IS NOT ENOUGH ROOM TO INCLUDE ANYTHING ELSE.
TWO OF THE GENTLEMEN ACCOMPANYING ME HAPPEN TO BE PRINTERS FROM BOSTON. THEY WILL BE GLAD TO ASSIST IN PREPARING THIS EVENING'S PAPER.
YOU'LL NOT NEED YOUR APPRENTICES THIS EVENING, MR. HALL. SEND THEM HOME EARLY.
NOW, AS FAR AS ROOM...

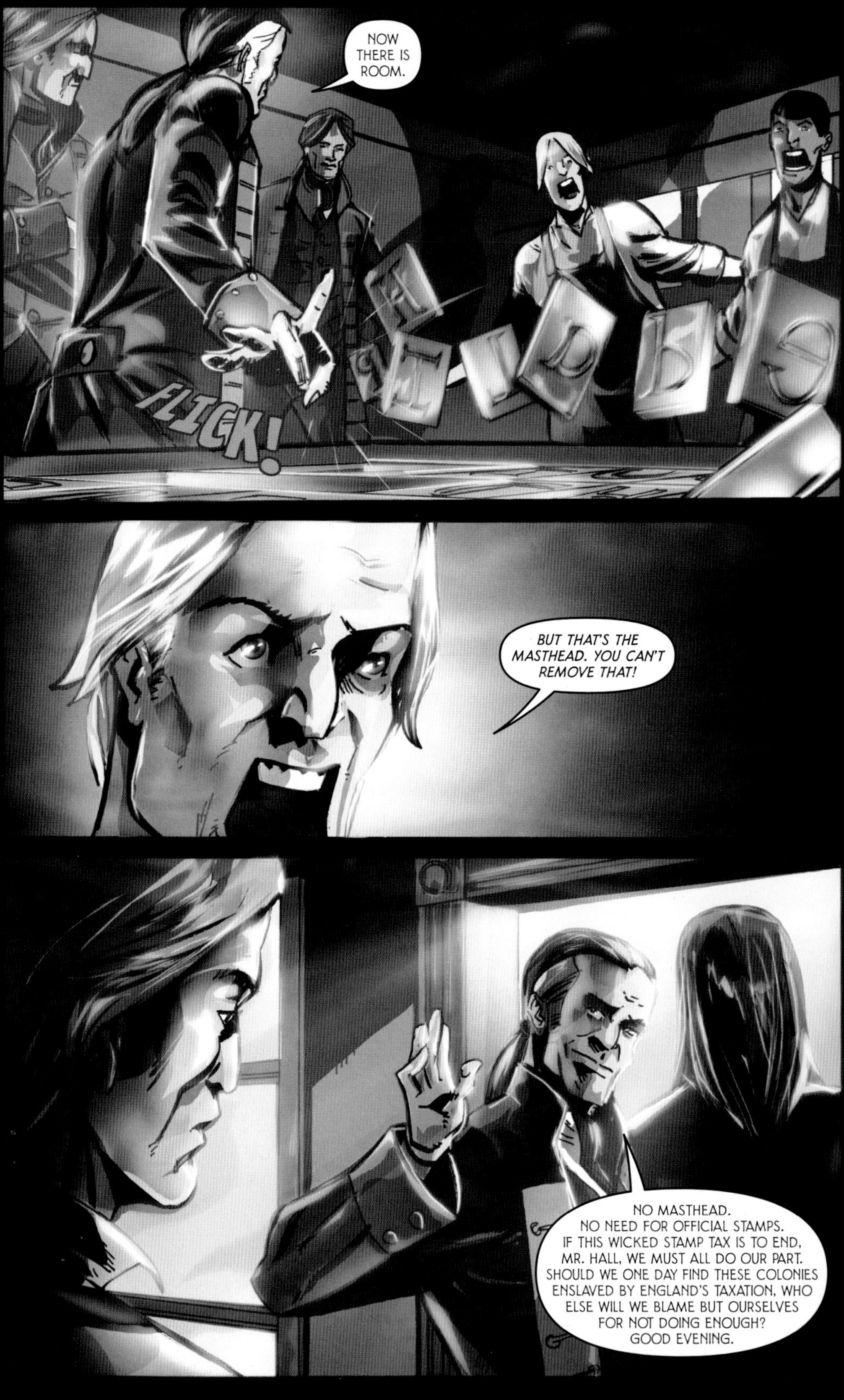
NOW THERE IS ROOM.
FLICK!
BUT THAT'S THE MASTHEAD. YOU CAN'T REMOVE THAT!
NO MASTHEAD. NO NEED FOR OFFICIAL STAMPS. IF THIS WICKED STAMP TAX IS TO END, MR. HALL, WE MUST ALL DO OUR PART. SHOULD WE ONE DAY FIND THESE COLONIES ENSLAVED BY ENGLAND'S TAXATION, WHO ELSE WILL WE BLAME BUT OURSELVES FOR NOT DOING ENOUGH? GOOD EVENING.

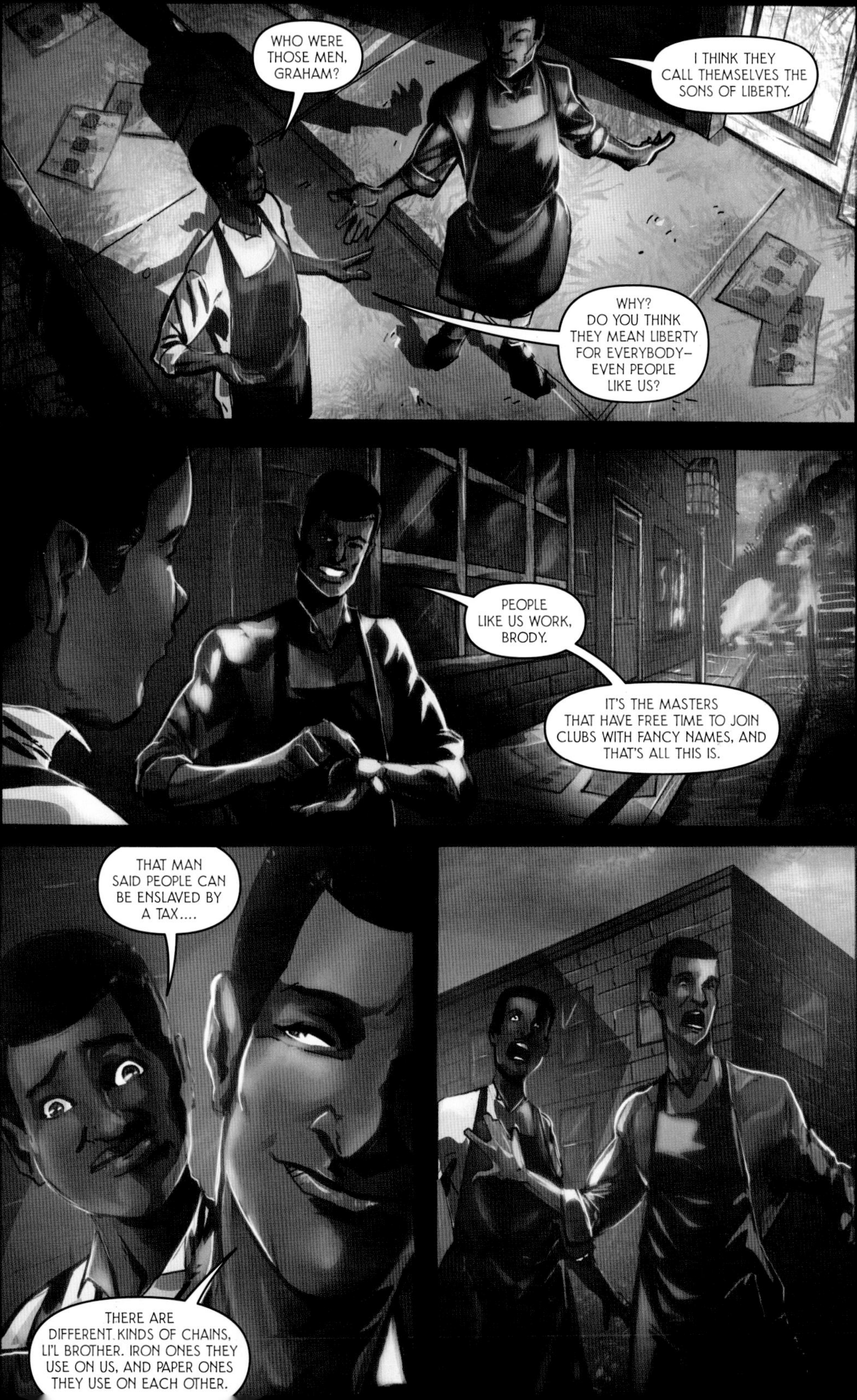
WHO WERE THOSE MEN, GRAHAM?
I THINK THEY CALL THEMSELVES THE SONS OF LIBERTY.
WHY? DO YOU THINK THEY MEAN LIBERTY FOR EVERYBODY—EVEN PEOPLE LIKE US?
PEOPLE LIKE US WORK, BRODY.
IT'S THE MASTERS THAT HAVE FREE TIME TO JOIN CLUBS WITH FANCY NAMES, AND THAT'S ALL THIS IS.
THAT MAN SAID PEOPLE CAN BE ENSLAVED BY A TAX....
THERE ARE DIFFERENT KINDS OF CHAINS, LI'L BROTHER. IRON ONES THEY USE ON US, AND PAPER ONES THEY USE ON EACH OTHER.

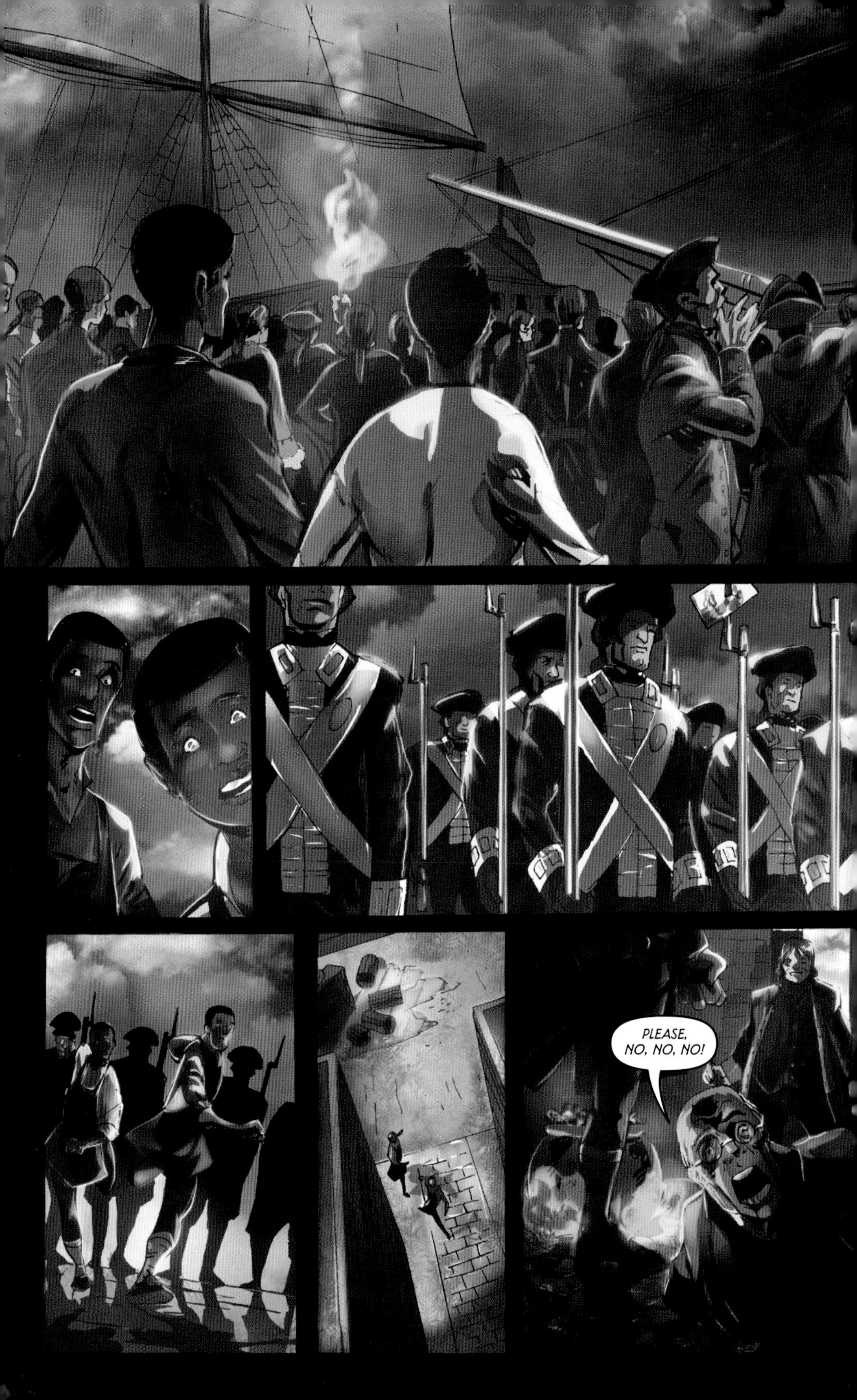
PLEASE, NO, NO, NO!

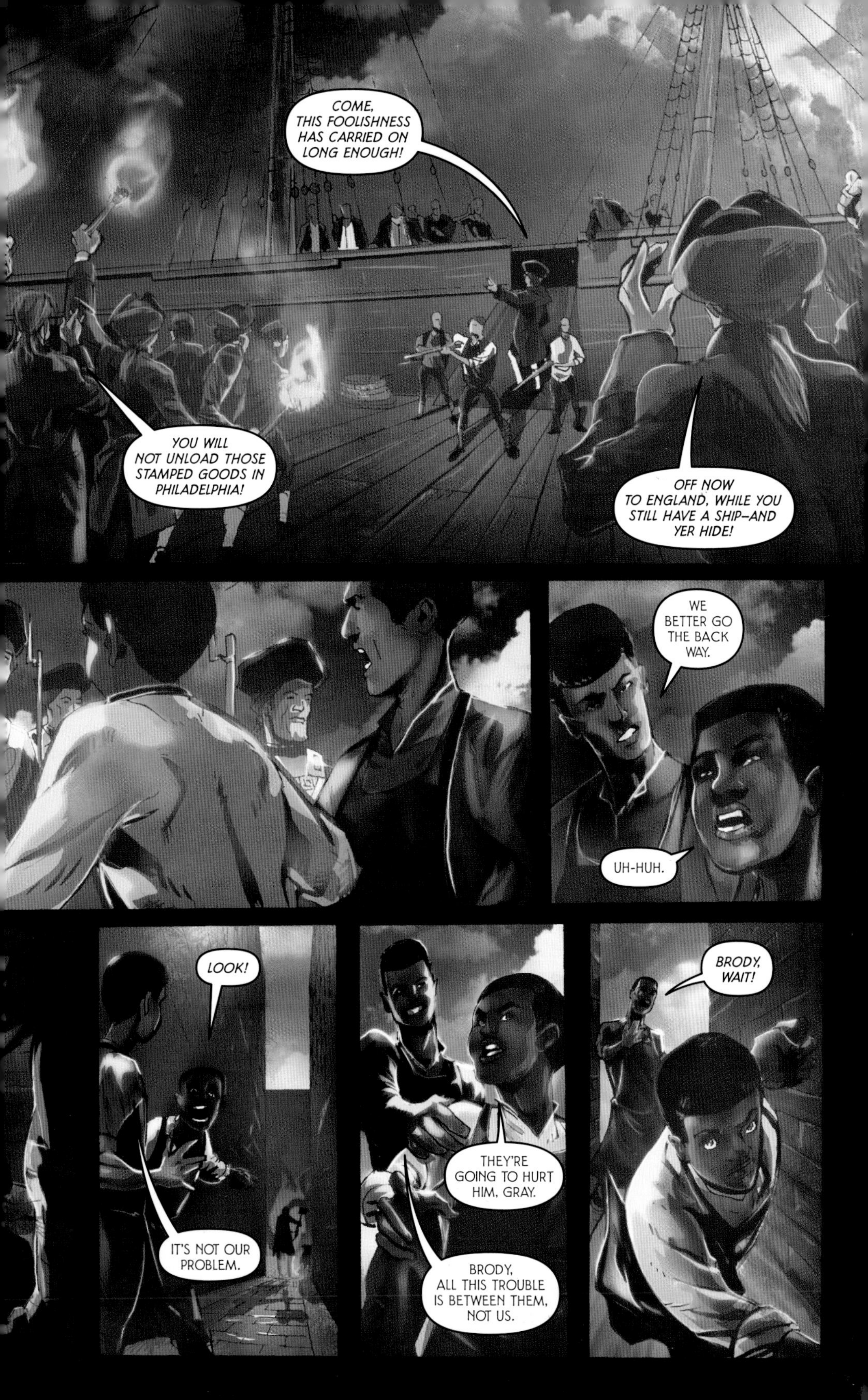
COME, THIS FOOLISHNESS HAS CARRIED ON LONG ENOUGH!
YOU WILL NOT UNLOAD THOSE STAMPED GOODS IN PHILADELPHIA!
OFF NOW TO ENGLAND, WHILE YOU STILL HAVE A SHIP—AND YER HIDE!
WE BETTER GO THE BACK WAY.
UH-HUH.
LOOK!
IT'S NOT OUR PROBLEM.
THEY'RE GOING TO HURT HIM, GRAY.
BRODY, ALL THIS TROUBLE IS BETWEEN THEM, NOT US.
BRODY, WAIT!

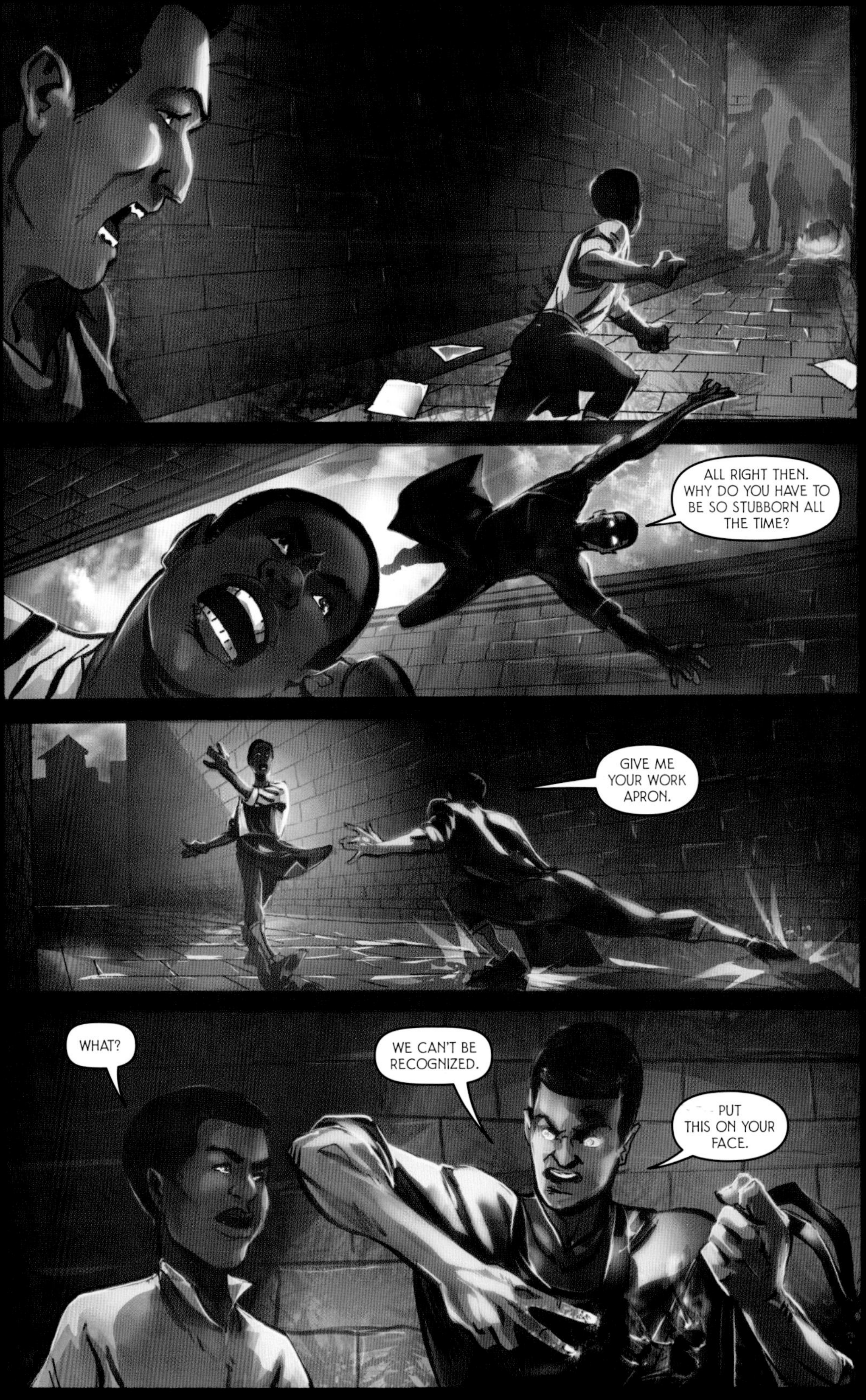
ALL RIGHT THEN. WHY DO YOU HAVE TO BE SO STUBBORN ALL THE TIME?
GIVE ME YOUR WORK APRON.
WHAT?
WE CAN'T BE RECOGNIZED.
PUT THIS ON YOUR FACE.

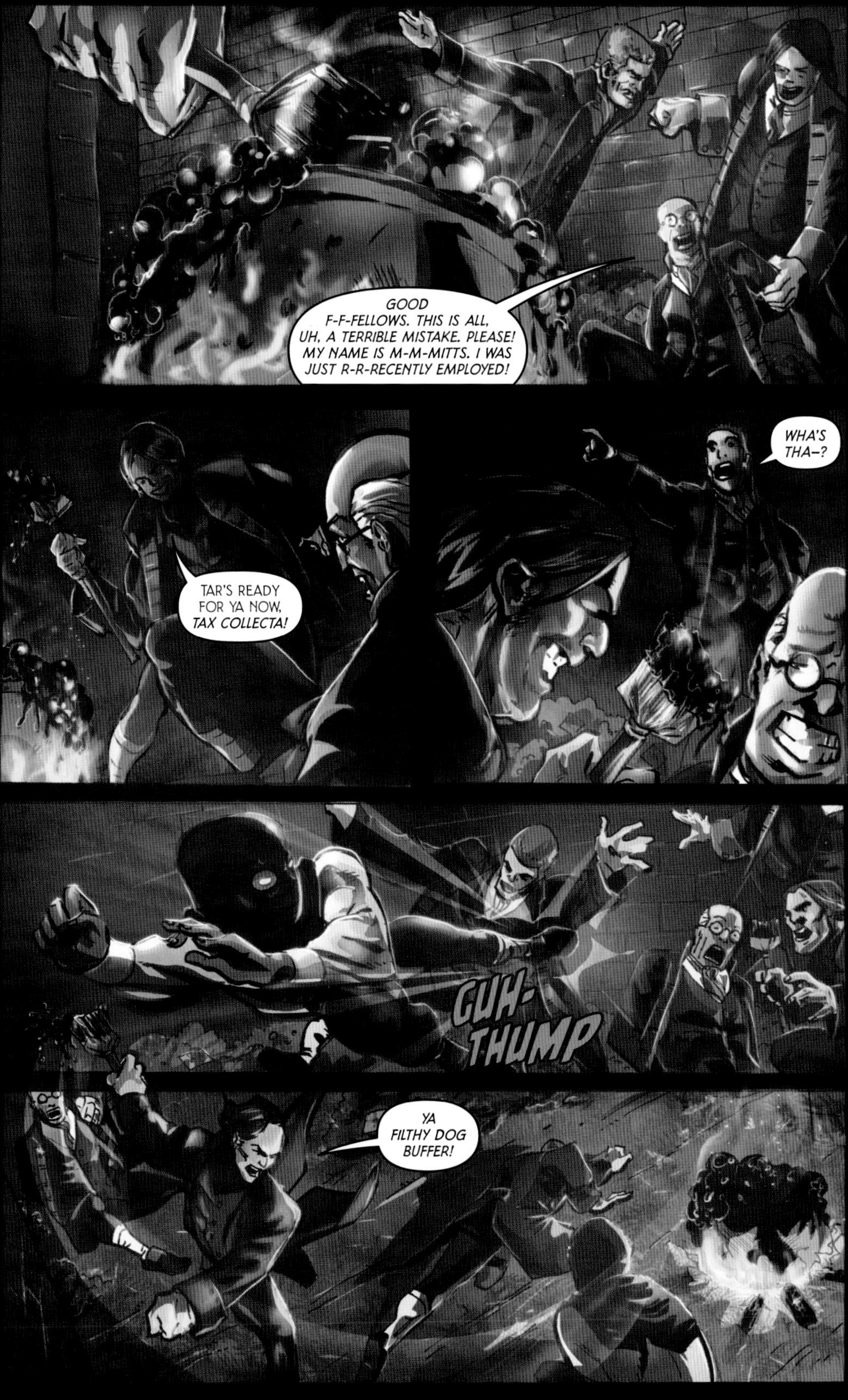
GOOD F-F-FELLOWS. THIS IS ALL, UH, A TERRIBLE MISTAKE. PLEASE! MY NAME IS M-M-MITTS. I WAS JUST R-R-RECENTLY EMPLOYED!
TAR'S READY FOR YA NOW, *TAX COLLECTA!*
WHA'S THA–?
GUH-THUMP
YA FILTHY DOG BUFFER!

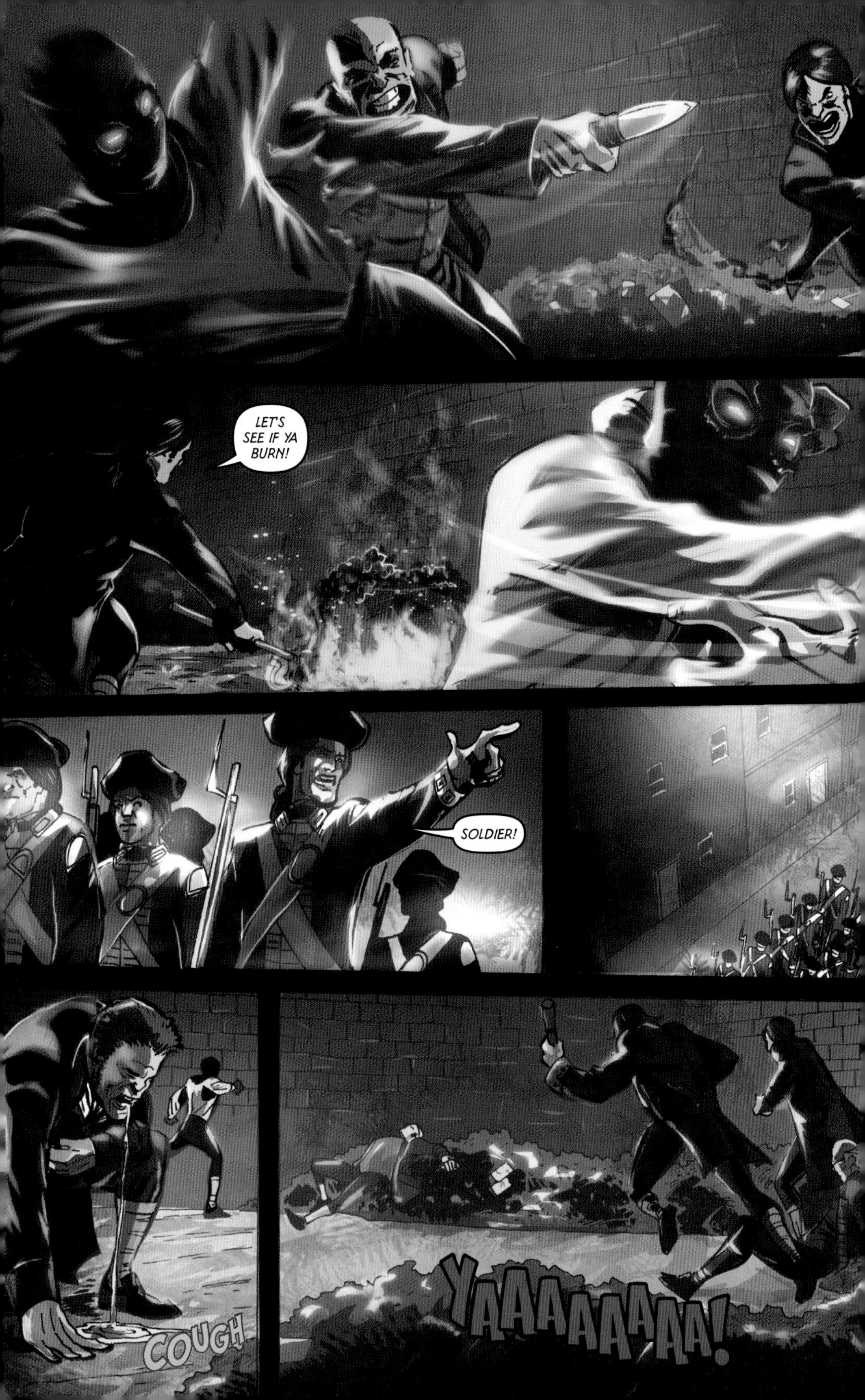
LET'S SEE IF YA BURN!
SOLDIER!
COUGH
YAAAAAAAAA!

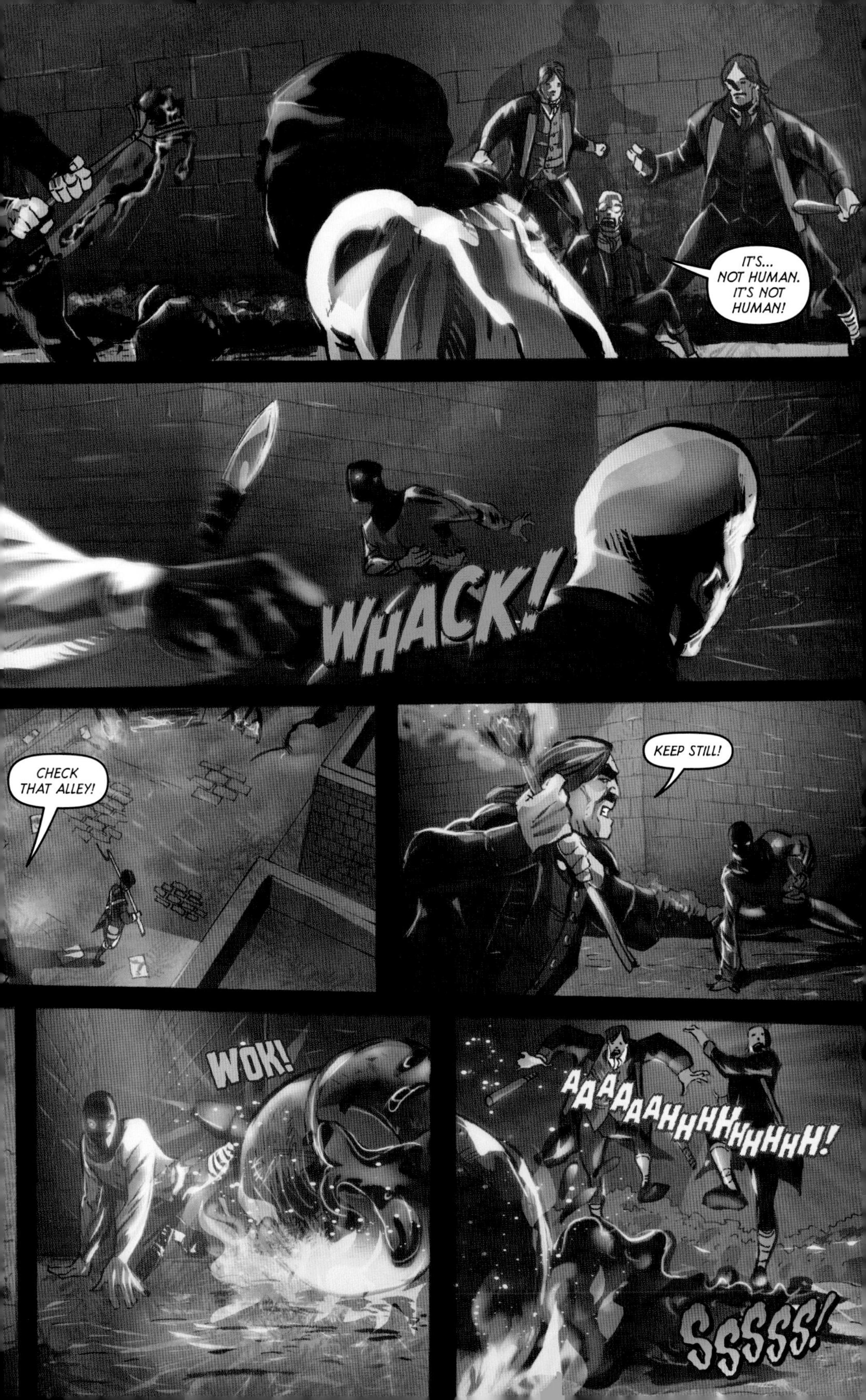
IT'S... NOT HUMAN. IT'S NOT HUMAN!
WHACK!
CHECK THAT ALLEY!
KEEP STILL!
WOK!
AAAAAHHHHHHHHH!
SSSSS!

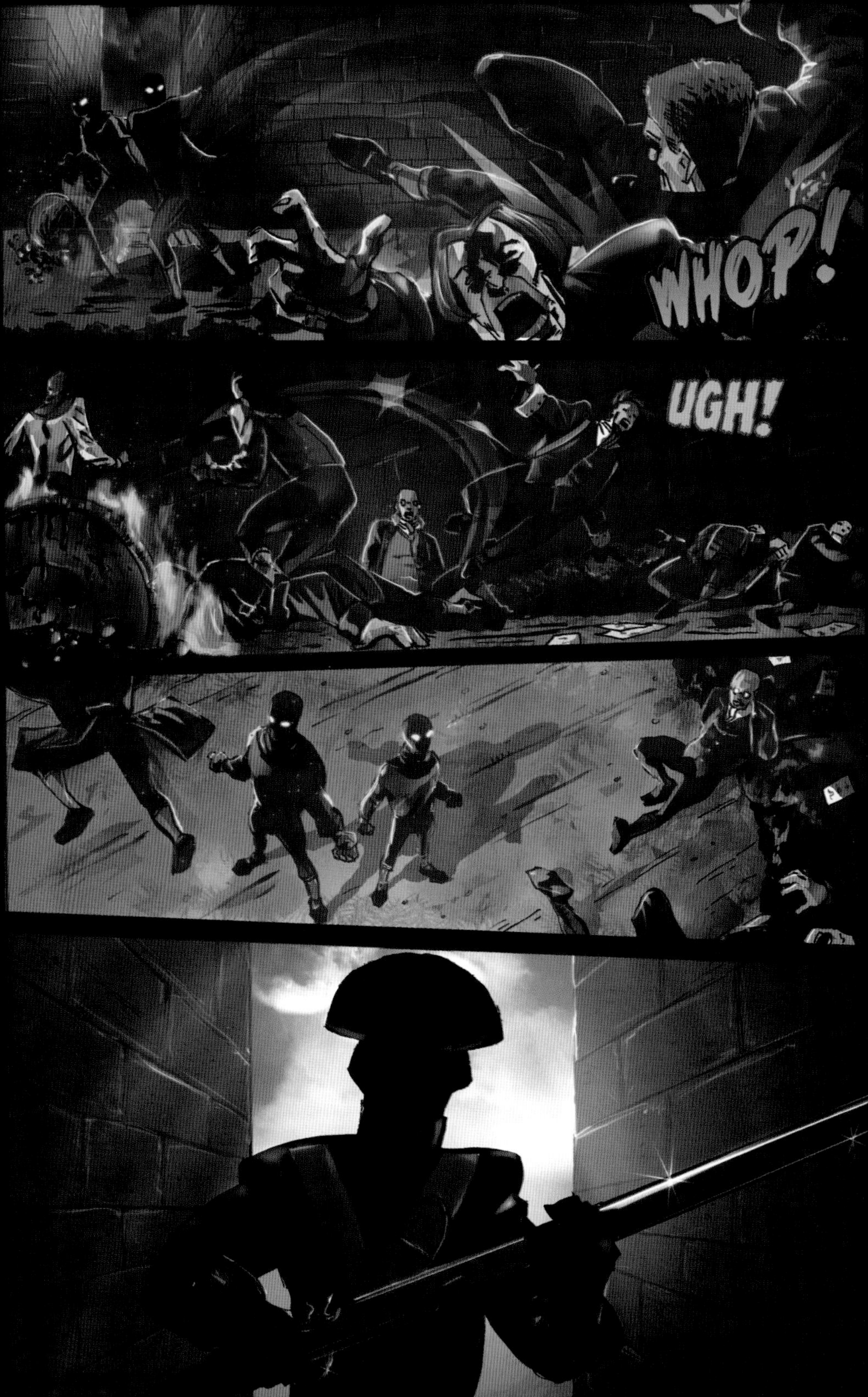
WHOP!
UGH!

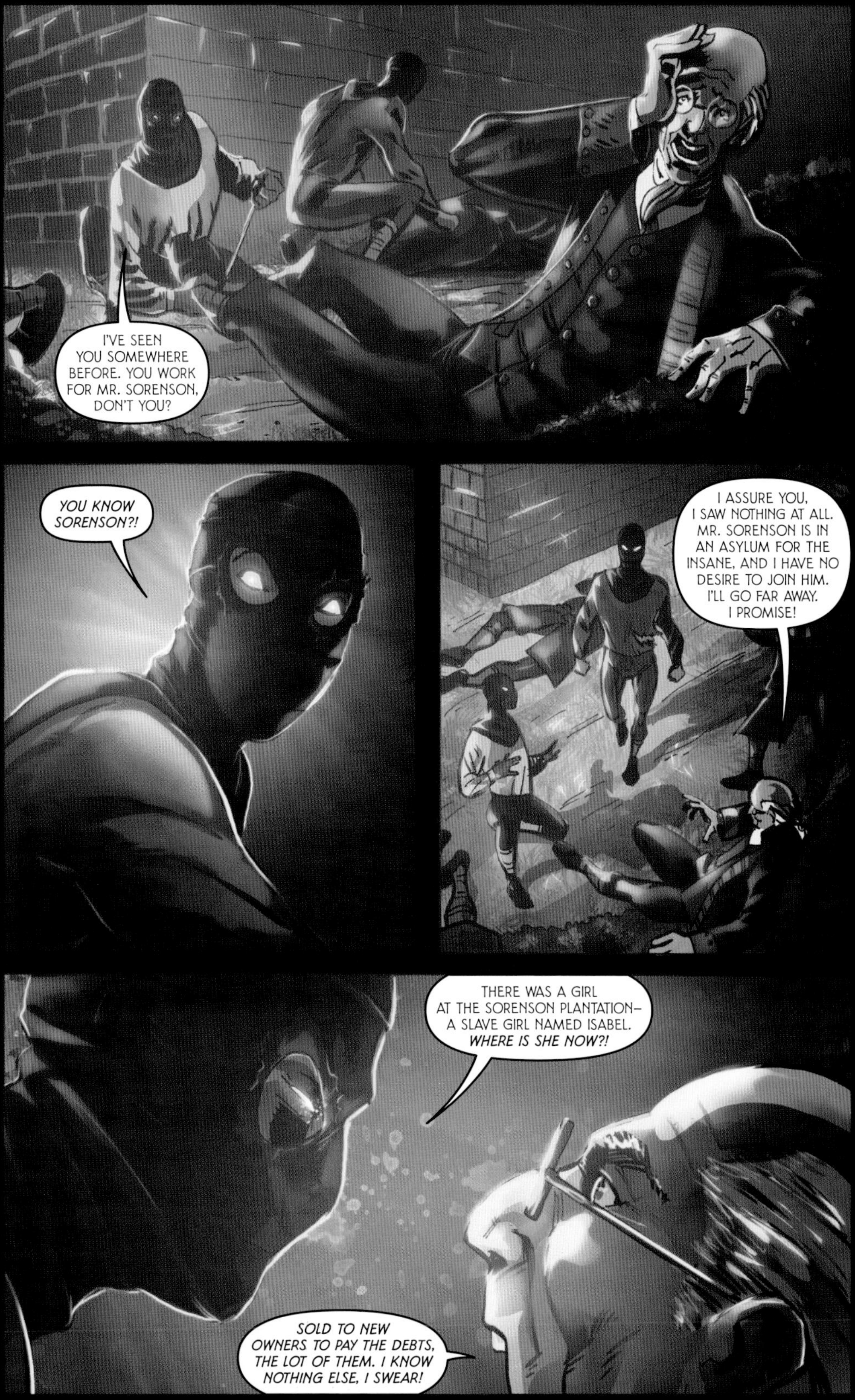
I'VE SEEN YOU SOMEWHERE BEFORE. YOU WORK FOR MR. SORENSON, DON'T YOU?
YOU KNOW SORENSON?!
I ASSURE YOU, I SAW NOTHING AT ALL. MR. SORENSON IS IN AN ASYLUM FOR THE INSANE, AND I HAVE NO DESIRE TO JOIN HIM. I'LL GO FAR AWAY. I PROMISE!
THERE WAS A GIRL AT THE SORENSON PLANTATION— A SLAVE GIRL NAMED ISABEL. *WHERE IS SHE NOW?!*
SOLD TO NEW OWNERS TO PAY THE DEBTS, THE LOT OF THEM. I KNOW NOTHING ELSE, I SWEAR!

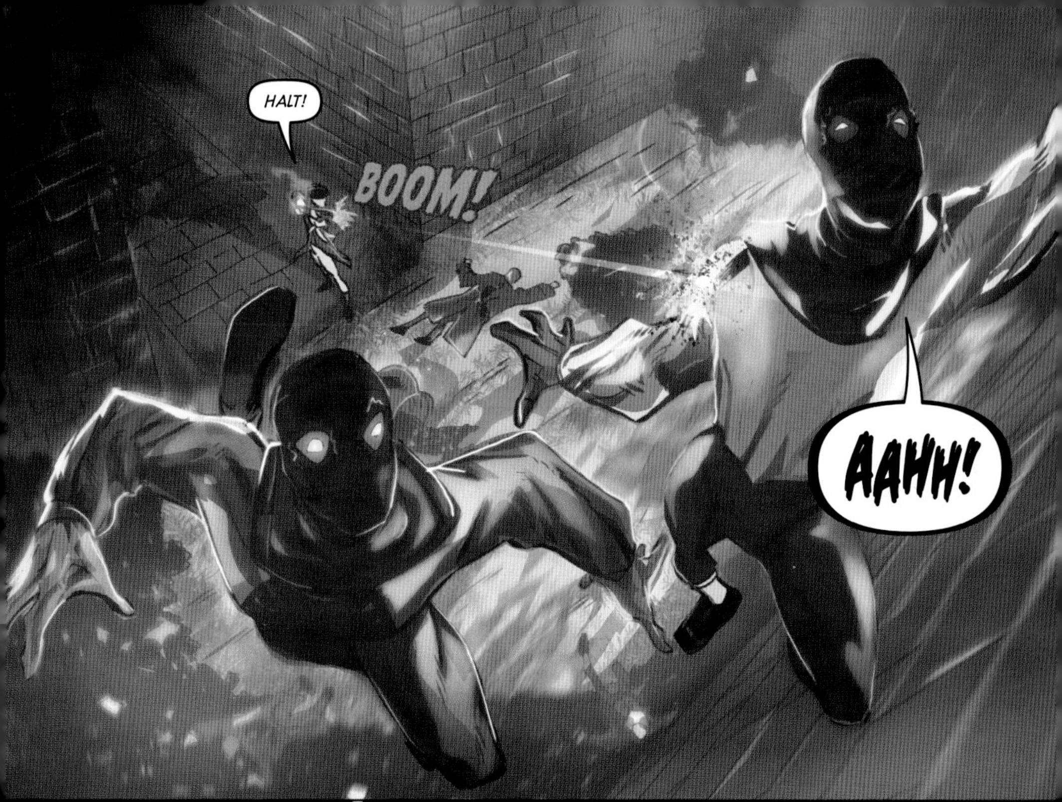
HALT!
BOOM!
AAHH!

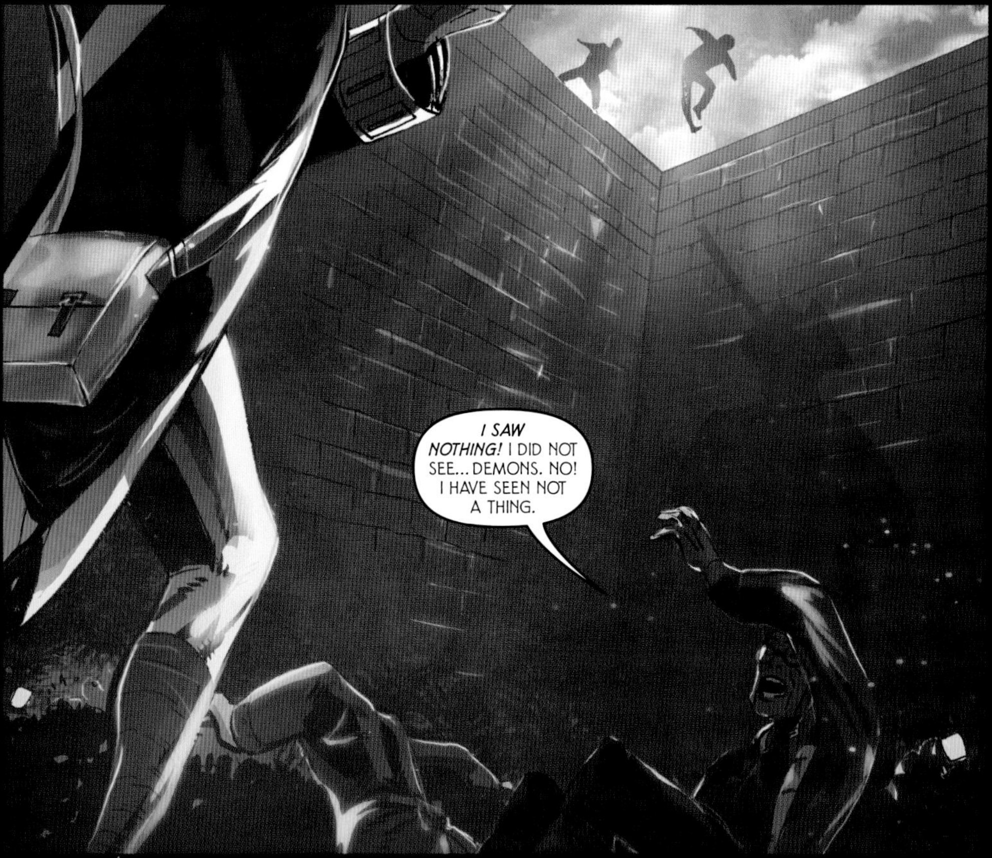
I SAW NOTHING! I DID NOT SEE... DEMONS. NO! I HAVE SEEN NOT A THING.

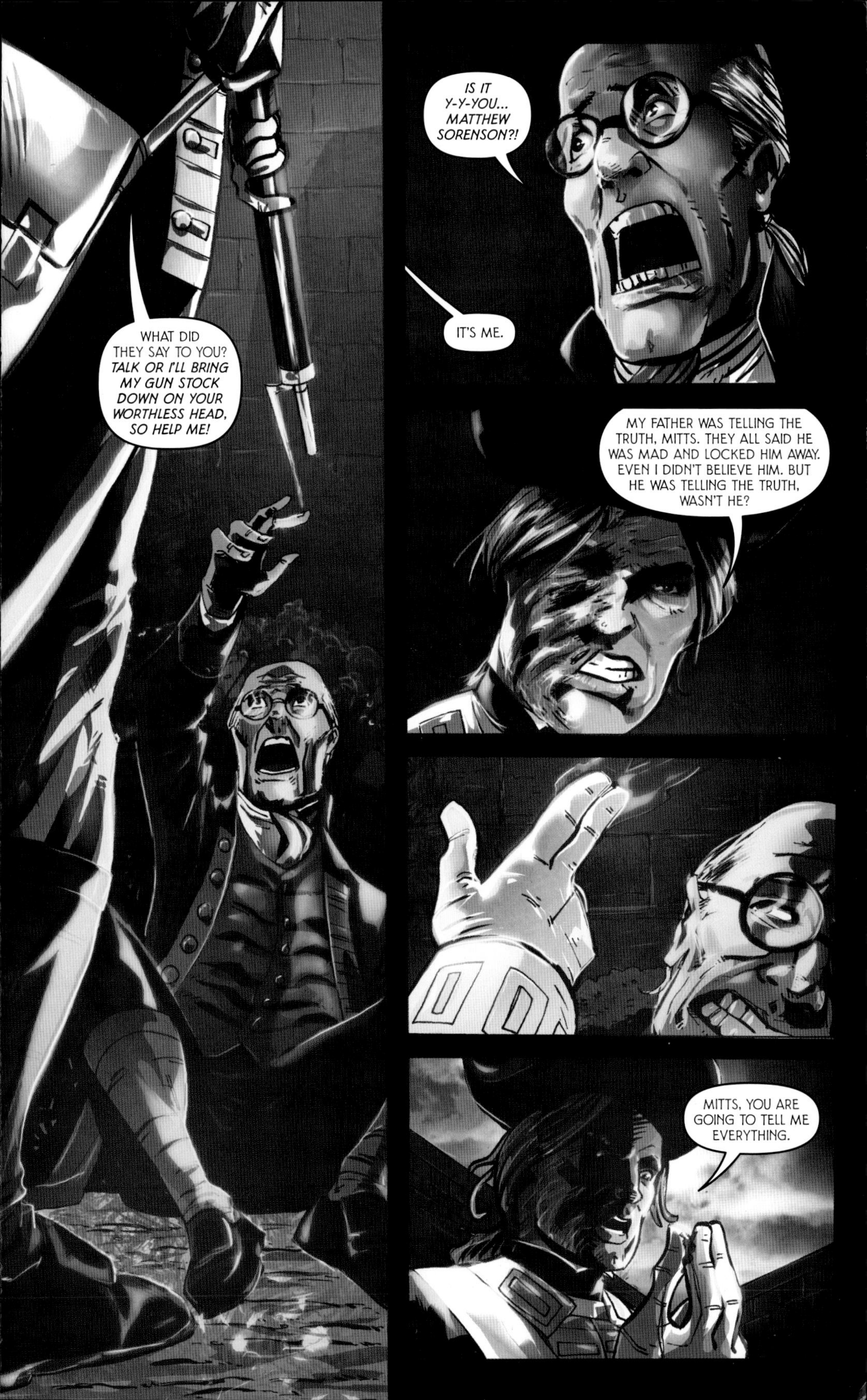
WHAT DID THEY SAY TO YOU? *TALK OR I'LL BRING MY GUN STOCK DOWN ON YOUR WORTHLESS HEAD, SO HELP ME!*
IS IT Y-Y-YOU... MATTHEW SORENSON?!
IT'S ME.
MY FATHER WAS TELLING THE TRUTH, MITTS. THEY ALL SAID HE WAS MAD AND LOCKED HIM AWAY. EVEN I DIDN'T BELIEVE HIM. BUT HE WAS TELLING THE TRUTH, WASN'T HE?
MITTS, YOU ARE GOING TO TELL ME EVERYTHING.

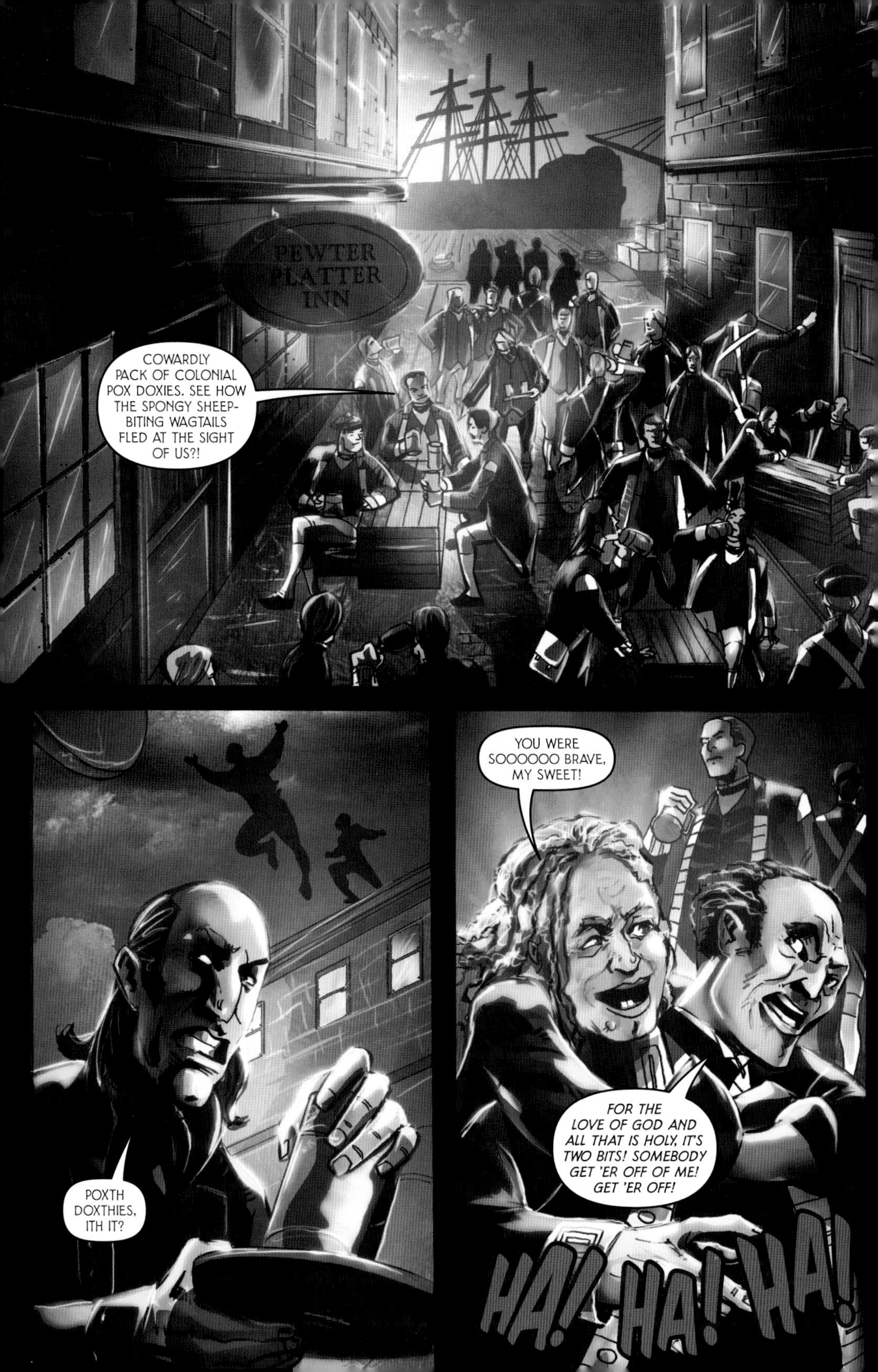
PEWTER PLATTER INN
COWARDLY PACK OF COLONIAL POX DOXIES. SEE HOW THE SPONGY SHEEP-BITING WAGTAILS FLED AT THE SIGHT OF US?!
POXTH DOXTHIES, ITH IT?
YOU WERE SOOOOOO BRAVE, MY SWEET!
FOR THE LOVE OF GOD AND ALL THAT IS HOLY, IT'S TWO BITS! SOMEBODY GET 'ER OFF OF ME! GET 'ER OFF!
HA! HA! HA!

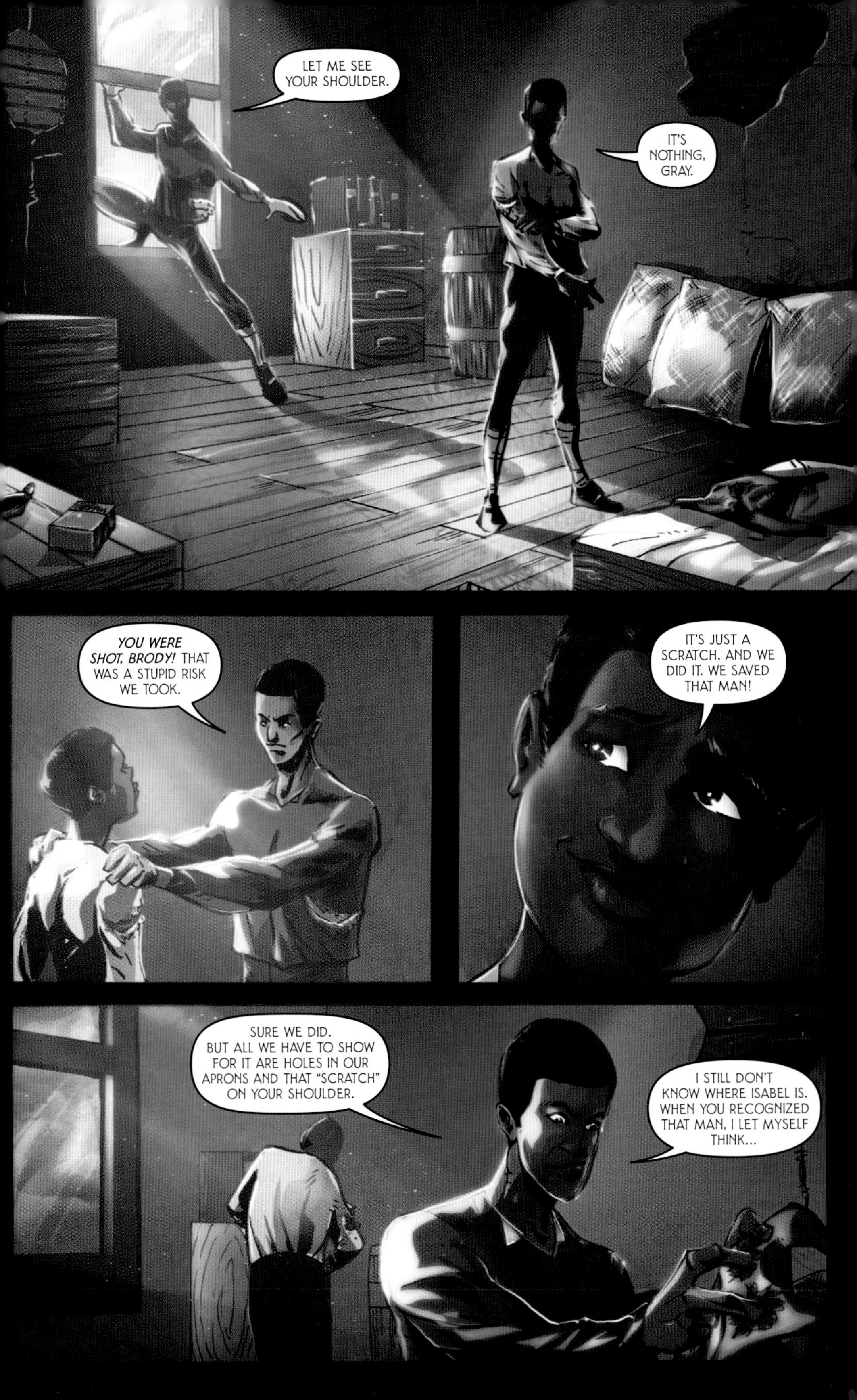

LET ME SEE YOUR SHOULDER.
IT'S NOTHING, GRAY.
YOU WERE SHOT, BRODY! THAT WAS A STUPID RISK WE TOOK.
IT'S JUST A SCRATCH. AND WE DID IT. WE SAVED THAT MAN!
SURE WE DID. BUT ALL WE HAVE TO SHOW FOR IT ARE HOLES IN OUR APRONS AND THAT "SCRATCH" ON YOUR SHOULDER.
I STILL DON'T KNOW WHERE ISABEL IS. WHEN YOU RECOGNIZED THAT MAN, I LET MYSELF THINK...

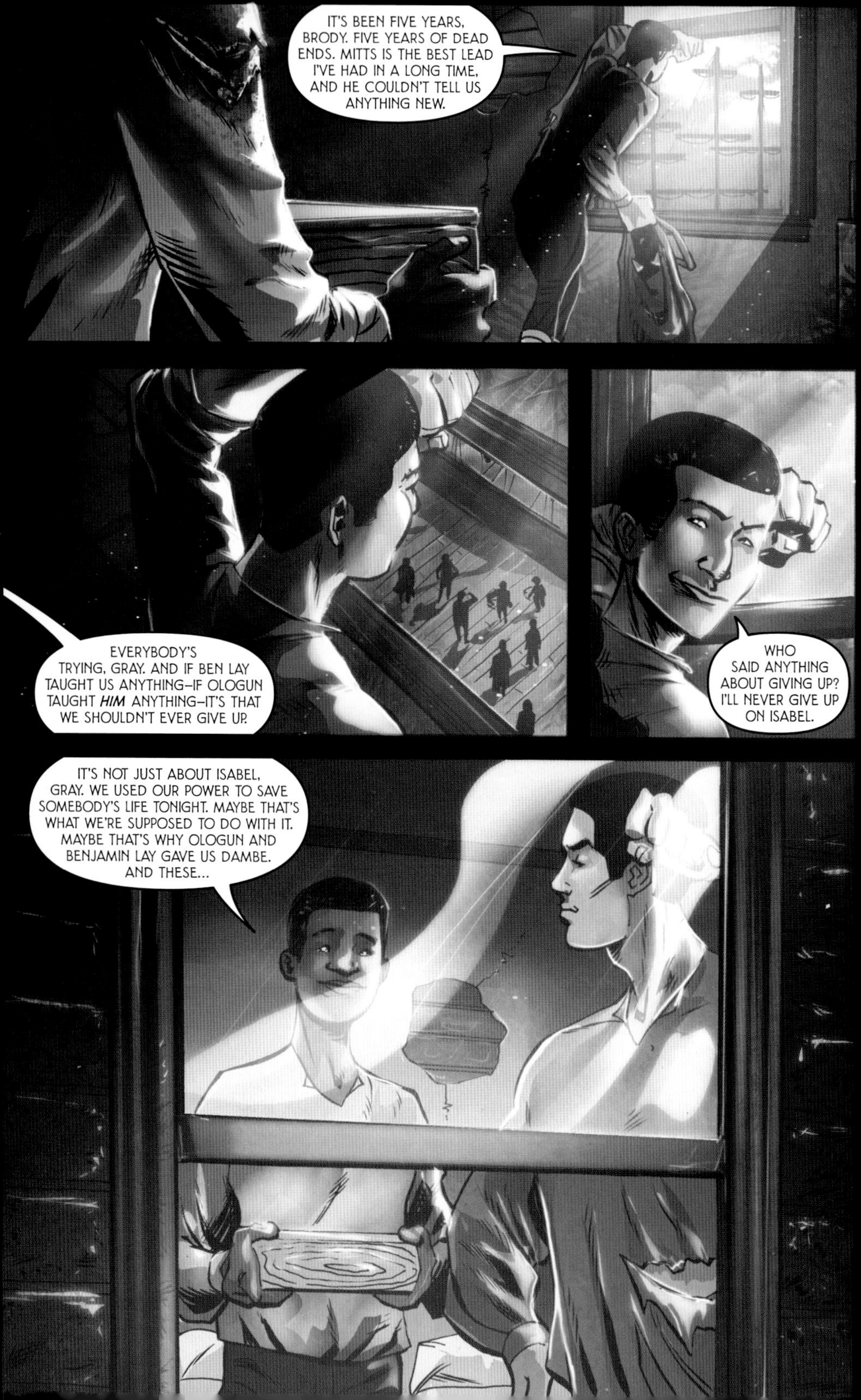
IT'S BEEN FIVE YEARS, BRODY. FIVE YEARS OF DEAD ENDS. MITTS IS THE BEST LEAD I'VE HAD IN A LONG TIME, AND HE COULDN'T TELL US ANYTHING NEW.
EVERYBODY'S TRYING, GRAY. AND IF BEN LAY TAUGHT US ANYTHING–IF OLOGUN TAUGHT *HIM* ANYTHING–IT'S THAT WE SHOULDN'T EVER GIVE UP.
WHO SAID ANYTHING ABOUT GIVING UP? I'LL NEVER GIVE UP ON ISABEL.
IT'S NOT JUST ABOUT ISABEL, GRAY. WE USED OUR POWER TO SAVE SOMEBODY'S LIFE TONIGHT. MAYBE THAT'S WHAT WE'RE SUPPOSED TO DO WITH IT. MAYBE THAT'S WHY OLOGUN AND BENJAMIN LAY GAVE US DAMBE. AND THESE...

I THINK IT'S TIME WE START CARRYING THESE WITH US, GRAY.

BRODY, WE ARE GOING TO FIND ISABEL, WE ARE GOING TO GET ON A SHIP, AND WE ARE GOING BACK TO AFRICA. THAT'S ALL THAT MATTERS.

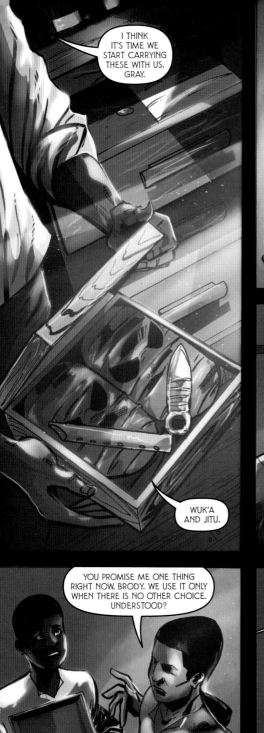

WUK'A AND JITU.

WHAT YOU TOLD ME ONCE IS TRUE, GRAY: *"SOMETIMES YOU HAVE TO FIGHT. SOMETIMES THERE'S NO CHOICE."* IT HAPPENED TONIGHT. IF IT HAPPENS AGAIN, WE HAVE TO BE READY FOR IT.

YOU PROMISE ME ONE THING RIGHT NOW, BRODY. WE USE IT ONLY WHEN THERE IS NO OTHER CHOICE. UNDERSTOOD?

YES.

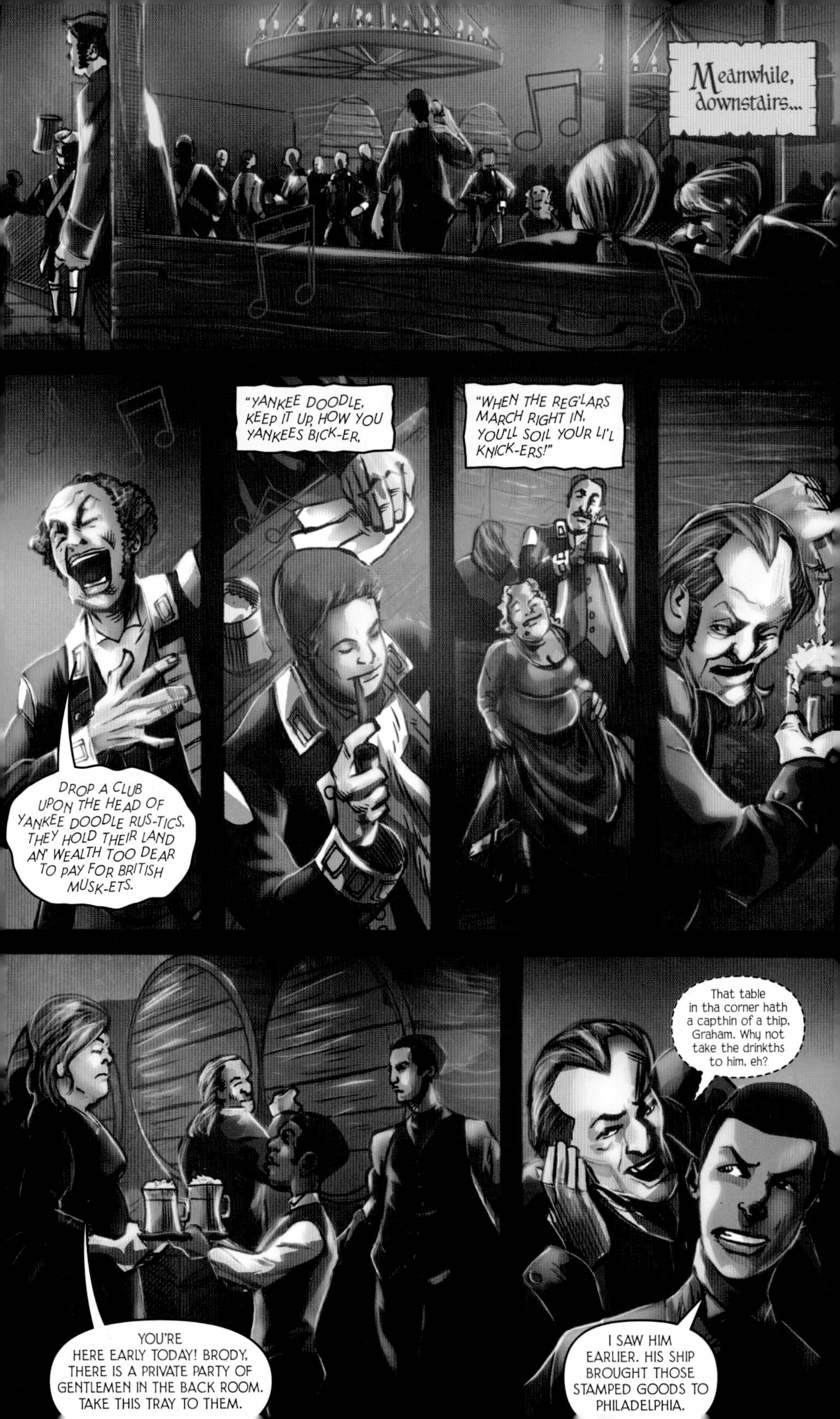
Meanwhile, downstairs...
DROP A CLUB UPON THE HEAD OF YANKEE DOODLE RUS-TICS, THEY HOLD THEIR LAND AN' WEALTH TOO DEAR TO PAY FOR BRITISH MUSK-ETS.
"YANKEE DOODLE, KEEP IT UP, HOW YOU YANKEES BICK-ER,
"WHEN THE REG'LARS MARCH RIGHT IN, YOU'LL SOIL YOUR LI'L KNICK-ERS!"
YOU'RE HERE EARLY TODAY! BRODY, THERE IS A PRIVATE PARTY OF GENTLEMEN IN THE BACK ROOM. TAKE THIS TRAY TO THEM.
That table in tha corner hath a capthin of a thip, Graham. Why not take the drinkths to him, eh?
I SAW HIM EARLIER. HIS SHIP BROUGHT THOSE STAMPED GOODS TO PHILADELPHIA.

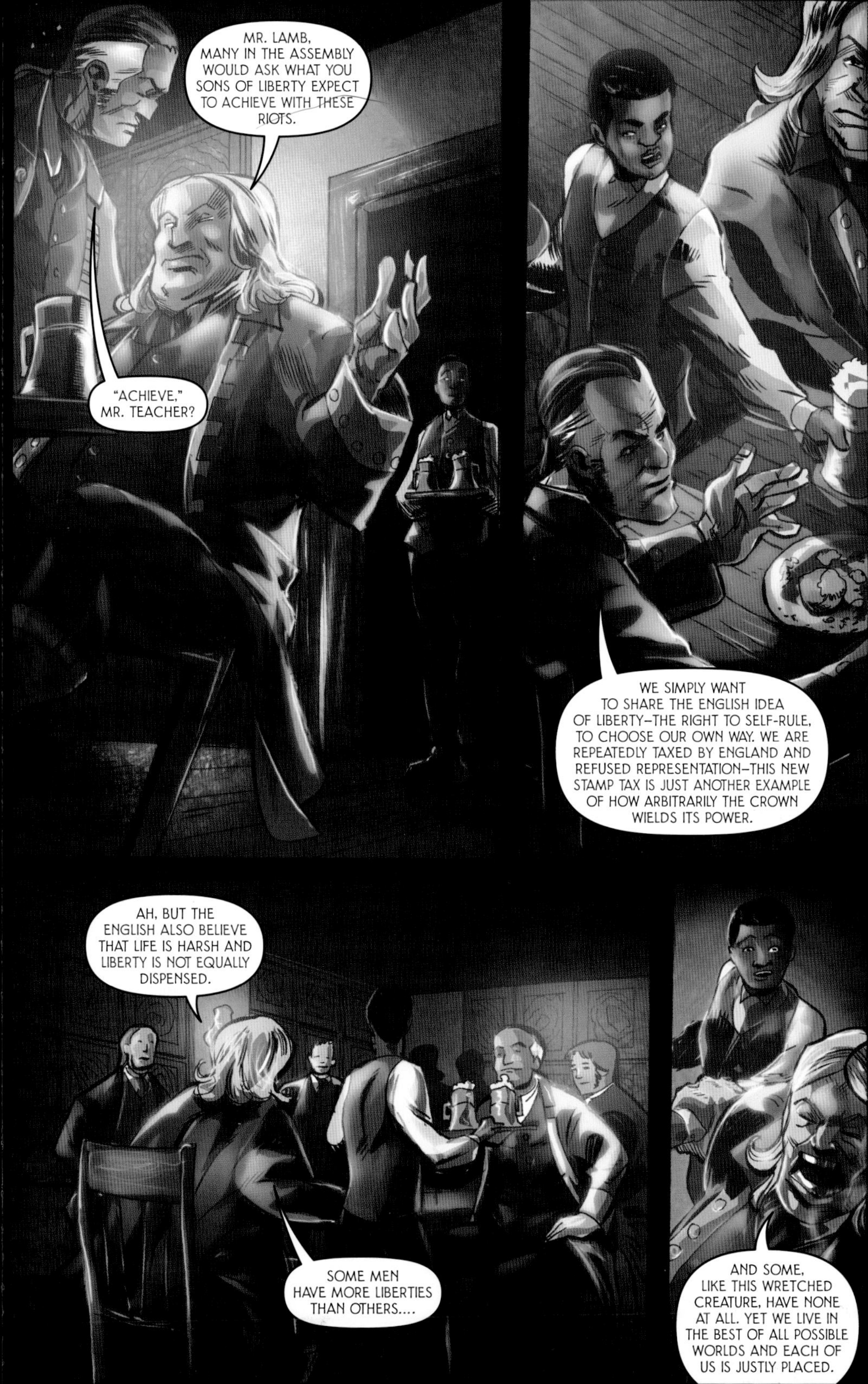

MR. LAMB, MANY IN THE ASSEMBLY WOULD ASK WHAT YOU SONS OF LIBERTY EXPECT TO ACHIEVE WITH THESE RIOTS.
"ACHIEVE," MR. TEACHER?
WE SIMPLY WANT TO SHARE THE ENGLISH IDEA OF LIBERTY—THE RIGHT TO SELF-RULE, TO CHOOSE OUR OWN WAY. WE ARE REPEATEDLY TAXED BY ENGLAND AND REFUSED REPRESENTATION—THIS NEW STAMP TAX IS JUST ANOTHER EXAMPLE OF HOW ARBITRARILY THE CROWN WIELDS ITS POWER.
AH, BUT THE ENGLISH ALSO BELIEVE THAT LIFE IS HARSH AND LIBERTY IS NOT EQUALLY DISPENSED.
SOME MEN HAVE MORE LIBERTIES THAN OTHERS....
AND SOME, LIKE THIS WRETCHED CREATURE, HAVE NONE AT ALL. YET WE LIVE IN THE BEST OF ALL POSSIBLE WORLDS AND EACH OF US IS JUSTLY PLACED.

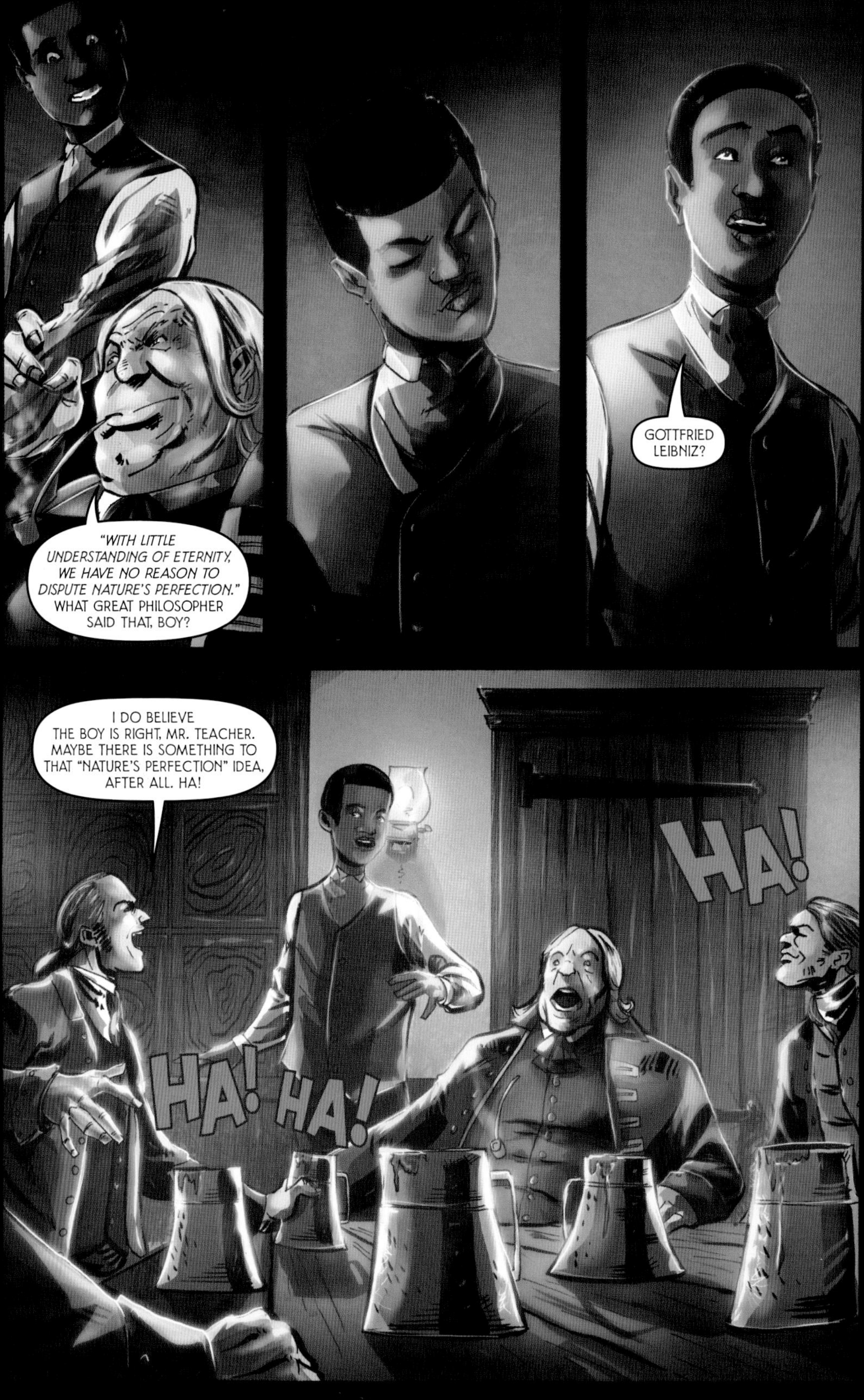
"WITH LITTLE UNDERSTANDING OF ETERNITY, WE HAVE NO REASON TO DISPUTE NATURE'S PERFECTION." WHAT GREAT PHILOSOPHER SAID THAT, BOY?
GOTTFRIED LEIBNIZ?
I DO BELIEVE THE BOY IS RIGHT, MR. TEACHER. MAYBE THERE IS SOMETHING TO THAT "NATURE'S PERFECTION" IDEA, AFTER ALL. HA!
HA!
HA! HA!

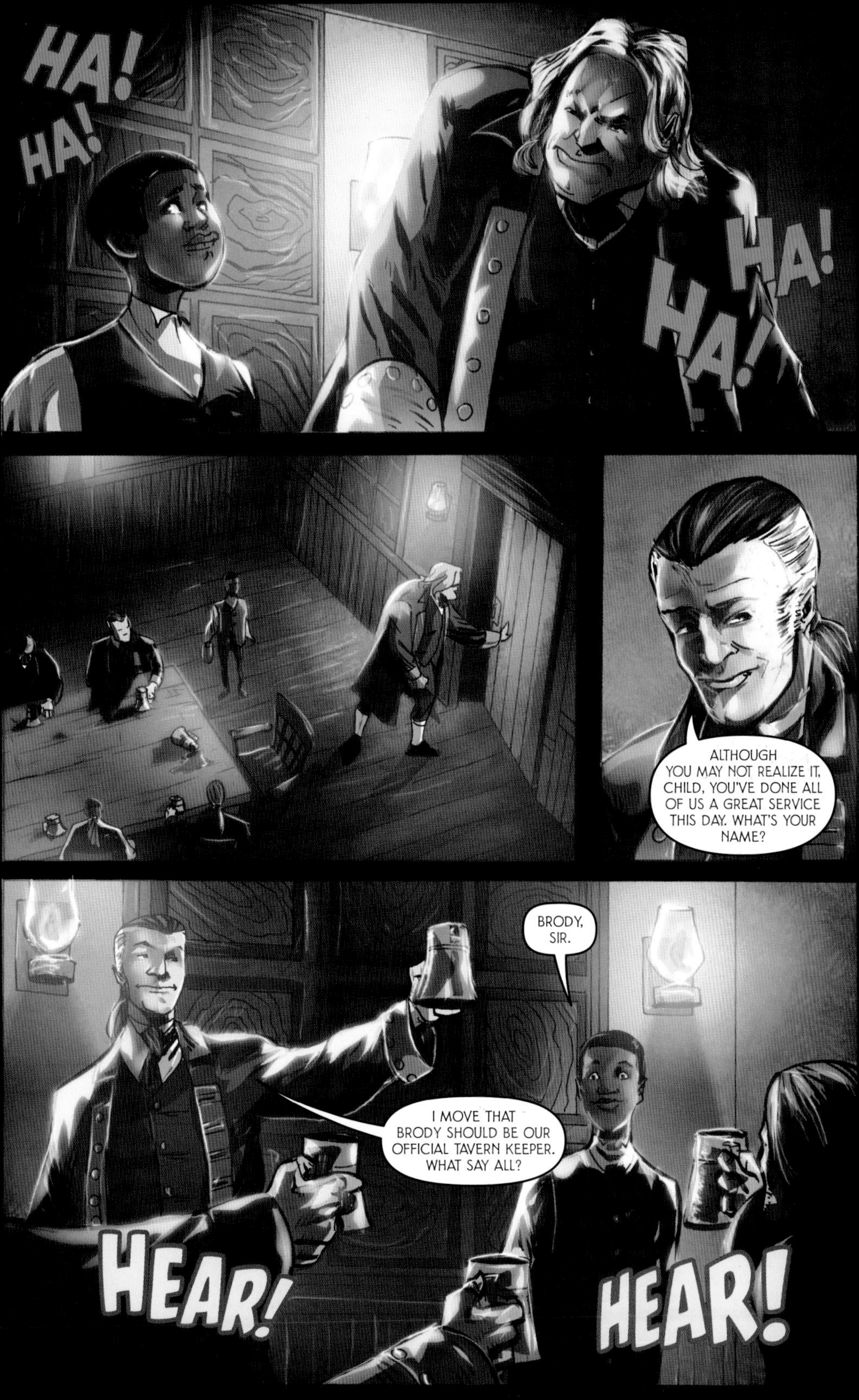
HA! HA!
HA! HA!
ALTHOUGH YOU MAY NOT REALIZE IT, CHILD, YOU'VE DONE ALL OF US A GREAT SERVICE THIS DAY. WHAT'S YOUR NAME?
BRODY, SIR.
I MOVE THAT BRODY SHOULD BE OUR OFFICIAL TAVERN KEEPER. WHAT SAY ALL?
HEAR! HEAR!

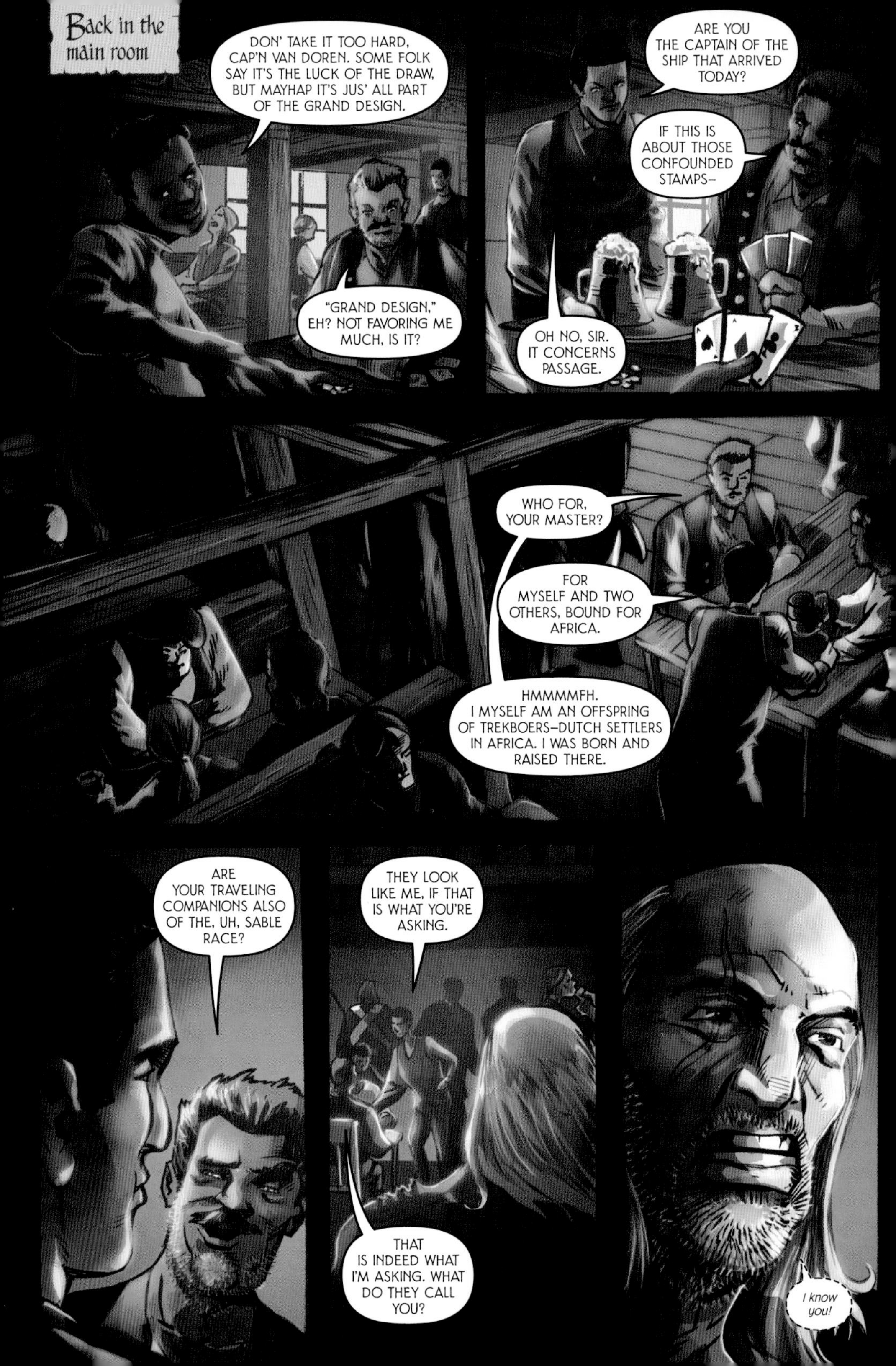
Back in the main room
DON' TAKE IT TOO HARD, CAP'N VAN DOREN. SOME FOLK SAY IT'S THE LUCK OF THE DRAW, BUT MAYHAP IT'S JUS' ALL PART OF THE GRAND DESIGN.
"GRAND DESIGN," EH? NOT FAVORING ME MUCH, IS IT?
ARE YOU THE CAPTAIN OF THE SHIP THAT ARRIVED TODAY?
IF THIS IS ABOUT THOSE CONFOUNDED STAMPS–
OH NO, SIR. IT CONCERNS PASSAGE.
WHO FOR, YOUR MASTER?
FOR MYSELF AND TWO OTHERS, BOUND FOR AFRICA.
HMMMMFH. I MYSELF AM AN OFFSPRING OF TREKBOERS–DUTCH SETTLERS IN AFRICA. I WAS BORN AND RAISED THERE.
ARE YOUR TRAVELING COMPANIONS ALSO OF THE, UH, SABLE RACE?
THEY LOOK LIKE ME, IF THAT IS WHAT YOU'RE ASKING.
THAT IS INDEED WHAT I'M ASKING. WHAT DO THEY CALL YOU?
I know you!

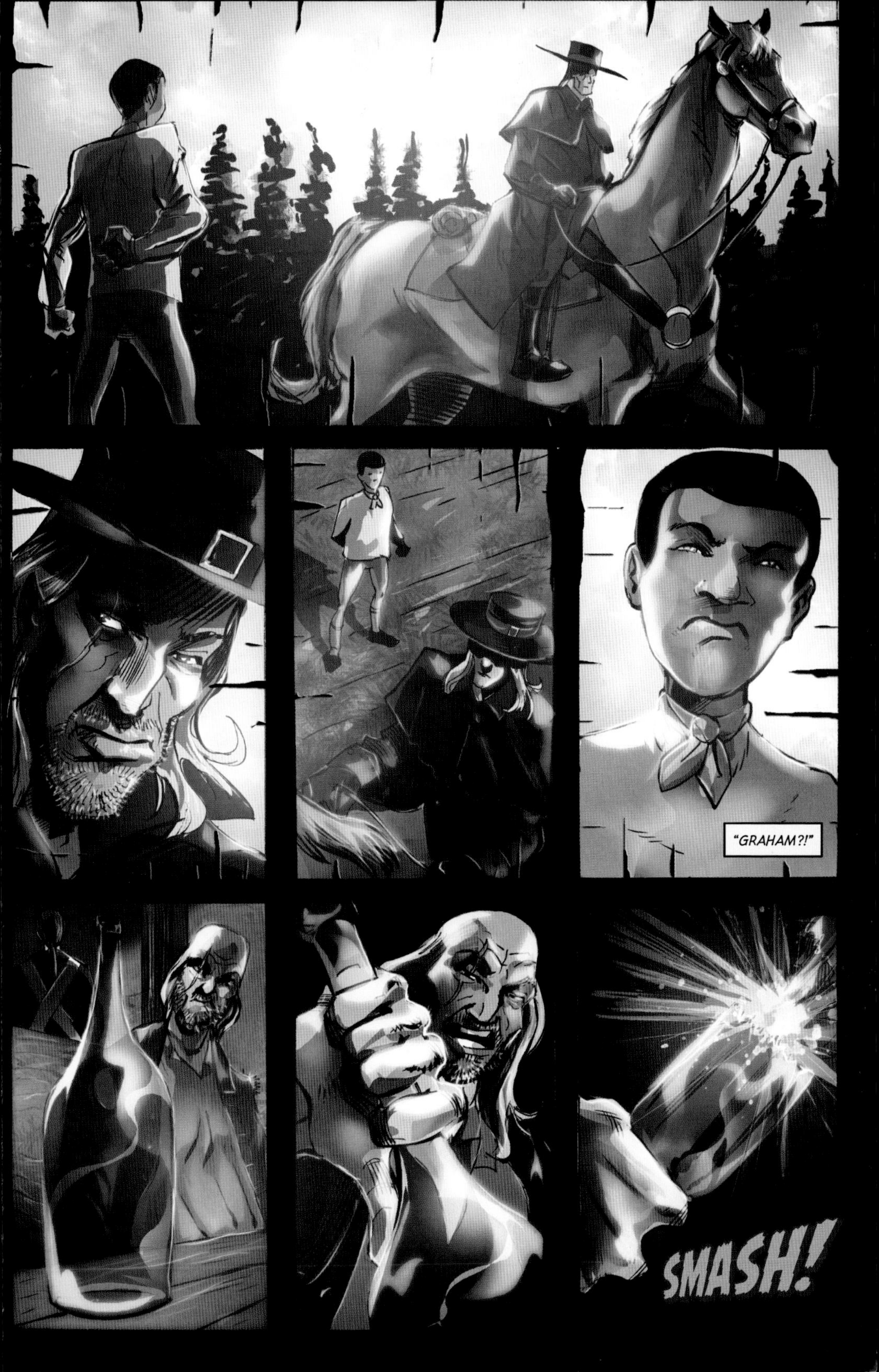
"GRAHAM?!"
SMASH!

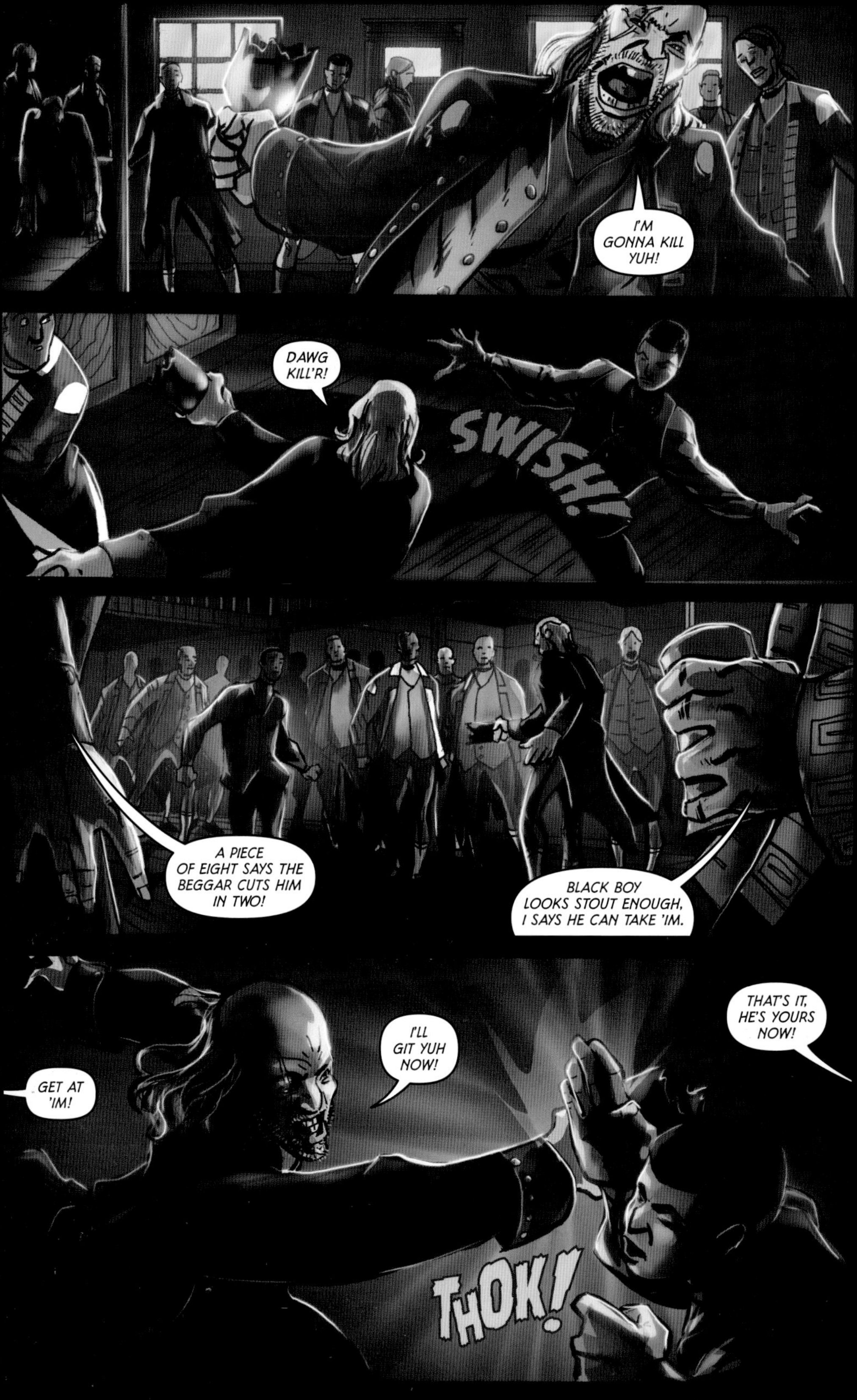
I'M GONNA KILL YUH!
DAWG KILL'R!
SWISH!
A PIECE OF EIGHT SAYS THE BEGGAR CUTS HIM IN TWO!
BLACK BOY LOOKS STOUT ENOUGH, I SAYS HE CAN TAKE 'IM.
GET AT 'IM!
I'LL GIT YUH NOW!
THAT'S IT, HE'S YOURS NOW!
THOK!

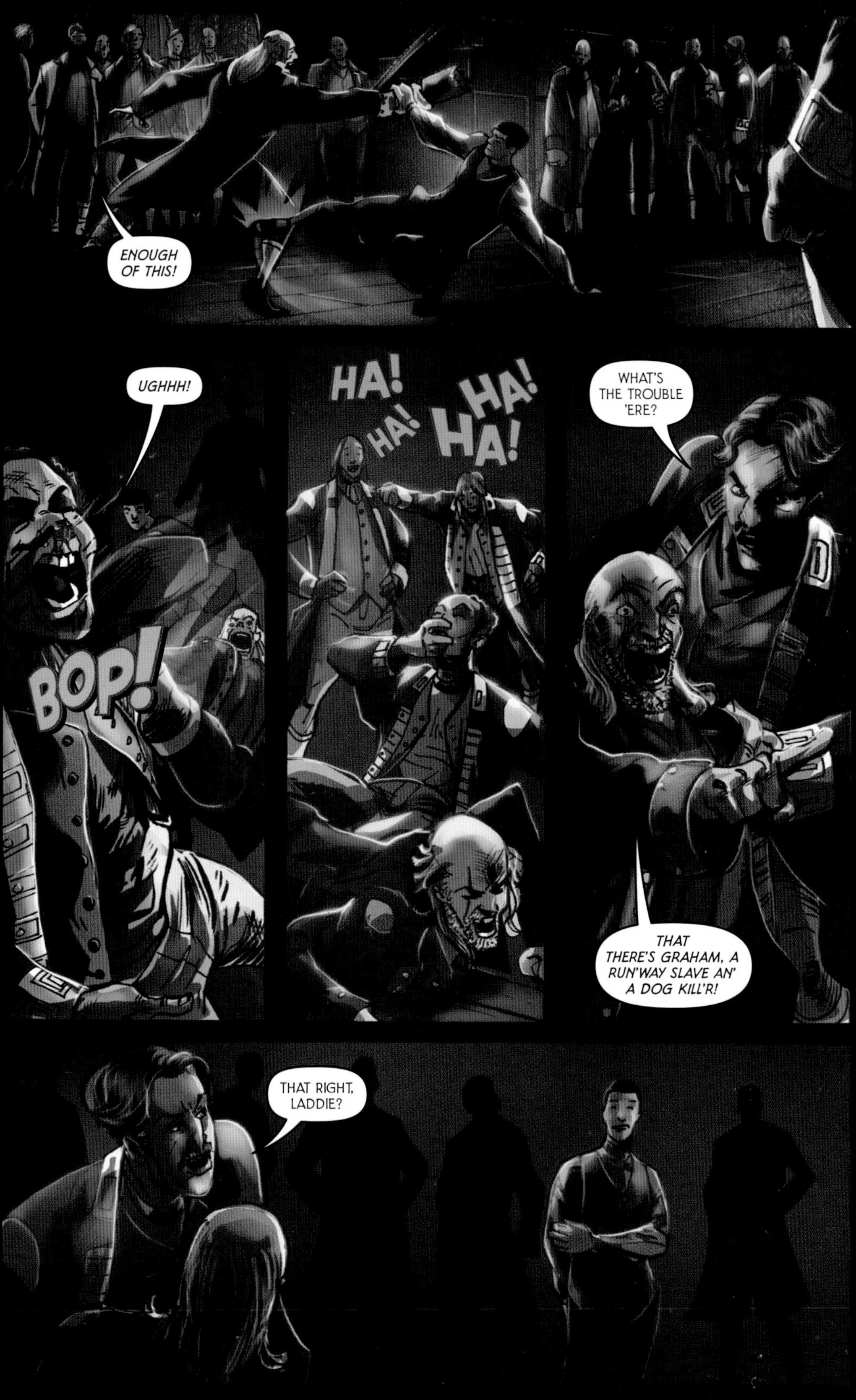
ENOUGH OF THIS!
UGHHH!
BOP!
HA! HA! HA! HA!
WHAT'S THE TROUBLE 'ERE?
THAT THERE'S GRAHAM, A RUN'WAY SLAVE AN' A DOG KILL'R!
THAT RIGHT, LADDIE?

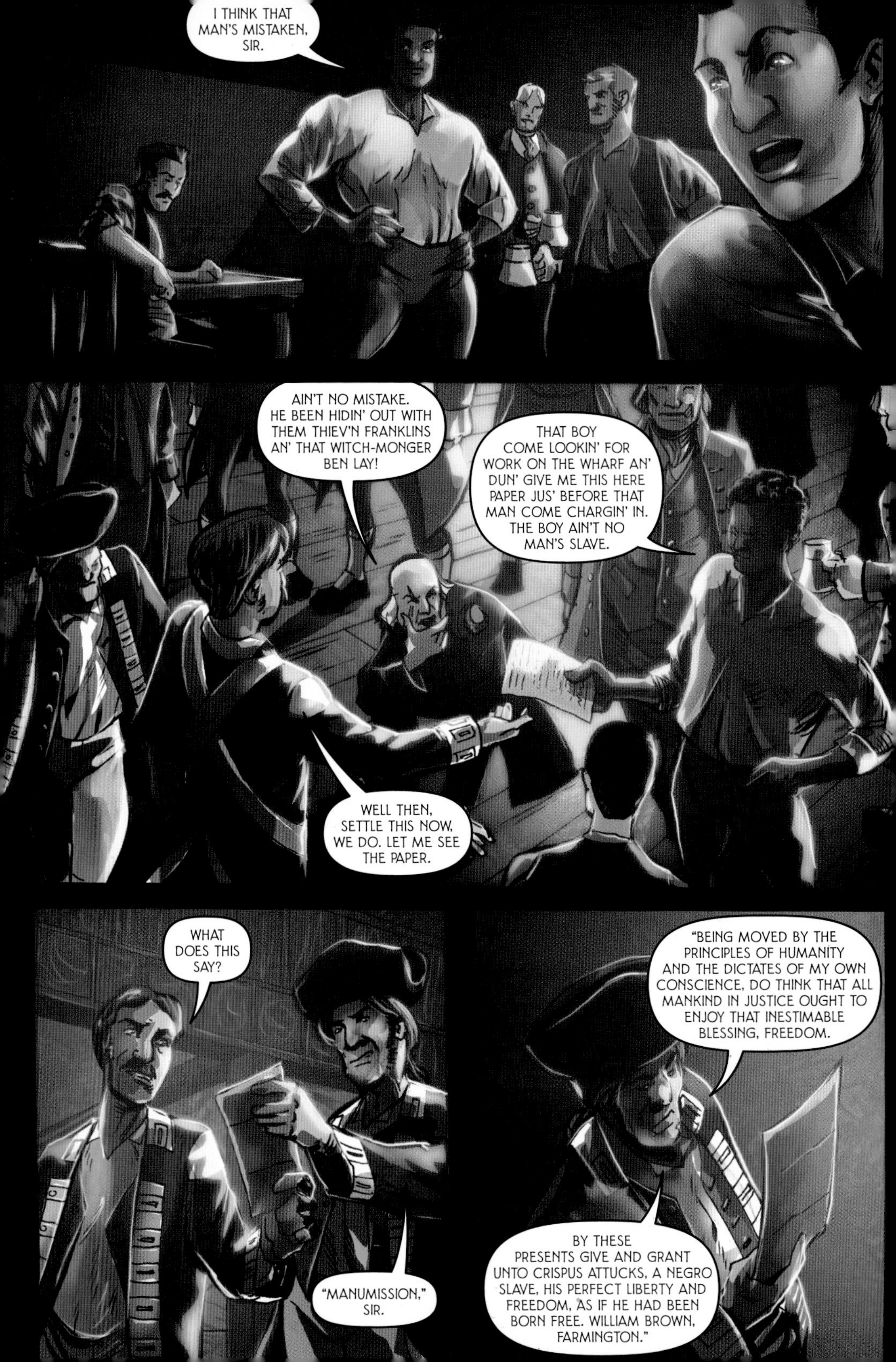
I THINK THAT MAN'S MISTAKEN, SIR.
AIN'T NO MISTAKE. HE BEEN HIDIN' OUT WITH THEM THIEV'N FRANKLINS AN' THAT WITCH-MONGER BEN LAY!
THAT BOY COME LOOKIN' FOR WORK ON THE WHARF AN' DUN' GIVE ME THIS HERE PAPER JUS' BEFORE THAT MAN COME CHARGIN' IN. THE BOY AIN'T NO MAN'S SLAVE.
WELL THEN, SETTLE THIS NOW, WE DO. LET ME SEE THE PAPER.
WHAT DOES THIS SAY?
"MANUMISSION," SIR.
"BEING MOVED BY THE PRINCIPLES OF HUMANITY AND THE DICTATES OF MY OWN CONSCIENCE, DO THINK THAT ALL MANKIND IN JUSTICE OUGHT TO ENJOY THAT INESTIMABLE BLESSING, FREEDOM.
BY THESE PRESENTS GIVE AND GRANT UNTO CRISPUS ATTUCKS, A NEGRO SLAVE, HIS PERFECT LIBERTY AND FREEDOM, AS IF HE HAD BEEN BORN FREE. WILLIAM BROWN, FARMINGTON."

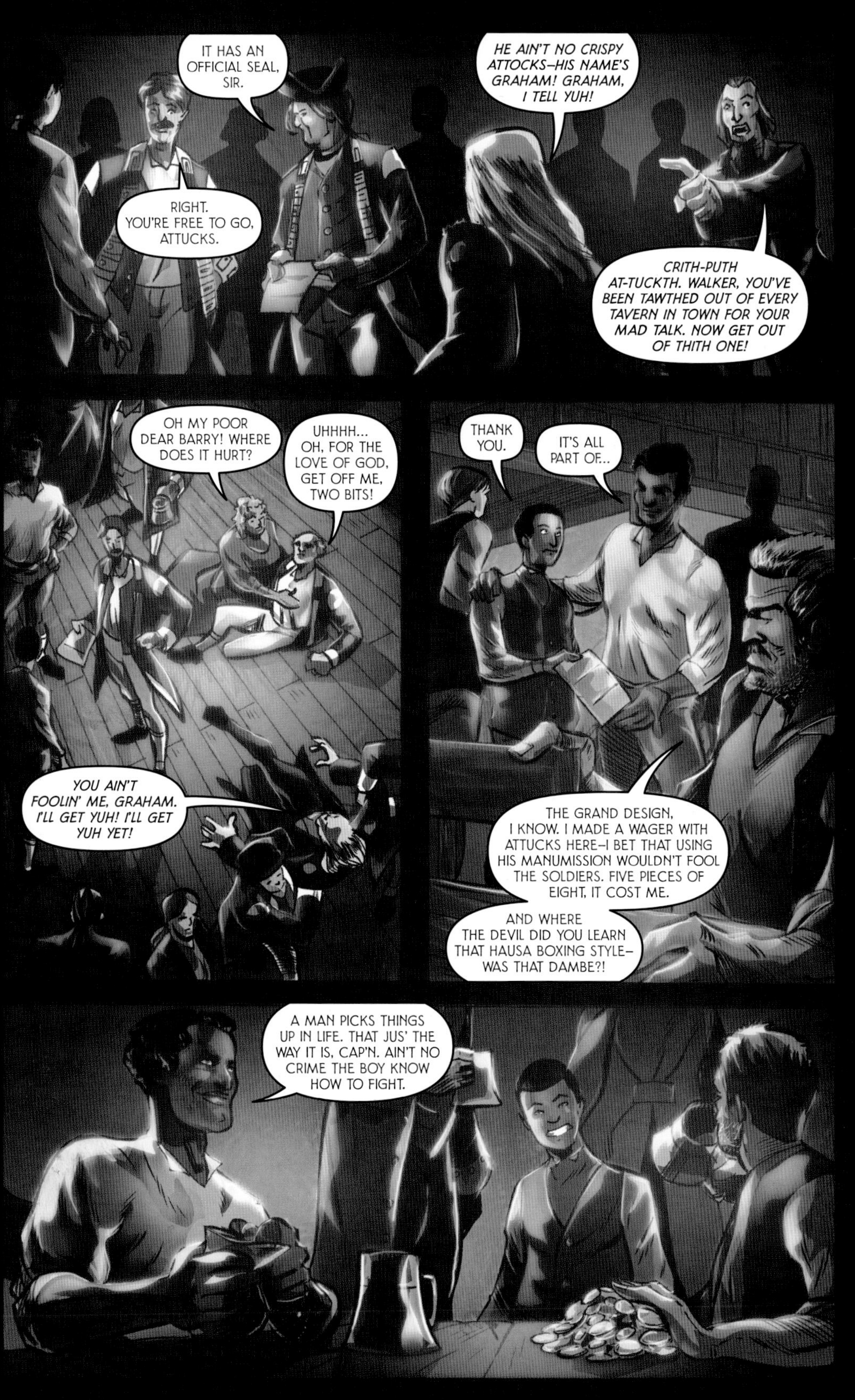
IT HAS AN OFFICIAL SEAL, SIR.
RIGHT. YOU'RE FREE TO GO, ATTUCKS.
HE AIN'T NO CRISPY ATTOCKS—HIS NAME'S GRAHAM! GRAHAM, I TELL YUH!
CRITH-PUTH AT-TUCKTH. WALKER, YOU'VE BEEN TAWTHED OUT OF EVERY TAVERN IN TOWN FOR YOUR MAD TALK. NOW GET OUT OF THITH ONE!
OH MY POOR DEAR BARRY! WHERE DOES IT HURT?
UHHHH... OH, FOR THE LOVE OF GOD, GET OFF ME, TWO BITS!
YOU AIN'T FOOLIN' ME, GRAHAM. I'LL GET YUH! I'LL GET YUH YET!
THANK YOU.
IT'S ALL PART OF...
THE GRAND DESIGN, I KNOW. I MADE A WAGER WITH ATTUCKS HERE—I BET THAT USING HIS MANUMISSION WOULDN'T FOOL THE SOLDIERS. FIVE PIECES OF EIGHT, IT COST ME.
AND WHERE THE DEVIL DID YOU LEARN THAT HAUSA BOXING STYLE—WAS THAT DAMBE?!
A MAN PICKS THINGS UP IN LIFE. THAT JUS' THE WAY IT IS, CAP'N. AIN'T NO CRIME THE BOY KNOW HOW TO FIGHT.

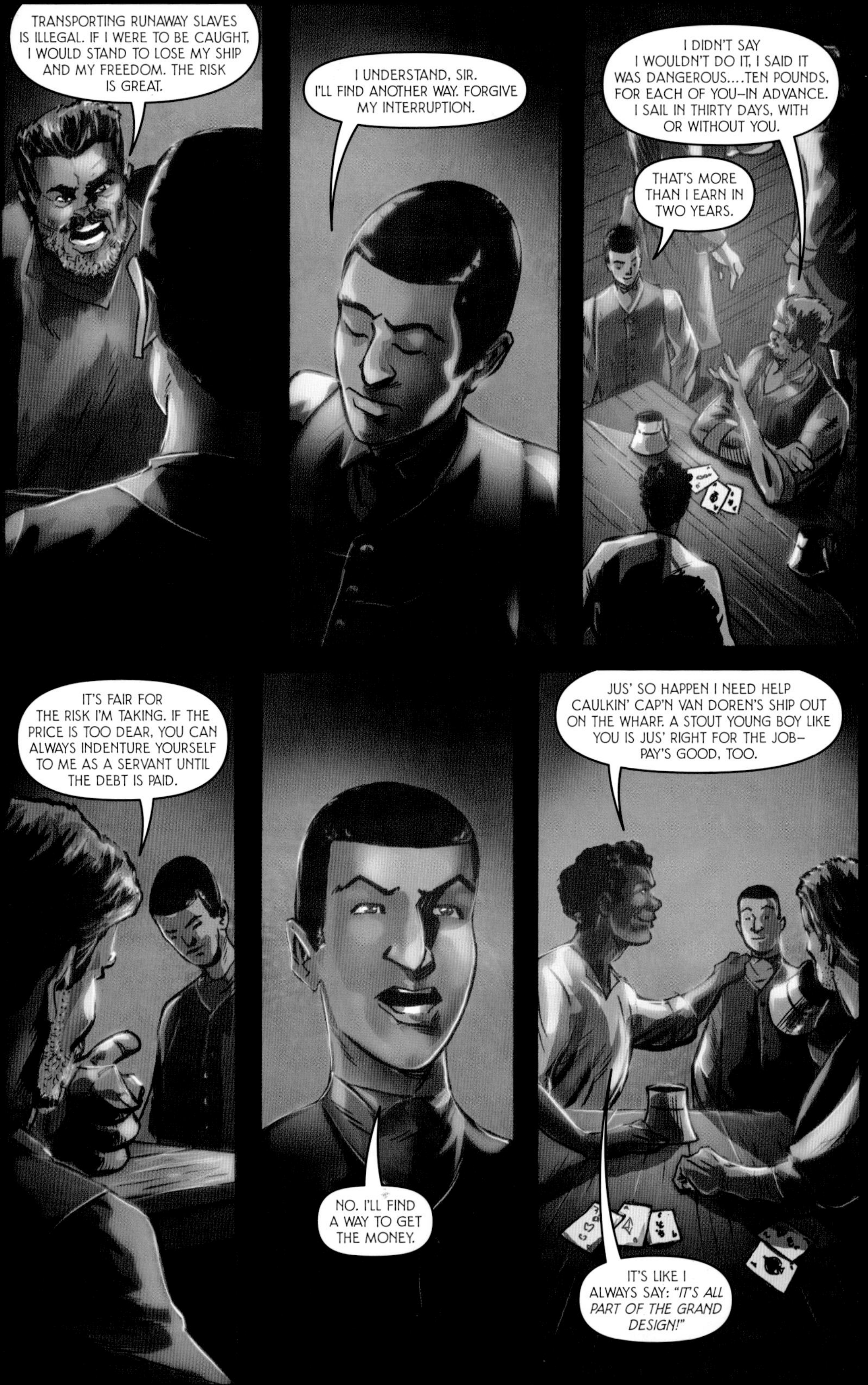
TRANSPORTING RUNAWAY SLAVES IS ILLEGAL. IF I WERE TO BE CAUGHT, I WOULD STAND TO LOSE MY SHIP AND MY FREEDOM. THE RISK IS GREAT.
I UNDERSTAND, SIR. I'LL FIND ANOTHER WAY. FORGIVE MY INTERRUPTION.
I DIDN'T SAY I WOULDN'T DO IT, I SAID IT WAS DANGEROUS....TEN POUNDS, FOR EACH OF YOU–IN ADVANCE. I SAIL IN THIRTY DAYS, WITH OR WITHOUT YOU.
THAT'S MORE THAN I EARN IN TWO YEARS.
IT'S FAIR FOR THE RISK I'M TAKING. IF THE PRICE IS TOO DEAR, YOU CAN ALWAYS INDENTURE YOURSELF TO ME AS A SERVANT UNTIL THE DEBT IS PAID.
NO. I'LL FIND A WAY TO GET THE MONEY.
JUS' SO HAPPEN I NEED HELP CAULKIN' CAP'N VAN DOREN'S SHIP OUT ON THE WHARF. A STOUT YOUNG BOY LIKE YOU IS JUS' RIGHT FOR THE JOB– PAY'S GOOD, TOO.
IT'S LIKE I ALWAYS SAY: *"IT'S ALL PART OF THE GRAND DESIGN!"*

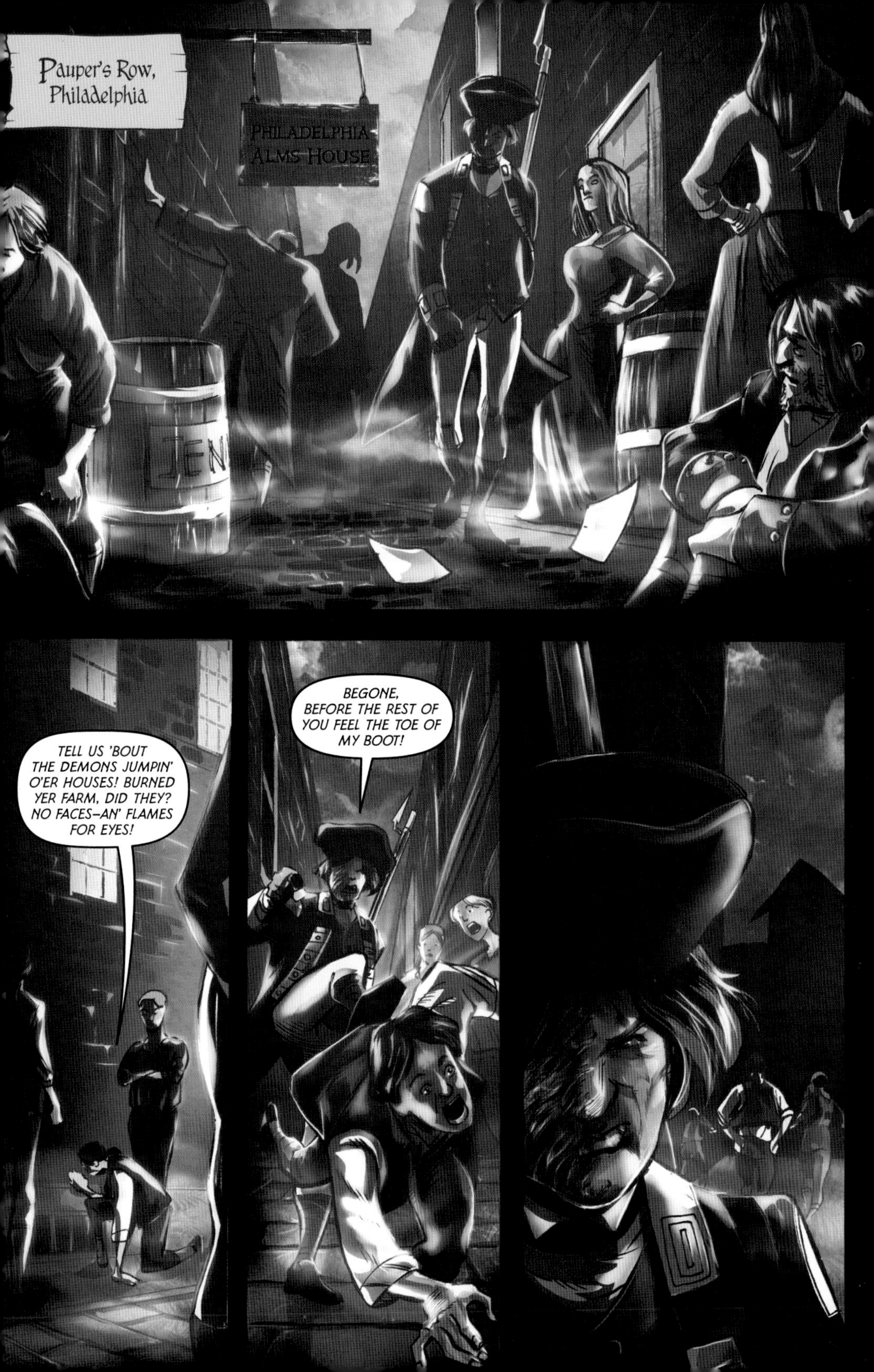
Pauper's Row, Philadelphia
PHILADELPHIA ALMS HOUSE
TELL US 'BOUT THE DEMONS JUMPIN' O'ER HOUSES! BURNED YER FARM, DID THEY? NO FACES–AN' FLAMES FOR EYES!
BEGONE, BEFORE THE REST OF YOU FEEL THE TOE OF MY BOOT!

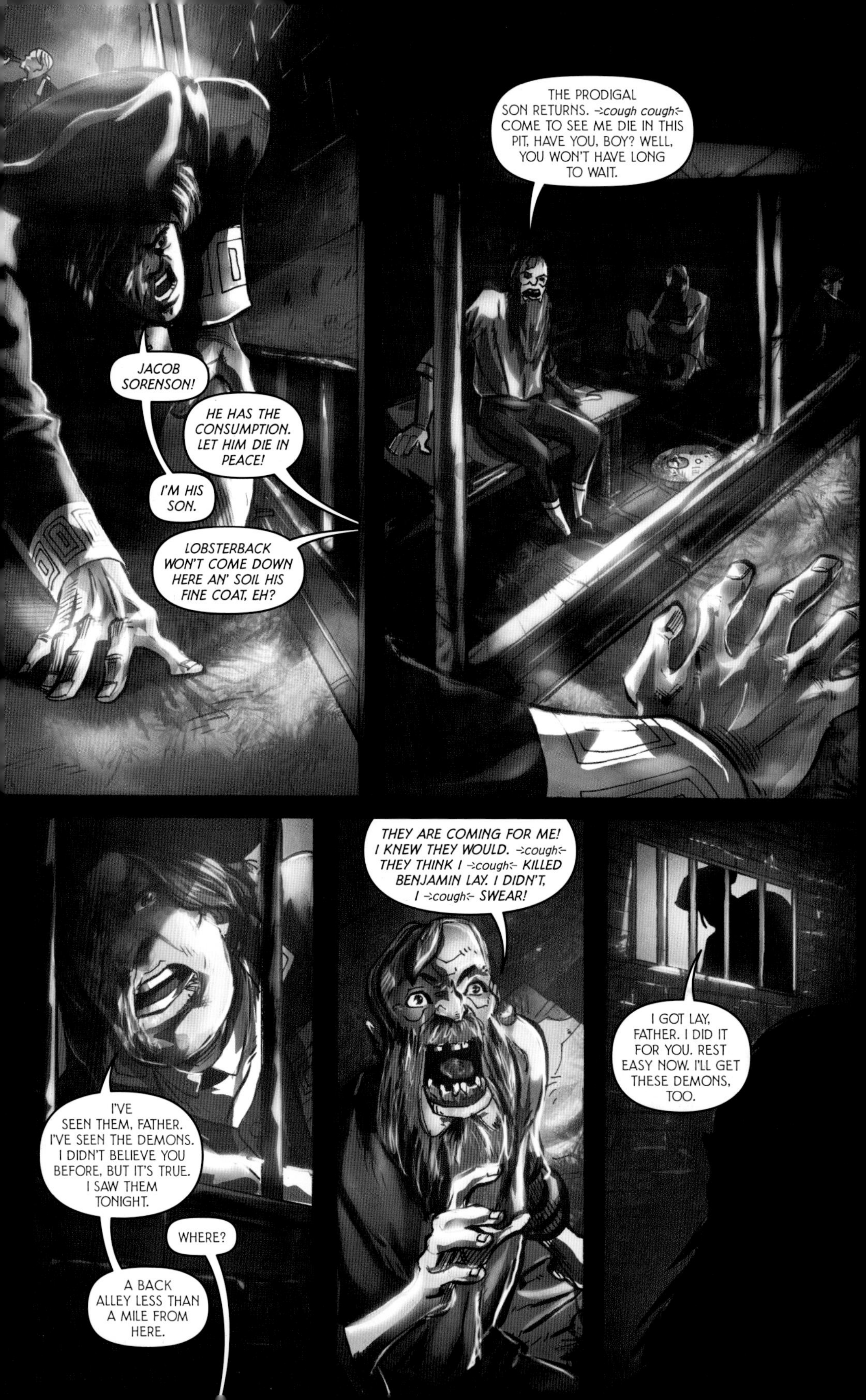
JACOB SORENSON!
HE HAS THE CONSUMPTION. LET HIM DIE IN PEACE!
I'M HIS SON.
LOBSTERBACK WON'T COME DOWN HERE AN' SOIL HIS FINE COAT, EH?
THE PRODIGAL SON RETURNS. ->cough cough<- COME TO SEE ME DIE IN THIS PIT, HAVE YOU, BOY? WELL, YOU WON'T HAVE LONG TO WAIT.
I'VE SEEN THEM, FATHER. I'VE SEEN THE DEMONS. I DIDN'T BELIEVE YOU BEFORE, BUT IT'S TRUE. I SAW THEM TONIGHT.
WHERE?
A BACK ALLEY LESS THAN A MILE FROM HERE.
THEY ARE COMING FOR ME! I KNEW THEY WOULD. ->cough<- THEY THINK I ->cough<- KILLED BENJAMIN LAY. I DIDN'T, I ->cough<- SWEAR!
I GOT LAY, FATHER. I DID IT FOR YOU. REST EASY NOW. I'LL GET THESE DEMONS, TOO.

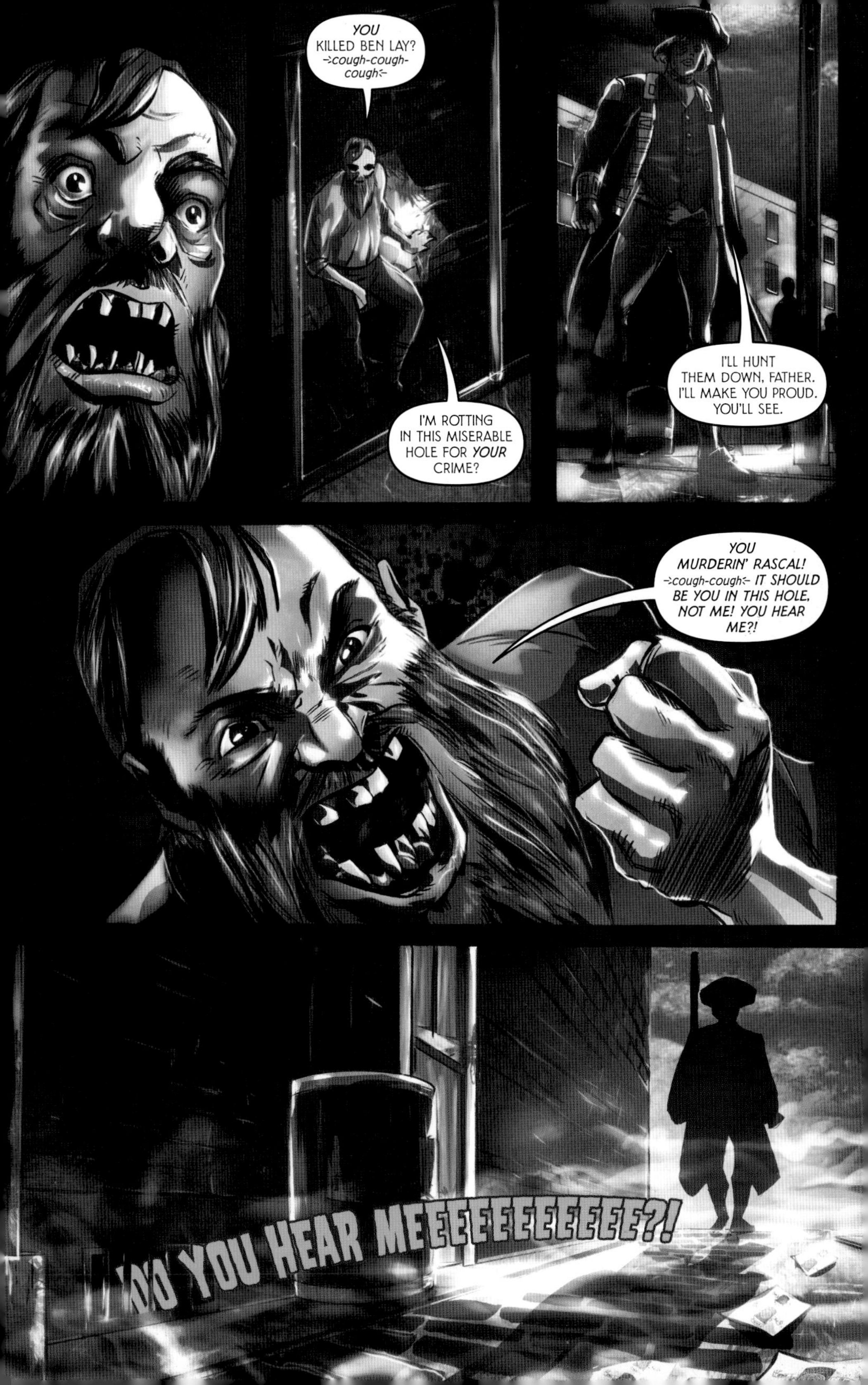
YOU KILLED BEN LAY? –cough-cough-cough–
I'M ROTTING IN THIS MISERABLE HOLE FOR *YOUR* CRIME?
I'LL HUNT THEM DOWN, FATHER. I'LL MAKE YOU PROUD. YOU'LL SEE.
YOU MURDERIN' RASCAL! –cough-cough– IT SHOULD BE YOU IN THIS HOLE, NOT ME! YOU HEAR ME?!
DO YOU HEAR MEEEEEEEEEEE?!

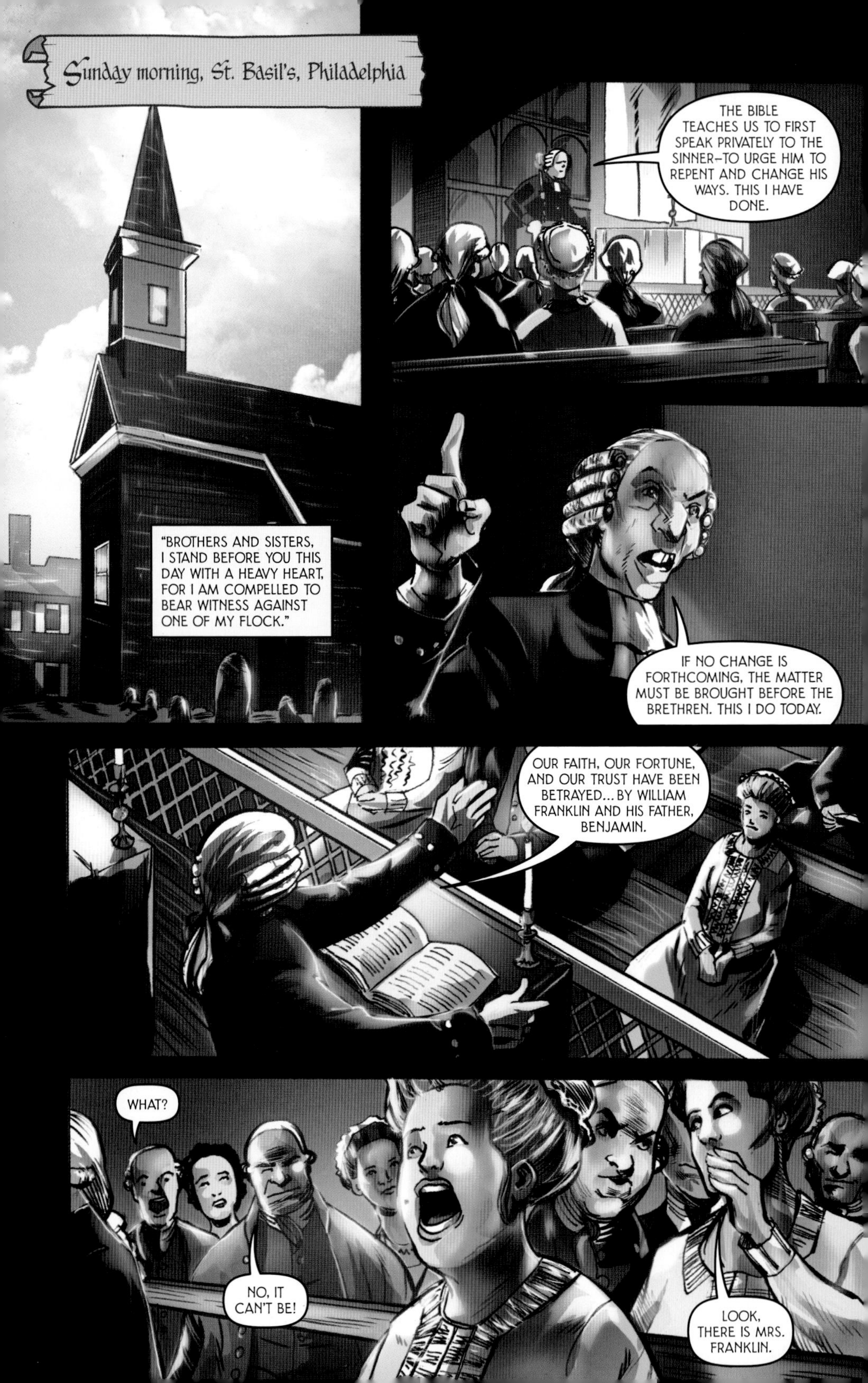
Sunday morning, St. Basil's, Philadelphia
THE BIBLE TEACHES US TO FIRST SPEAK PRIVATELY TO THE SINNER—TO URGE HIM TO REPENT AND CHANGE HIS WAYS. THIS I HAVE DONE.
"BROTHERS AND SISTERS, I STAND BEFORE YOU THIS DAY WITH A HEAVY HEART, FOR I AM COMPELLED TO BEAR WITNESS AGAINST ONE OF MY FLOCK."
IF NO CHANGE IS FORTHCOMING, THE MATTER MUST BE BROUGHT BEFORE THE BRETHREN. THIS I DO TODAY.
OUR FAITH, OUR FORTUNE, AND OUR TRUST HAVE BEEN BETRAYED... BY WILLIAM FRANKLIN AND HIS FATHER, BENJAMIN.
WHAT?
NO, IT CAN'T BE!
LOOK, THERE IS MRS. FRANKLIN.

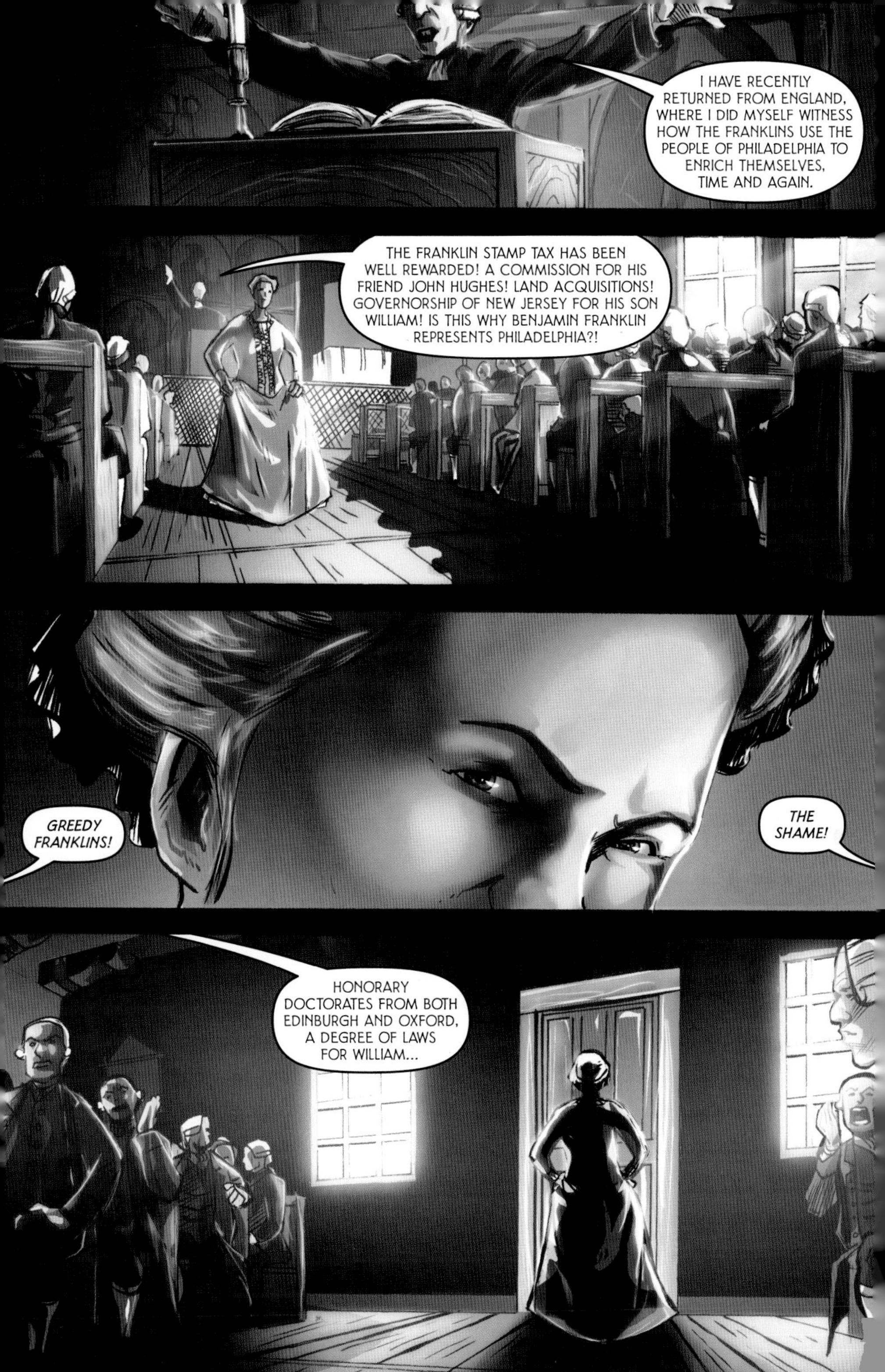
I HAVE RECENTLY RETURNED FROM ENGLAND, WHERE I DID MYSELF WITNESS HOW THE FRANKLINS USE THE PEOPLE OF PHILADELPHIA TO ENRICH THEMSELVES, TIME AND AGAIN.
THE FRANKLIN STAMP TAX HAS BEEN WELL REWARDED! A COMMISSION FOR HIS FRIEND JOHN HUGHES! LAND ACQUISITIONS! GOVERNORSHIP OF NEW JERSEY FOR HIS SON WILLIAM! IS THIS WHY BENJAMIN FRANKLIN REPRESENTS PHILADELPHIA?!
GREEDY FRANKLINS!
THE SHAME!
HONORARY DOCTORATES FROM BOTH EDINBURGH AND OXFORD, A DEGREE OF LAWS FOR WILLIAM...

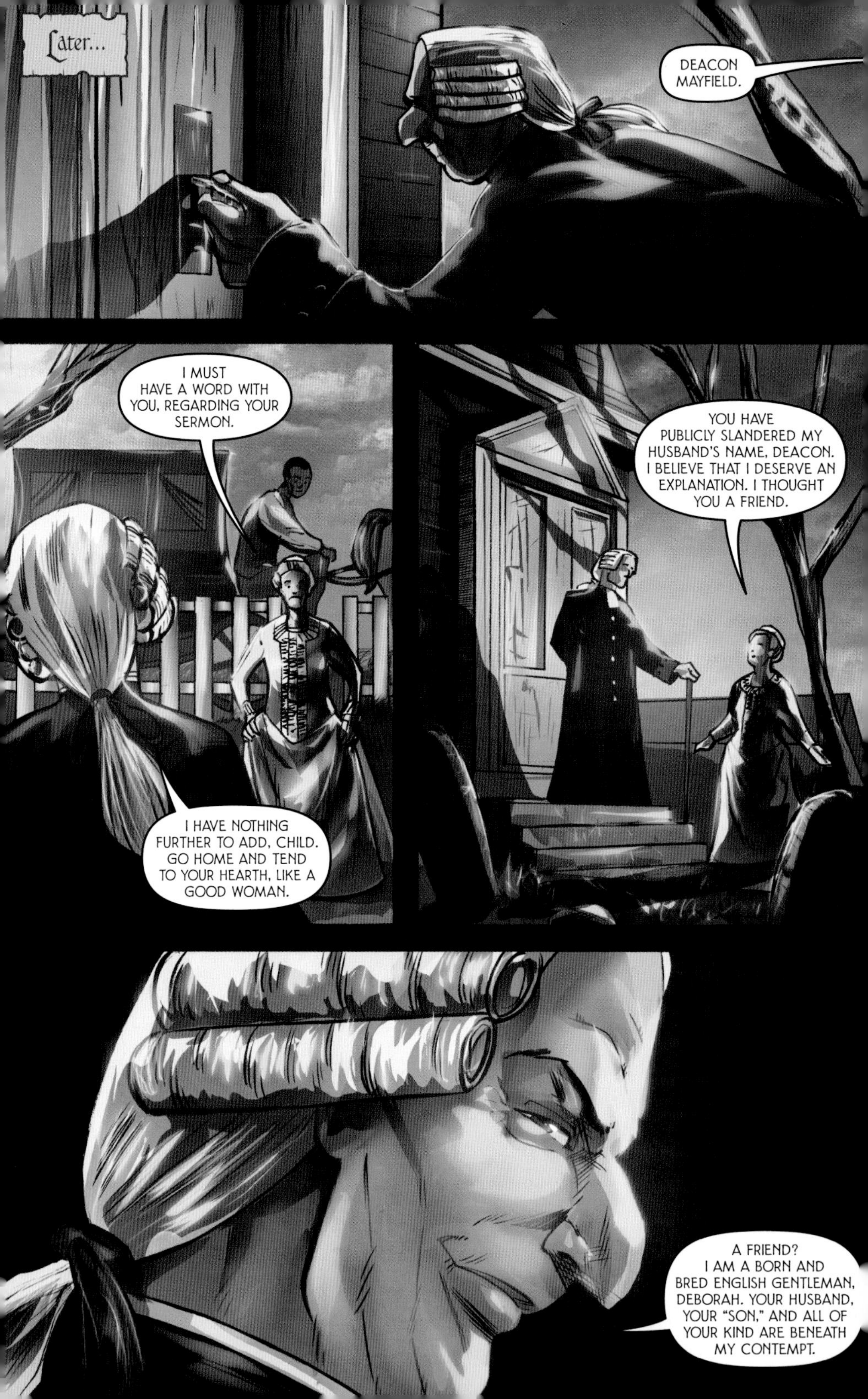
Later...
DEACON MAYFIELD.
I MUST HAVE A WORD WITH YOU, REGARDING YOUR SERMON.
I HAVE NOTHING FURTHER TO ADD, CHILD. GO HOME AND TEND TO YOUR HEARTH, LIKE A GOOD WOMAN.
YOU HAVE PUBLICLY SLANDERED MY HUSBAND'S NAME, DEACON. I BELIEVE THAT I DESERVE AN EXPLANATION. I THOUGHT YOU A FRIEND.
A FRIEND? I AM A BORN AND BRED ENGLISH GENTLEMAN, DEBORAH. YOUR HUSBAND, YOUR "SON," AND ALL OF YOUR KIND ARE BENEATH MY CONTEMPT.

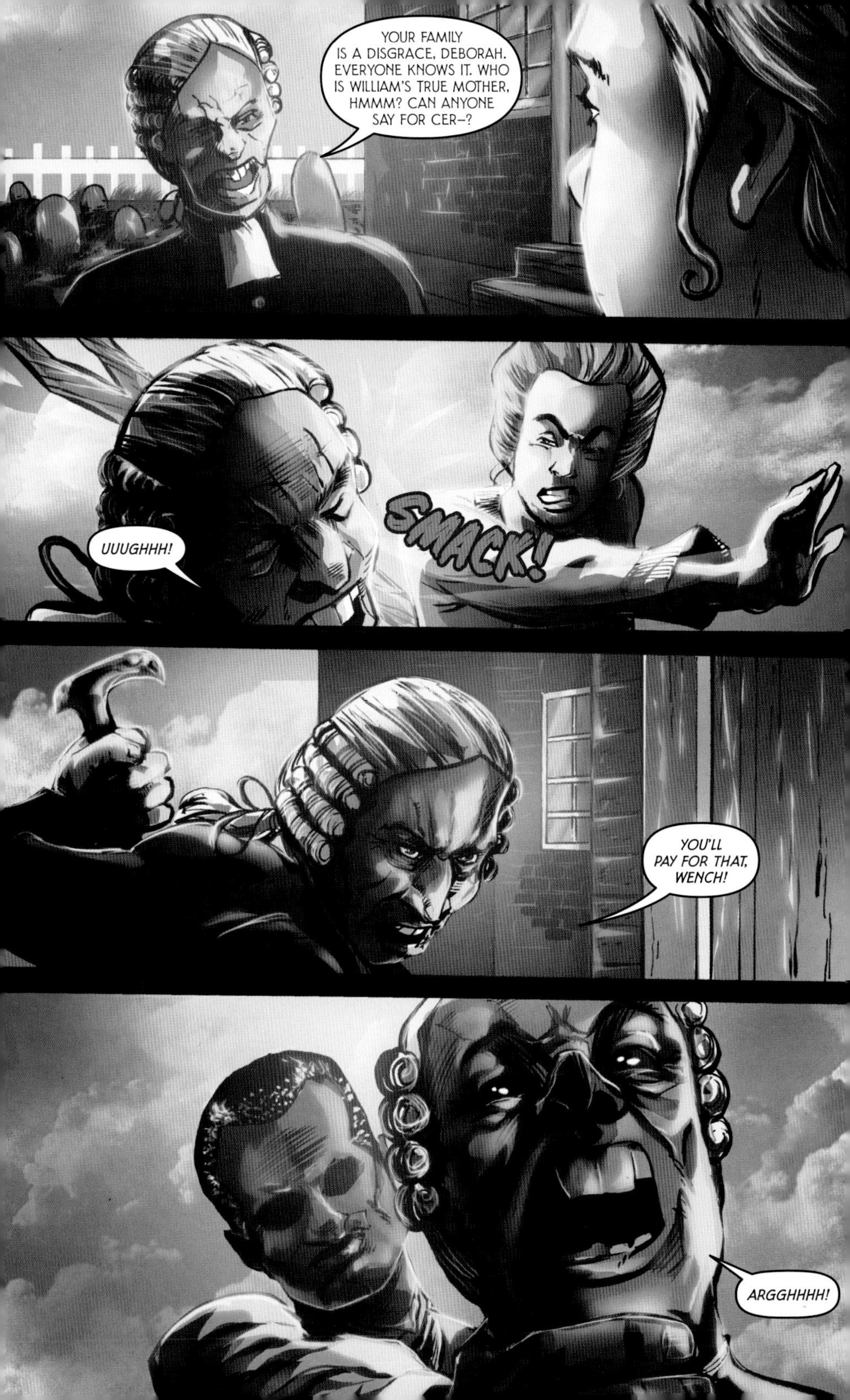
YOUR FAMILY IS A DISGRACE, DEBORAH. EVERYONE KNOWS IT. WHO IS WILLIAM'S TRUE MOTHER, HMMM? CAN ANYONE SAY FOR CER–?
SMACK!
UUUGHHH!
YOU'LL PAY FOR THAT, WENCH!
ARGGHHHH!

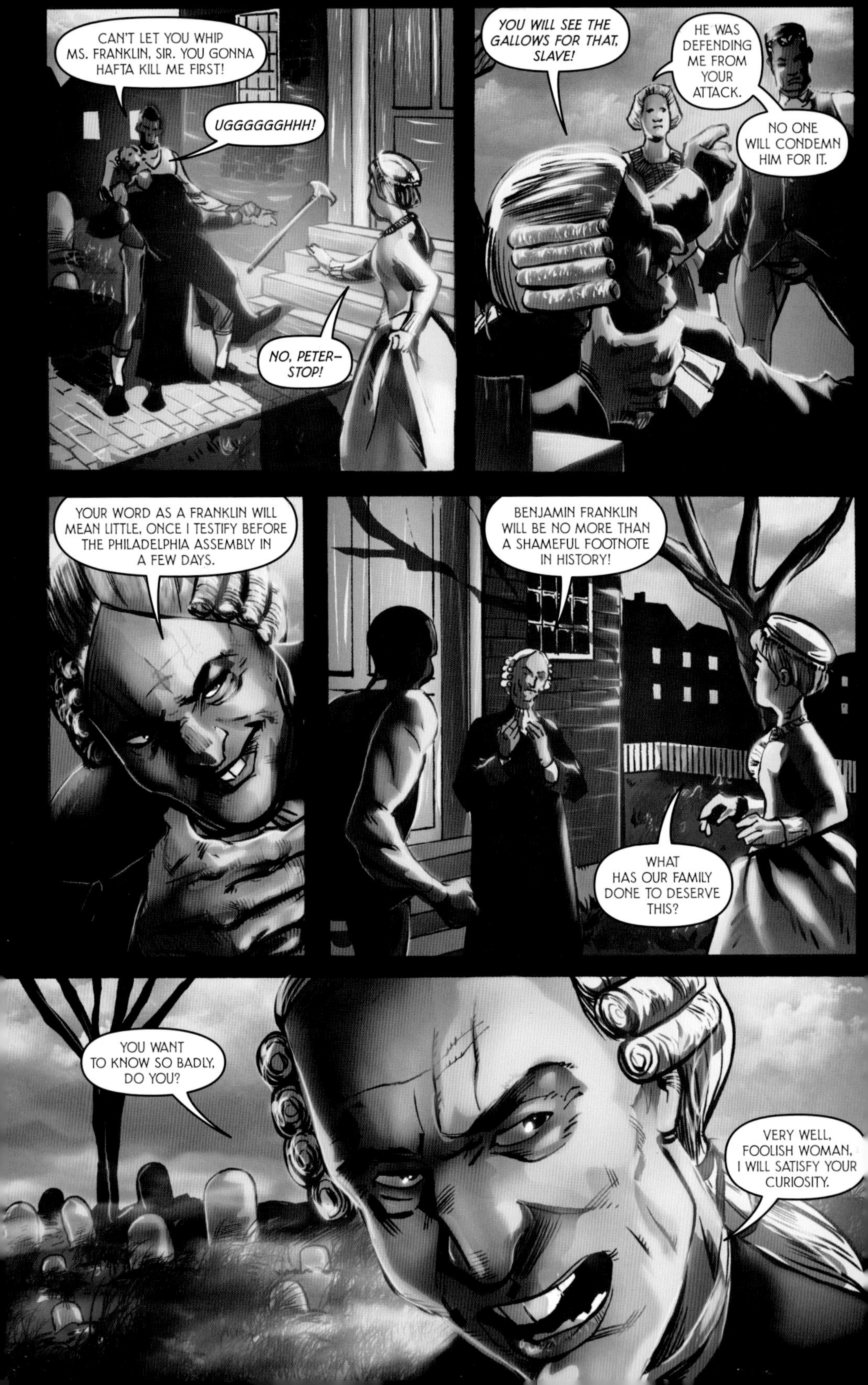

CAN'T LET YOU WHIP MS. FRANKLIN, SIR. YOU GONNA HAFTA KILL ME FIRST!
UGGGGGGHHH!
NO, PETER– STOP!
YOU WILL SEE THE GALLOWS FOR THAT, SLAVE!
HE WAS DEFENDING ME FROM YOUR ATTACK.
NO ONE WILL CONDEMN HIM FOR IT.
YOUR WORD AS A FRANKLIN WILL MEAN LITTLE, ONCE I TESTIFY BEFORE THE PHILADELPHIA ASSEMBLY IN A FEW DAYS.
BENJAMIN FRANKLIN WILL BE NO MORE THAN A SHAMEFUL FOOTNOTE IN HISTORY!
WHAT HAS OUR FAMILY DONE TO DESERVE THIS?
YOU WANT TO KNOW SO BADLY, DO YOU?
VERY WELL, FOOLISH WOMAN, I WILL SATISFY YOUR CURIOSITY.

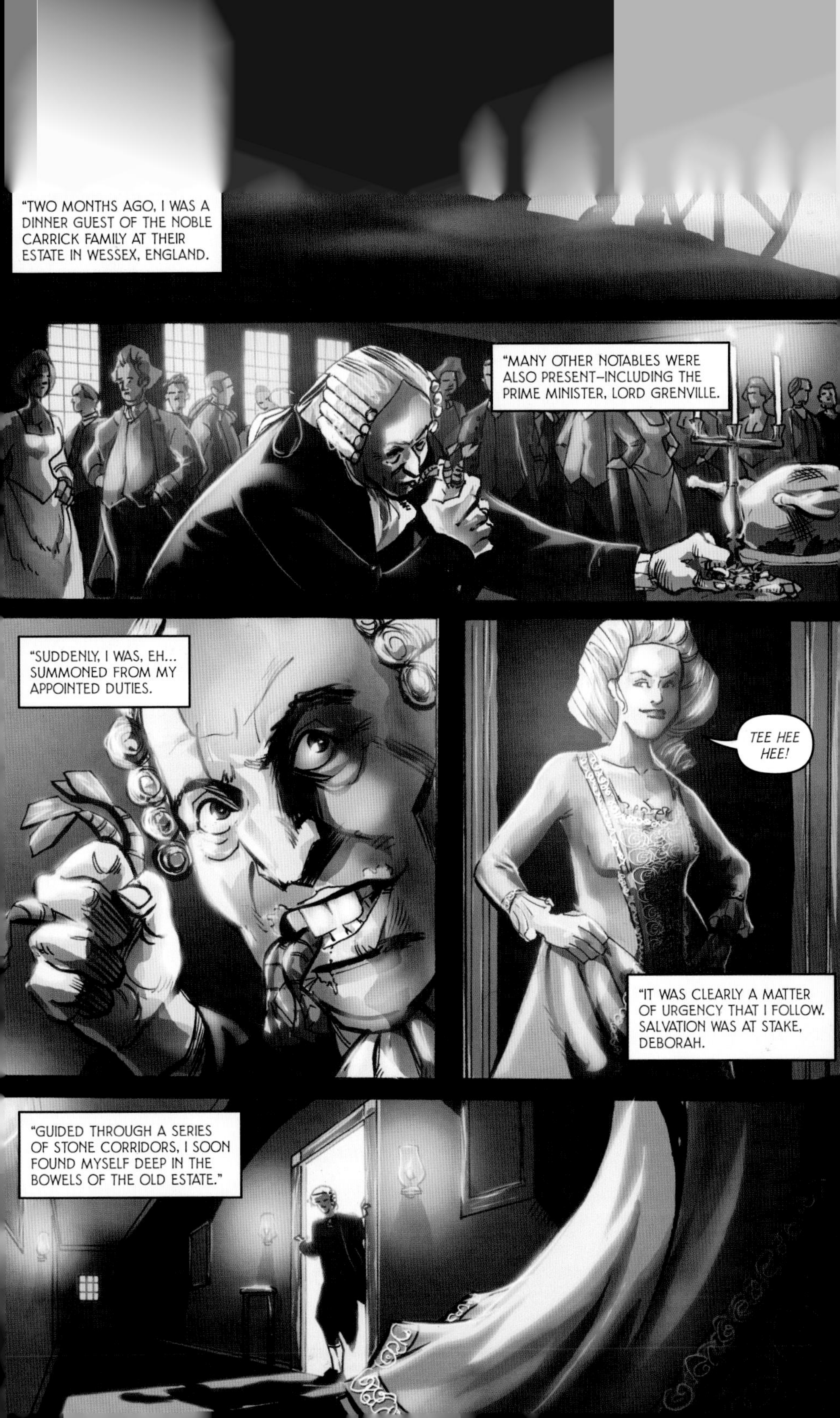
"TWO MONTHS AGO, I WAS A DINNER GUEST OF THE NOBLE CARRICK FAMILY AT THEIR ESTATE IN WESSEX, ENGLAND.
"MANY OTHER NOTABLES WERE ALSO PRESENT—INCLUDING THE PRIME MINISTER, LORD GRENVILLE.
"SUDDENLY, I WAS, EH... SUMMONED FROM MY APPOINTED DUTIES.
TEE HEE HEE!
"IT WAS CLEARLY A MATTER OF URGENCY THAT I FOLLOW. SALVATION WAS AT STAKE, DEBORAH.
"GUIDED THROUGH A SERIES OF STONE CORRIDORS, I SOON FOUND MYSELF DEEP IN THE BOWELS OF THE OLD ESTATE."

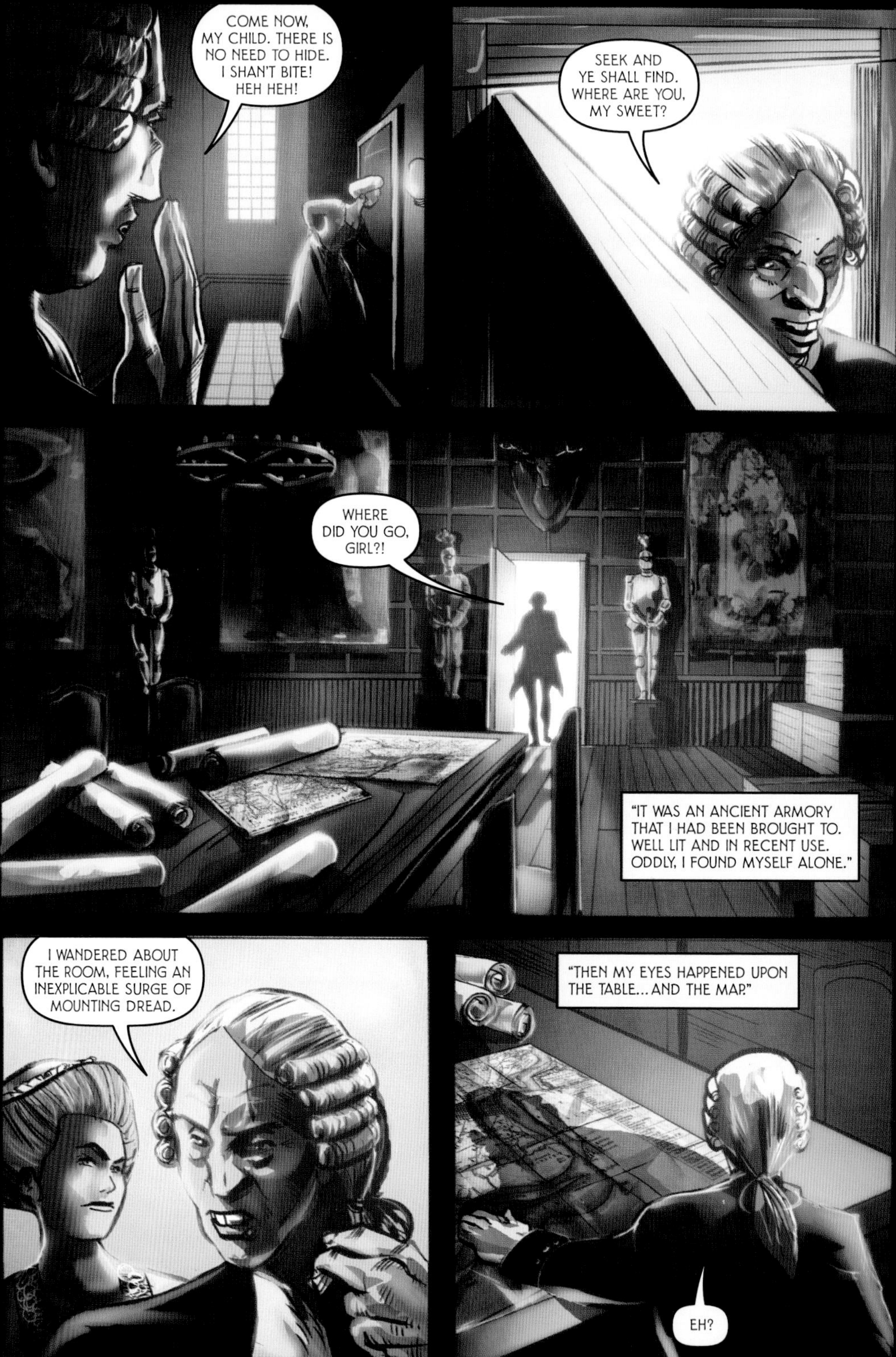
COME NOW, MY CHILD. THERE IS NO NEED TO HIDE. I SHAN'T BITE! HEH HEH!
SEEK AND YE SHALL FIND. WHERE ARE YOU, MY SWEET?
WHERE DID YOU GO, GIRL?!
"IT WAS AN ANCIENT ARMORY THAT I HAD BEEN BROUGHT TO. WELL LIT AND IN RECENT USE. ODDLY, I FOUND MYSELF ALONE."
I WANDERED ABOUT THE ROOM, FEELING AN INEXPLICABLE SURGE OF MOUNTING DREAD.
"THEN MY EYES HAPPENED UPON THE TABLE... AND THE MAP."
EH?

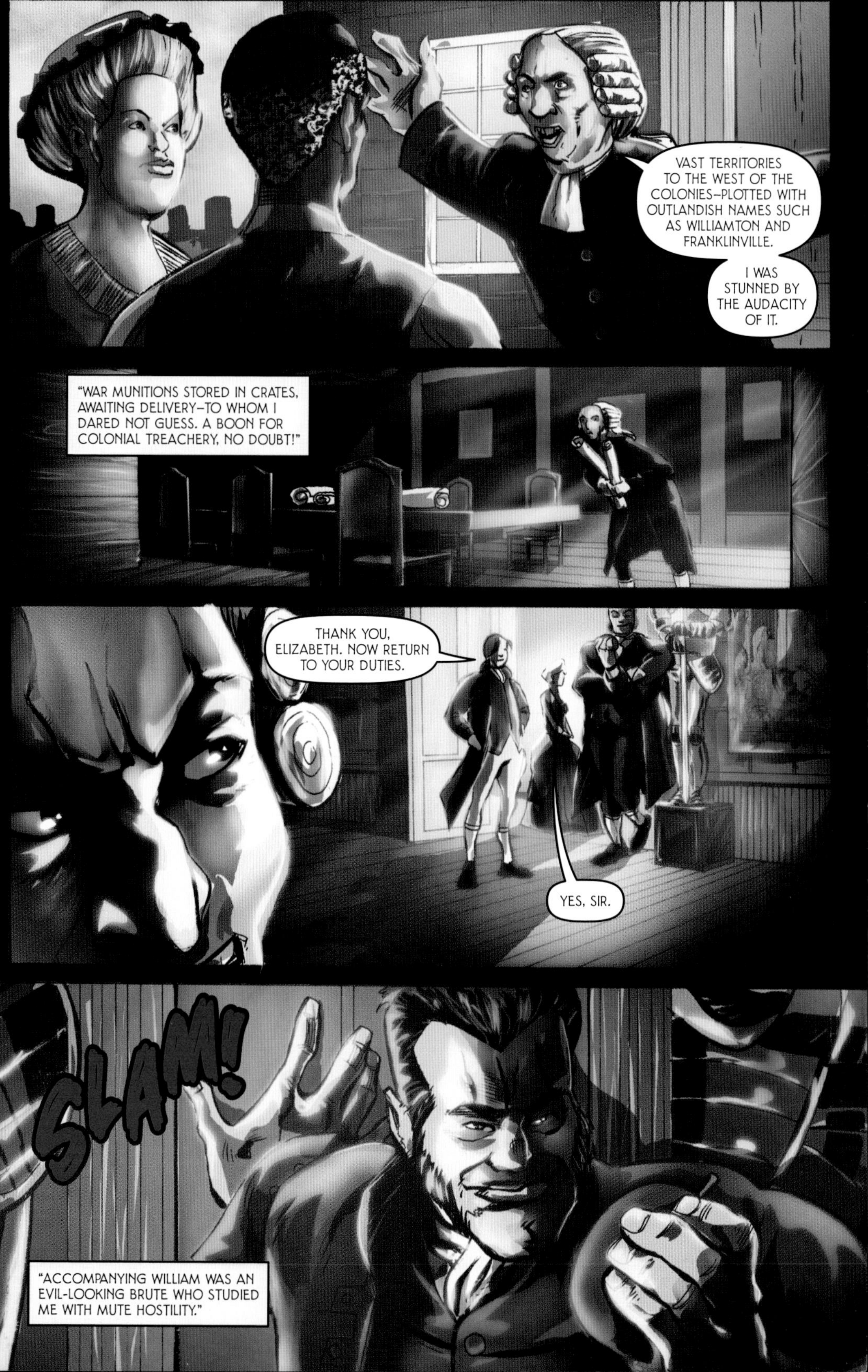
VAST TERRITORIES TO THE WEST OF THE COLONIES—PLOTTED WITH OUTLANDISH NAMES SUCH AS WILLIAMTON AND FRANKLINVILLE.
I WAS STUNNED BY THE AUDACITY OF IT.
"WAR MUNITIONS STORED IN CRATES, AWAITING DELIVERY—TO WHOM I DARED NOT GUESS. A BOON FOR COLONIAL TREACHERY, NO DOUBT!"
THANK YOU, ELIZABETH. NOW RETURN TO YOUR DUTIES.
YES, SIR.
SLAM!
"ACCOMPANYING WILLIAM WAS AN EVIL-LOOKING BRUTE WHO STUDIED ME WITH MUTE HOSTILITY."

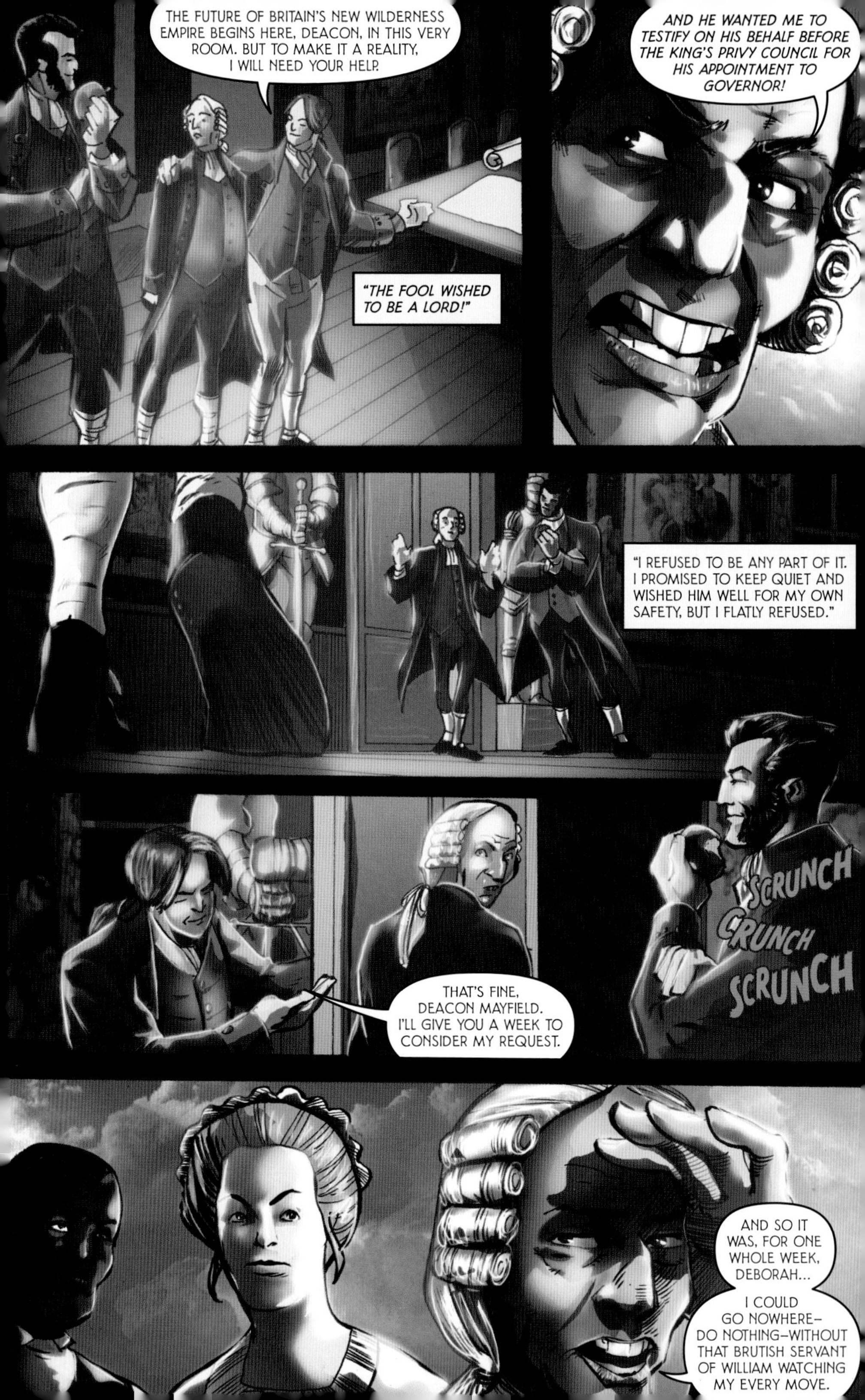
THE FUTURE OF BRITAIN'S NEW WILDERNESS EMPIRE BEGINS HERE, DEACON, IN THIS VERY ROOM. BUT TO MAKE IT A REALITY, I WILL NEED YOUR HELP.
"THE FOOL WISHED TO BE A LORD!"
AND HE WANTED ME TO TESTIFY ON HIS BEHALF BEFORE THE KING'S PRIVY COUNCIL FOR HIS APPOINTMENT TO GOVERNOR!
"I REFUSED TO BE ANY PART OF IT. I PROMISED TO KEEP QUIET AND WISHED HIM WELL FOR MY OWN SAFETY, BUT I FLATLY REFUSED."
THAT'S FINE, DEACON MAYFIELD. I'LL GIVE YOU A WEEK TO CONSIDER MY REQUEST.
SCRUNCH
CRUNCH
SCRUNCH
AND SO IT WAS, FOR ONE WHOLE WEEK, DEBORAH...
I COULD GO NOWHERE—DO NOTHING—WITHOUT THAT BRUTISH SERVANT OF WILLIAM WATCHING MY EVERY MOVE.

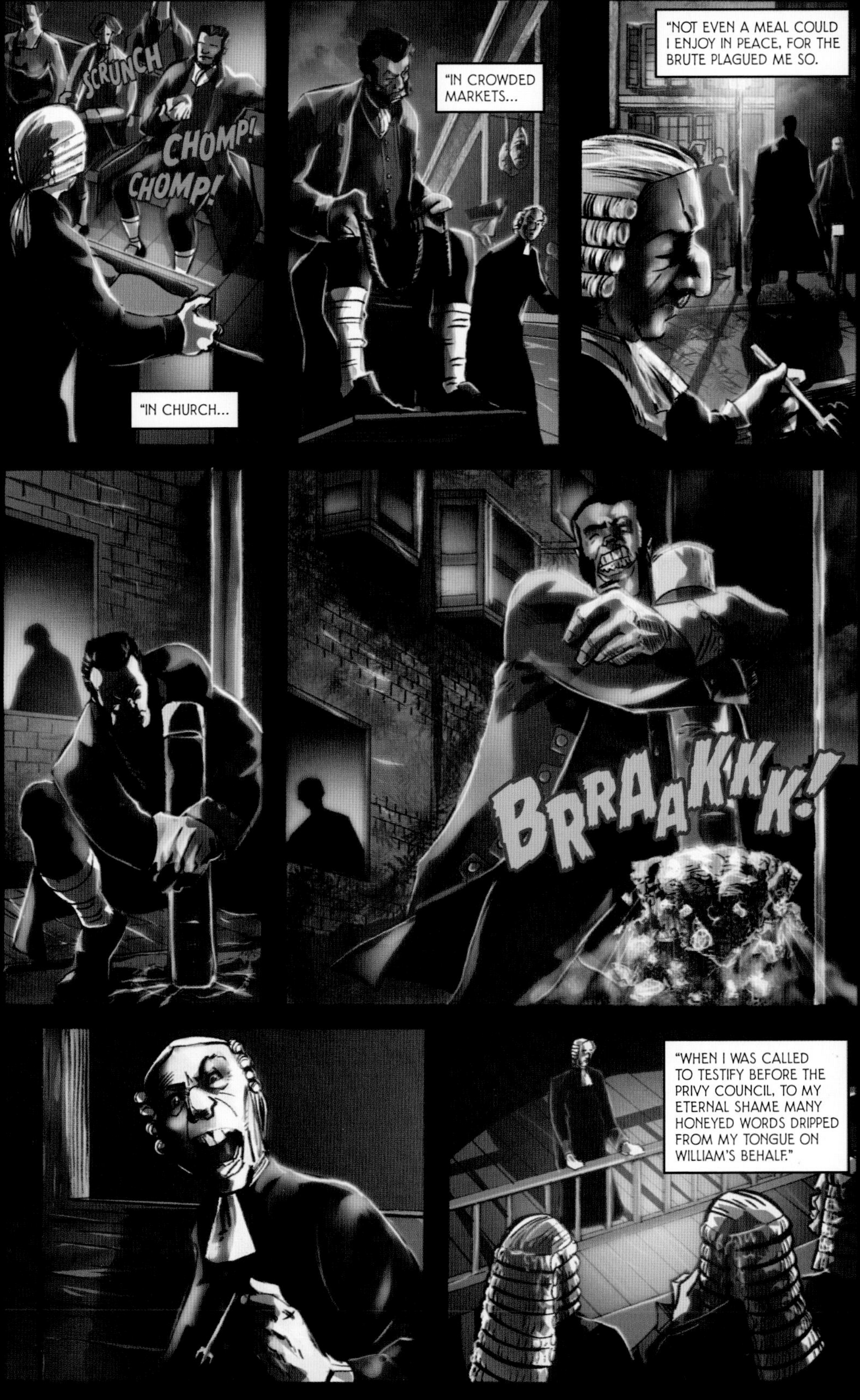
SCRUNCH
CHOMP!
CHOMP!
"IN CHURCH...
"IN CROWDED MARKETS...
"NOT EVEN A MEAL COULD I ENJOY IN PEACE, FOR THE BRUTE PLAGUED ME SO.
BRRAAKKKK!
"WHEN I WAS CALLED TO TESTIFY BEFORE THE PRIVY COUNCIL, TO MY ETERNAL SHAME MANY HONEYED WORDS DRIPPED FROM MY TONGUE ON WILLIAM'S BEHALF."

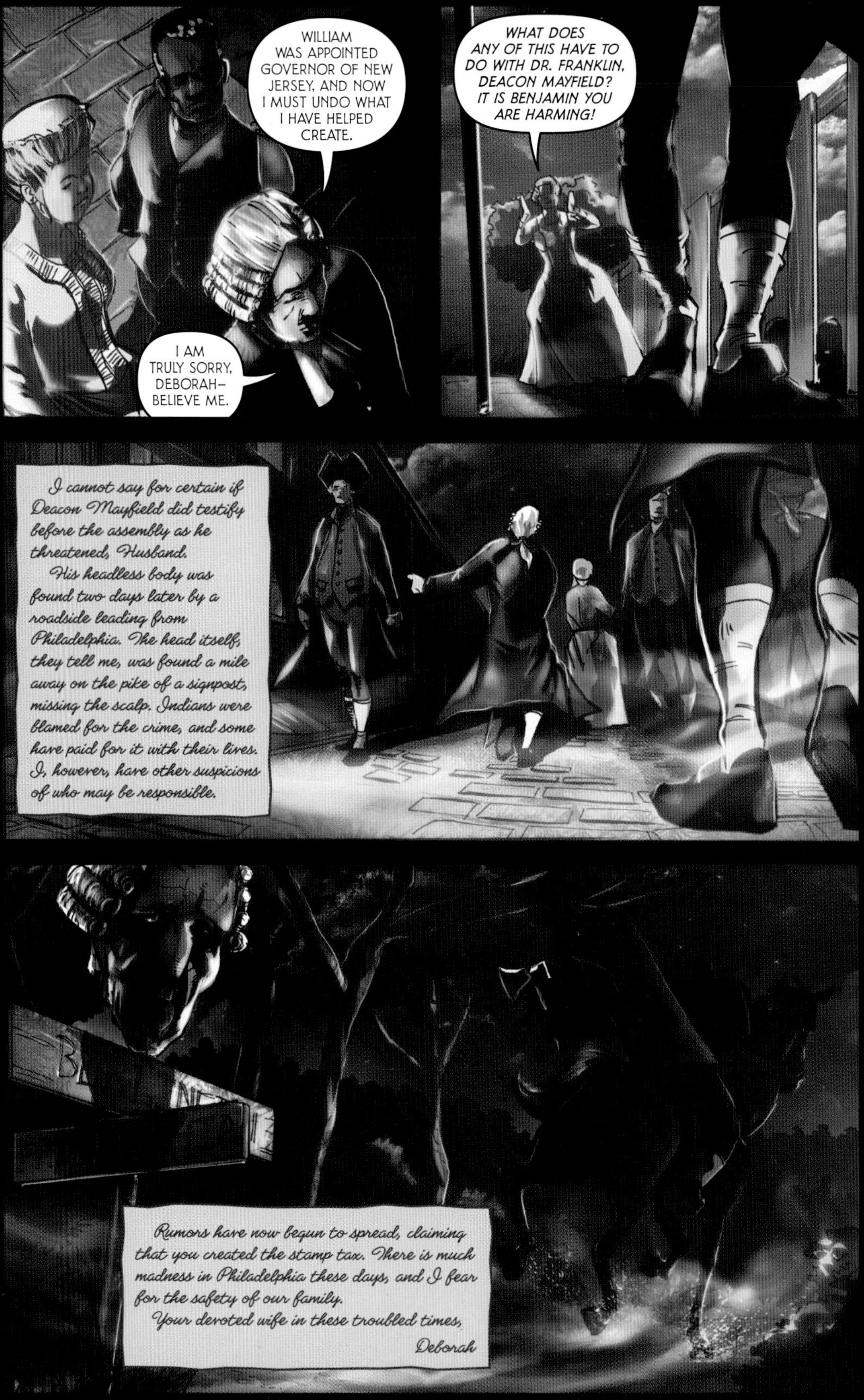

WILLIAM WAS APPOINTED GOVERNOR OF NEW JERSEY, AND NOW I MUST UNDO WHAT I HAVE HELPED CREATE.
I AM TRULY SORRY, DEBORAH— BELIEVE ME.
WHAT DOES ANY OF THIS HAVE TO DO WITH DR. FRANKLIN, DEACON MAYFIELD? IT IS BENJAMIN YOU ARE HARMING!
I cannot say for certain if Deacon Mayfield did testify before the assembly as he threatened, Husband.
His headless body was found two days later by a roadside leading from Philadelphia. The head itself, they tell me, was found a mile away on the pike of a signpost, missing the scalp. Indians were blamed for the crime, and some have paid for it with their lives. I, however, have other suspicions of who may be responsible.
Rumors have now begun to spread, claiming that you created the stamp tax. There is much madness in Philadelphia these days, and I fear for the safety of our family.
Your devoted wife in these troubled times,
Deborah

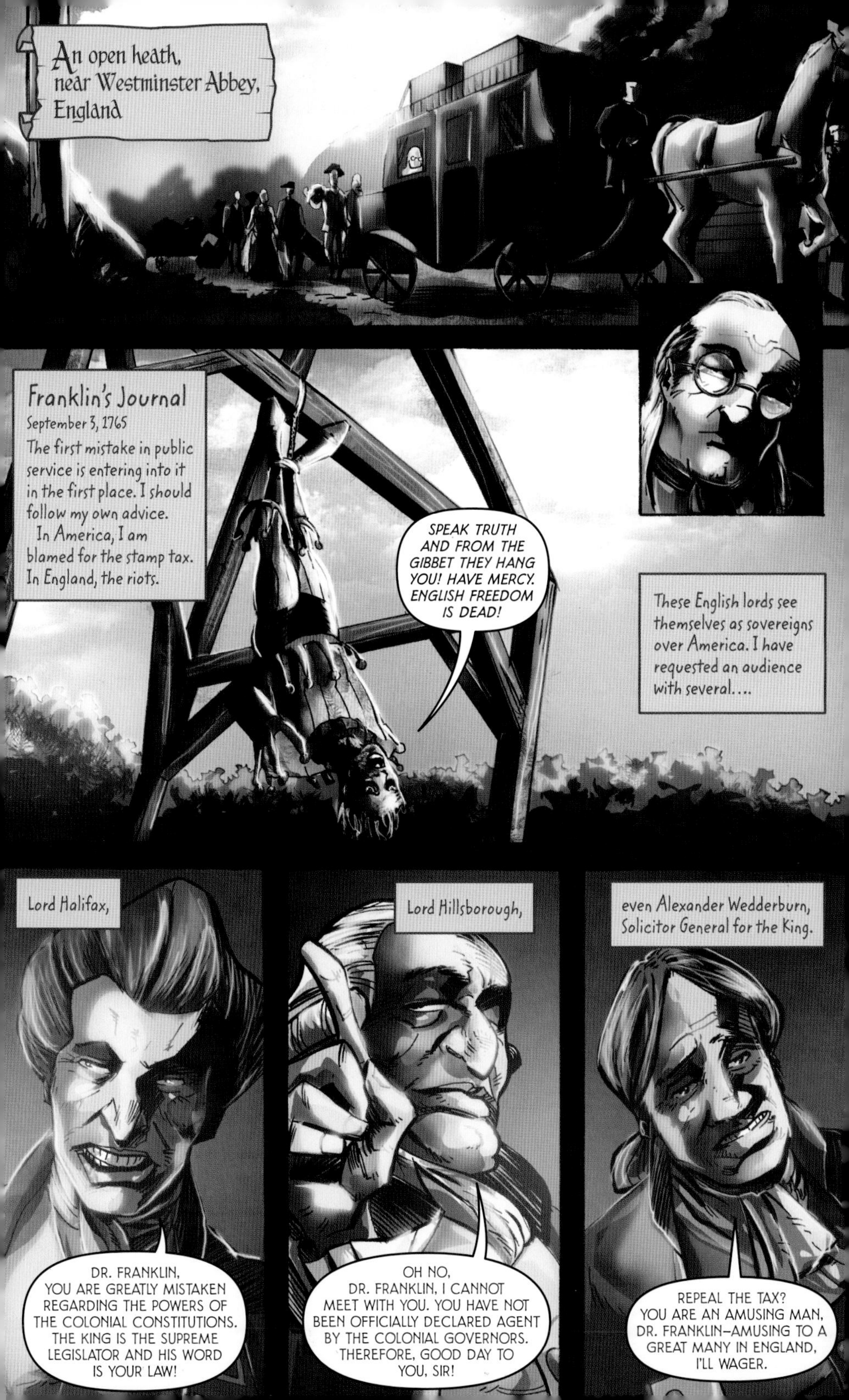
An open heath, near Westminster Abbey, England
Franklin's Journal
September 3, 1765
The first mistake in public service is entering into it in the first place. I should follow my own advice.
In America, I am blamed for the stamp tax. In England, the riots.
SPEAK TRUTH AND FROM THE GIBBET THEY HANG YOU! HAVE MERCY. ENGLISH FREEDOM IS DEAD!
These English lords see themselves as sovereigns over America. I have requested an audience with several....
Lord Halifax,
DR. FRANKLIN, YOU ARE GREATLY MISTAKEN REGARDING THE POWERS OF THE COLONIAL CONSTITUTIONS. THE KING IS THE SUPREME LEGISLATOR AND HIS WORD IS YOUR LAW!
Lord Hillsborough,
OH NO, DR. FRANKLIN, I CANNOT MEET WITH YOU. YOU HAVE NOT BEEN OFFICIALLY DECLARED AGENT BY THE COLONIAL GOVERNORS. THEREFORE, GOOD DAY TO YOU, SIR!
even Alexander Wedderburn, Solicitor General for the King.
REPEAL THE TAX? YOU ARE AN AMUSING MAN, DR. FRANKLIN—AMUSING TO A GREAT MANY IN ENGLAND, I'LL WAGER.

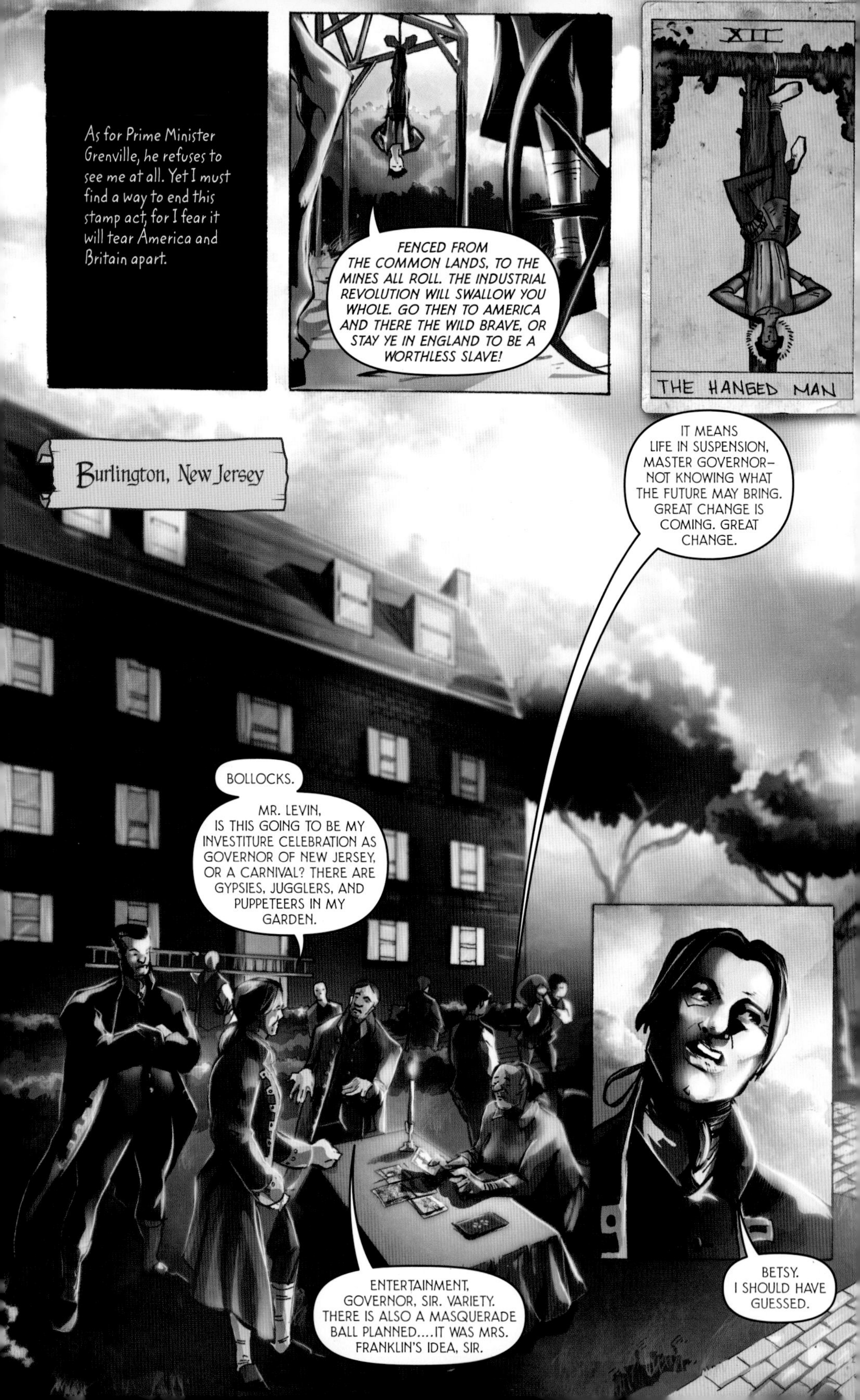
As for Prime Minister Grenville, he refuses to see me at all. Yet I must find a way to end this stamp act, for I fear it will tear America and Britain apart.
FENCED FROM THE COMMON LANDS, TO THE MINES ALL ROLL. THE INDUSTRIAL REVOLUTION WILL SWALLOW YOU WHOLE. GO THEN TO AMERICA AND THERE THE WILD BRAVE, OR STAY YE IN ENGLAND TO BE A WORTHLESS SLAVE!
XII
THE HANGED MAN
Burlington, New Jersey
IT MEANS LIFE IN SUSPENSION, MASTER GOVERNOR— NOT KNOWING WHAT THE FUTURE MAY BRING. GREAT CHANGE IS COMING. GREAT CHANGE.
BOLLOCKS.
MR. LEVIN, IS THIS GOING TO BE MY INVESTITURE CELEBRATION AS GOVERNOR OF NEW JERSEY, OR A CARNIVAL? THERE ARE GYPSIES, JUGGLERS, AND PUPPETEERS IN MY GARDEN.
ENTERTAINMENT, GOVERNOR, SIR. VARIETY. THERE IS ALSO A MASQUERADE BALL PLANNED....IT WAS MRS. FRANKLIN'S IDEA, SIR.
BETSY. I SHOULD HAVE GUESSED.

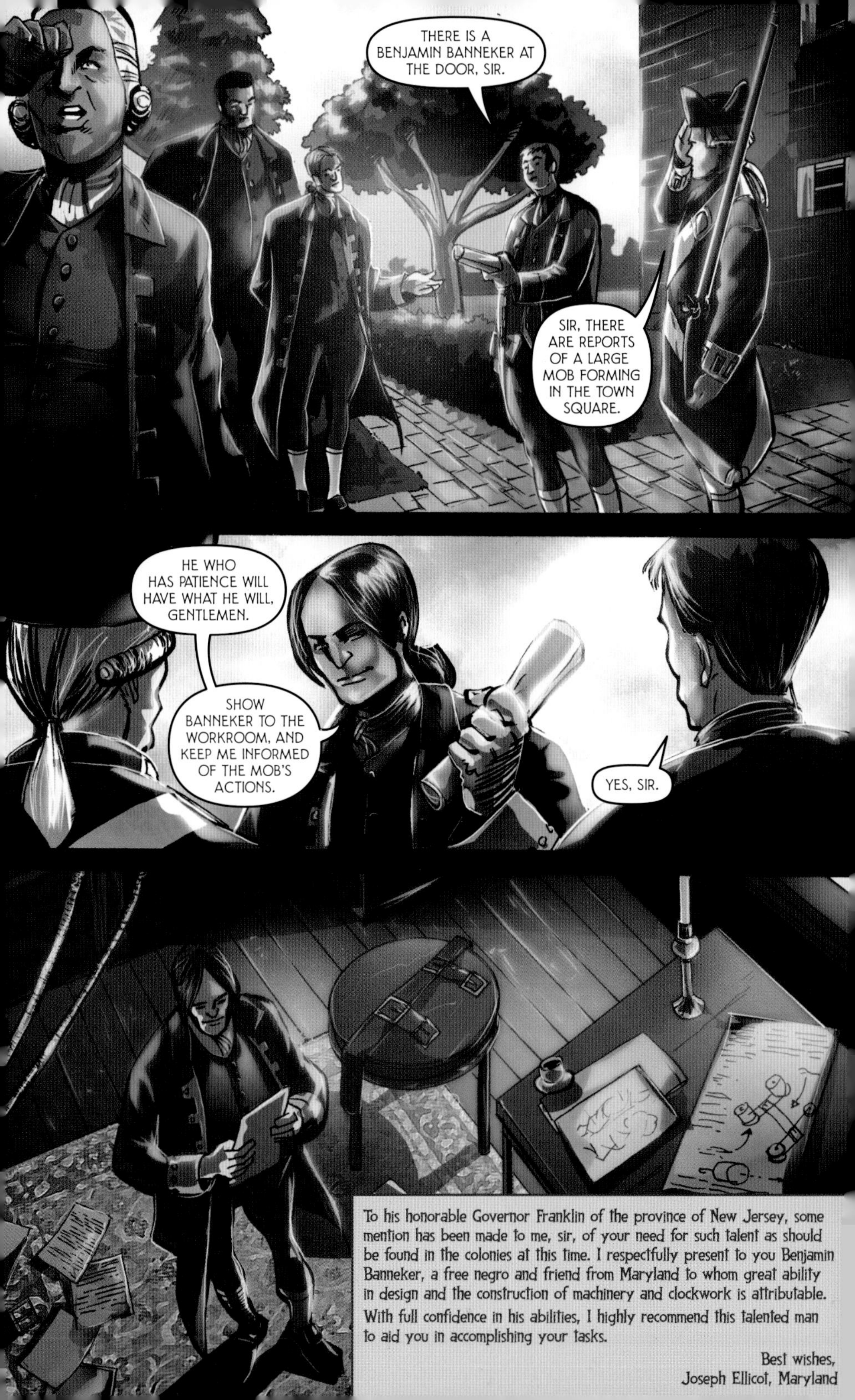
THERE IS A BENJAMIN BANNEKER AT THE DOOR, SIR.
SIR, THERE ARE REPORTS OF A LARGE MOB FORMING IN THE TOWN SQUARE.
HE WHO HAS PATIENCE WILL HAVE WHAT HE WILL, GENTLEMEN.
SHOW BANNEKER TO THE WORKROOM, AND KEEP ME INFORMED OF THE MOB'S ACTIONS.
YES, SIR.
To his honorable Governor Franklin of the province of New Jersey, some mention has been made to me, sir, of your need for such talent as should be found in the colonies at this time. I respectfully present to you Benjamin Banneker, a free negro and friend from Maryland to whom great ability in design and the construction of machinery and clockwork is attributable. With full confidence in his abilities, I highly recommend this talented man to aid you in accomplishing your tasks.
Best wishes,
Joseph Ellicot, Maryland

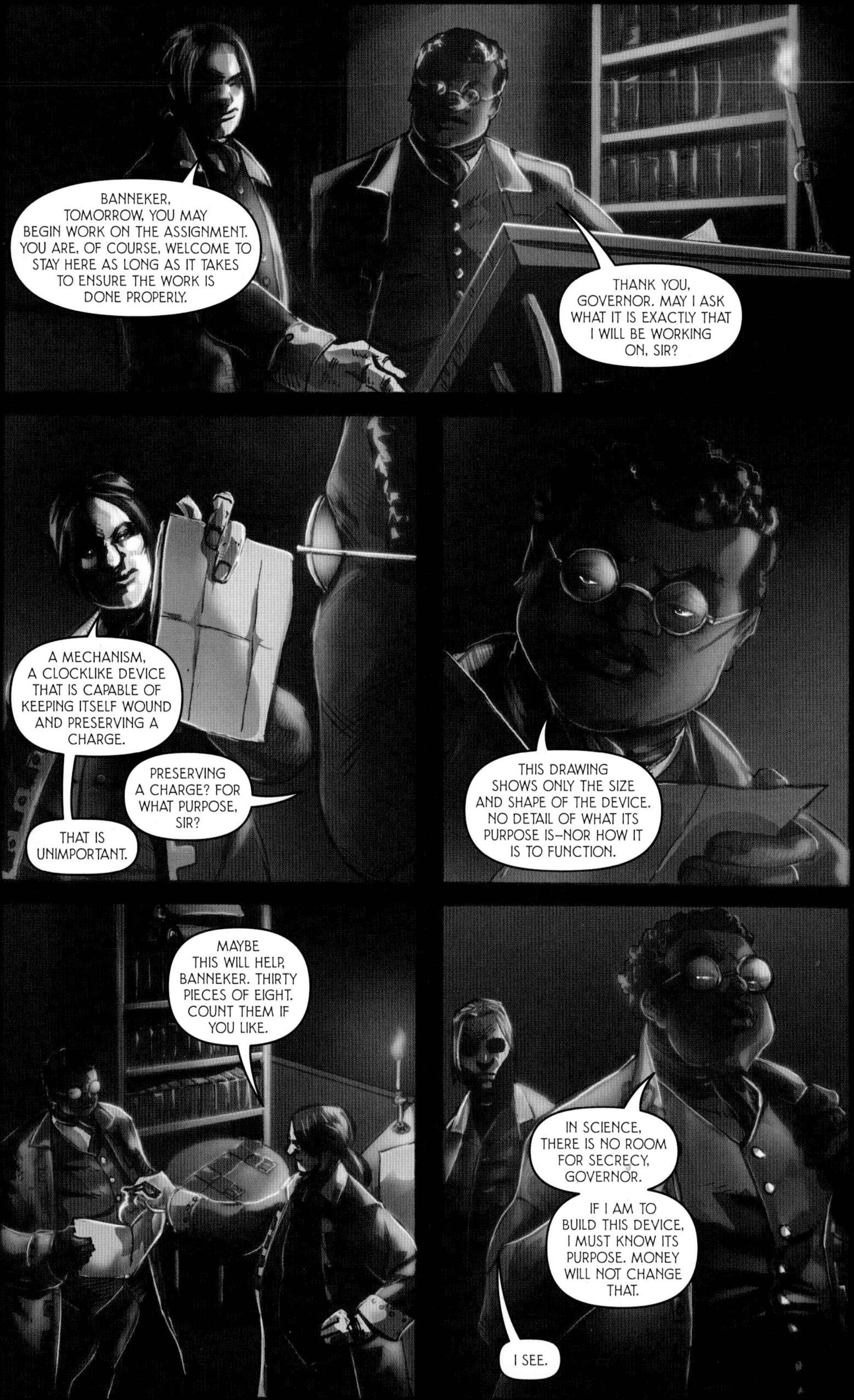
BANNEKER, TOMORROW, YOU MAY BEGIN WORK ON THE ASSIGNMENT. YOU ARE, OF COURSE, WELCOME TO STAY HERE AS LONG AS IT TAKES TO ENSURE THE WORK IS DONE PROPERLY.
THANK YOU, GOVERNOR. MAY I ASK WHAT IT IS EXACTLY THAT I WILL BE WORKING ON, SIR?
A MECHANISM, A CLOCKLIKE DEVICE THAT IS CAPABLE OF KEEPING ITSELF WOUND AND PRESERVING A CHARGE.
PRESERVING A CHARGE? FOR WHAT PURPOSE, SIR?
THAT IS UNIMPORTANT.
THIS DRAWING SHOWS ONLY THE SIZE AND SHAPE OF THE DEVICE. NO DETAIL OF WHAT ITS PURPOSE IS—NOR HOW IT IS TO FUNCTION.
MAYBE THIS WILL HELP, BANNEKER. THIRTY PIECES OF EIGHT. COUNT THEM IF YOU LIKE.
IN SCIENCE, THERE IS NO ROOM FOR SECRECY, GOVERNOR.
IF I AM TO BUILD THIS DEVICE, I MUST KNOW ITS PURPOSE. MONEY WILL NOT CHANGE THAT.
I SEE.

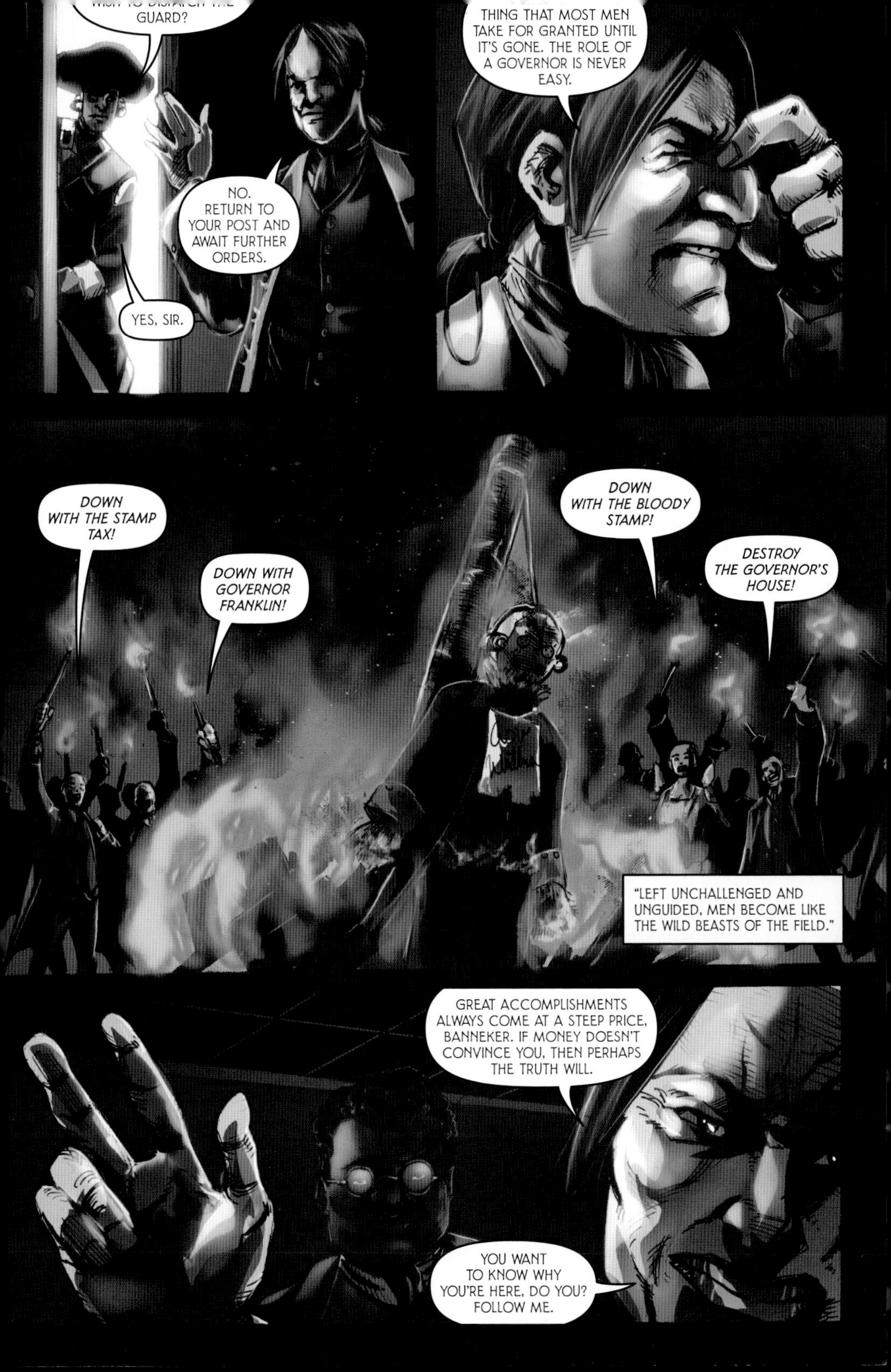
GUARD?
NO. RETURN TO YOUR POST AND AWAIT FURTHER ORDERS.
YES, SIR.
THING THAT MOST MEN TAKE FOR GRANTED UNTIL IT'S GONE. THE ROLE OF A GOVERNOR IS NEVER EASY.
DOWN WITH THE STAMP TAX!
DOWN WITH GOVERNOR FRANKLIN!
DOWN WITH THE BLOODY STAMP!
DESTROY THE GOVERNOR'S HOUSE!
"LEFT UNCHALLENGED AND UNGUIDED, MEN BECOME LIKE THE WILD BEASTS OF THE FIELD."
GREAT ACCOMPLISHMENTS ALWAYS COME AT A STEEP PRICE, BANNEKER. IF MONEY DOESN'T CONVINCE YOU, THEN PERHAPS THE TRUTH WILL.
YOU WANT TO KNOW WHY YOU'RE HERE, DO YOU? FOLLOW ME.

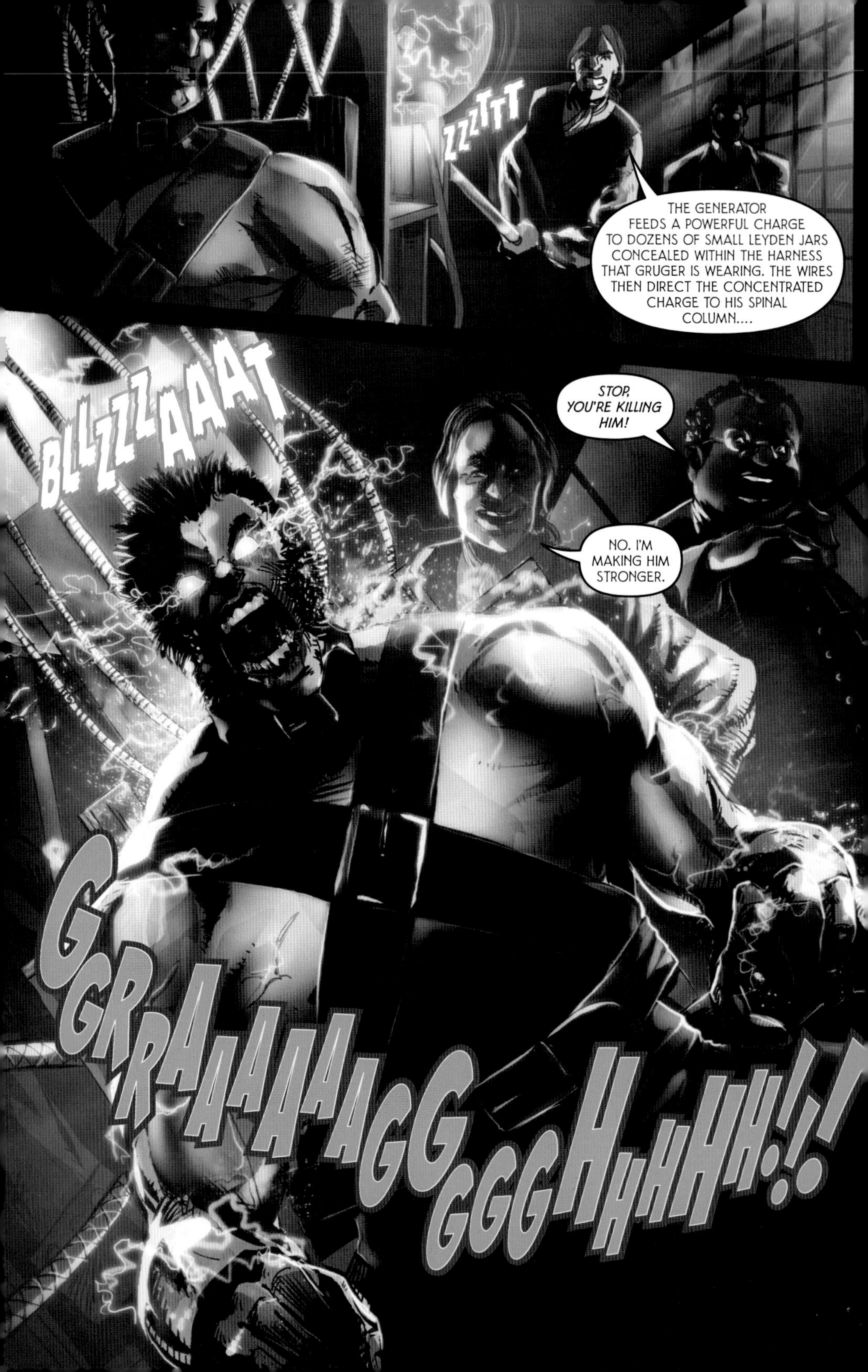
ZZZTTT
THE GENERATOR FEEDS A POWERFUL CHARGE TO DOZENS OF SMALL LEYDEN JARS CONCEALED WITHIN THE HARNESS THAT GRUGER IS WEARING. THE WIRES THEN DIRECT THE CONCENTRATED CHARGE TO HIS SPINAL COLUMN....
BLLZZZAAAT
STOP, YOU'RE KILLING HIM!
NO. I'M MAKING HIM STRONGER.
GGRRAAAAAAGGGGGHHHHH!!!

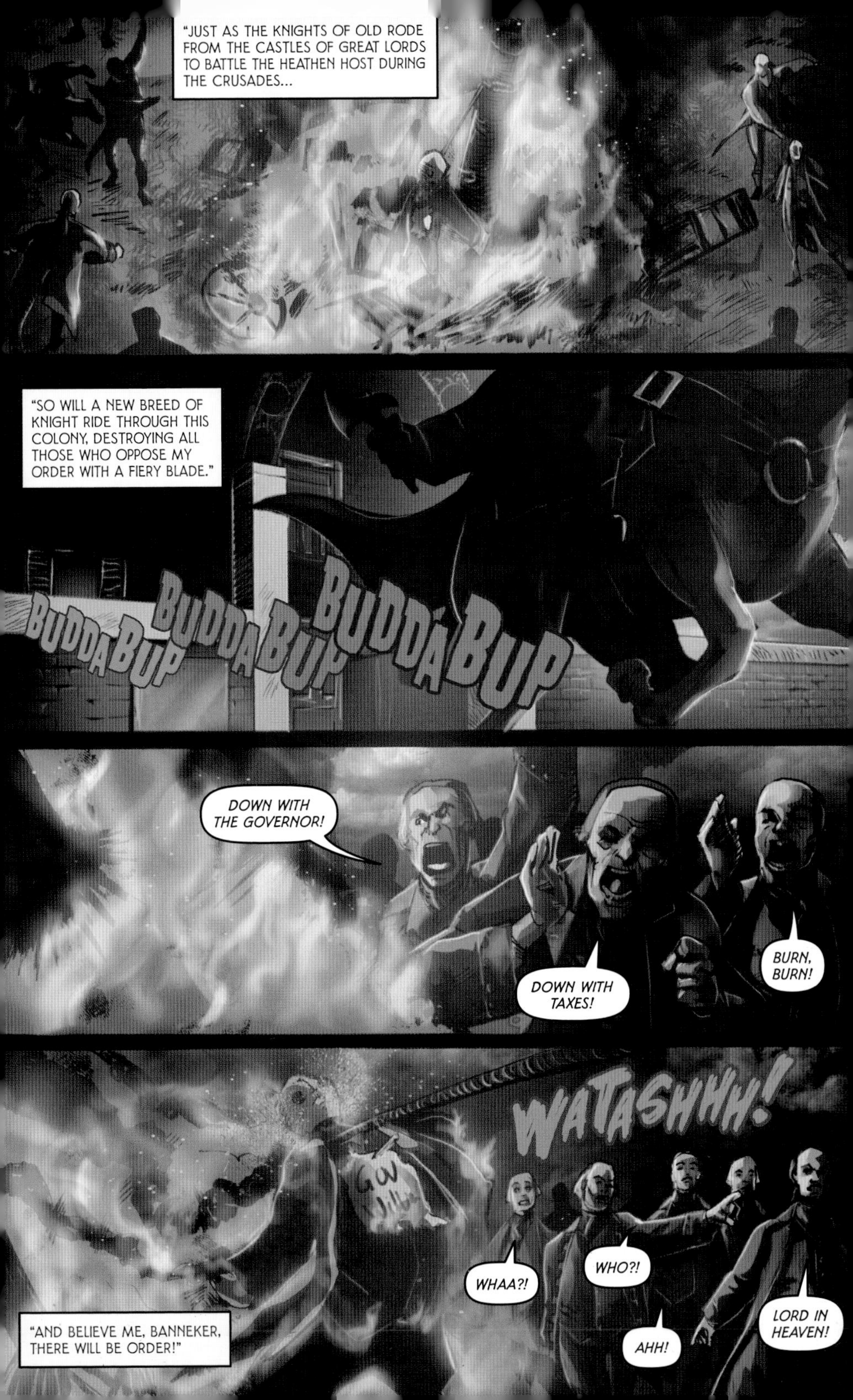
"JUST AS THE KNIGHTS OF OLD RODE FROM THE CASTLES OF GREAT LORDS TO BATTLE THE HEATHEN HOST DURING THE CRUSADES...
"SO WILL A NEW BREED OF KNIGHT RIDE THROUGH THIS COLONY, DESTROYING ALL THOSE WHO OPPOSE MY ORDER WITH A FIERY BLADE."
BUDDA BUP BUDDA BUP BUDDA BUP
DOWN WITH THE GOVERNOR!
DOWN WITH TAXES!
BURN, BURN!
WATASHHH!
WHAA?!
WHO?!
AHH!
LORD IN HEAVEN!
"AND BELIEVE ME, BANNEKER, THERE WILL BE ORDER!"

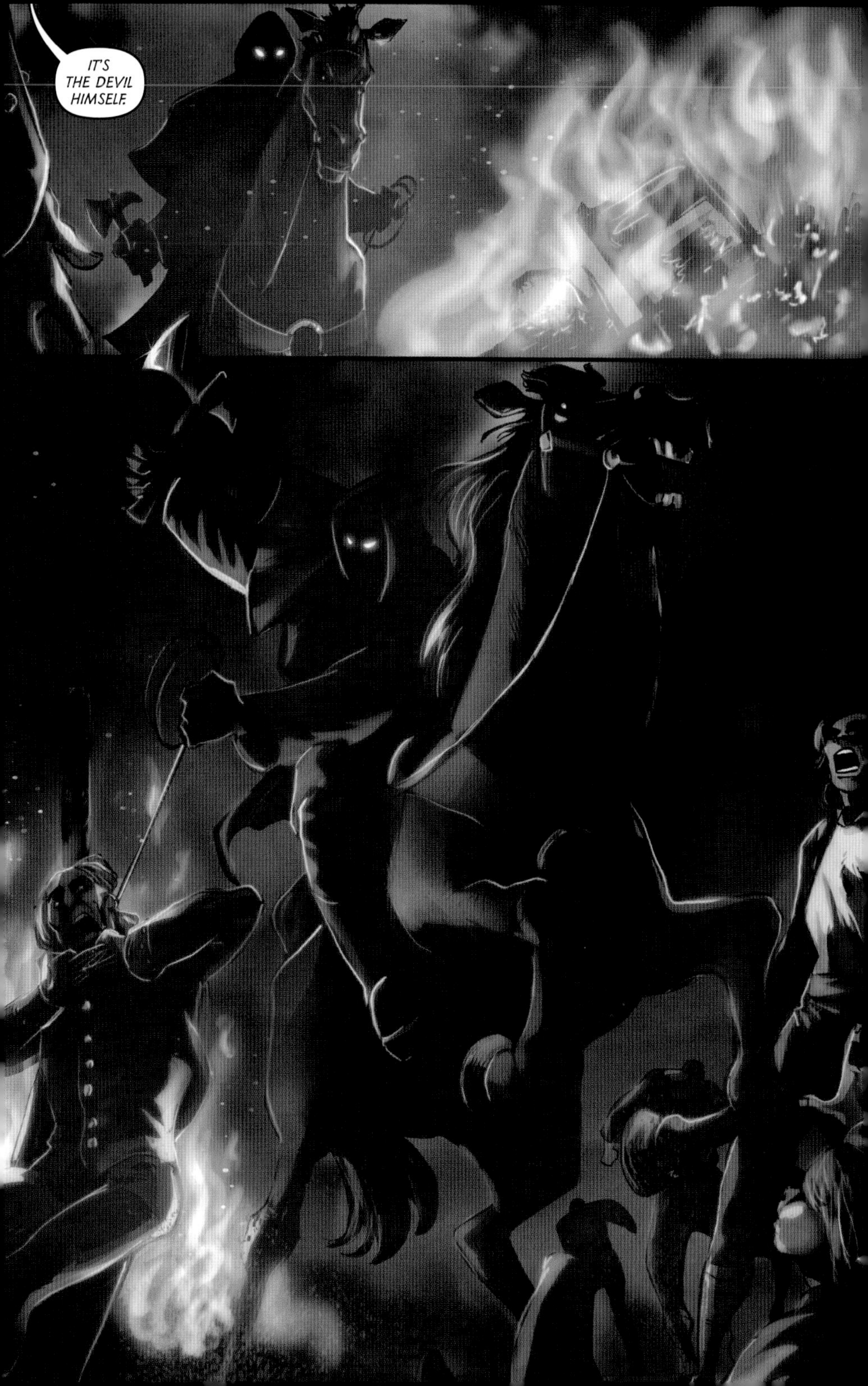
IT'S THE DEVIL HIMSELF.

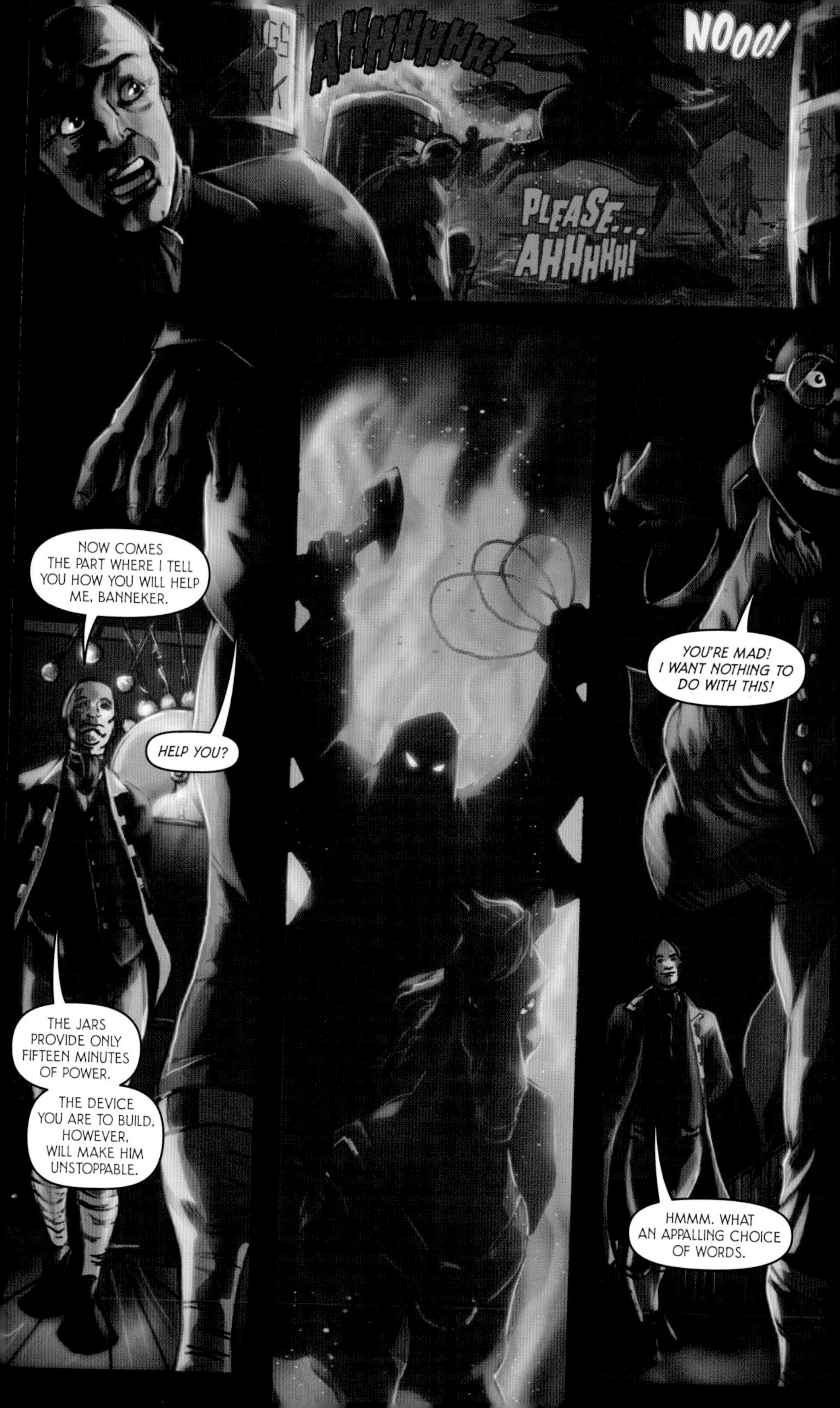
AHHHHHH!
NOOO!
PLEASE... AHHHHH!
NOW COMES THE PART WHERE I TELL YOU HOW YOU WILL HELP ME, BANNEKER.
HELP YOU?
YOU'RE MAD! I WANT NOTHING TO DO WITH THIS!
THE JARS PROVIDE ONLY FIFTEEN MINUTES OF POWER.
THE DEVICE YOU ARE TO BUILD, HOWEVER, WILL MAKE HIM UNSTOPPABLE.
HMMM. WHAT AN APPALLING CHOICE OF WORDS.

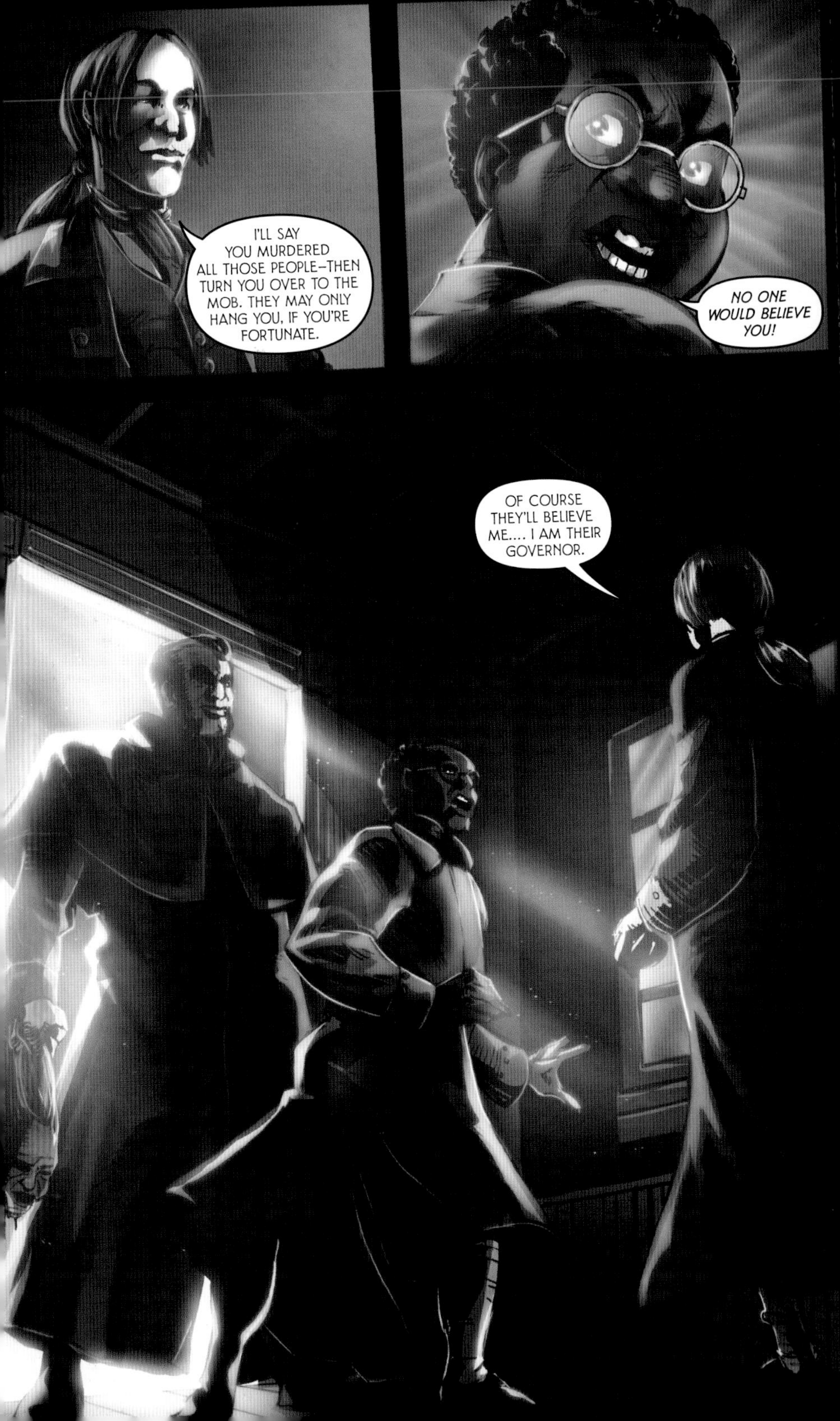
I'LL SAY YOU MURDERED ALL THOSE PEOPLE—THEN TURN YOU OVER TO THE MOB. THEY MAY ONLY HANG YOU, IF YOU'RE FORTUNATE.
NO ONE WOULD BELIEVE YOU!
OF COURSE THEY'LL BELIEVE ME.... I AM THEIR GOVERNOR.

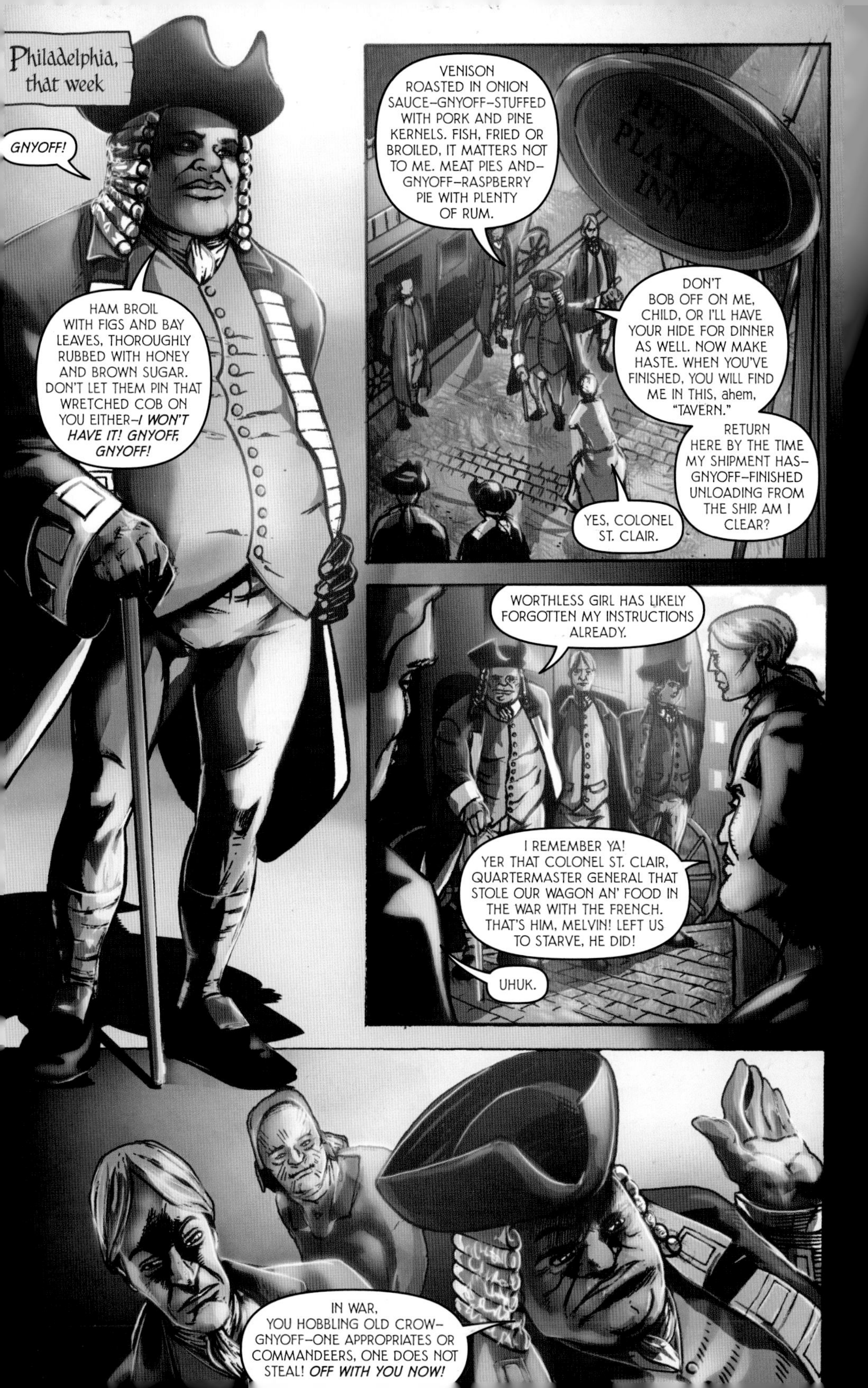
Philadelphia, that week
GNYOFF!
HAM BROIL WITH FIGS AND BAY LEAVES, THOROUGHLY RUBBED WITH HONEY AND BROWN SUGAR. DON'T LET THEM PIN THAT WRETCHED COB ON YOU EITHER–*I WON'T HAVE IT! GNYOFF, GNYOFF!*
VENISON ROASTED IN ONION SAUCE–GNYOFF–STUFFED WITH PORK AND PINE KERNELS. FISH, FRIED OR BROILED, IT MATTERS NOT TO ME. MEAT PIES AND–GNYOFF–RASPBERRY PIE WITH PLENTY OF RUM.
DON'T BOB OFF ON ME, CHILD, OR I'LL HAVE YOUR HIDE FOR DINNER AS WELL. NOW MAKE HASTE. WHEN YOU'VE FINISHED, YOU WILL FIND ME IN THIS, ahem, "TAVERN."
RETURN HERE BY THE TIME MY SHIPMENT HAS–GNYOFF–FINISHED UNLOADING FROM THE SHIP. AM I CLEAR?
YES, COLONEL ST. CLAIR.
WORTHLESS GIRL HAS LIKELY FORGOTTEN MY INSTRUCTIONS ALREADY.
I REMEMBER YA! YER THAT COLONEL ST. CLAIR, QUARTERMASTER GENERAL THAT STOLE OUR WAGON AN' FOOD IN THE WAR WITH THE FRENCH. THAT'S HIM, MELVIN! LEFT US TO STARVE, HE DID!
UHUK.
IN WAR, YOU HOBBLING OLD CROW–GNYOFF–ONE APPROPRIATES OR COMMANDEERS, ONE DOES NOT STEAL! *OFF WITH YOU NOW!*

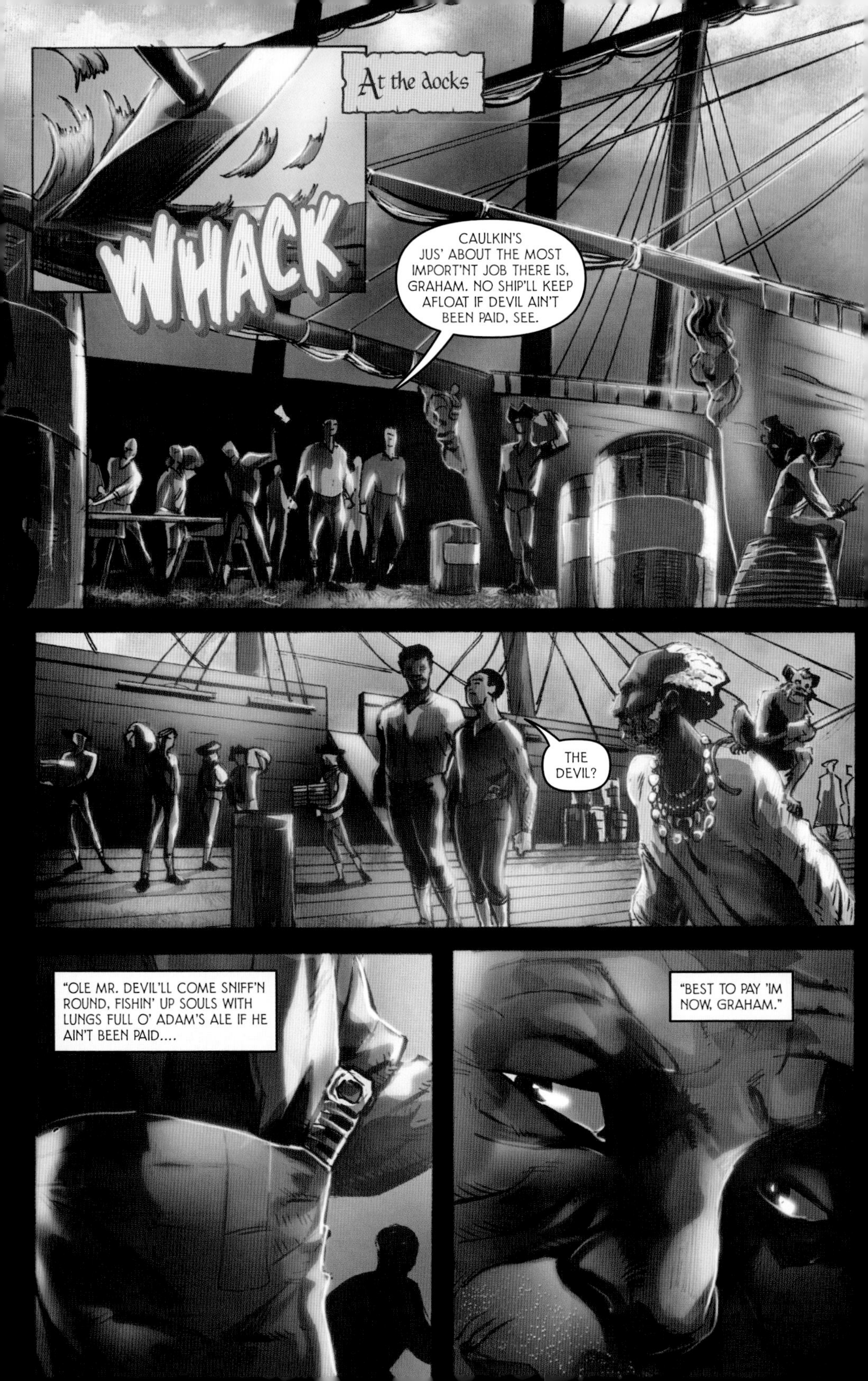
At the docks
WHACK
CAULKIN'S JUS' ABOUT THE MOST IMPORT'NT JOB THERE IS, GRAHAM. NO SHIP'LL KEEP AFLOAT IF DEVIL AIN'T BEEN PAID, SEE.
THE DEVIL?
"OLE MR. DEVIL'LL COME SNIFF'N ROUND, FISHIN' UP SOULS WITH LUNGS FULL O' ADAM'S ALE IF HE AIN'T BEEN PAID....
"BEST TO PAY 'IM NOW, GRAHAM."

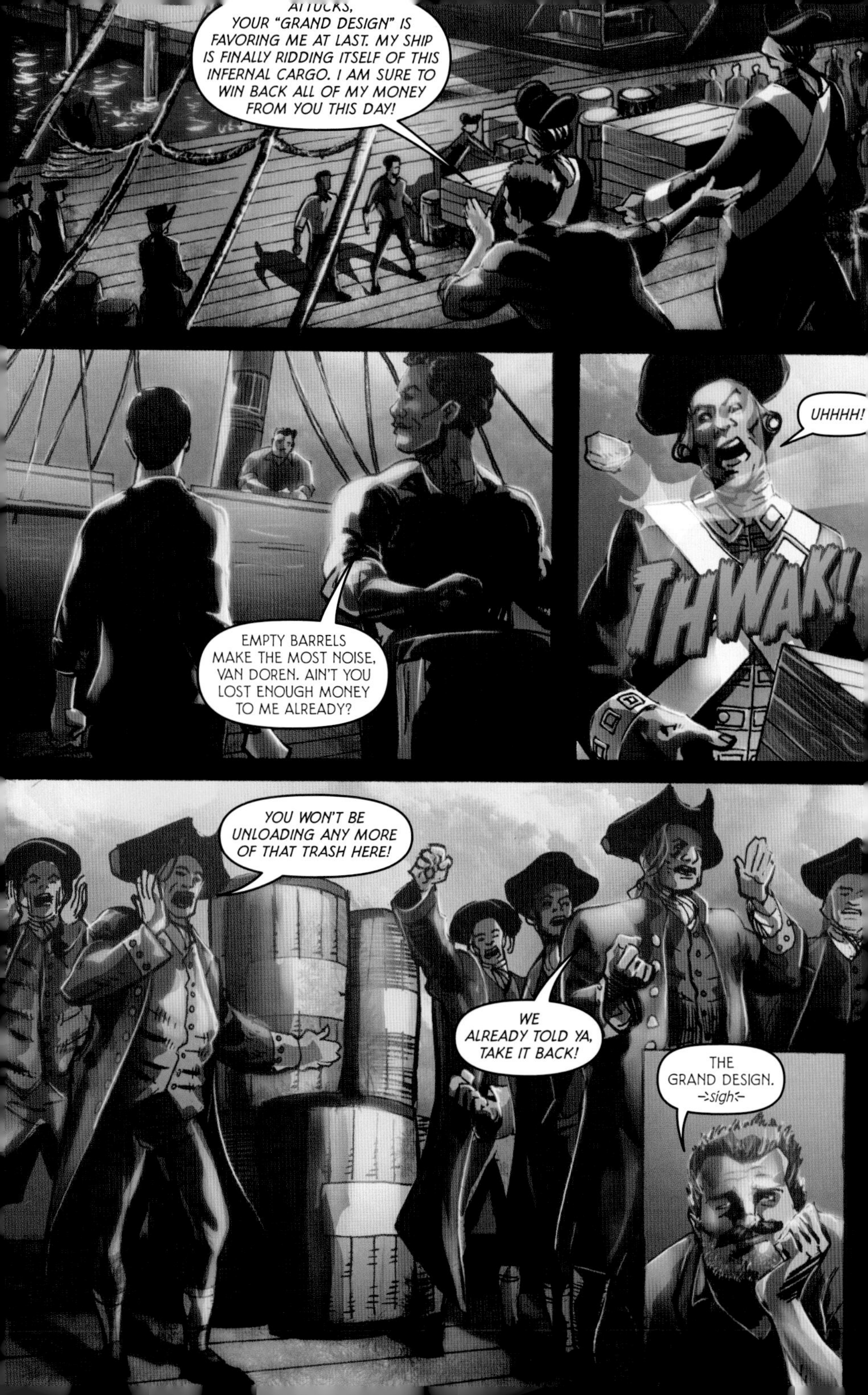
ATTUCKS, YOUR "GRAND DESIGN" IS FAVORING ME AT LAST. MY SHIP IS FINALLY RIDDING ITSELF OF THIS INFERNAL CARGO. I AM SURE TO WIN BACK ALL OF MY MONEY FROM YOU THIS DAY!
EMPTY BARRELS MAKE THE MOST NOISE, VAN DOREN. AIN'T YOU LOST ENOUGH MONEY TO ME ALREADY?
UHHHH!
THWAK!
YOU WON'T BE UNLOADING ANY MORE OF THAT TRASH HERE!
WE ALREADY TOLD YA, TAKE IT BACK!
THE GRAND DESIGN.
sigh

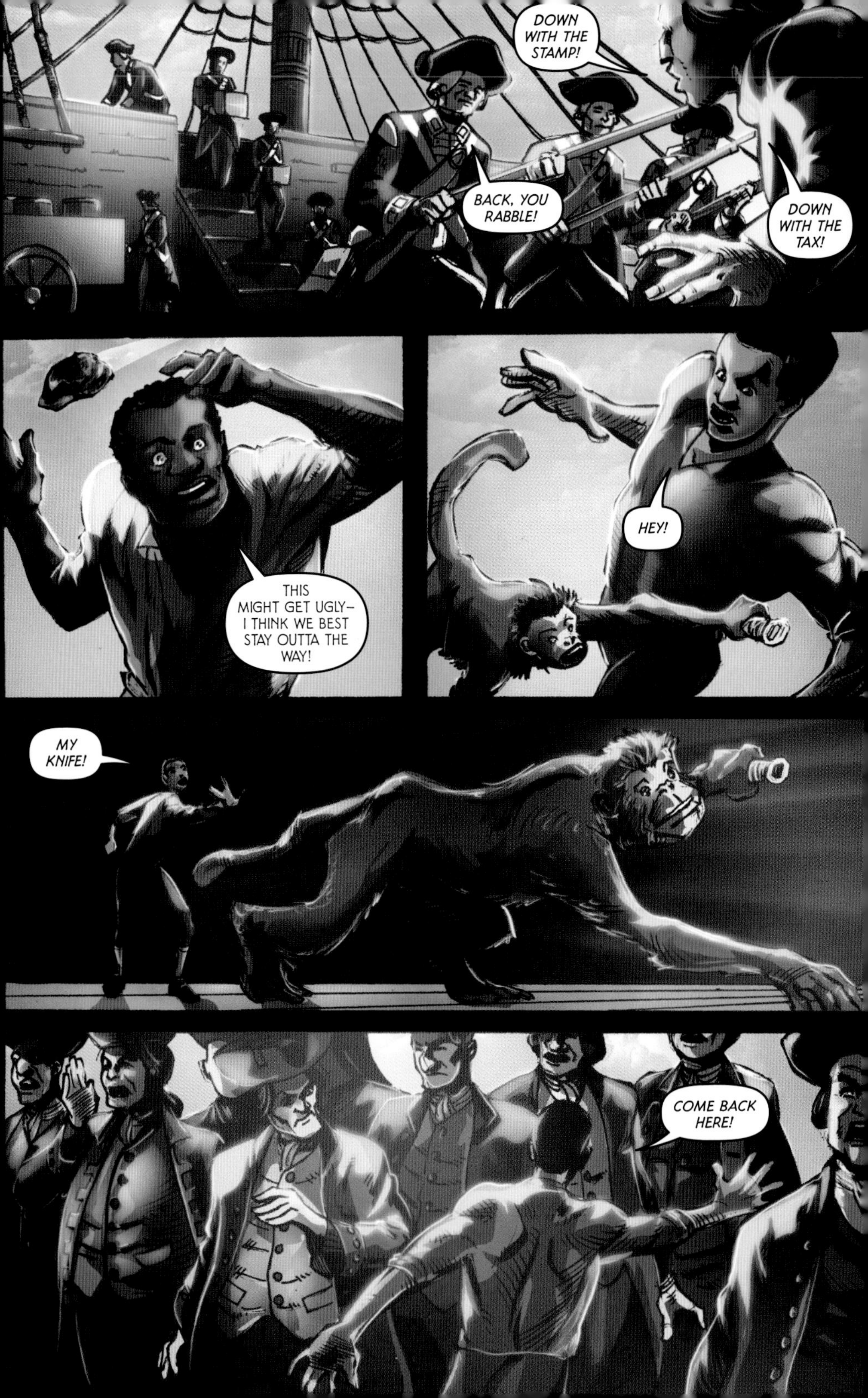
DOWN WITH THE STAMP!
BACK, YOU RABBLE!
DOWN WITH THE TAX!
THIS MIGHT GET UGLY— I THINK WE BEST STAY OUTTA THE WAY!
HEY!
MY KNIFE!
COME BACK HERE!

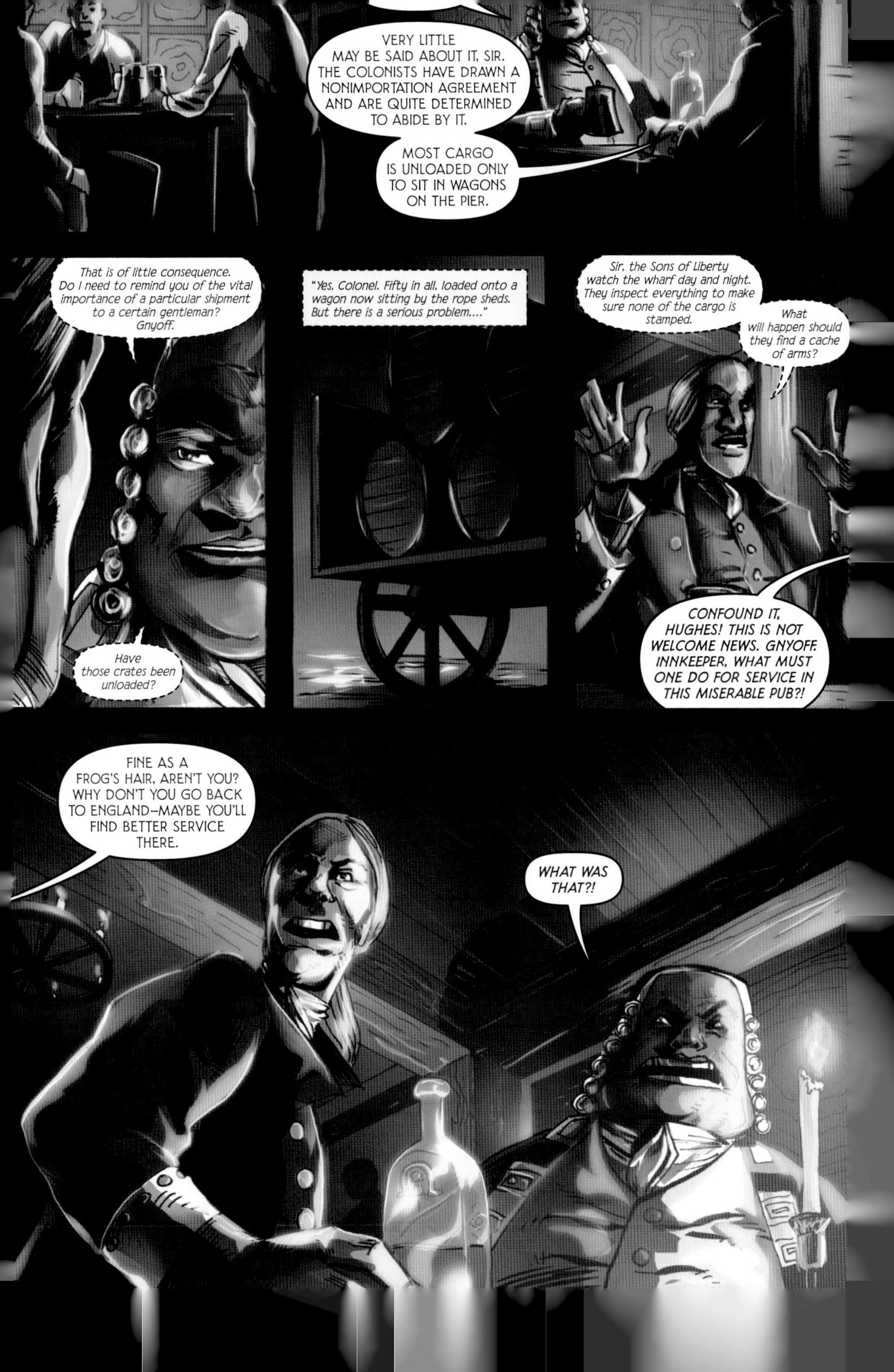
VERY LITTLE MAY BE SAID ABOUT IT, SIR. THE COLONISTS HAVE DRAWN A NONIMPORTATION AGREEMENT AND ARE QUITE DETERMINED TO ABIDE BY IT.
MOST CARGO IS UNLOADED ONLY TO SIT IN WAGONS ON THE PIER.
That is of little consequence. Do I need to remind you of the vital importance of a particular shipment to a certain gentleman? Gnyoff.
Have those crates been unloaded?
"Yes, Colonel. Fifty in all, loaded onto a wagon now sitting by the rope sheds. But there is a serious problem...."
Sir, the Sons of Liberty watch the wharf day and night. They inspect everything to make sure none of the cargo is stamped.
What will happen should they find a cache of arms?
CONFOUND IT, HUGHES! THIS IS NOT WELCOME NEWS. GNYOFF. INNKEEPER, WHAT MUST ONE DO FOR SERVICE IN THIS MISERABLE PUB?!
FINE AS A FROG'S HAIR, AREN'T YOU? WHY DON'T YOU GO BACK TO ENGLAND—MAYBE YOU'LL FIND BETTER SERVICE THERE.
WHAT WAS THAT?!

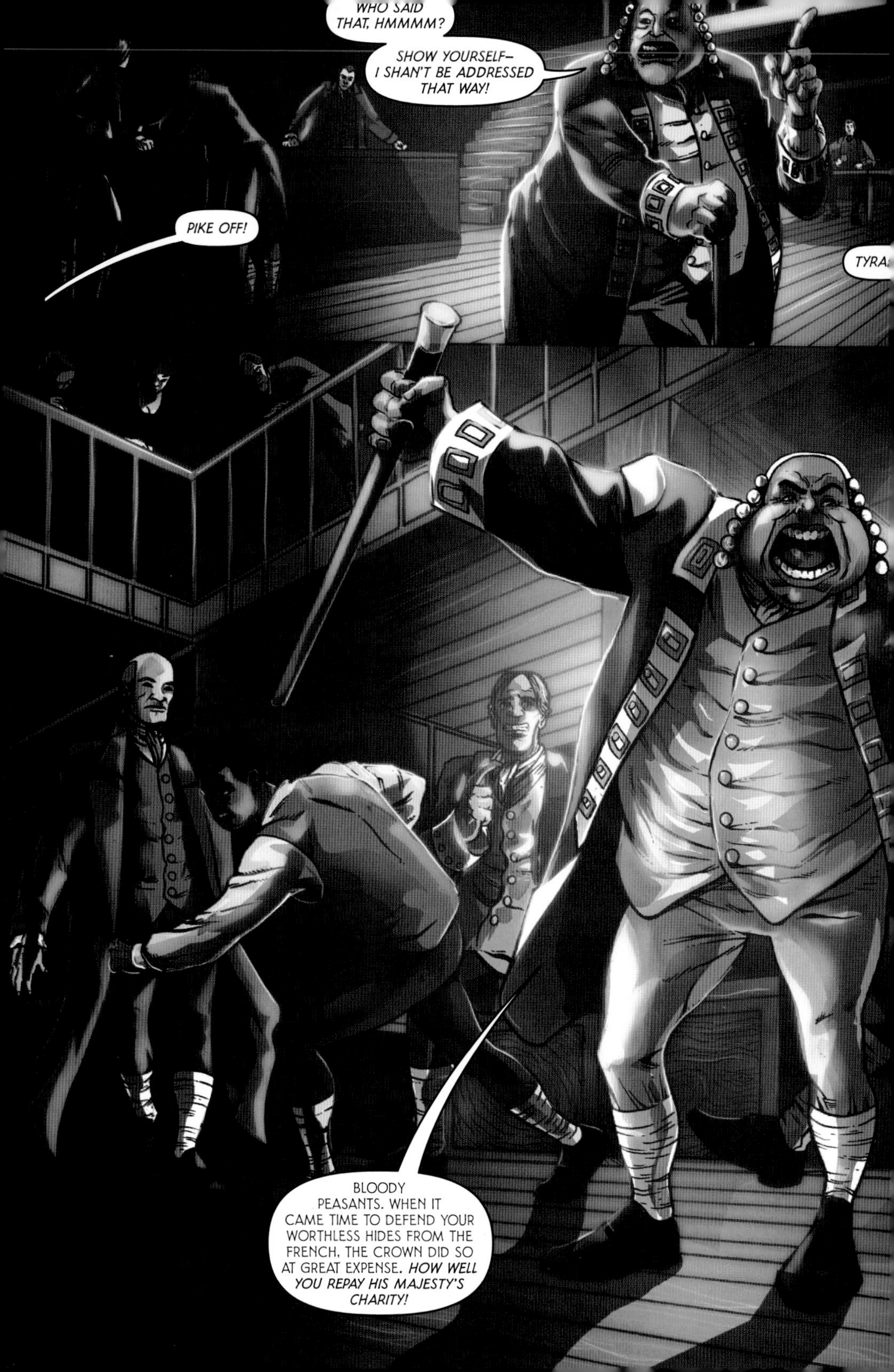
WHO SAID THAT, HMMMM?
SHOW YOURSELF— I SHAN'T BE ADDRESSED THAT WAY!
PIKE OFF!
TYRA
BLOODY PEASANTS. WHEN IT CAME TIME TO DEFEND YOUR WORTHLESS HIDES FROM THE FRENCH, THE CROWN DID SO AT GREAT EXPENSE. *HOW WELL YOU REPAY HIS MAJESTY'S CHARITY!*

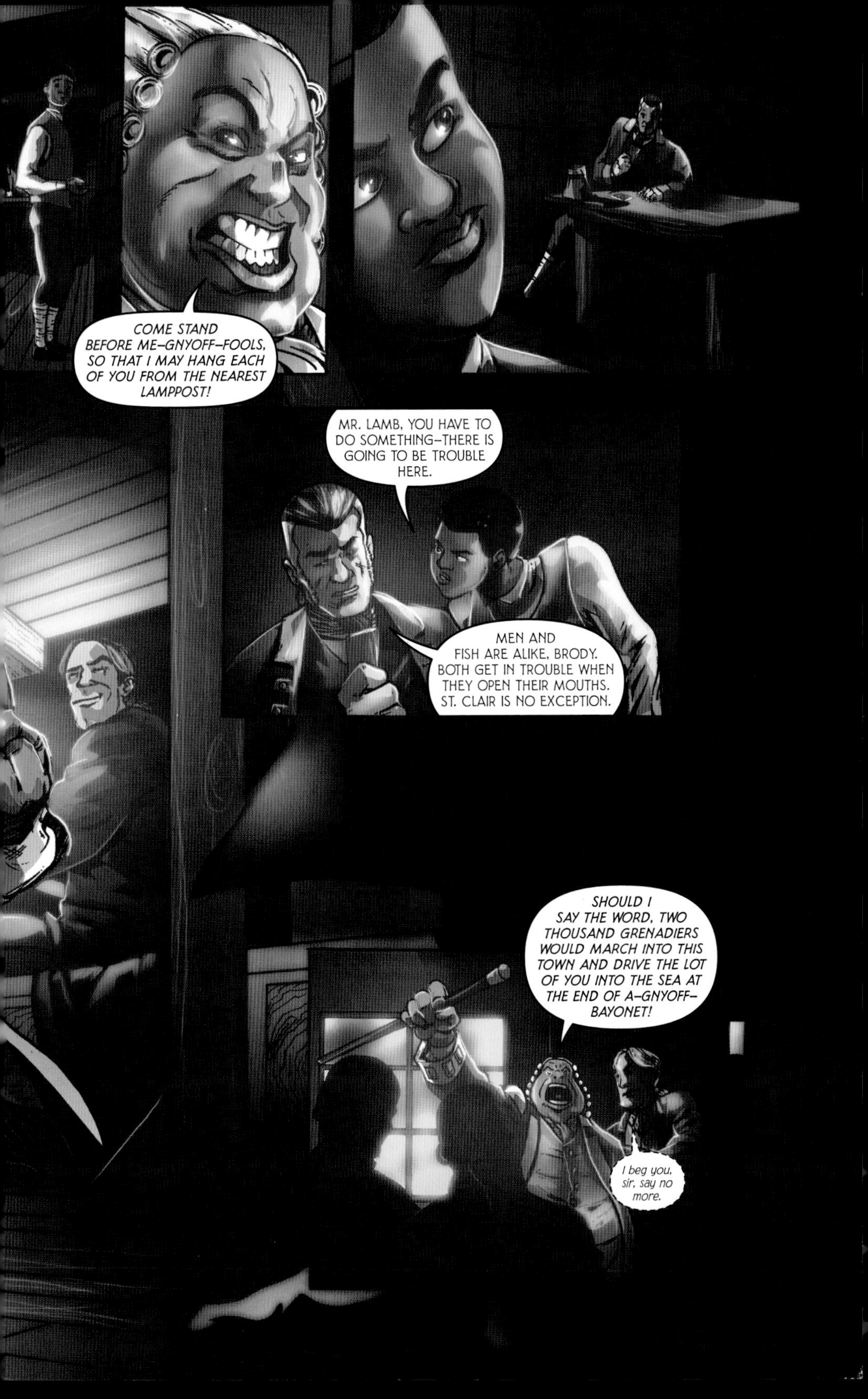
COME STAND BEFORE ME—GNYOFF—FOOLS, SO THAT I MAY HANG EACH OF YOU FROM THE NEAREST LAMPPOST!
MR. LAMB, YOU HAVE TO DO SOMETHING—THERE IS GOING TO BE TROUBLE HERE.
MEN AND FISH ARE ALIKE, BRODY. BOTH GET IN TROUBLE WHEN THEY OPEN THEIR MOUTHS. ST. CLAIR IS NO EXCEPTION.
SHOULD I SAY THE WORD, TWO THOUSAND GRENADIERS WOULD MARCH INTO THIS TOWN AND DRIVE THE LOT OF YOU INTO THE SEA AT THE END OF A—GNYOFF—BAYONET!
I beg you, sir, say no more.

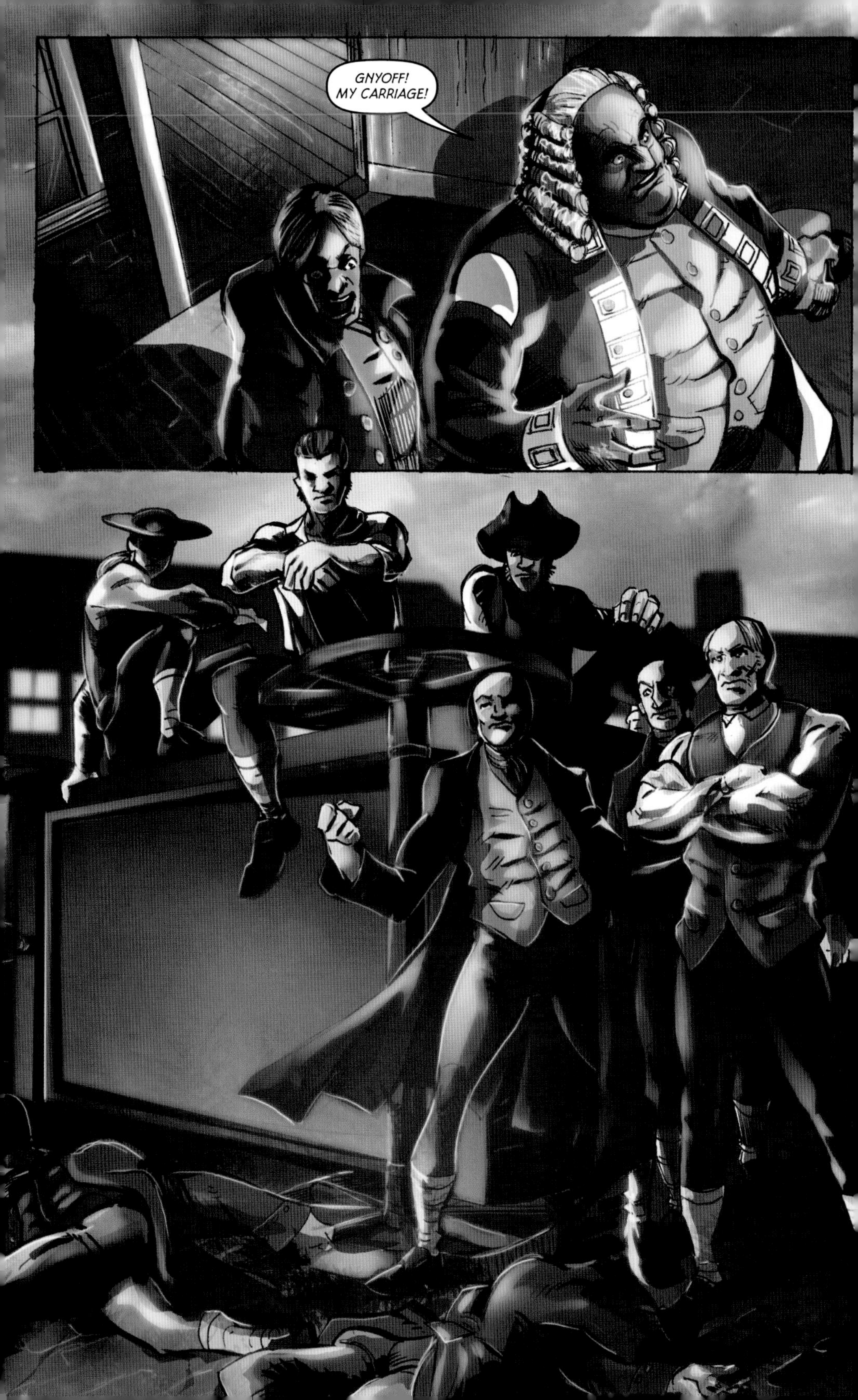
GNYOFF!
MY CARRIAGE!

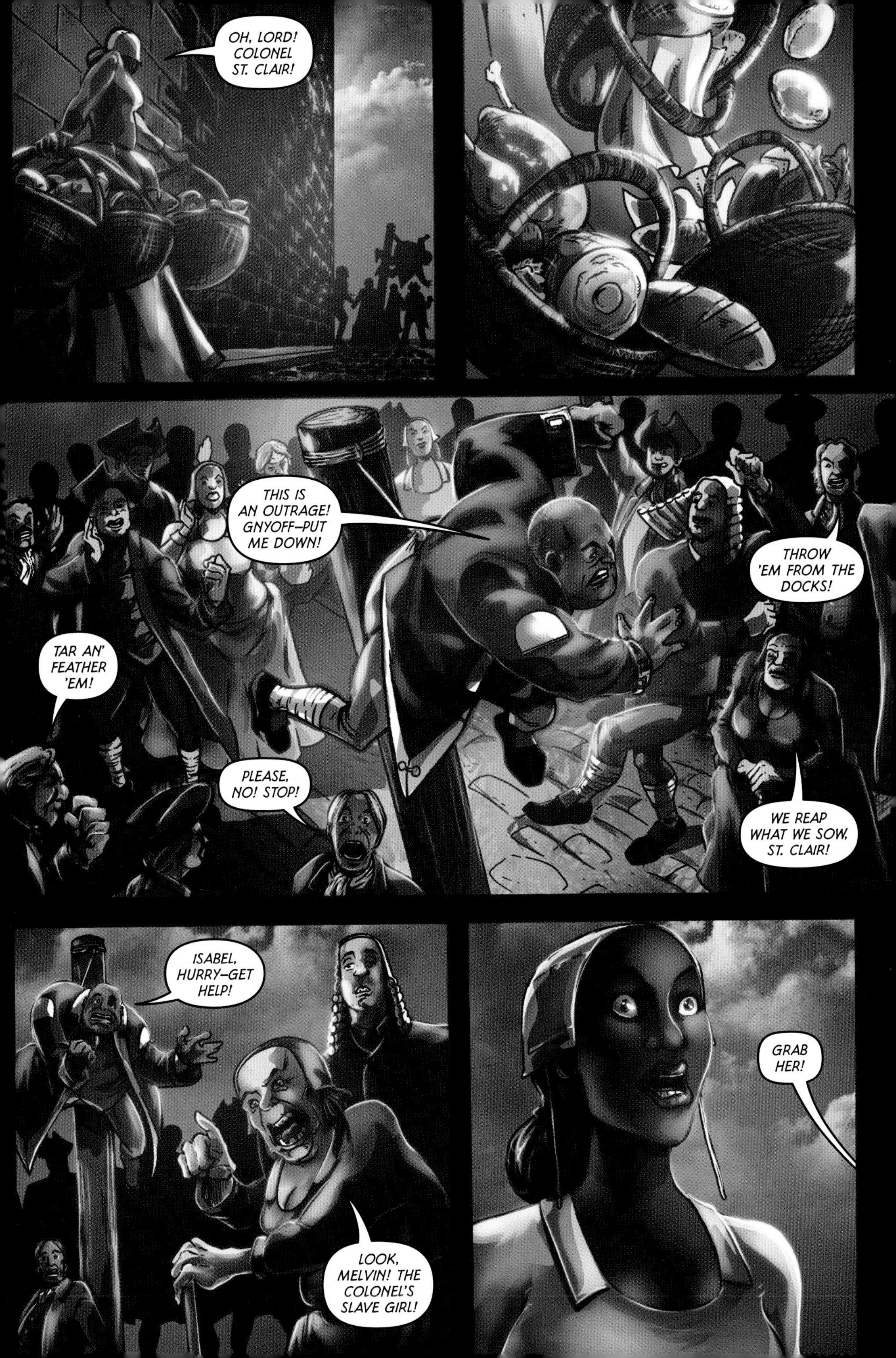
OH, LORD! COLONEL ST. CLAIR!
THIS IS AN OUTRAGE! GNYOFF—PUT ME DOWN!
THROW 'EM FROM THE DOCKS!
TAR AN' FEATHER 'EM!
PLEASE, NO! STOP!
WE REAP WHAT WE SOW, ST. CLAIR!
ISABEL, HURRY—GET HELP!
LOOK, MELVIN! THE COLONEL'S SLAVE GIRL!
GRAB HER!

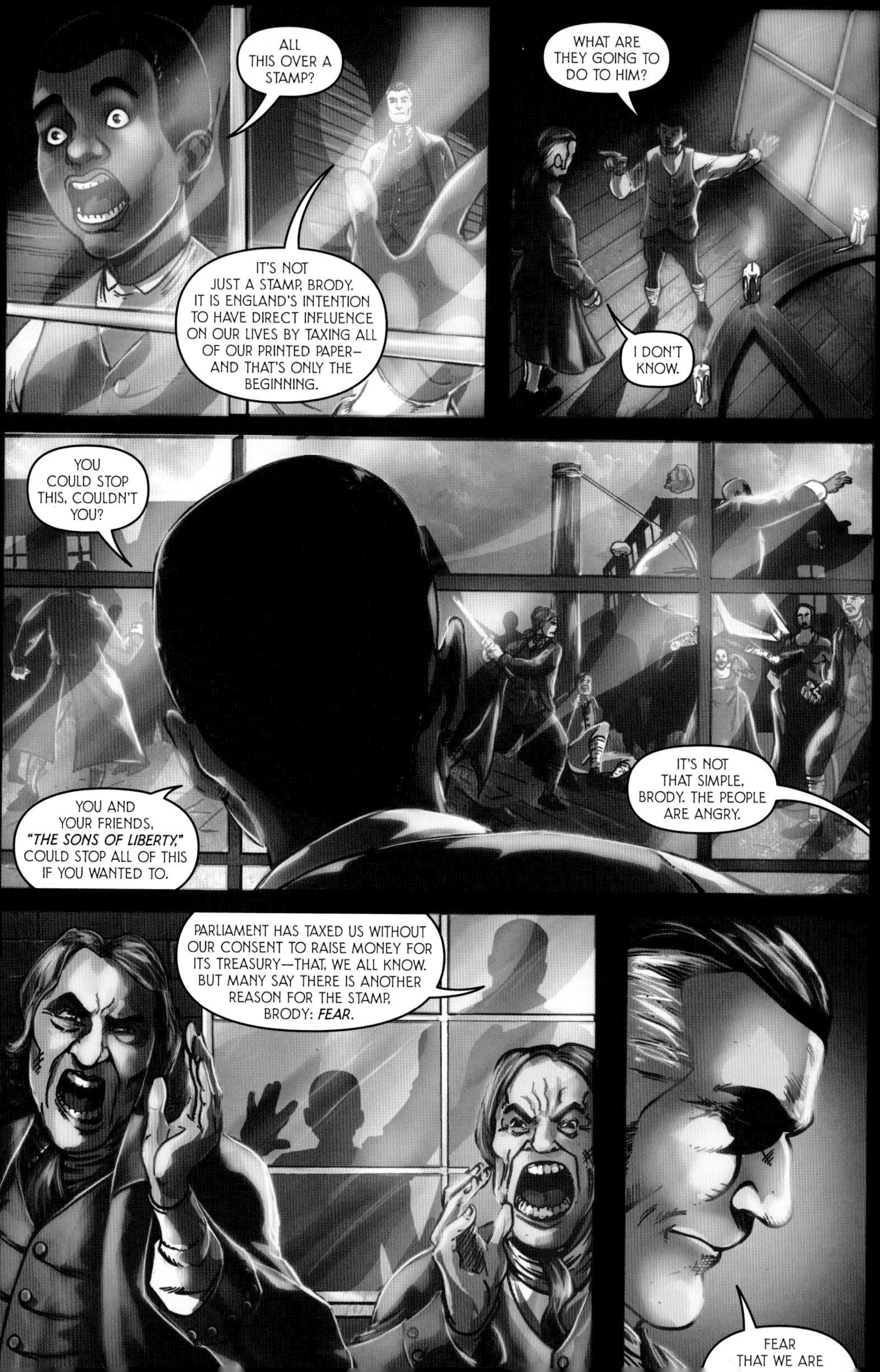
ALL THIS OVER A STAMP?
IT'S NOT JUST A STAMP, BRODY. IT IS ENGLAND'S INTENTION TO HAVE DIRECT INFLUENCE ON OUR LIVES BY TAXING ALL OF OUR PRINTED PAPER—AND THAT'S ONLY THE BEGINNING.
WHAT ARE THEY GOING TO DO TO HIM?
I DON'T KNOW.
YOU COULD STOP THIS, COULDN'T YOU?
YOU AND YOUR FRIENDS, *"THE SONS OF LIBERTY,"* COULD STOP ALL OF THIS IF YOU WANTED TO.
IT'S NOT THAT SIMPLE, BRODY. THE PEOPLE ARE ANGRY.
PARLIAMENT HAS TAXED US WITHOUT OUR CONSENT TO RAISE MONEY FOR ITS TREASURY—THAT, WE ALL KNOW. BUT MANY SAY THERE IS ANOTHER REASON FOR THE STAMP, BRODY: *FEAR*.
FEAR THAT WE ARE

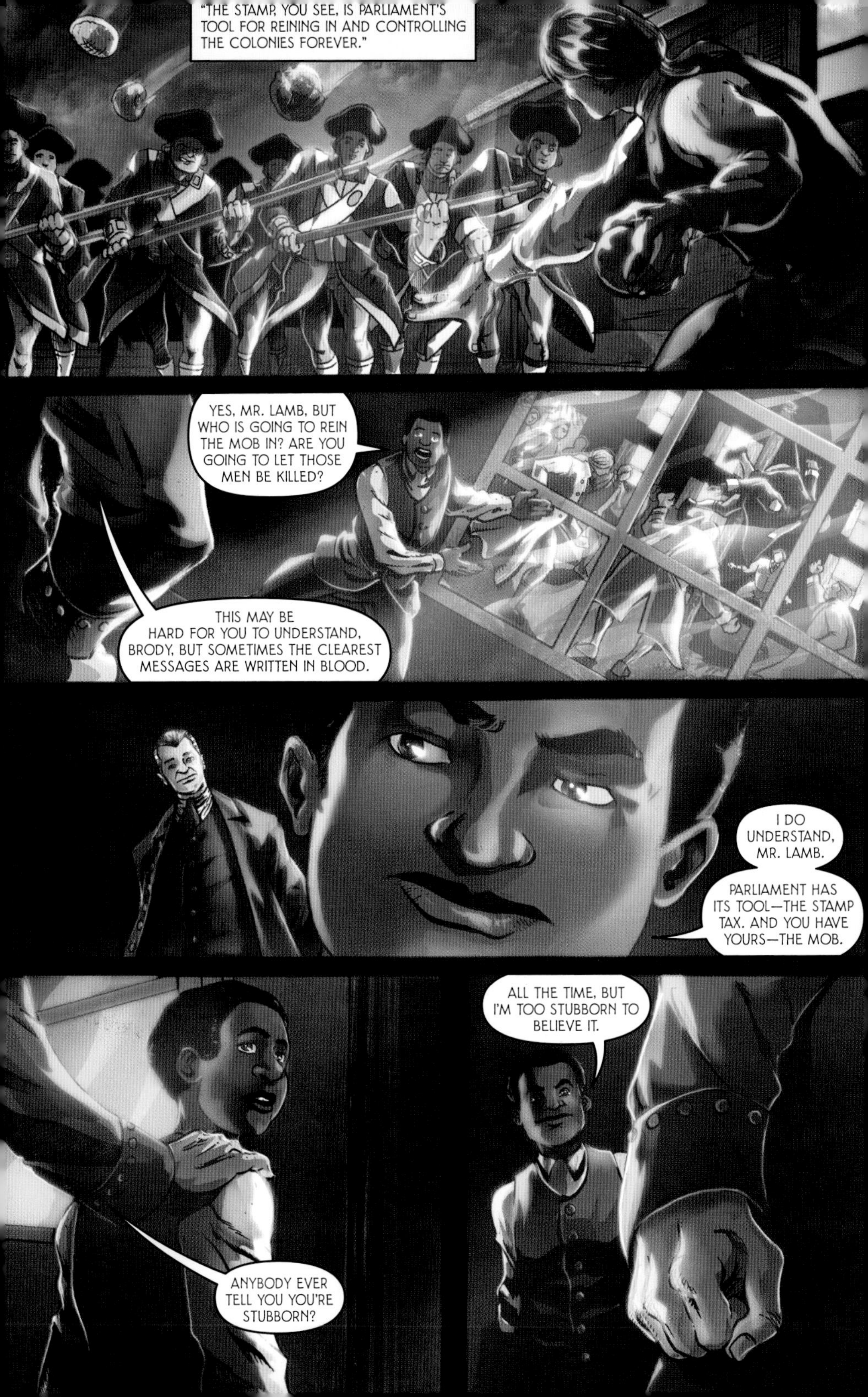
"THE STAMP, YOU SEE, IS PARLIAMENT'S TOOL FOR REINING IN AND CONTROLLING THE COLONIES FOREVER."
YES, MR. LAMB, BUT WHO IS GOING TO REIN THE MOB IN? ARE YOU GOING TO LET THOSE MEN BE KILLED?
THIS MAY BE HARD FOR YOU TO UNDERSTAND, BRODY, BUT SOMETIMES THE CLEAREST MESSAGES ARE WRITTEN IN BLOOD.
I DO UNDERSTAND, MR. LAMB.
PARLIAMENT HAS ITS TOOL—THE STAMP TAX. AND YOU HAVE YOURS—THE MOB.
ANYBODY EVER TELL YOU YOU'RE STUBBORN?
ALL THE TIME, BUT I'M TOO STUBBORN TO BELIEVE IT.

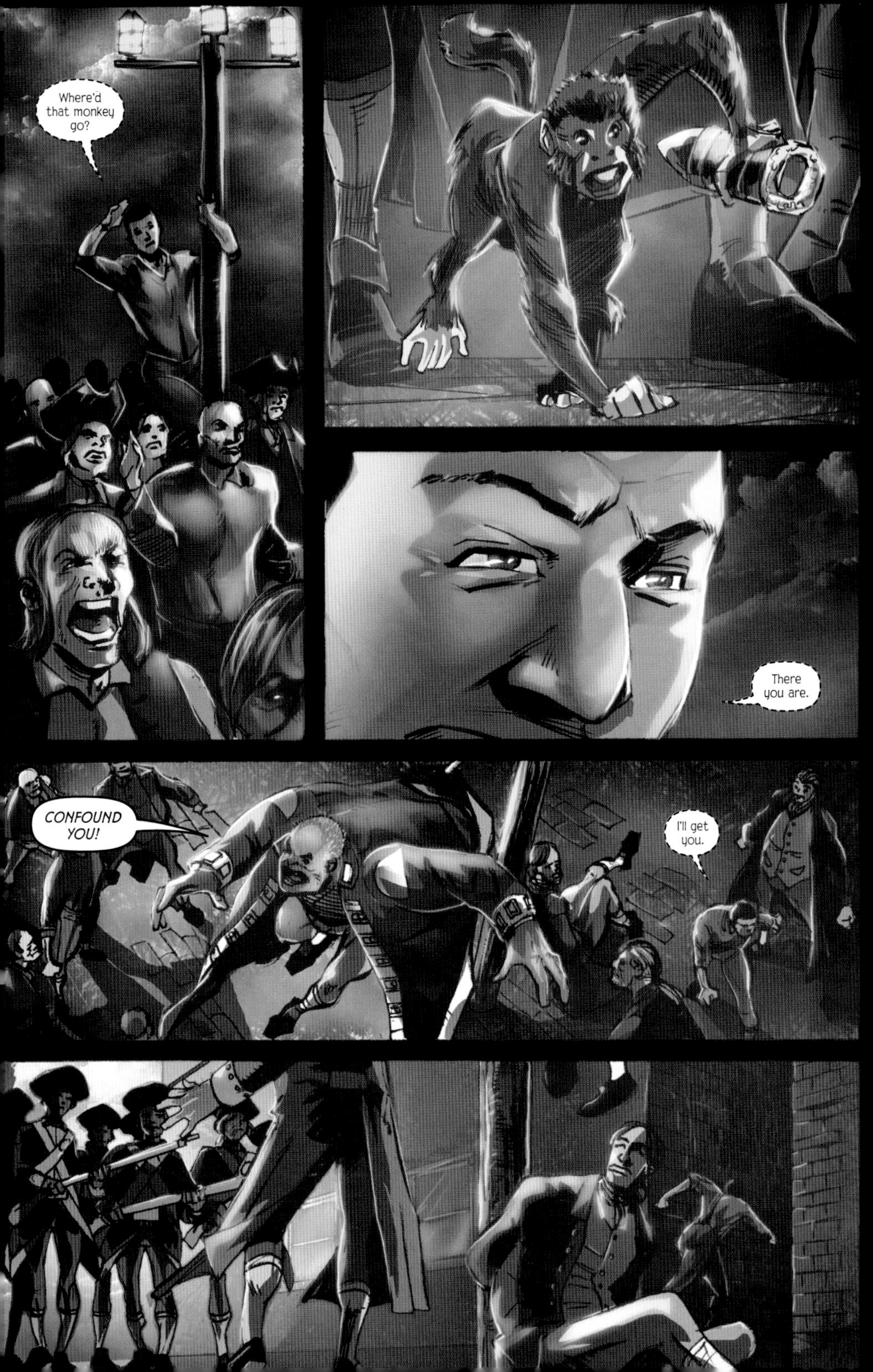
Where'd that monkey go?
There you are.
CONFOUND YOU!
I'll get you.

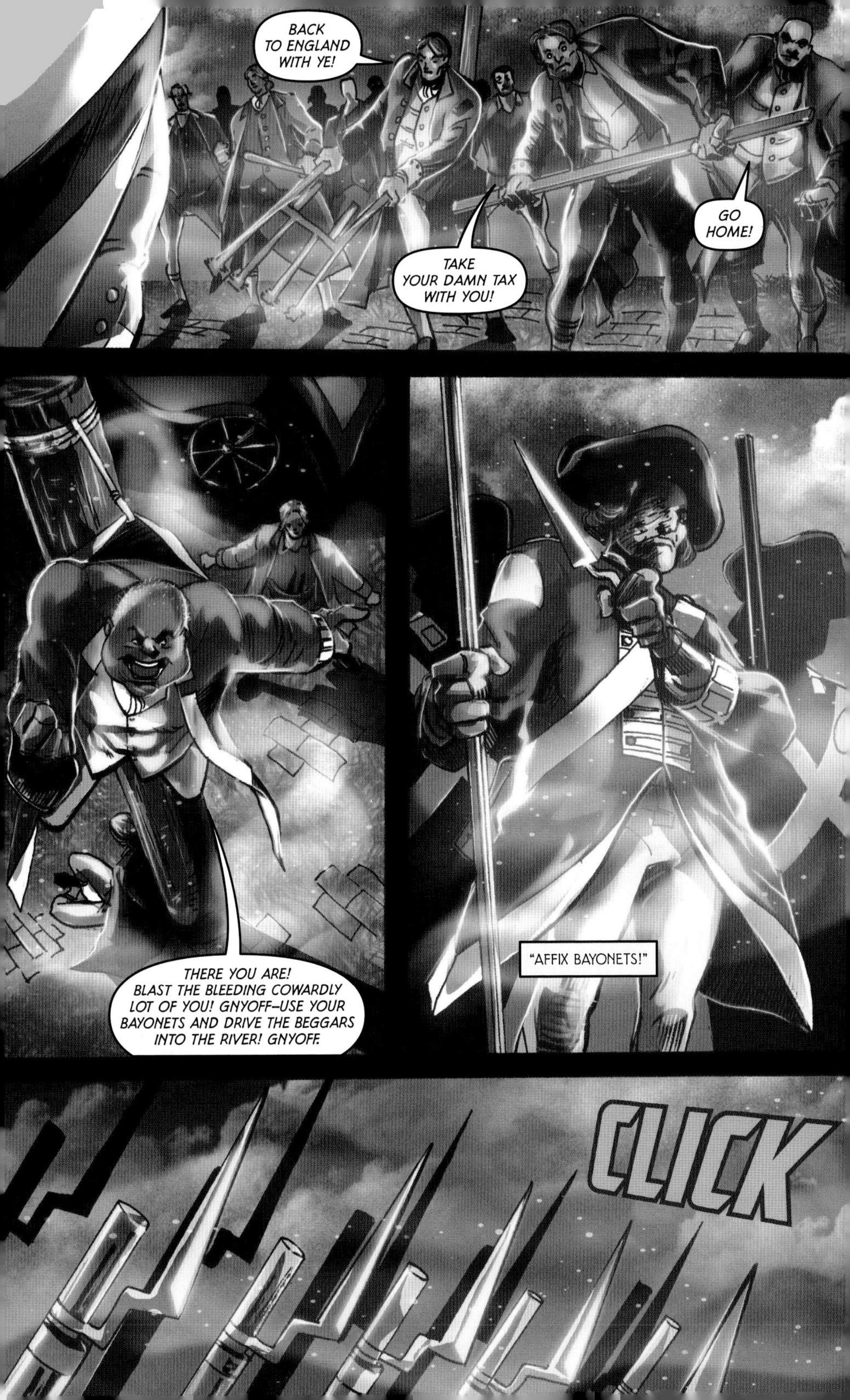
BACK TO ENGLAND WITH YE!
TAKE YOUR DAMN TAX WITH YOU!
GO HOME!
THERE YOU ARE! BLAST THE BLEEDING COWARDLY LOT OF YOU! GNYOFF—USE YOUR BAYONETS AND DRIVE THE BEGGARS INTO THE RIVER! GNYOFF.
"AFFIX BAYONETS!"
CLICK

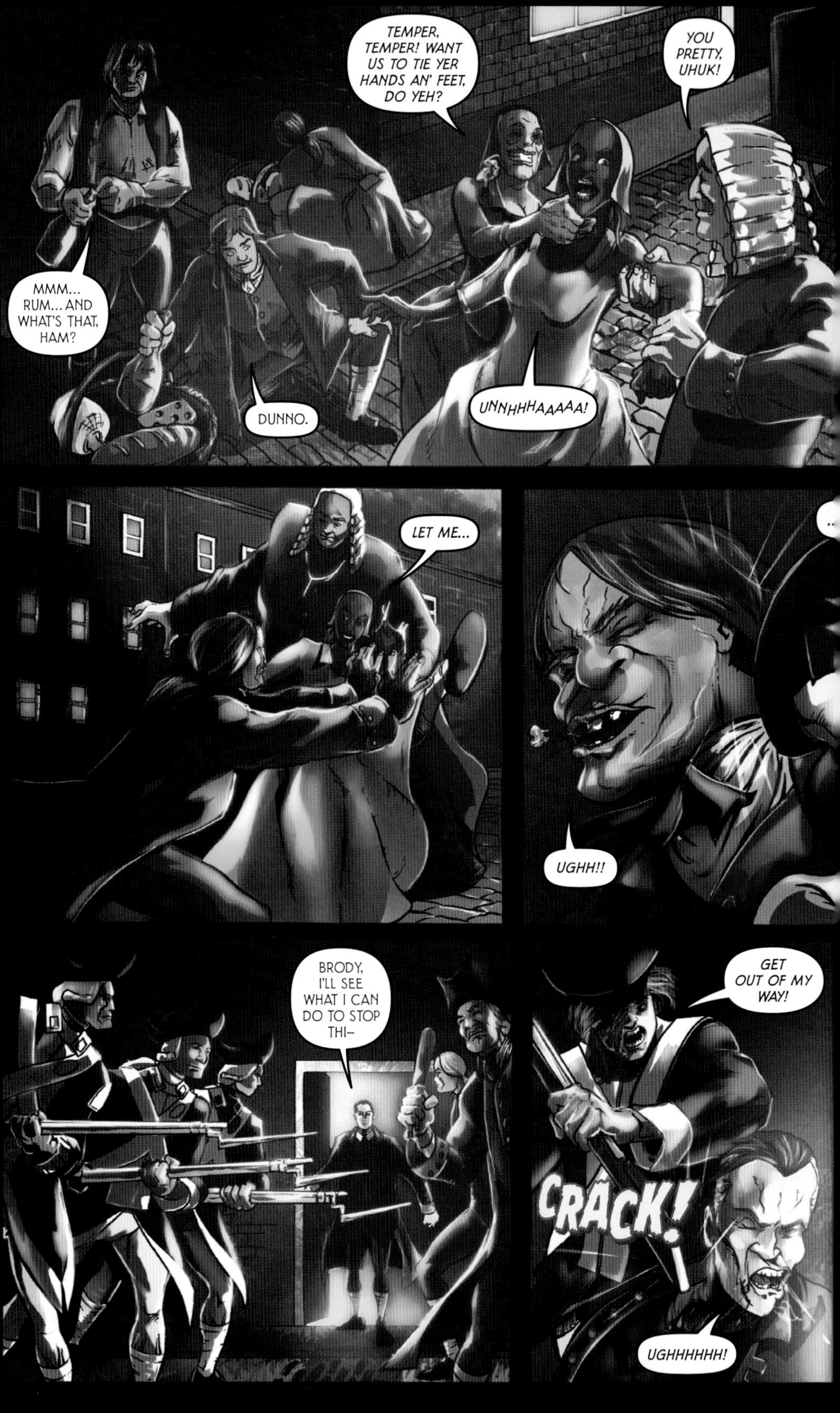
TEMPER, TEMPER! WANT US TO TIE YER HANDS AN' FEET, DO YEH?
YOU PRETTY, UHUK!
MMM... RUM... AND WHAT'S THAT, HAM?
DUNNO.
UNNHHHAAAAA!
LET ME...
UGHH!!
BRODY, I'LL SEE WHAT I CAN DO TO STOP THI–
GET OUT OF MY WAY!
CRACK!
UGHHHHHH!

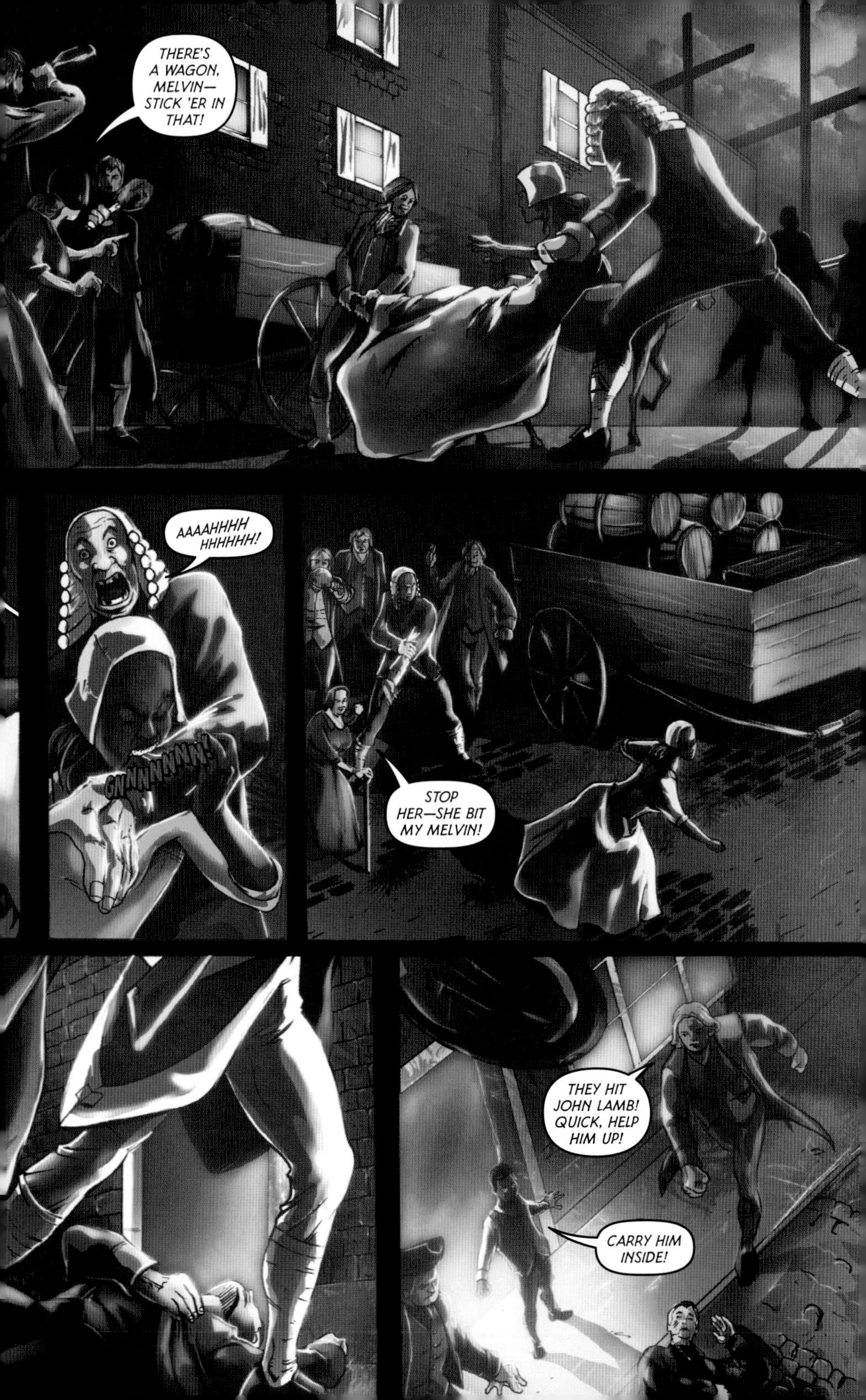
THERE'S A WAGON, MELVIN—STICK 'ER IN THAT!
AAAAHHHH HHHHHH!
GNNNNNNN!
STOP HER—SHE BIT MY MELVIN!
THEY HIT JOHN LAMB! QUICK, HELP HIM UP!
CARRY HIM INSIDE!

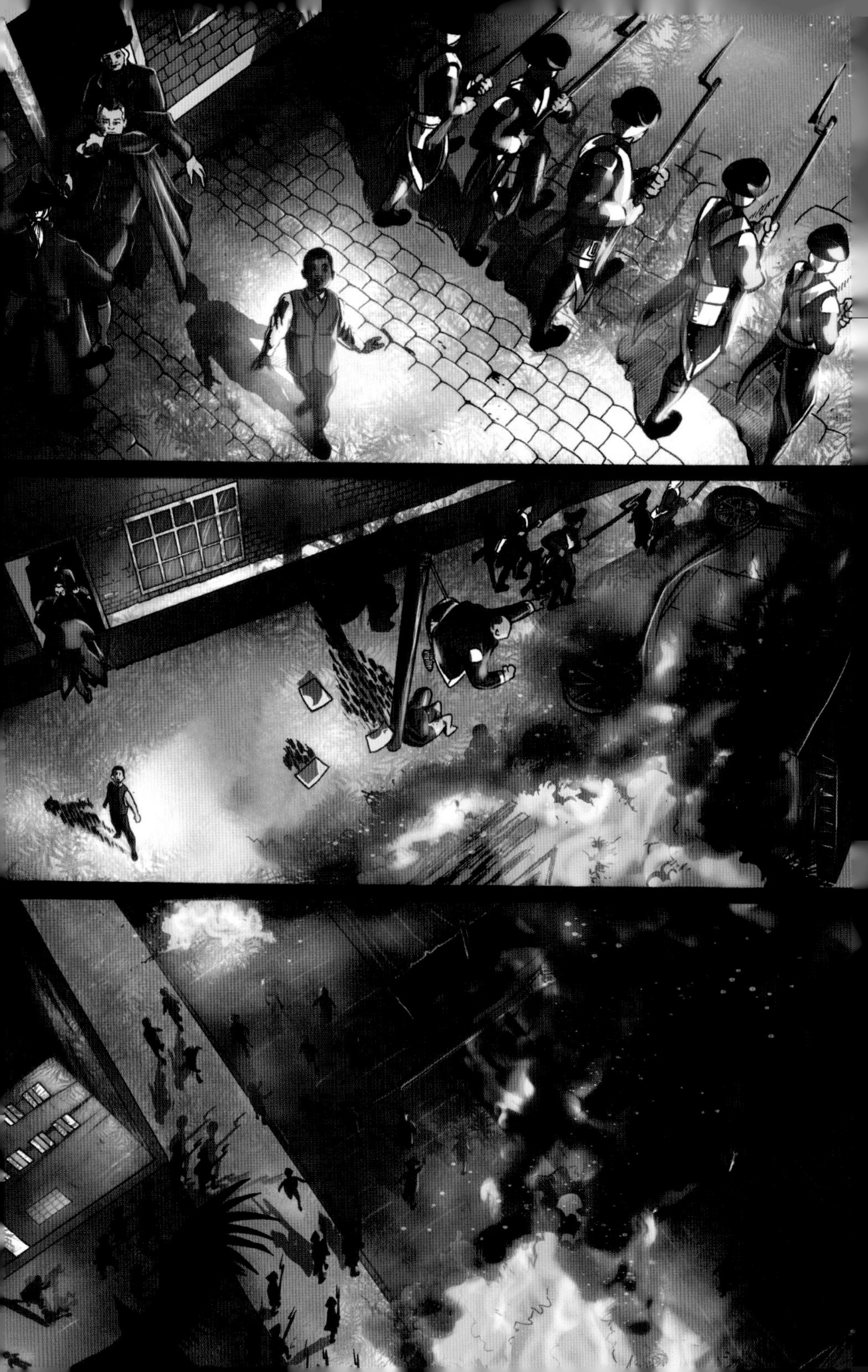

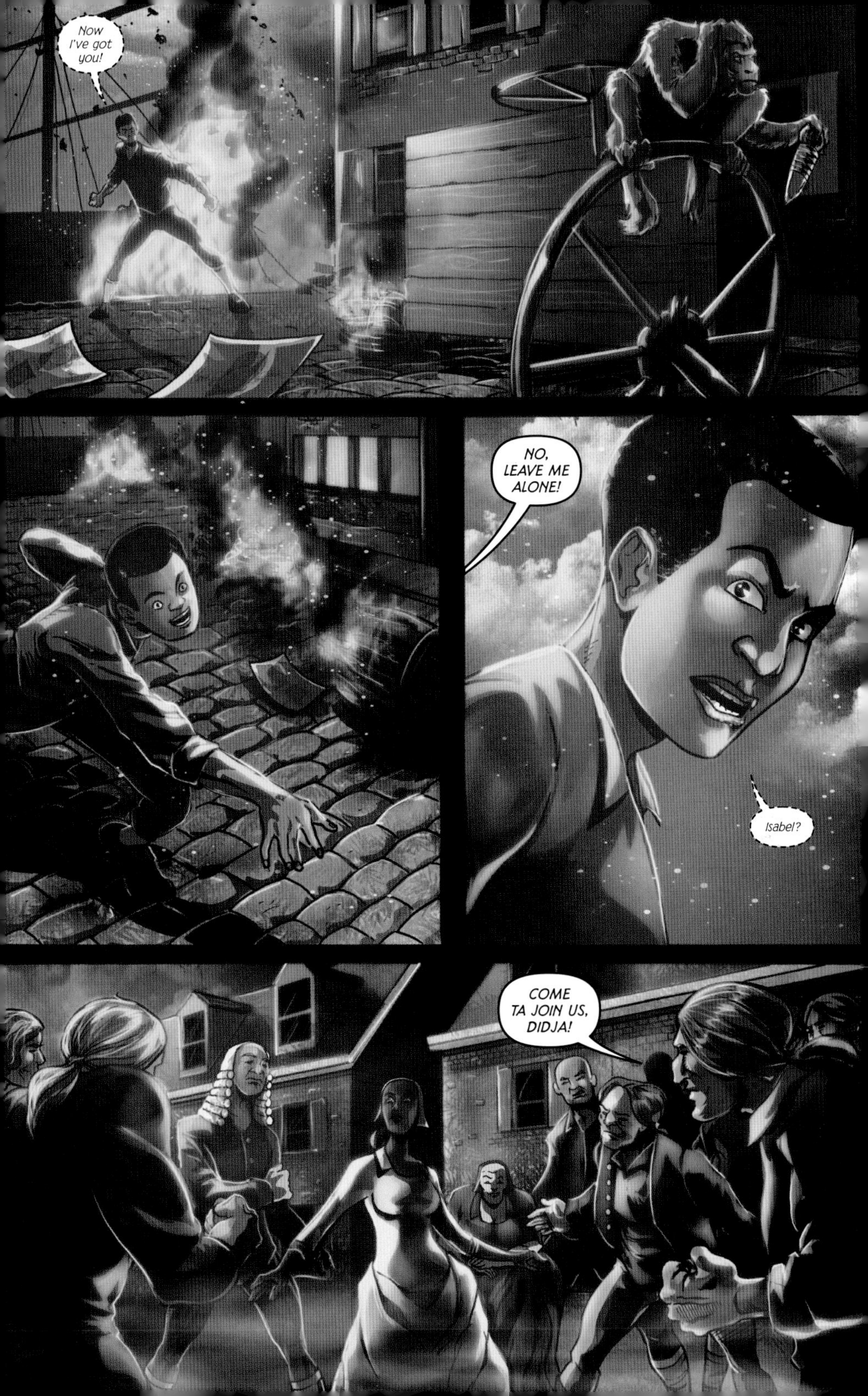
Now I've got you!
NO, LEAVE ME ALONE!
Isabel?
COME TA JOIN US, DIDJA!

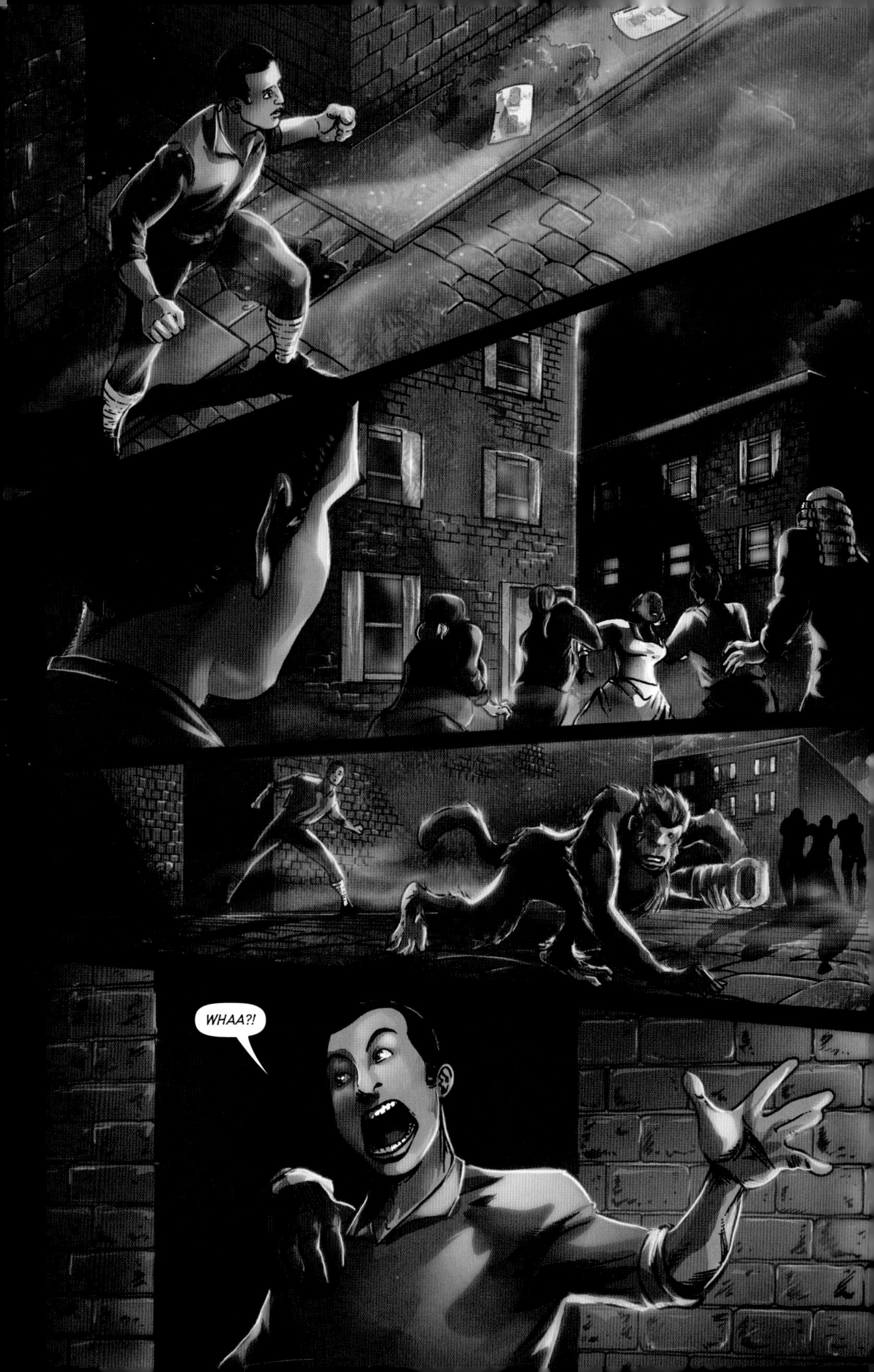
WHAA?!

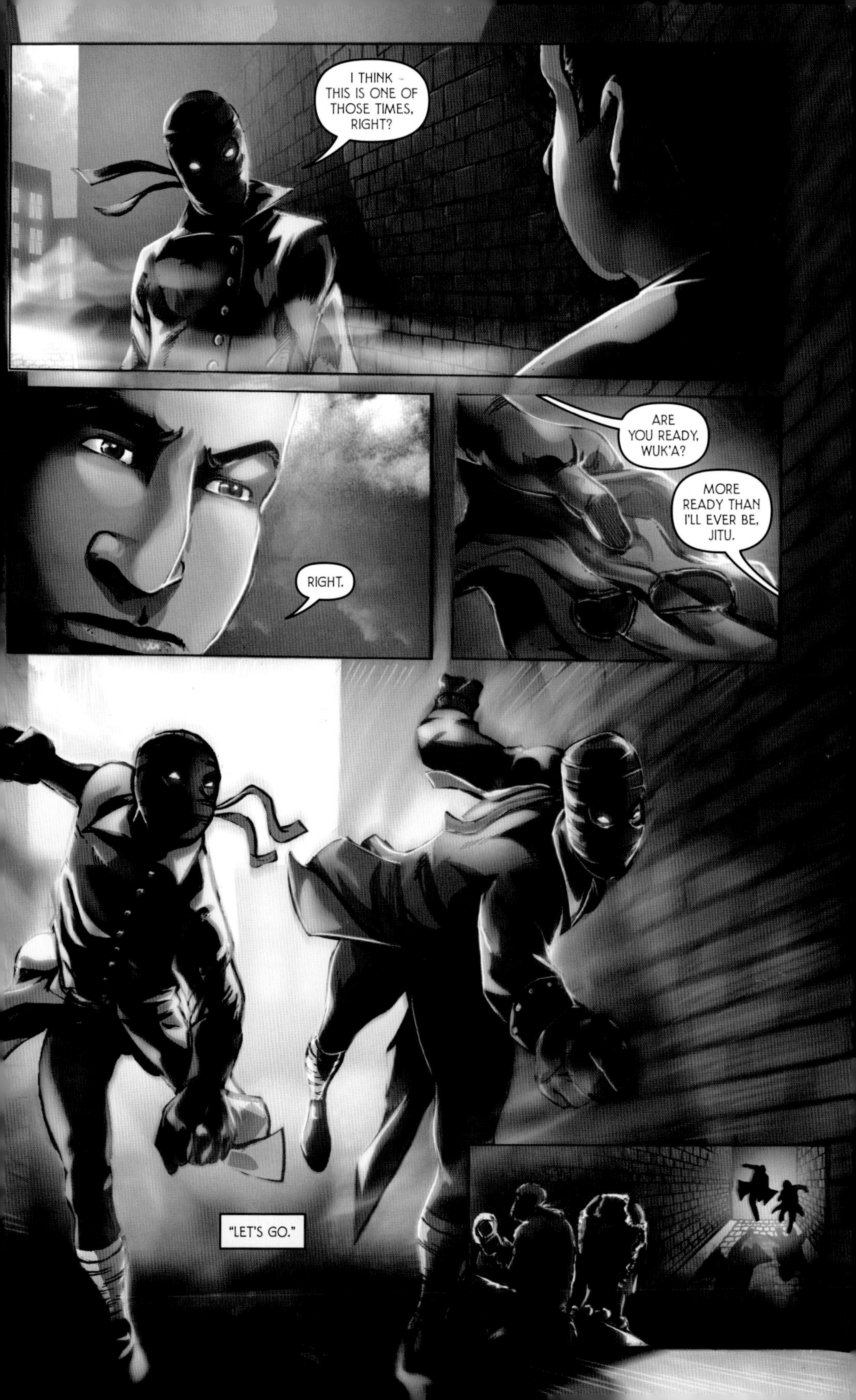
I THINK THIS IS ONE OF THOSE TIMES, RIGHT?
RIGHT.
ARE YOU READY, WUK'A?
MORE READY THAN I'LL EVER BE, JITU.
"LET'S GO."

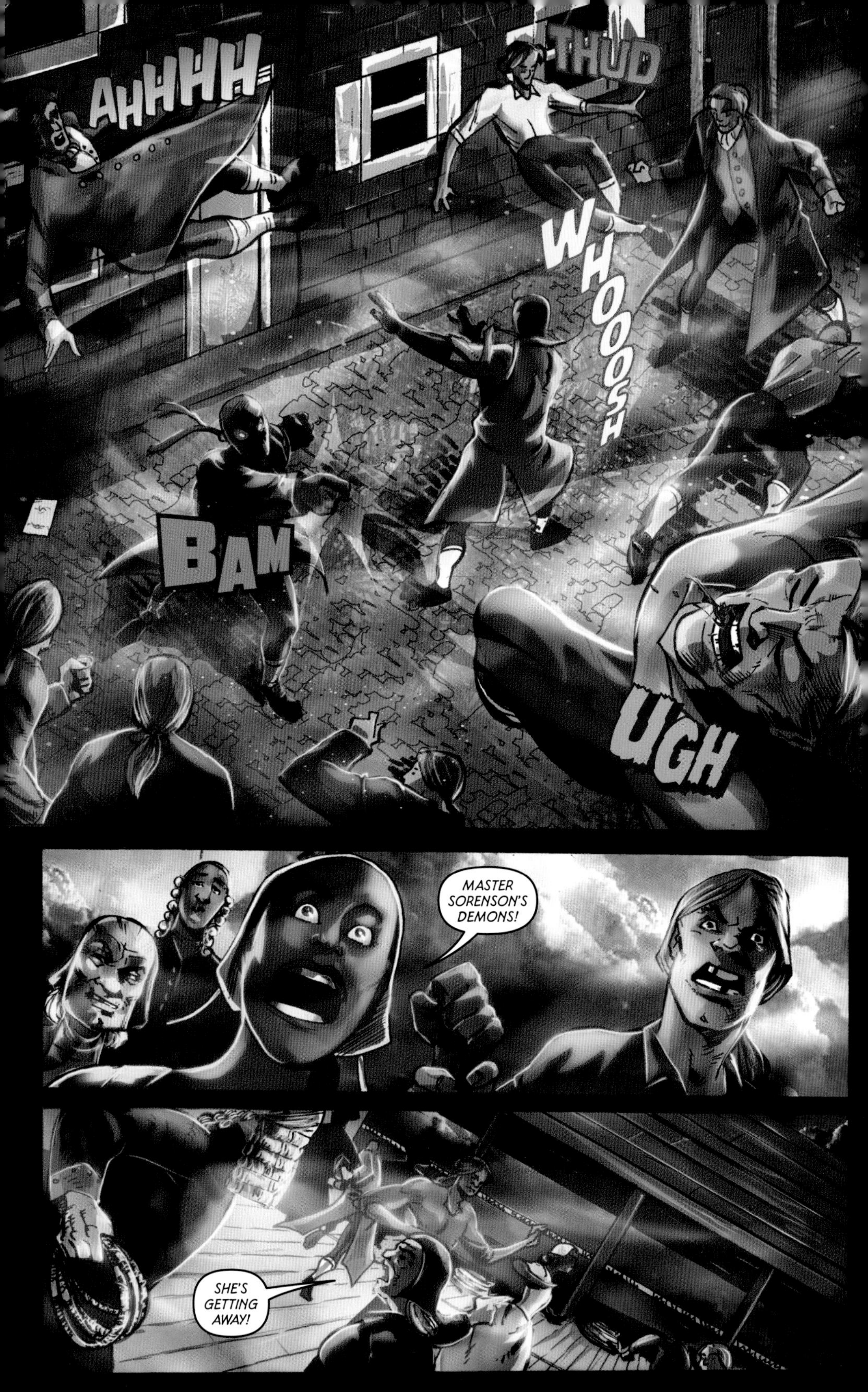
AHHHH
THUD
WHOOOSH
BAM
UGH
MASTER SORENSON'S DEMONS!
SHE'S GETTING AWAY!

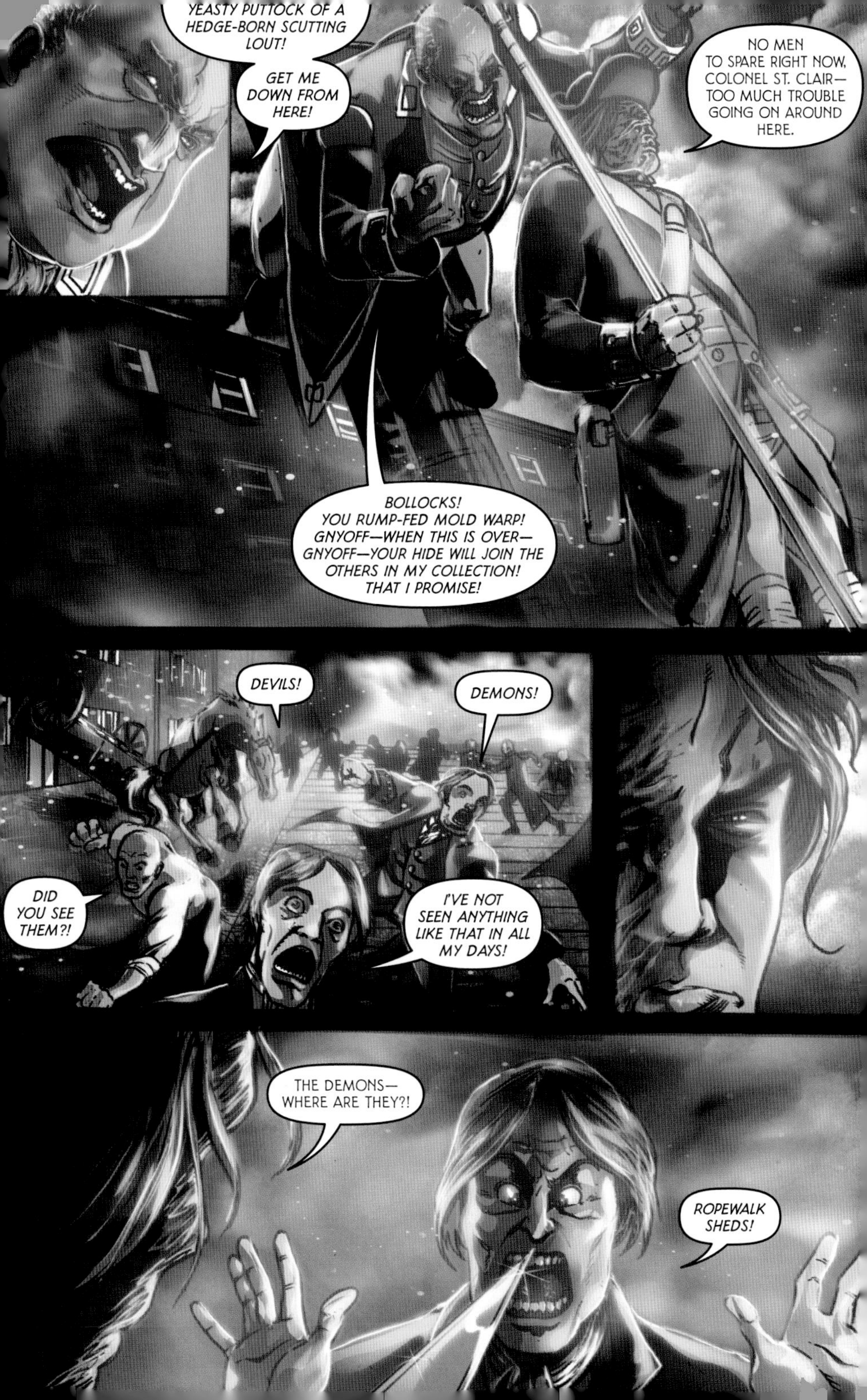
YEASTY PUTTOCK OF A HEDGE-BORN SCUTTING LOUT!
GET ME DOWN FROM HERE!
NO MEN TO SPARE RIGHT NOW, COLONEL ST. CLAIR— TOO MUCH TROUBLE GOING ON AROUND HERE.
BOLLOCKS! YOU RUMP-FED MOLD WARP! GNYOFF—WHEN THIS IS OVER— GNYOFF—YOUR HIDE WILL JOIN THE OTHERS IN MY COLLECTION! THAT I PROMISE!
DEVILS!
DEMONS!
DID YOU SEE THEM?!
I'VE NOT SEEN ANYTHING LIKE THAT IN ALL MY DAYS!
THE DEMONS— WHERE ARE THEY?!
ROPEWALK SHEDS!

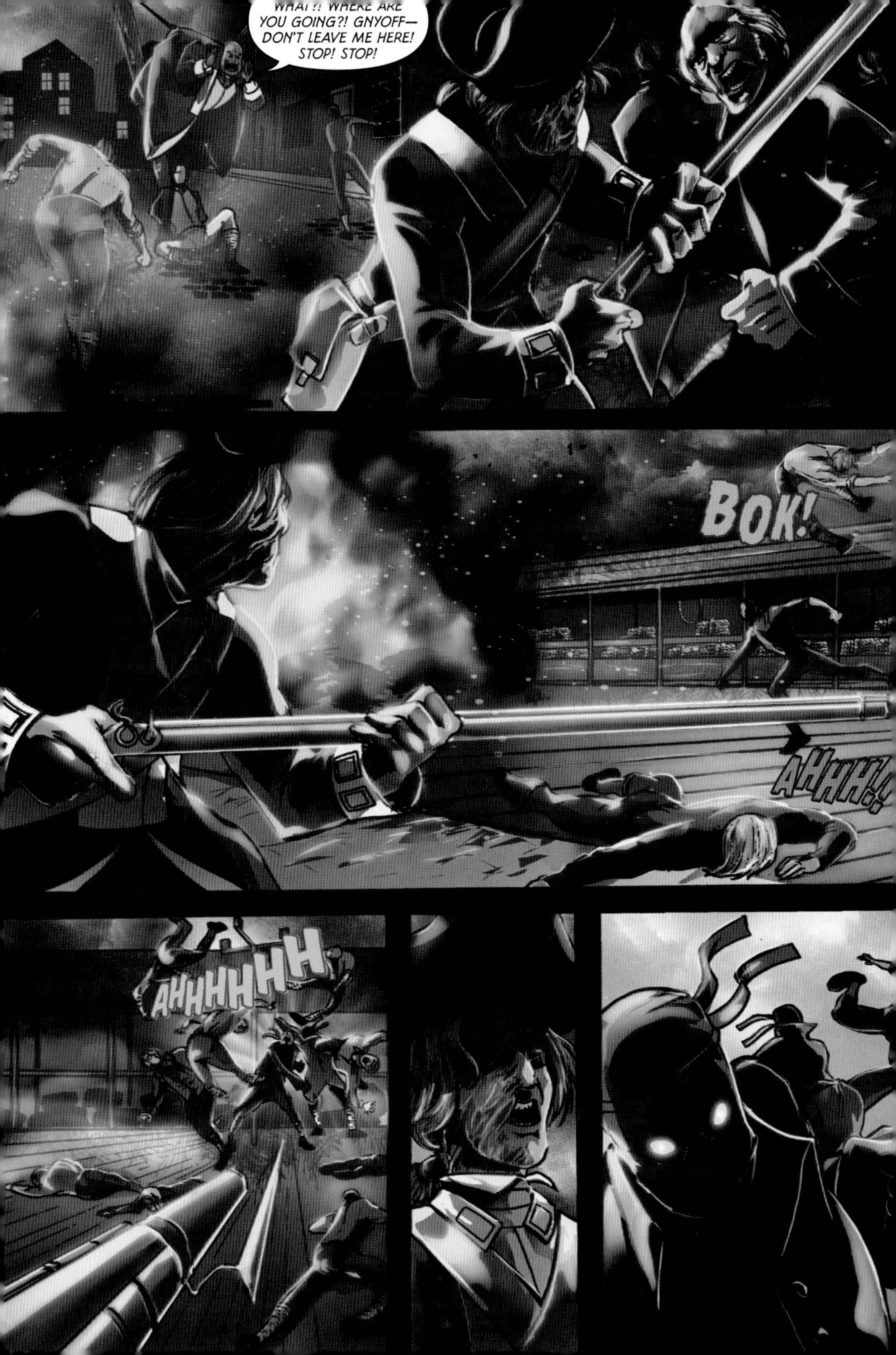
WHAT?! WHERE ARE YOU GOING?! GNYOFF— DON'T LEAVE ME HERE! STOP! STOP!
BOK!
AHHH!!
AHHHHHH

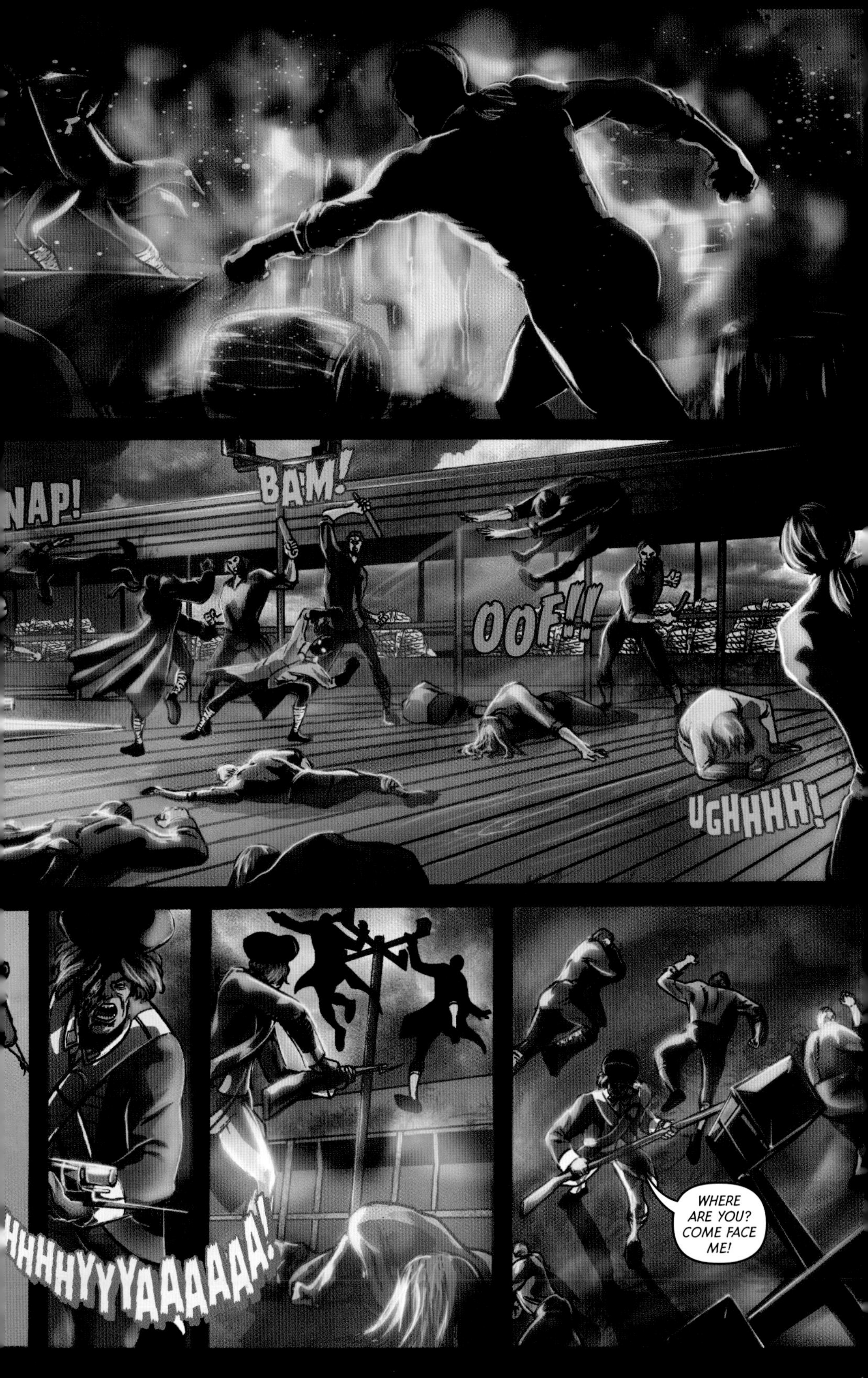
NAP!
BAM!
OOF!!
UGHHHH!
HHHHYYYAAAAAA!
WHERE ARE YOU? COME FACE ME!

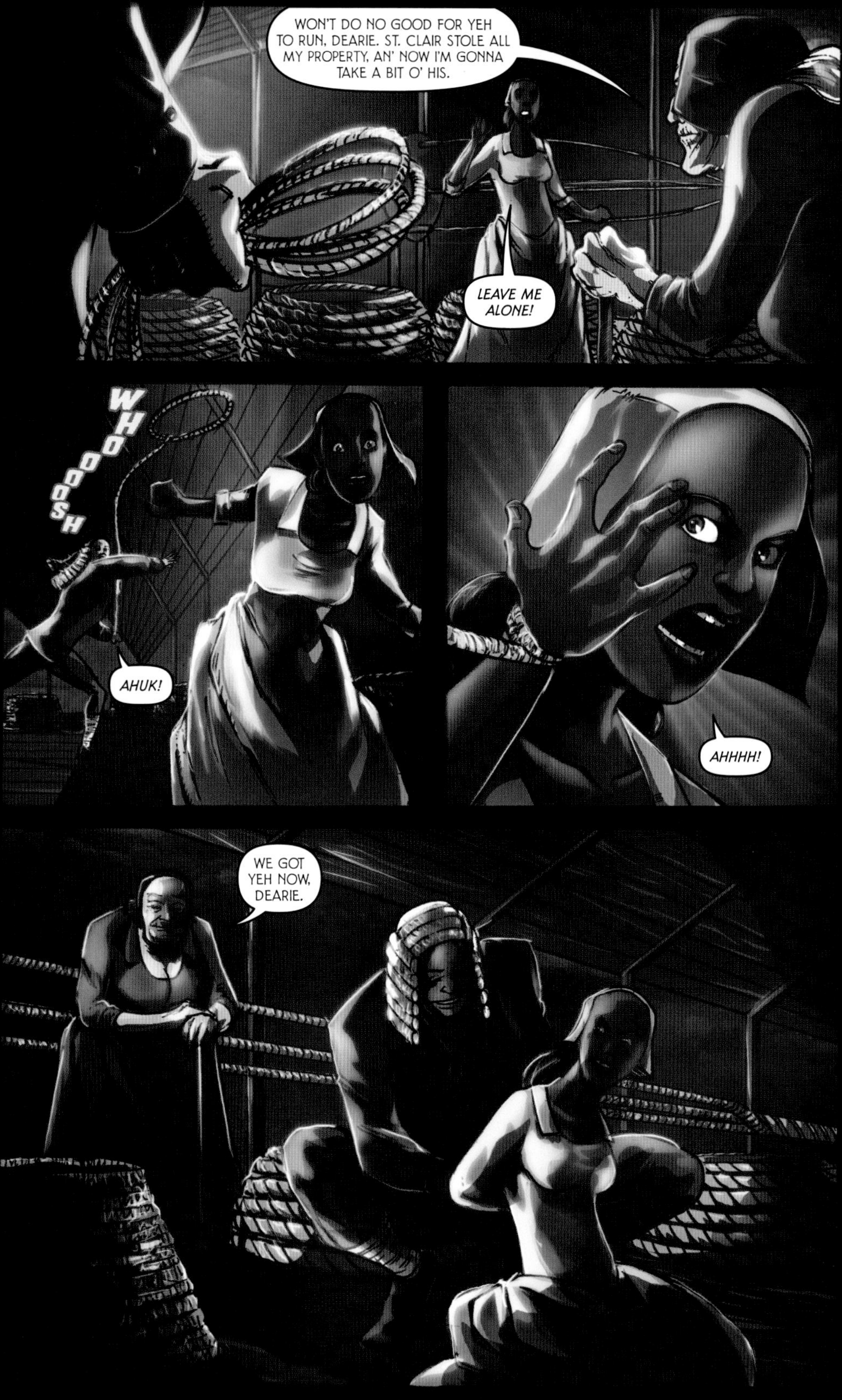
WON'T DO NO GOOD FOR YEH TO RUN, DEARIE. ST. CLAIR STOLE ALL MY PROPERTY, AN' NOW I'M GONNA TAKE A BIT O' HIS.
LEAVE ME ALONE!
WHOOOOSH
AHUK!
AHHHH!
WE GOT YEH NOW, DEARIE.

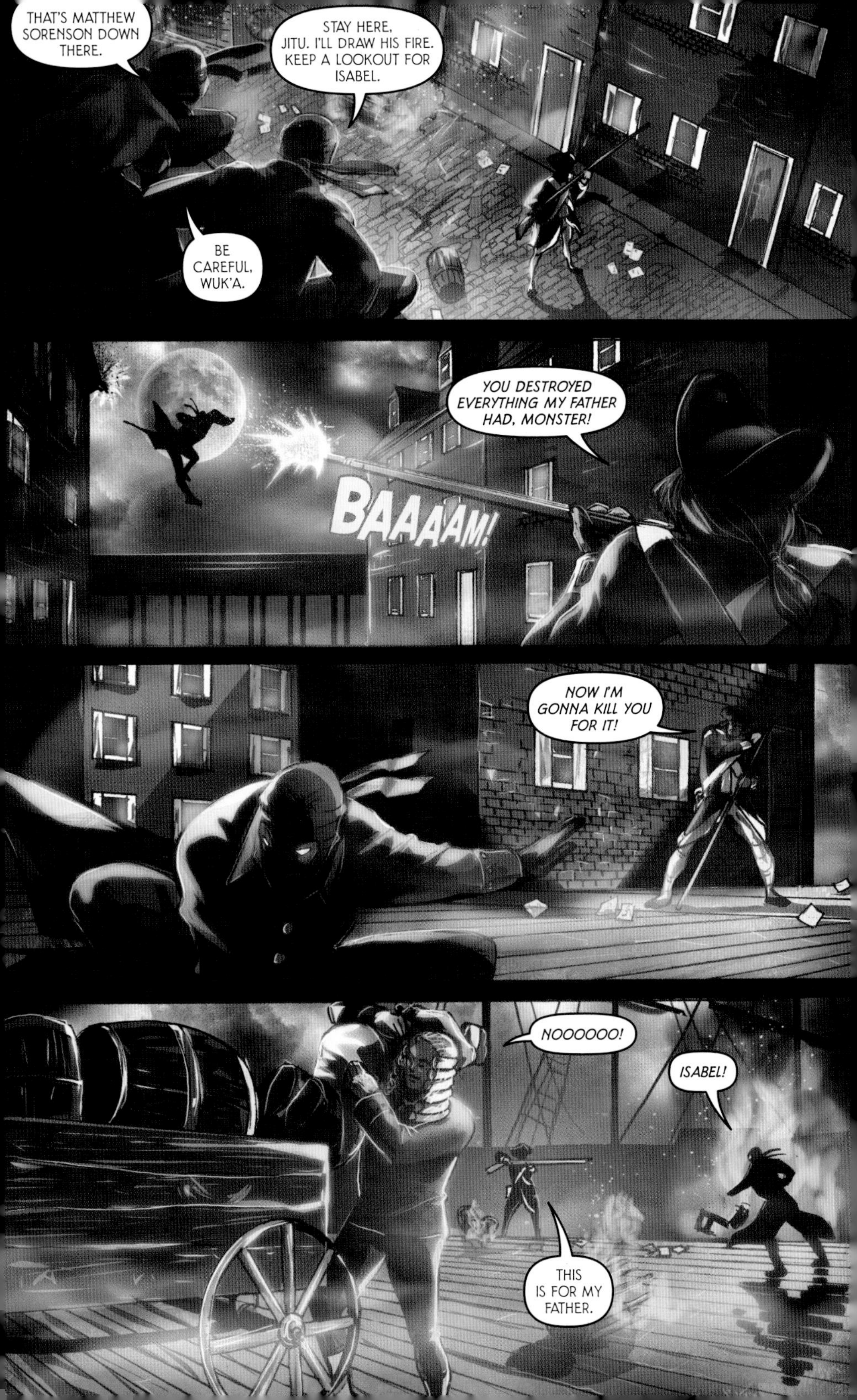
THAT'S MATTHEW SORENSON DOWN THERE.
STAY HERE, JITU. I'LL DRAW HIS FIRE. KEEP A LOOKOUT FOR ISABEL.
BE CAREFUL, WUK'A.
YOU DESTROYED EVERYTHING MY FATHER HAD, MONSTER!
BAAAAM!
NOW I'M GONNA KILL YOU FOR IT!
NOOOOOO!
ISABEL!
THIS IS FOR MY FATHER.

WHUUUMP!

BAAAM!

SSCRRASHH!

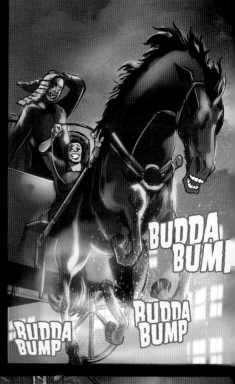

BUDDA BUMP

BUDDA BUMP

BUDDA BUMP

WUK'A, WAIT!

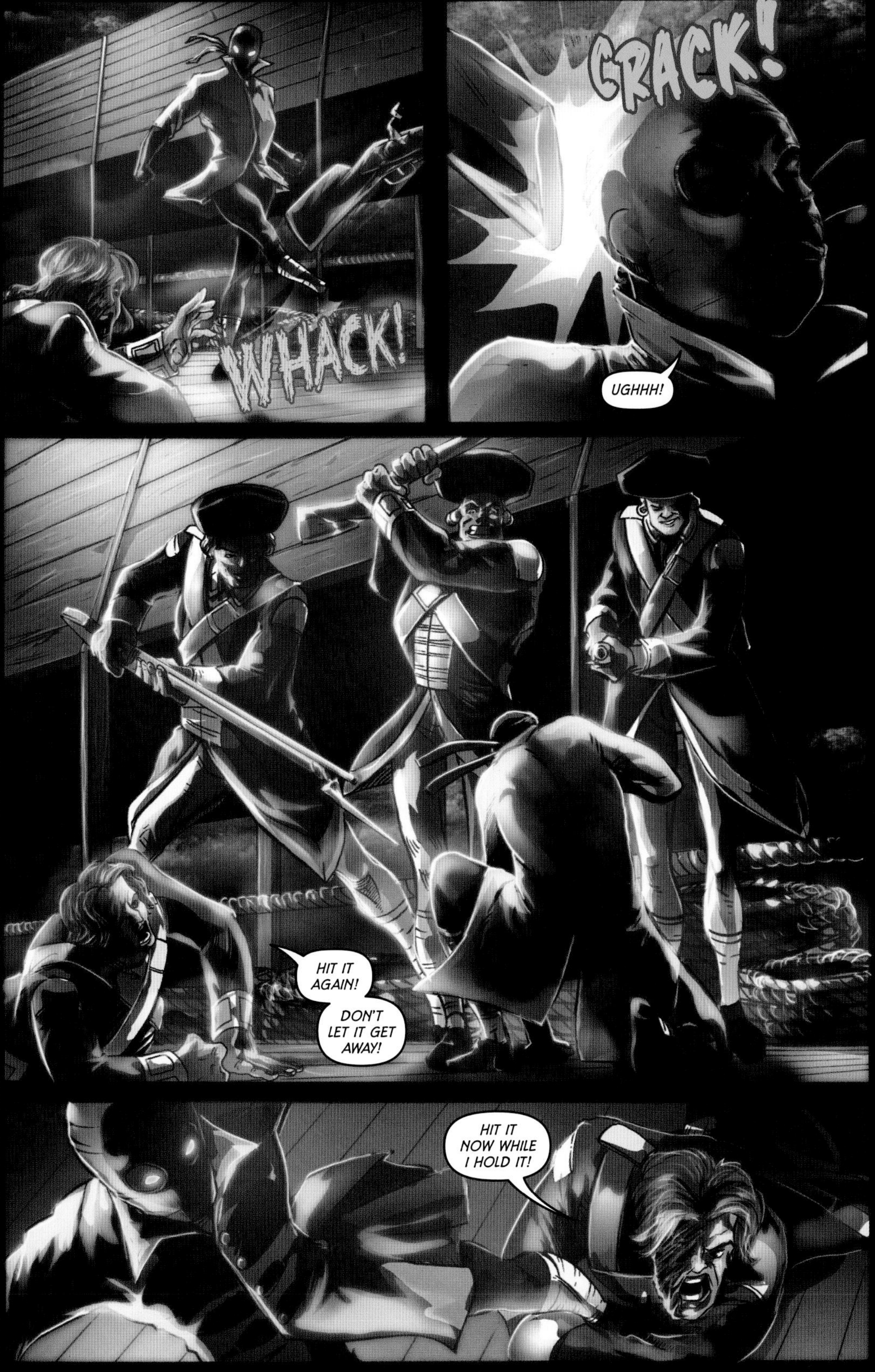
WHACK!
CRACK!
UGHHH!
HIT IT AGAIN!
DON'T LET IT GET AWAY!
HIT IT NOW WHILE I HOLD IT!

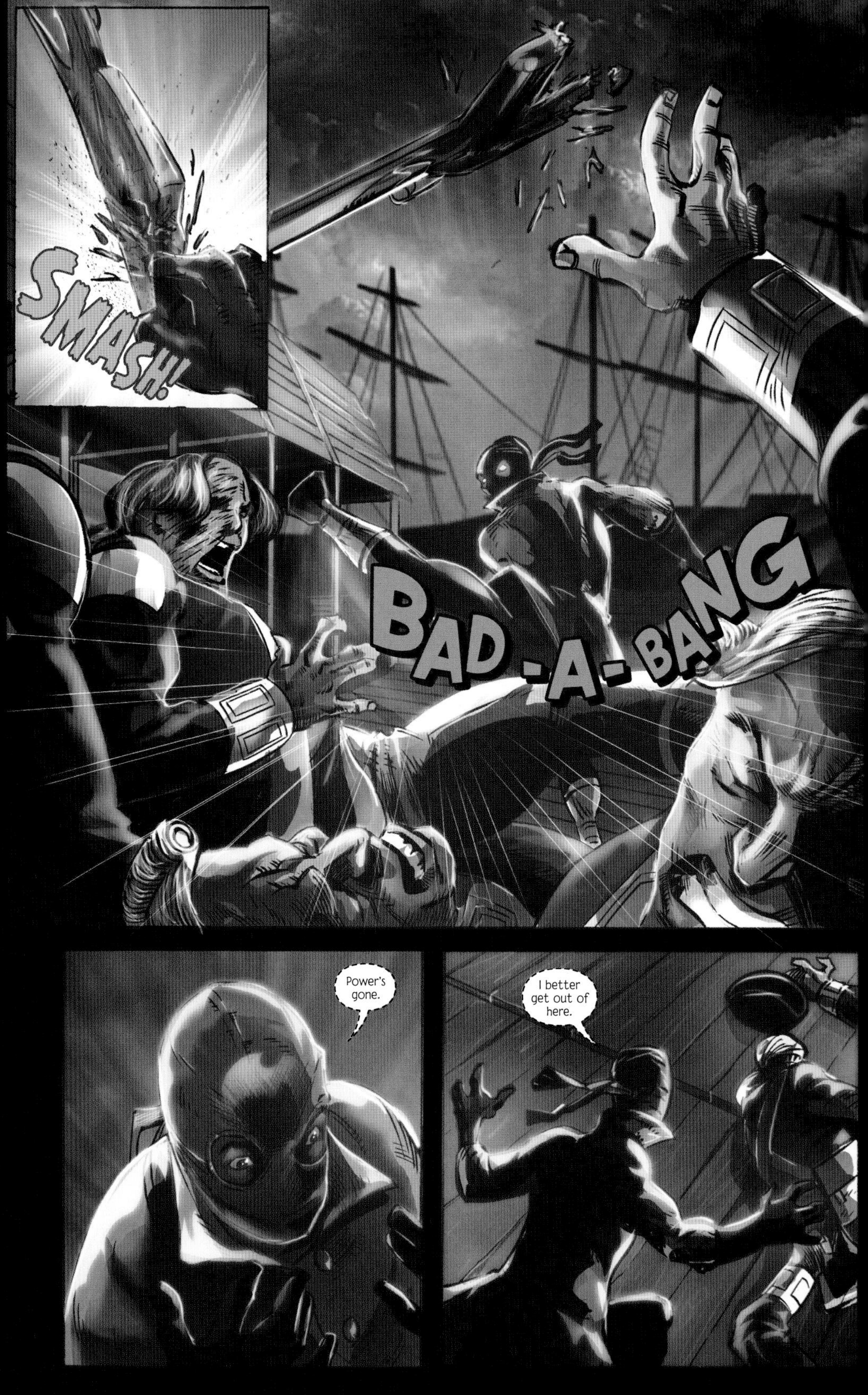
SMASH!
BAD-A-BANG
Power's gone.
I better get out of here.

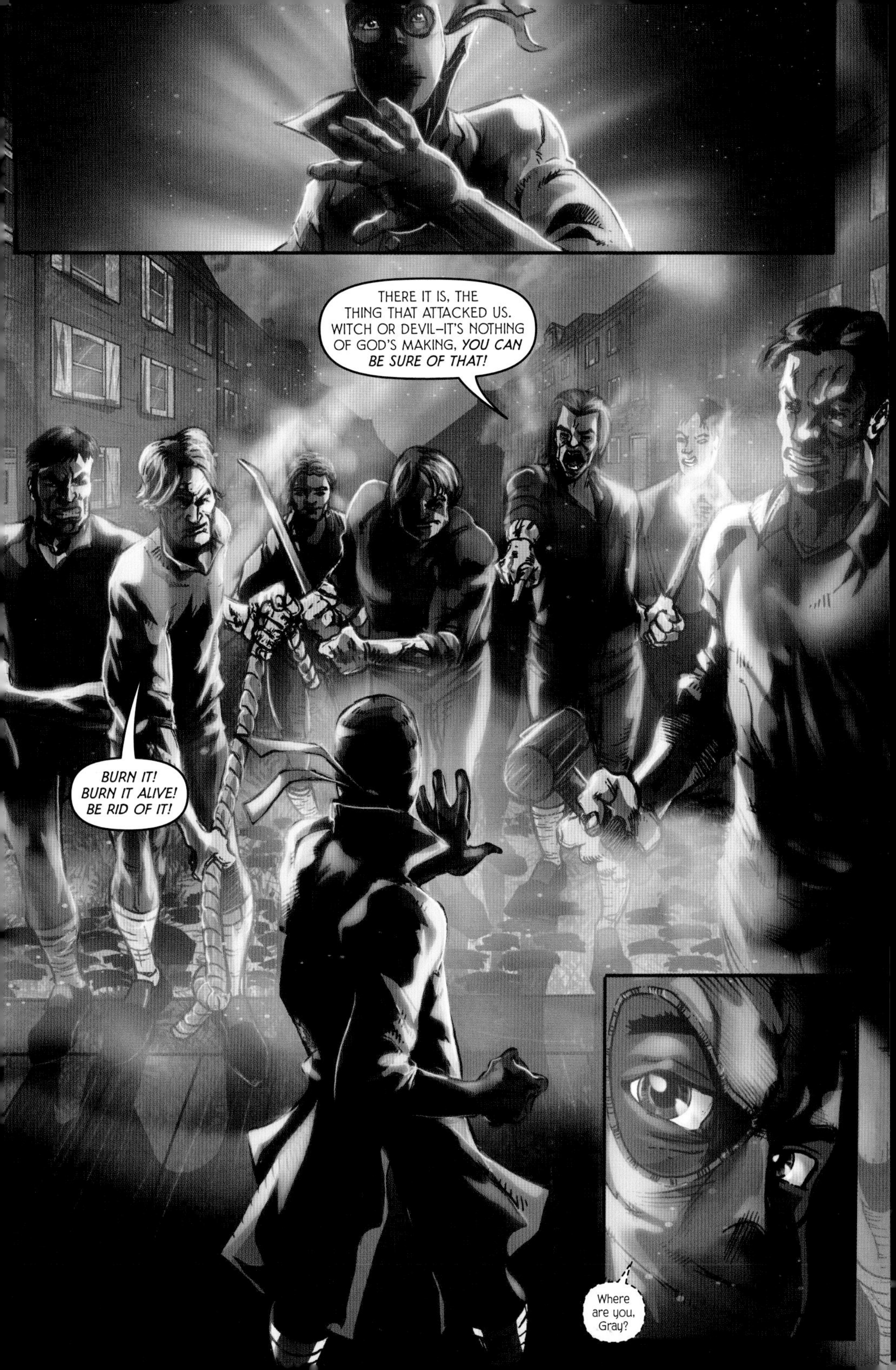
THERE IT IS, THE THING THAT ATTACKED US. WITCH OR DEVIL–IT'S NOTHING OF GOD'S MAKING, *YOU CAN BE SURE OF THAT!*
BURN IT! BURN IT ALIVE! BE RID OF IT!
Where are you, Gray?

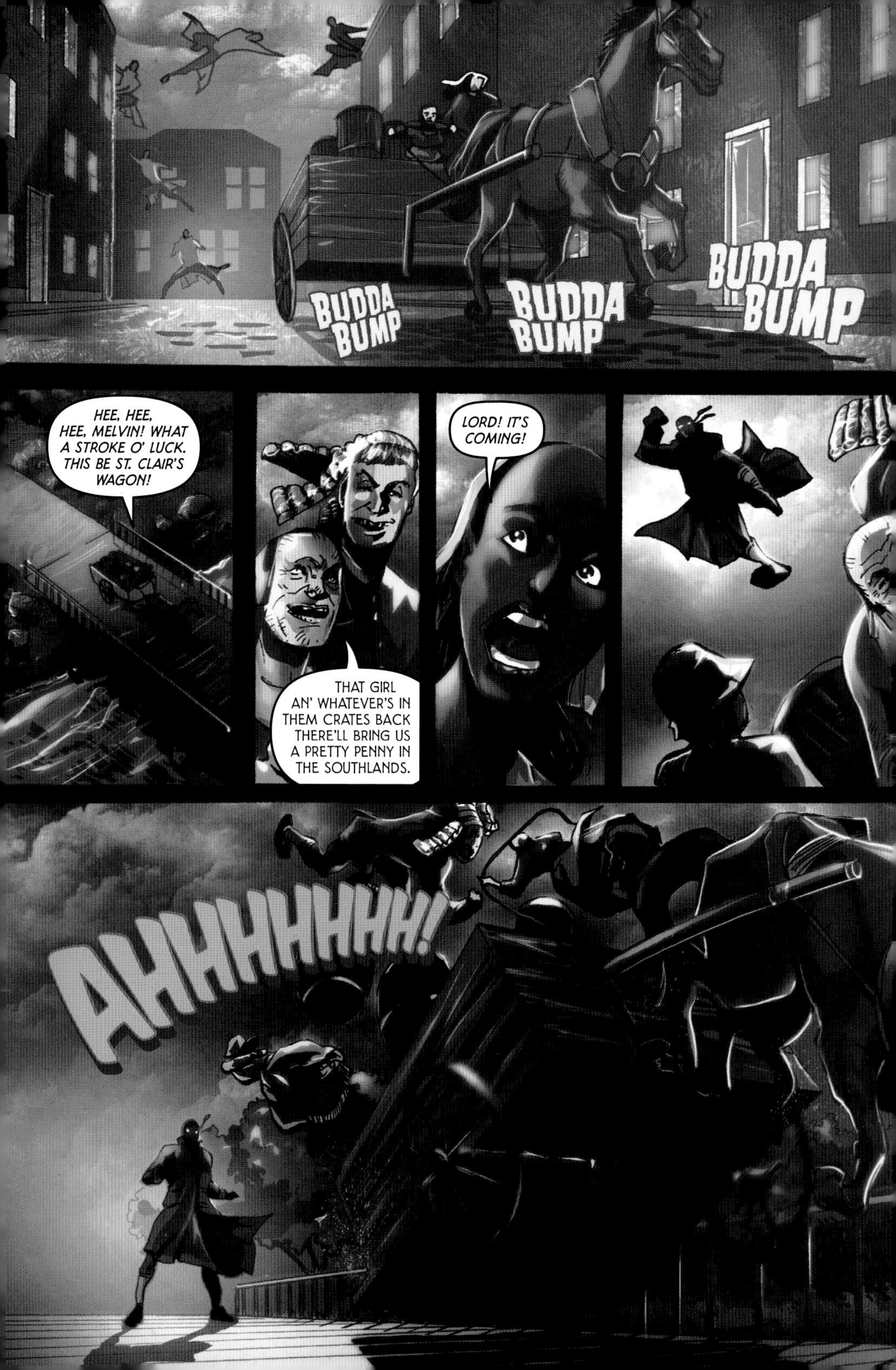
BUDDA BUMP
BUDDA BUMP
BUDDA BUMP
HEE, HEE, HEE, MELVIN! WHAT A STROKE O' LUCK. THIS BE ST. CLAIR'S WAGON!
THAT GIRL AN' WHATEVER'S IN THEM CRATES BACK THERE'LL BRING US A PRETTY PENNY IN THE SOUTHLANDS.
LORD! IT'S COMING!
AHHHHHHH!

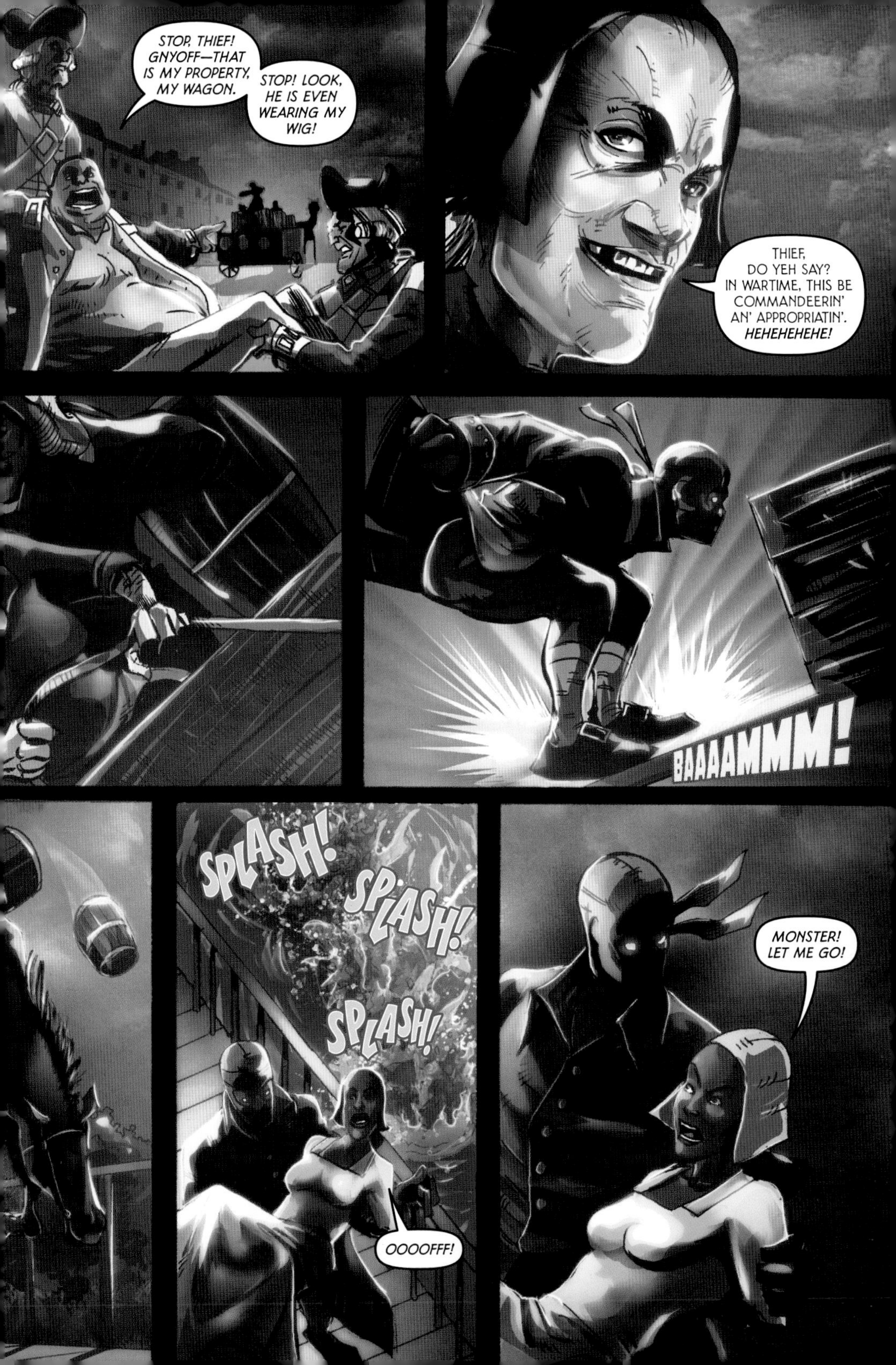
STOP, THIEF! GNYOFF—THAT IS MY PROPERTY, MY WAGON.
STOP! LOOK, HE IS EVEN WEARING MY WIG!
THIEF, DO YEH SAY? IN WARTIME, THIS BE COMMANDEERIN' AN' APPROPRIATIN'. HEHEHEHEHE!
BAAAMMM!
SPLASH!
SPLASH!
SPLASH!
OOOOFFF!
MONSTER! LET ME GO!

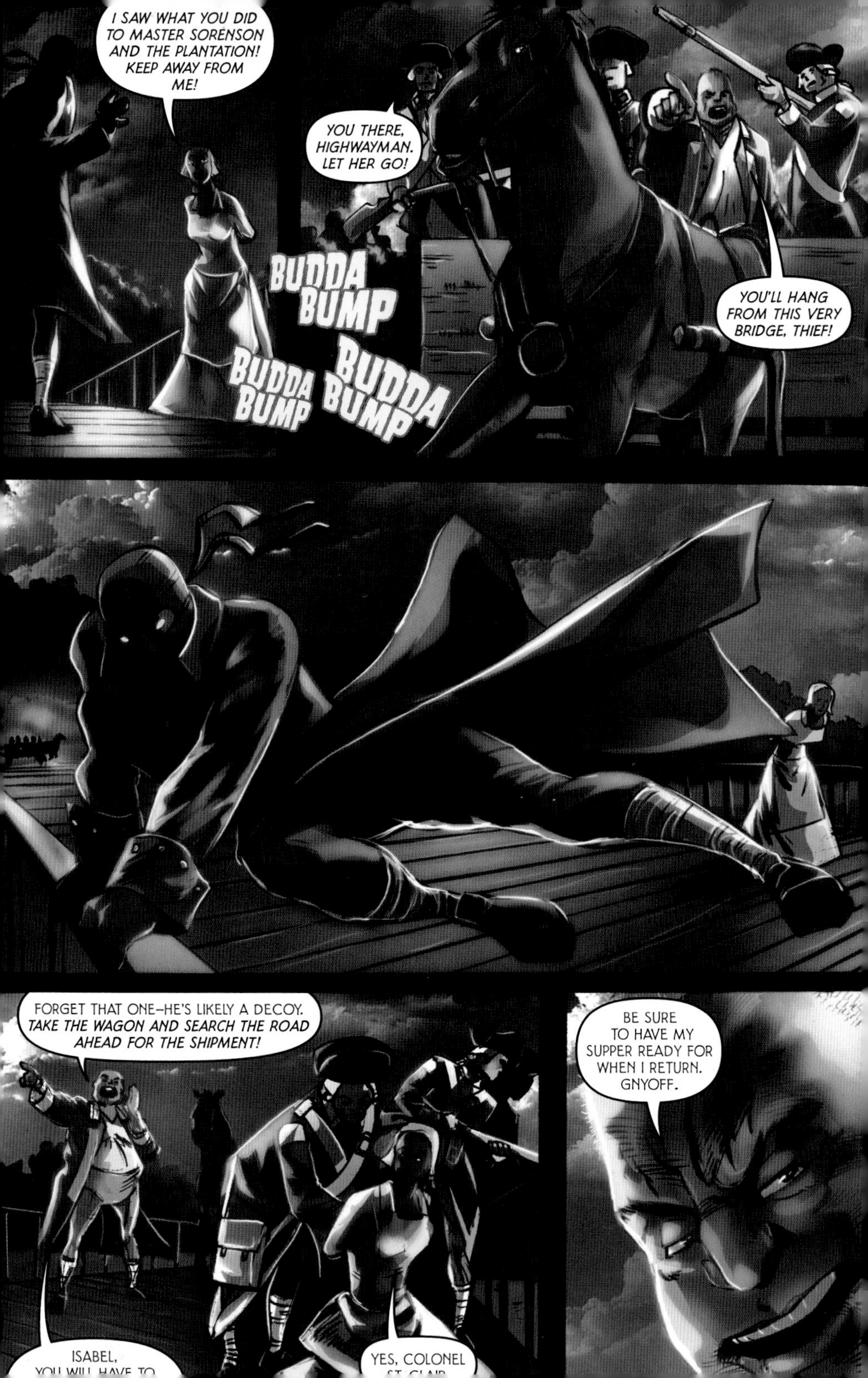
I SAW WHAT YOU DID TO MASTER SORENSON AND THE PLANTATION! KEEP AWAY FROM ME!
YOU THERE, HIGHWAYMAN. LET HER GO!
BUDDA BUMP
BUDDA BUMP
BUDDA BUMP
YOU'LL HANG FROM THIS VERY BRIDGE, THIEF!
FORGET THAT ONE–HE'S LIKELY A DECOY. *TAKE THE WAGON AND SEARCH THE ROAD AHEAD FOR THE SHIPMENT!*
BE SURE TO HAVE MY SUPPER READY FOR WHEN I RETURN. GNYOFF.
ISABEL,
YES, COLONEL

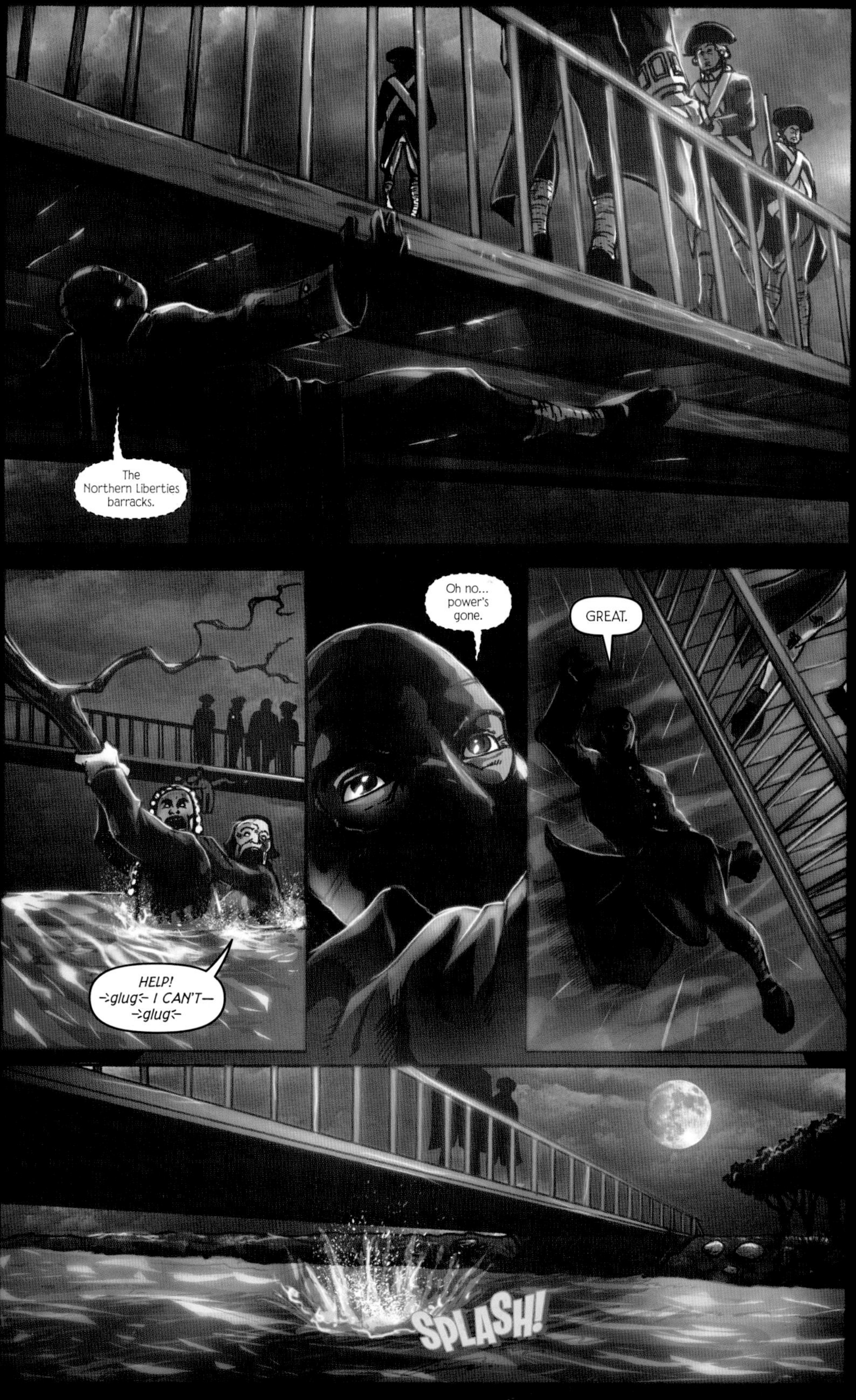
The Northern Liberties barracks.
HELP! ->glug<- I CAN'T— ->glug<-
Oh no... power's gone.
GREAT.
SPLASH!

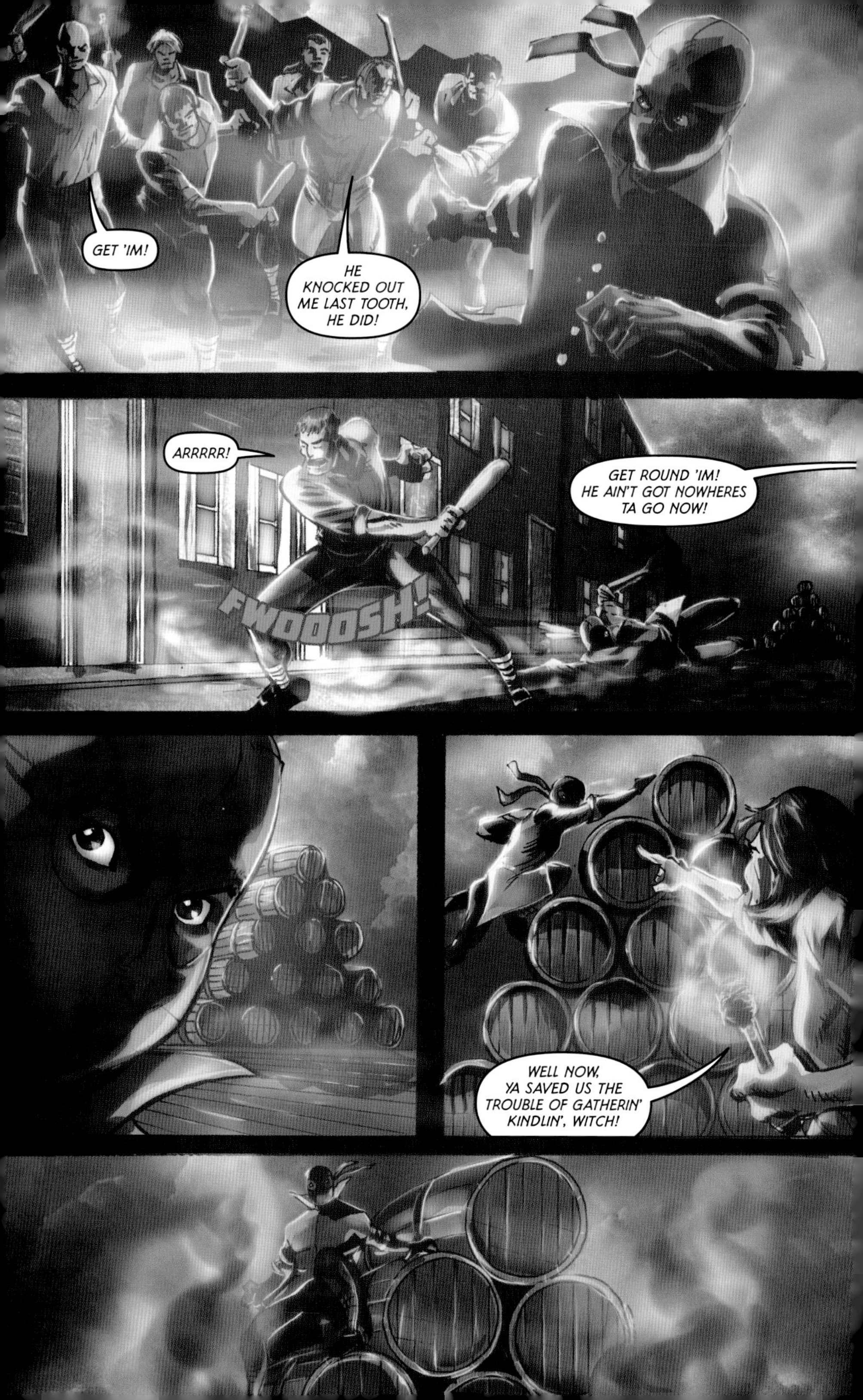

GET 'IM!
HE KNOCKED OUT ME LAST TOOTH, HE DID!
ARRRRR!
GET ROUND 'IM! HE AIN'T GOT NOWHERES TA GO NOW!
FWOOOSH!
WELL NOW, YA SAVED US THE TROUBLE OF GATHERIN' KINDLIN', WITCH!

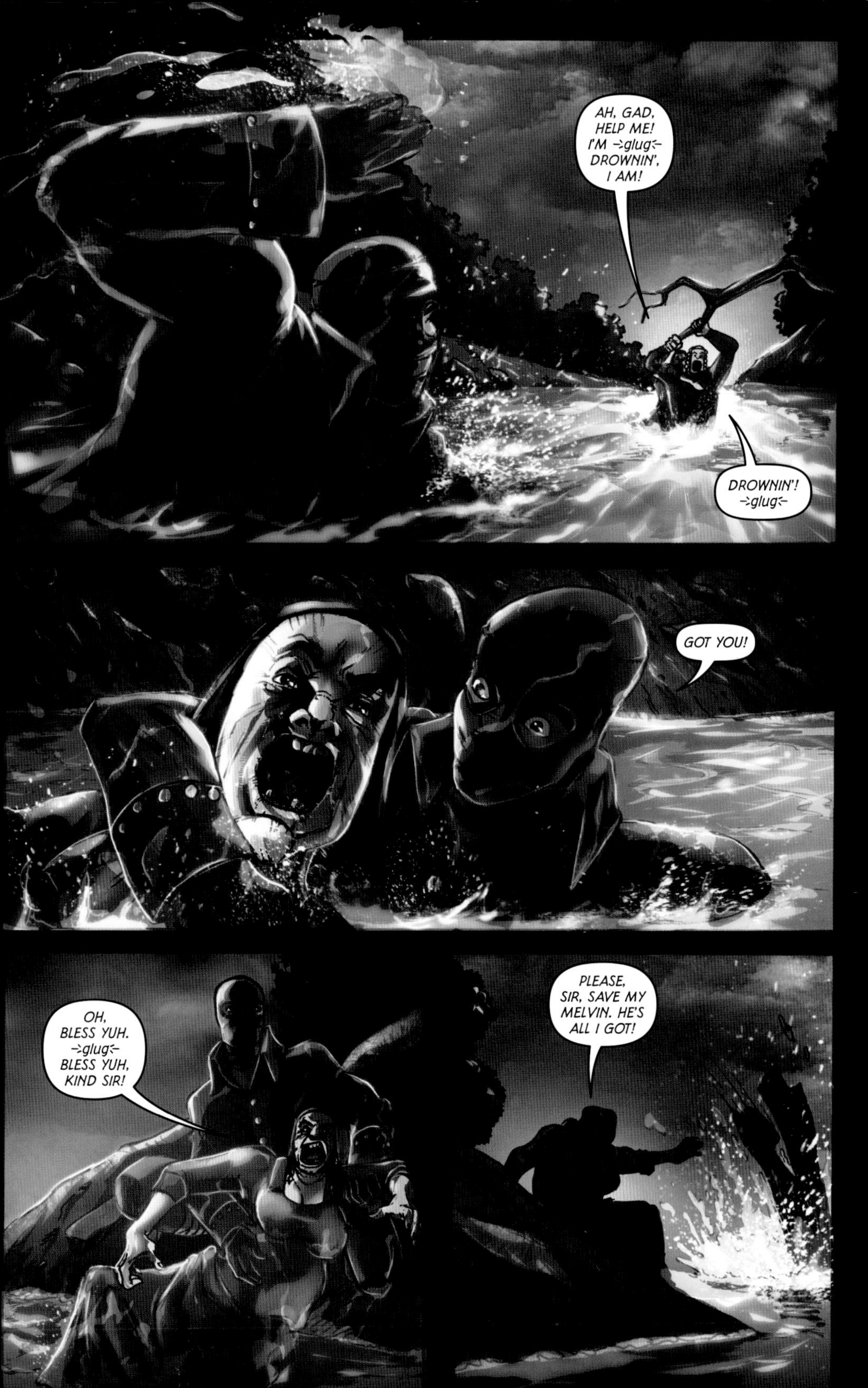
AH, GAD, HELP ME! I'M ->glug<- DROWNIN', I AM!
DROWNIN'! ->glug<-
GOT YOU!
OH, BLESS YUH. ->glug<- BLESS YUH, KIND SIR!
PLEASE, SIR, SAVE MY MELVIN. HE'S ALL I GOT!

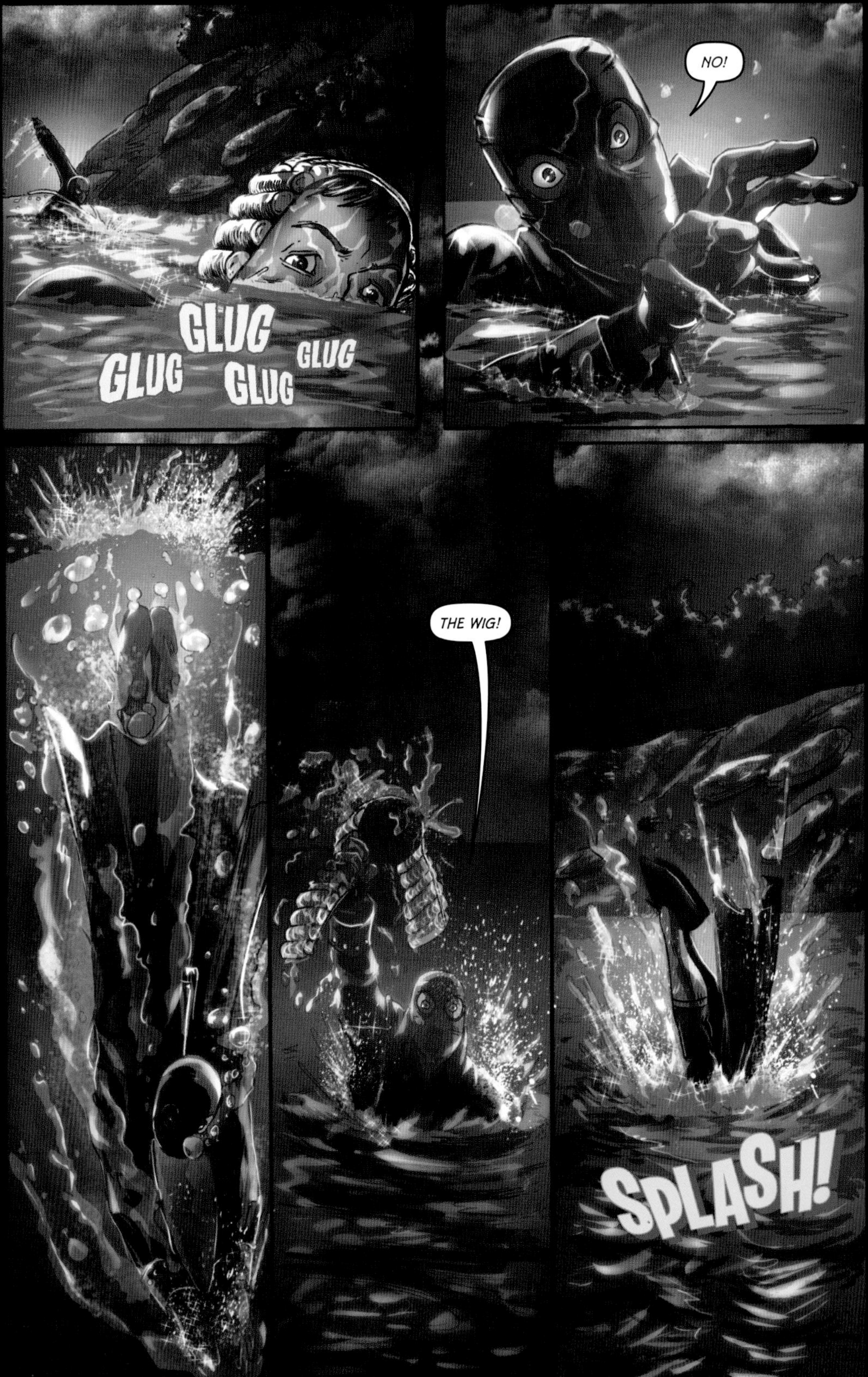
GLUG
GLUG
GLUG
GLUG
NO!
THE WIG!
SPLASH!

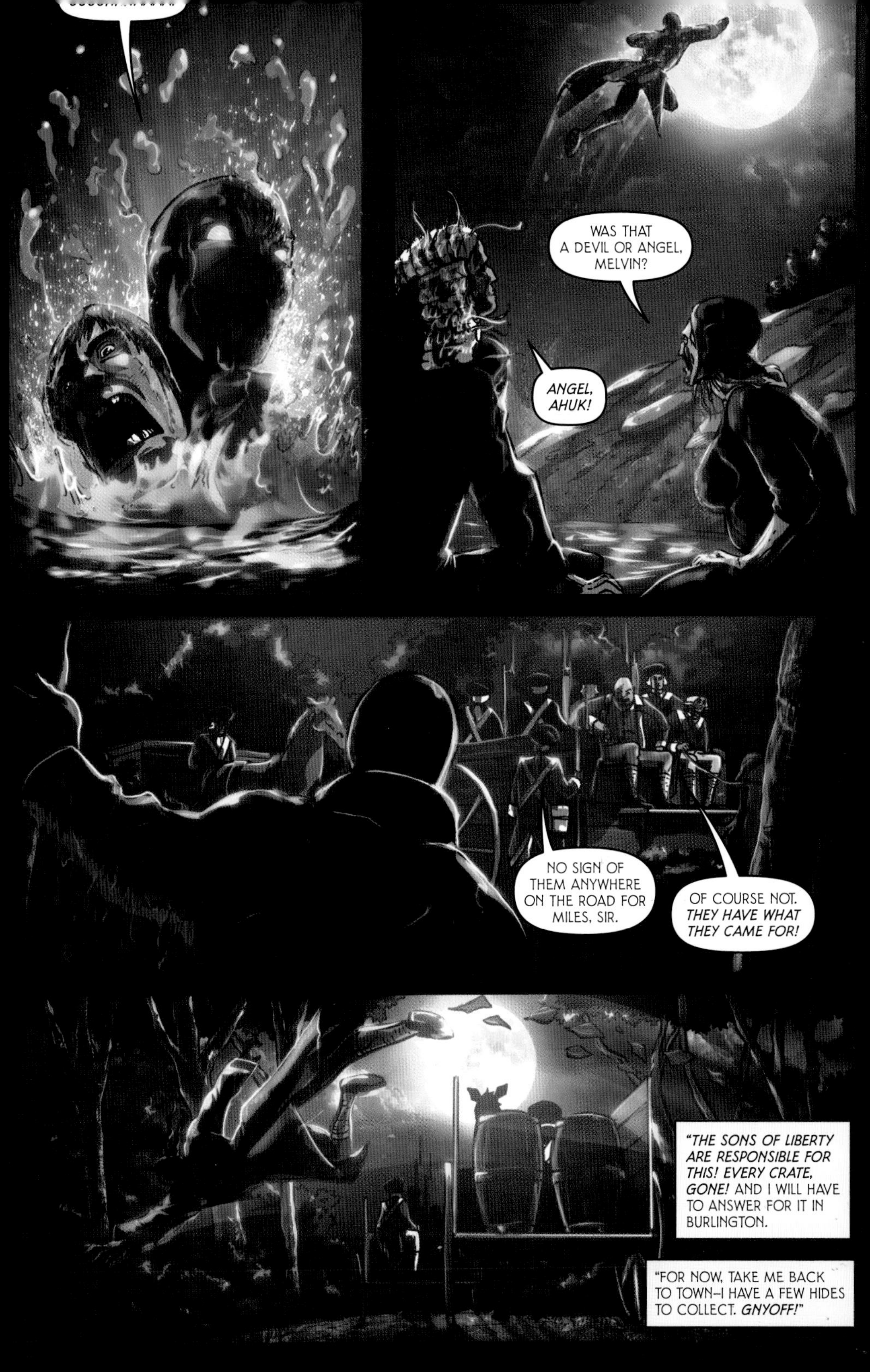
WAS THAT A DEVIL OR ANGEL, MELVIN?
ANGEL, AHUK!
NO SIGN OF THEM ANYWHERE ON THE ROAD FOR MILES, SIR.
OF COURSE NOT. THEY HAVE WHAT THEY CAME FOR!
"THE SONS OF LIBERTY ARE RESPONSIBLE FOR THIS! EVERY CRATE, GONE! AND I WILL HAVE TO ANSWER FOR IT IN BURLINGTON.
"FOR NOW, TAKE ME BACK TO TOWN—I HAVE A FEW HIDES TO COLLECT. GNYOFF!"

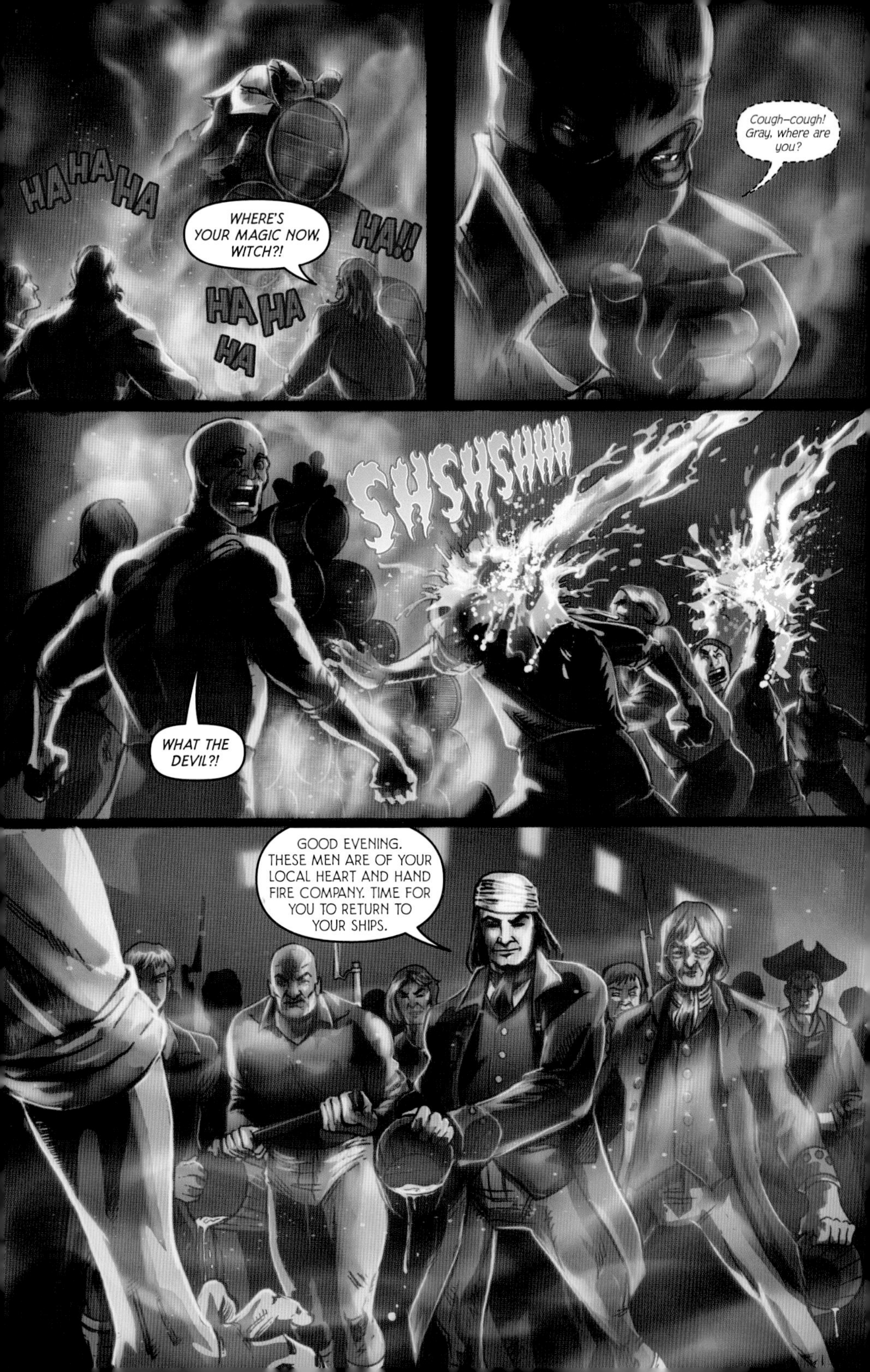
HAHAHA
WHERE'S YOUR MAGIC NOW, WITCH?!
HA!!
HAHA HA
Cough—cough! Gray, where are you?
SHSHSHHH
WHAT THE DEVIL?!
GOOD EVENING. THESE MEN ARE OF YOUR LOCAL HEART AND HAND FIRE COMPANY. TIME FOR YOU TO RETURN TO YOUR SHIPS.

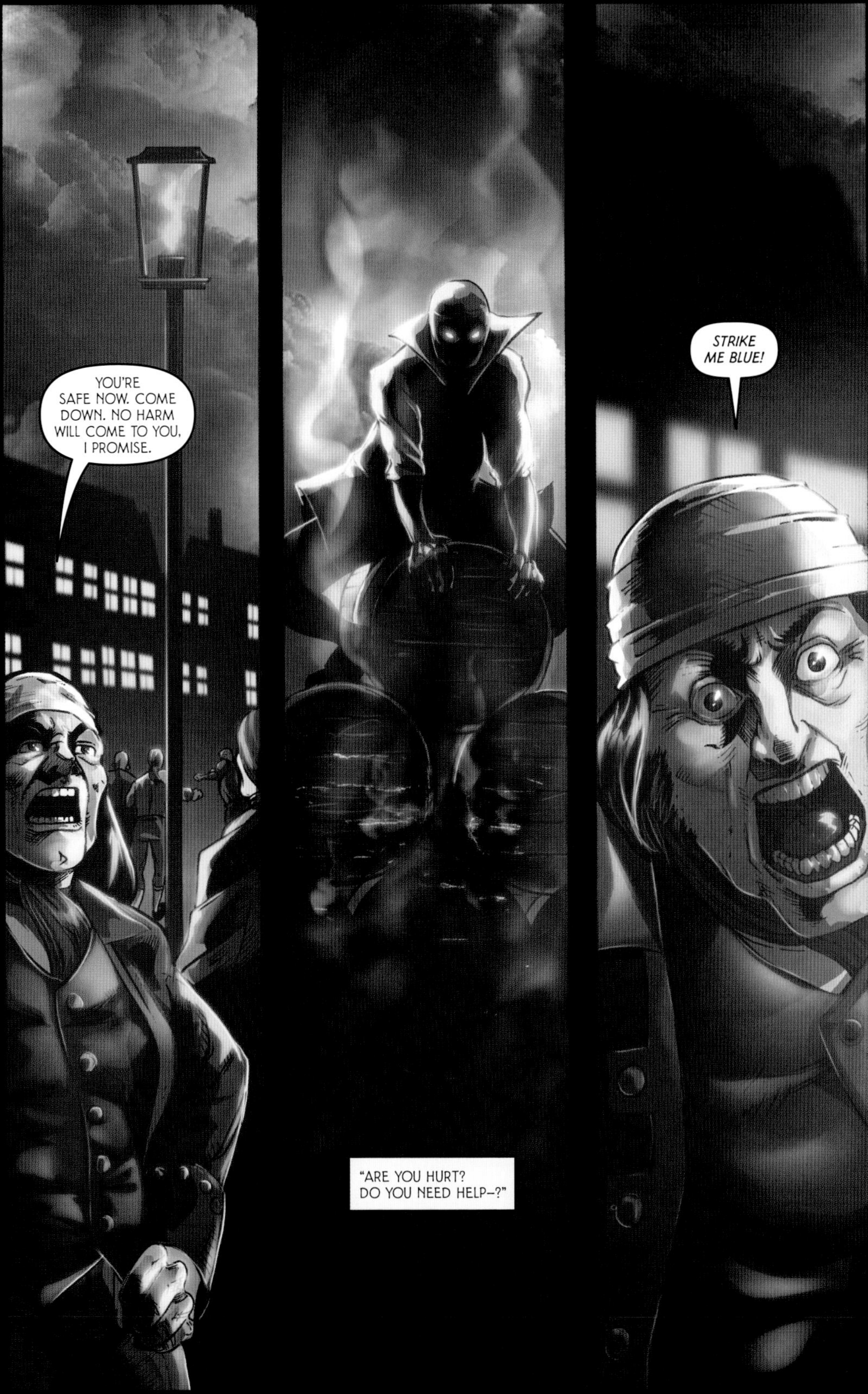
YOU'RE SAFE NOW. COME DOWN. NO HARM WILL COME TO YOU, I PROMISE.
"ARE YOU HURT? DO YOU NEED HELP–?"
STRIKE ME BLUE!

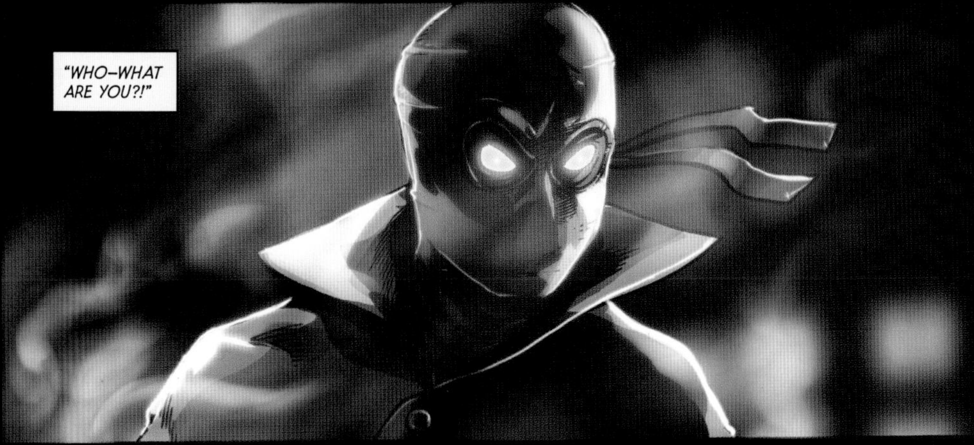
"WHO–WHAT
ARE YOU?!"

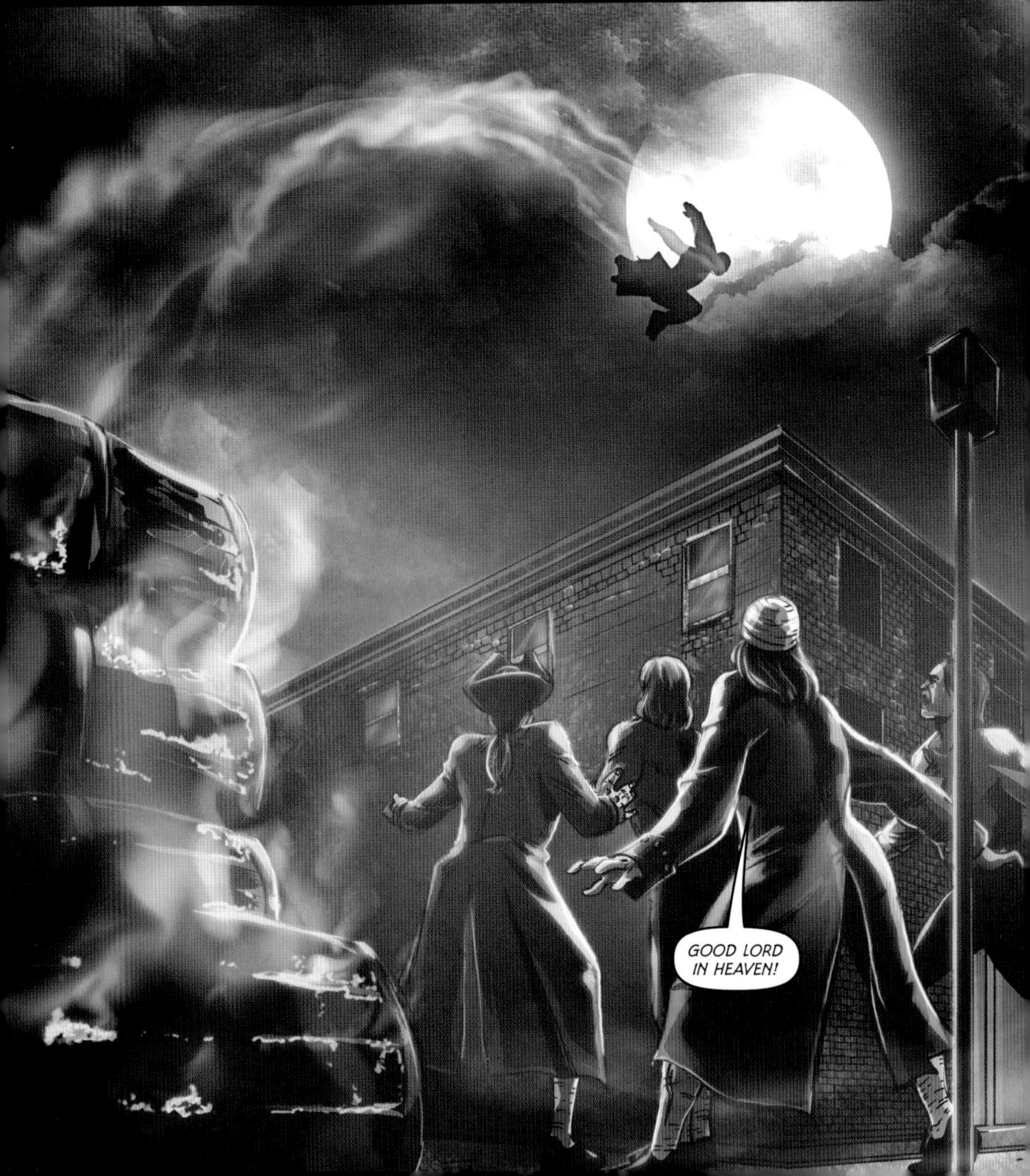
GOOD LORD
IN HEAVEN!

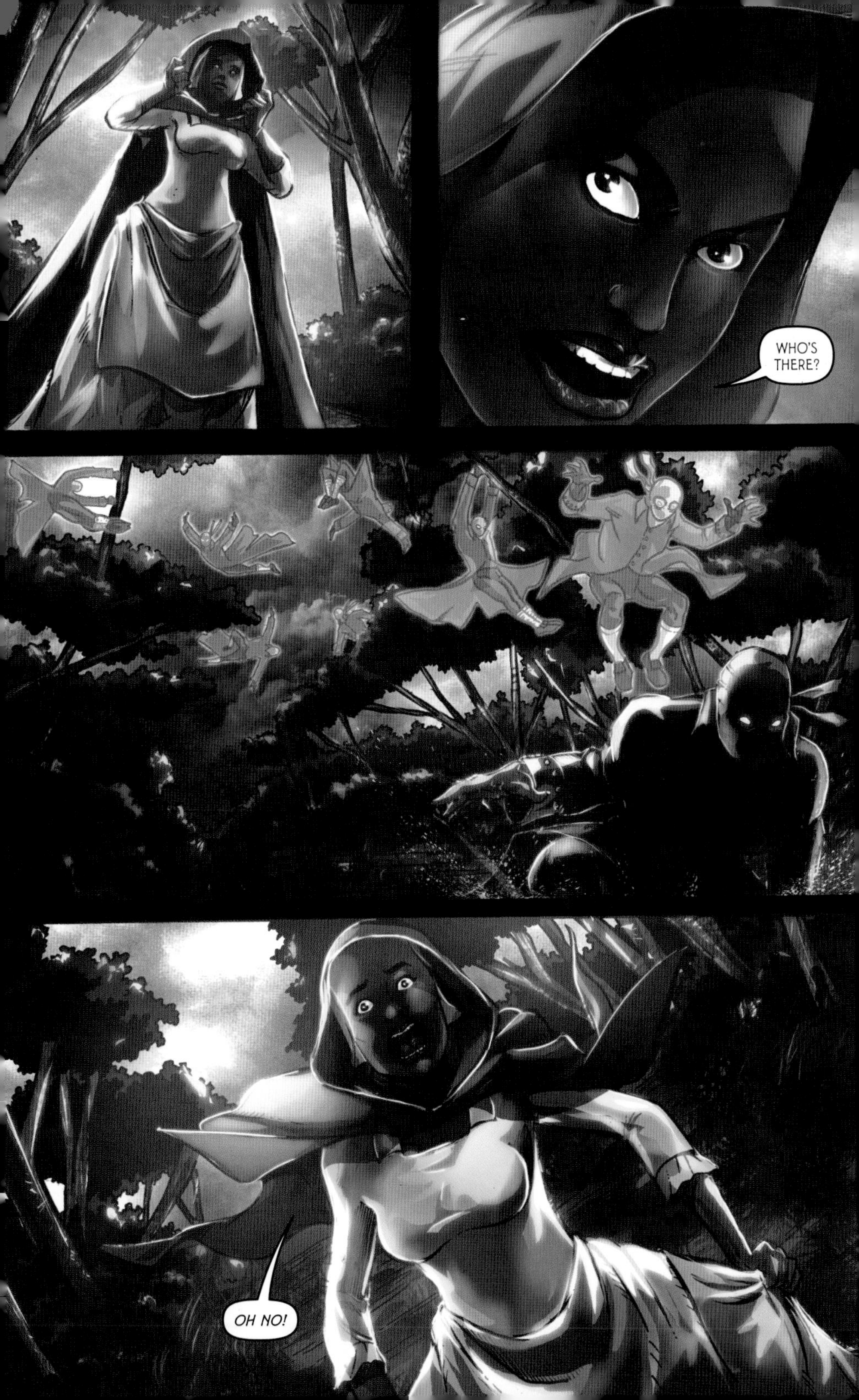
WHO'S THERE?
OH NO!

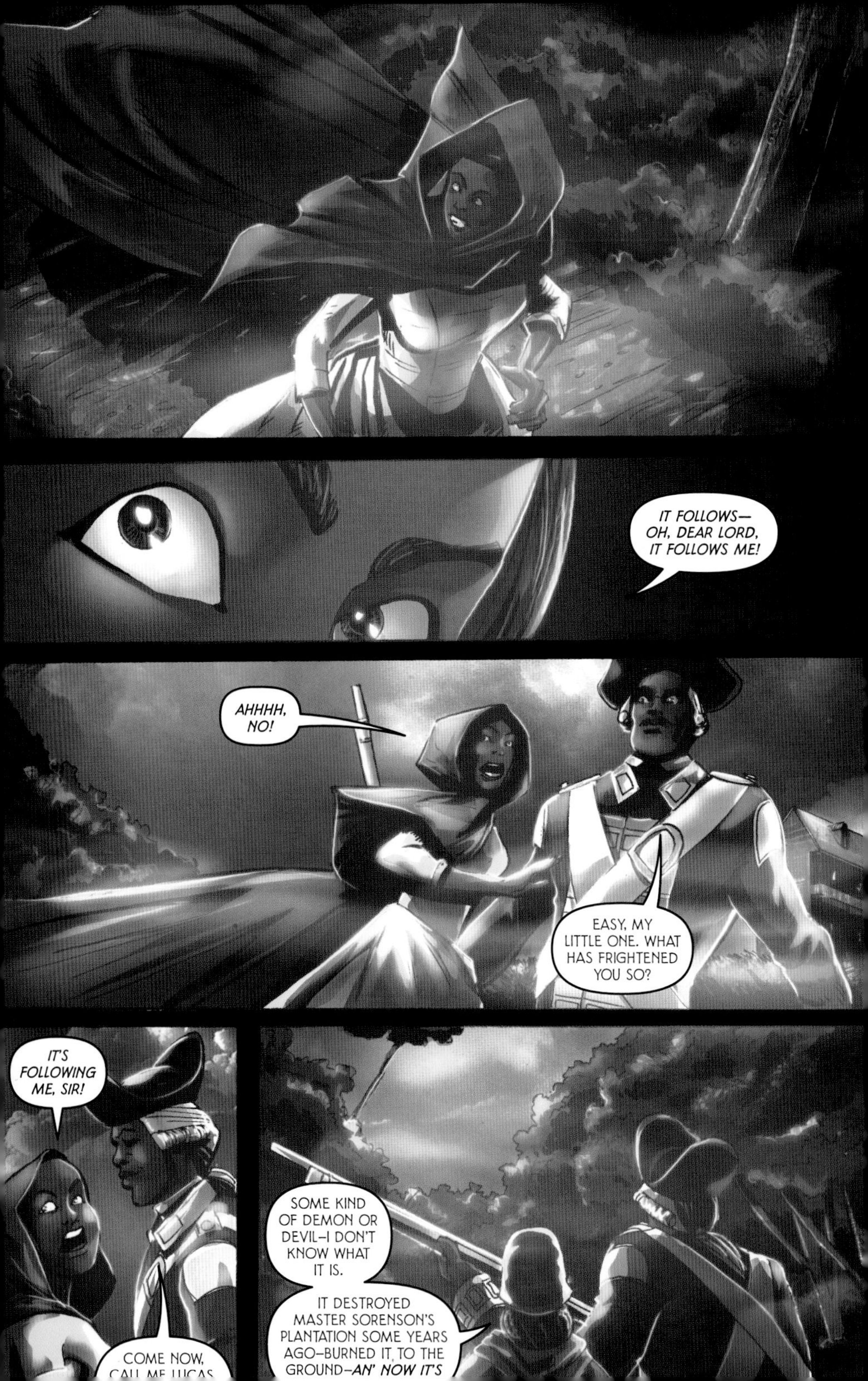
IT FOLLOWS—
OH, DEAR LORD,
IT FOLLOWS ME!
AHHHH,
NO!
EASY, MY
LITTLE ONE. WHAT
HAS FRIGHTENED
YOU SO?
IT'S
FOLLOWING
ME, SIR!
COME NOW,
SOME KIND
OF DEMON OR
DEVIL—I DON'T
KNOW WHAT
IT IS.
IT DESTROYED
MASTER SORENSON'S
PLANTATION SOME YEARS
AGO—BURNED IT TO THE
GROUND—AN' NOW IT'S

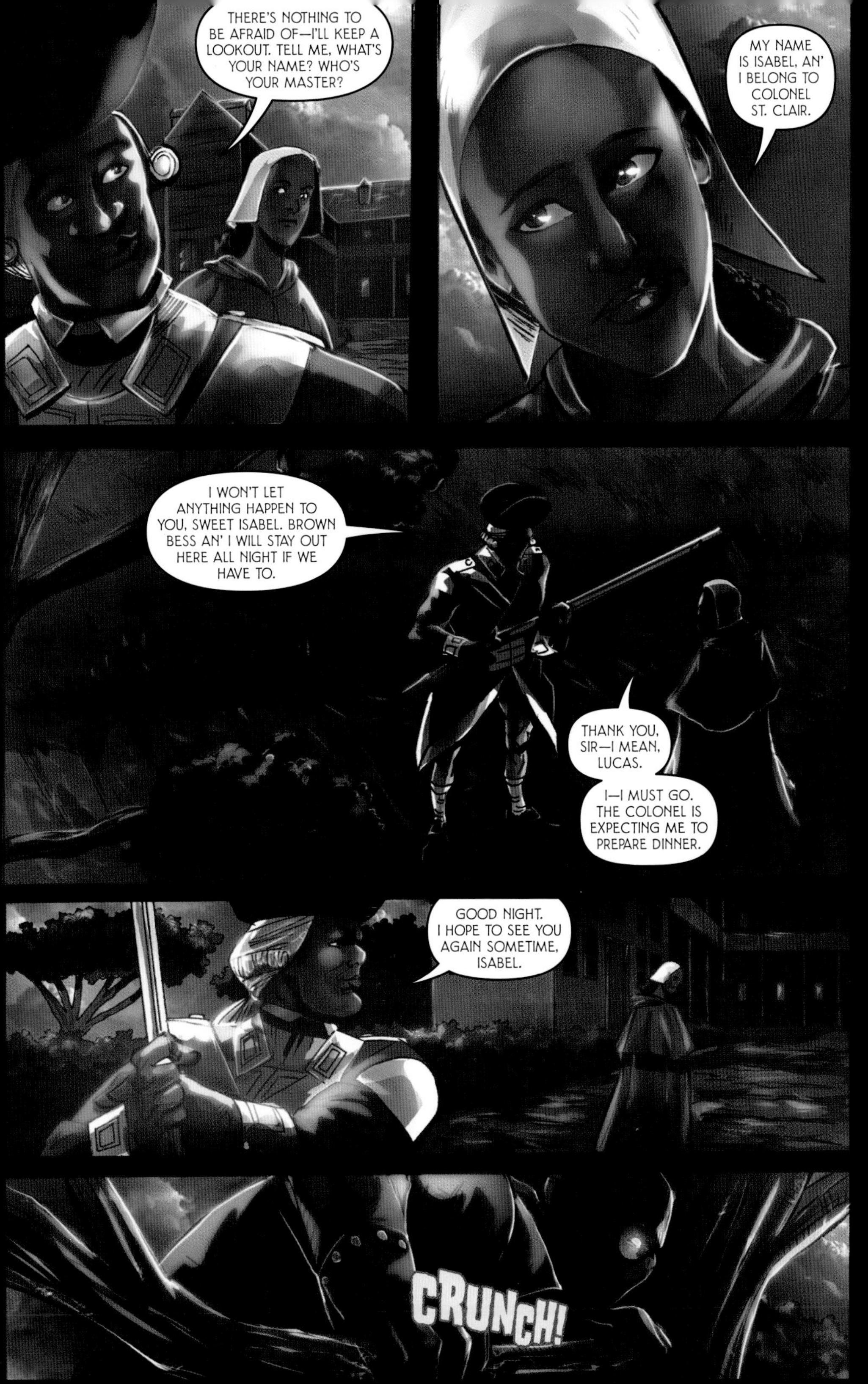
THERE'S NOTHING TO BE AFRAID OF—I'LL KEEP A LOOKOUT. TELL ME, WHAT'S YOUR NAME? WHO'S YOUR MASTER?
MY NAME IS ISABEL, AN' I BELONG TO COLONEL ST. CLAIR.
I WON'T LET ANYTHING HAPPEN TO YOU, SWEET ISABEL. BROWN BESS AN' I WILL STAY OUT HERE ALL NIGHT IF WE HAVE TO.
THANK YOU, SIR—I MEAN, LUCAS.
I—I MUST GO. THE COLONEL IS EXPECTING ME TO PREPARE DINNER.
GOOD NIGHT. I HOPE TO SEE YOU AGAIN SOMETIME, ISABEL.
CRUNCH!

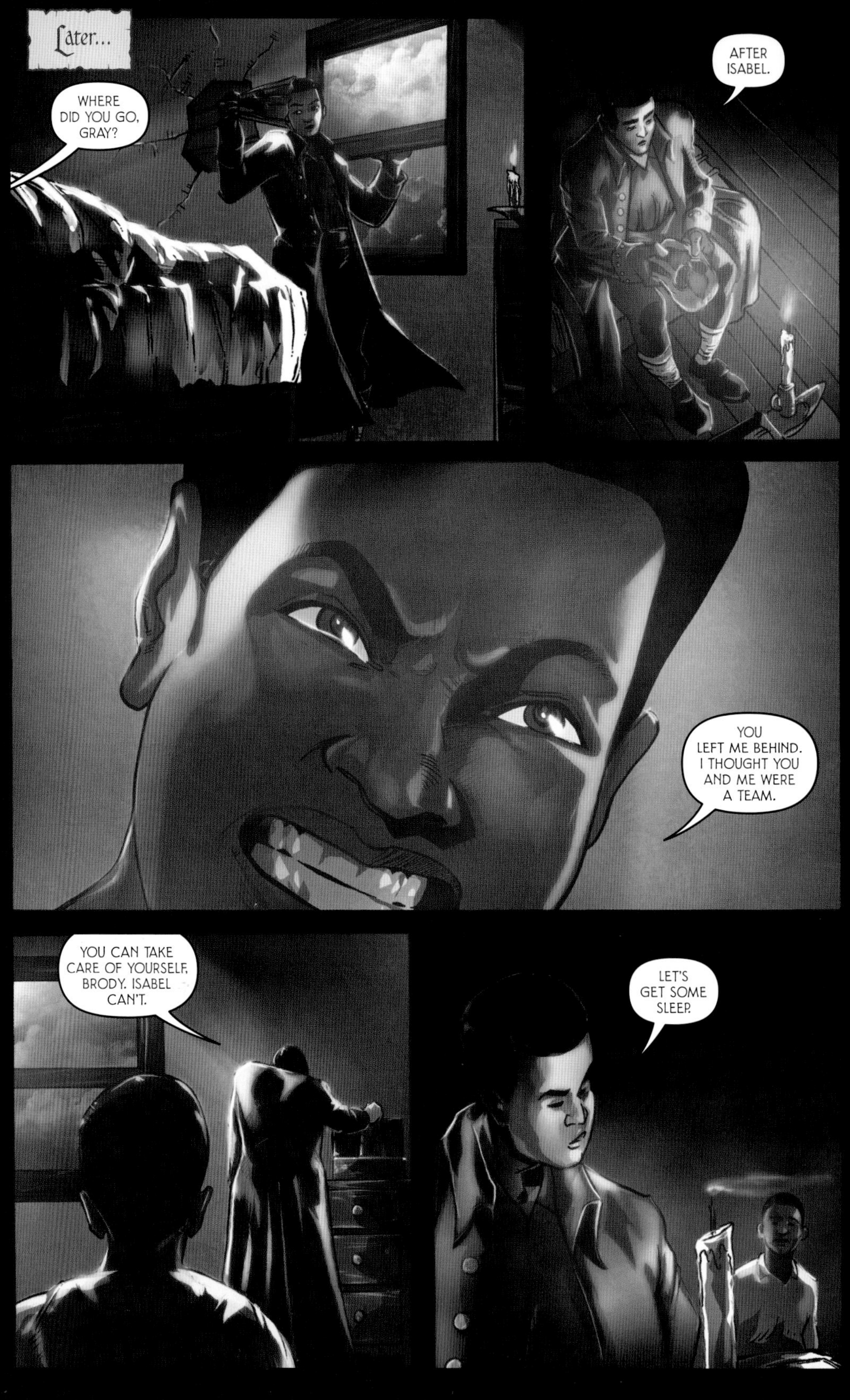
Later...
WHERE DID YOU GO, GRAY?
AFTER ISABEL.
YOU LEFT ME BEHIND. I THOUGHT YOU AND ME WERE A TEAM.
YOU CAN TAKE CARE OF YOURSELF, BRODY. ISABEL CAN'T.
LET'S GET SOME SLEEP.

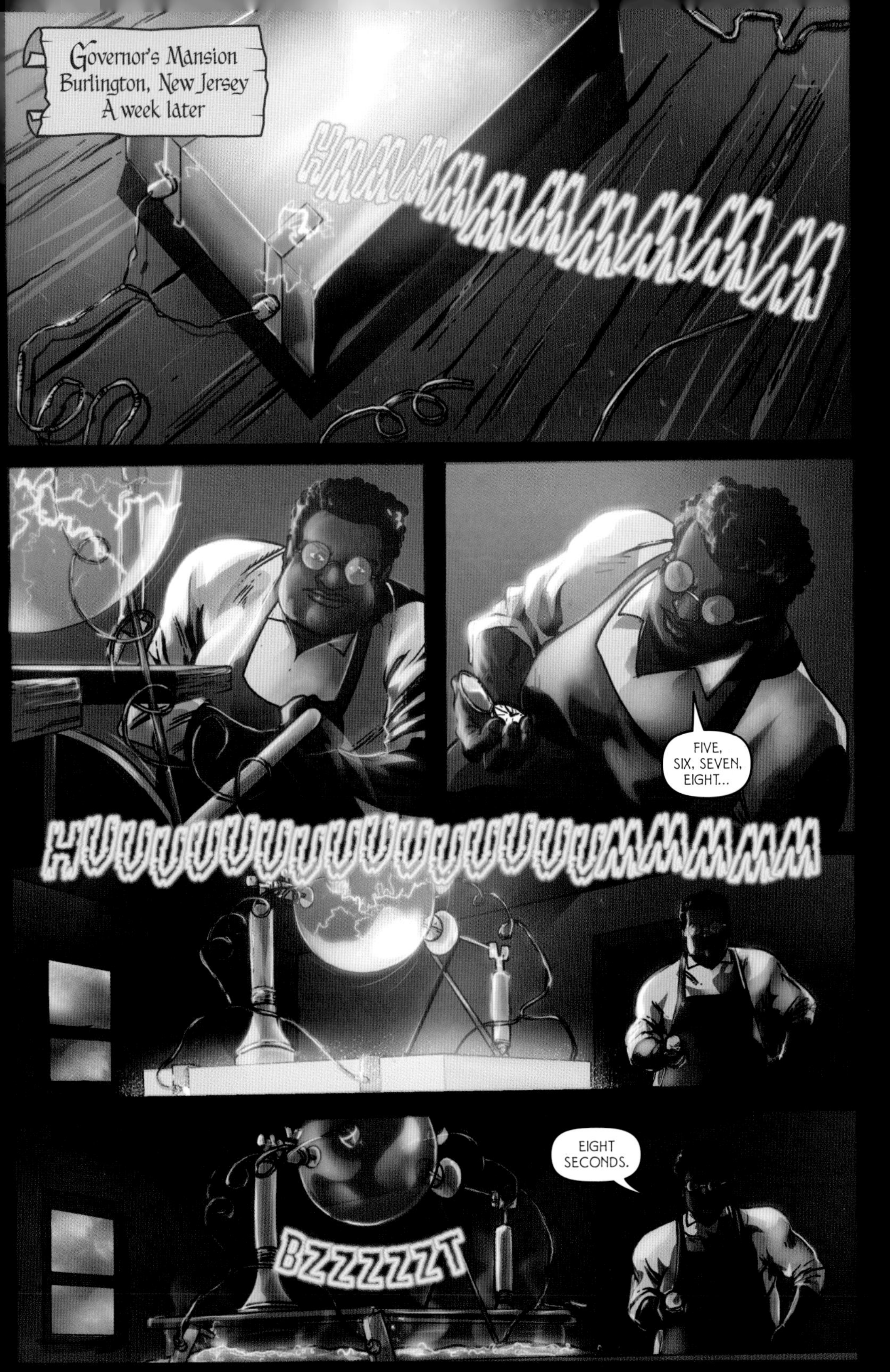
Governor's Mansion
Burlington, New Jersey
A week later
FIVE, SIX, SEVEN, EIGHT...
EIGHT SECONDS.
BZZZZZZT

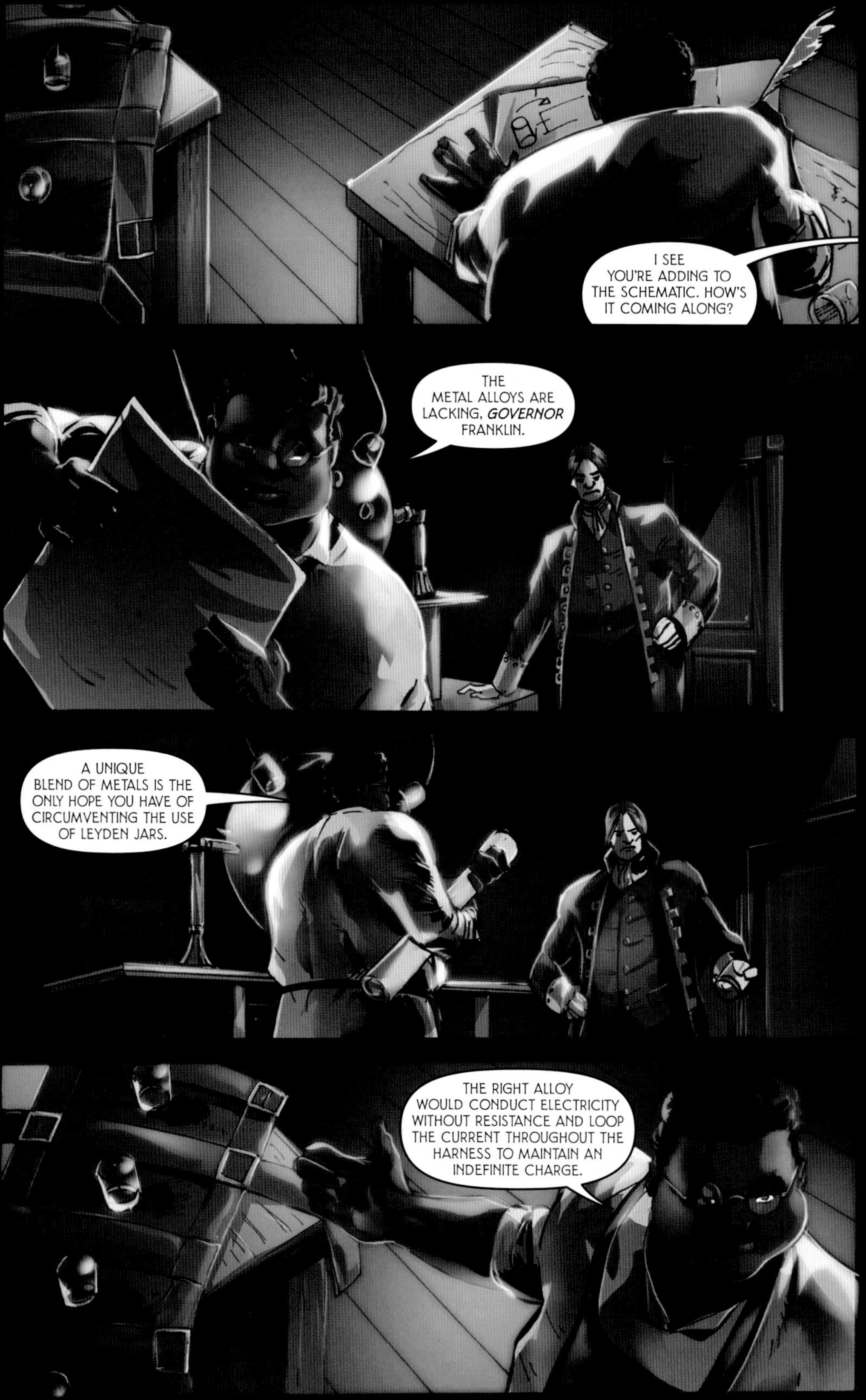
I SEE YOU'RE ADDING TO THE SCHEMATIC. HOW'S IT COMING ALONG?
THE METAL ALLOYS ARE LACKING, *GOVERNOR* FRANKLIN.
A UNIQUE BLEND OF METALS IS THE ONLY HOPE YOU HAVE OF CIRCUMVENTING THE USE OF LEYDEN JARS.
THE RIGHT ALLOY WOULD CONDUCT ELECTRICITY WITHOUT RESISTANCE AND LOOP THE CURRENT THROUGHOUT THE HARNESS TO MAINTAIN AN INDEFINITE CHARGE.

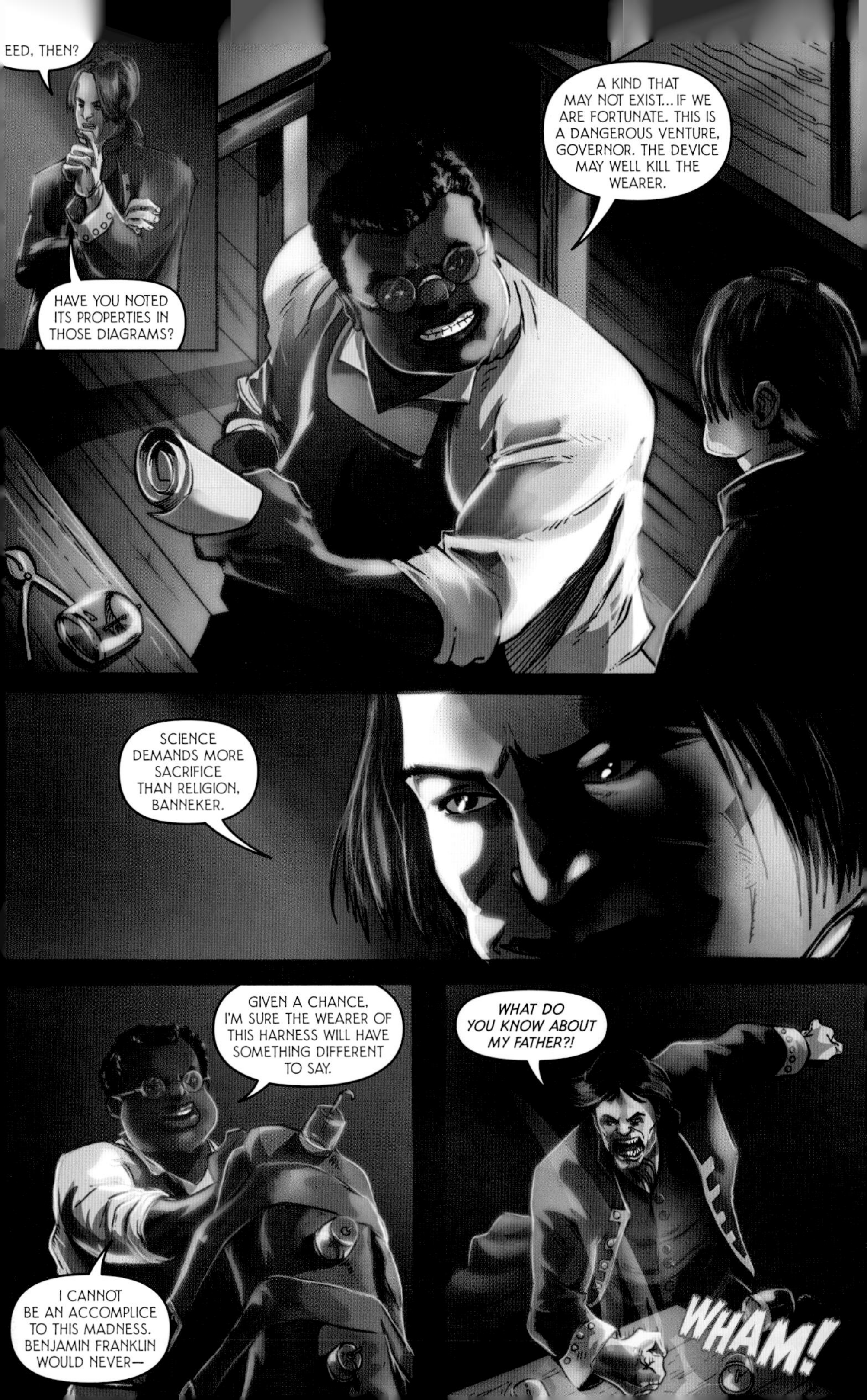
EED, THEN?
HAVE YOU NOTED ITS PROPERTIES IN THOSE DIAGRAMS?
A KIND THAT MAY NOT EXIST... IF WE ARE FORTUNATE. THIS IS A DANGEROUS VENTURE, GOVERNOR. THE DEVICE MAY WELL KILL THE WEARER.
SCIENCE DEMANDS MORE SACRIFICE THAN RELIGION, BANNEKER.
GIVEN A CHANCE, I'M SURE THE WEARER OF THIS HARNESS WILL HAVE SOMETHING DIFFERENT TO SAY.
I CANNOT BE AN ACCOMPLICE TO THIS MADNESS. BENJAMIN FRANKLIN WOULD NEVER—
WHAT DO YOU KNOW ABOUT MY FATHER?!
WHAM!

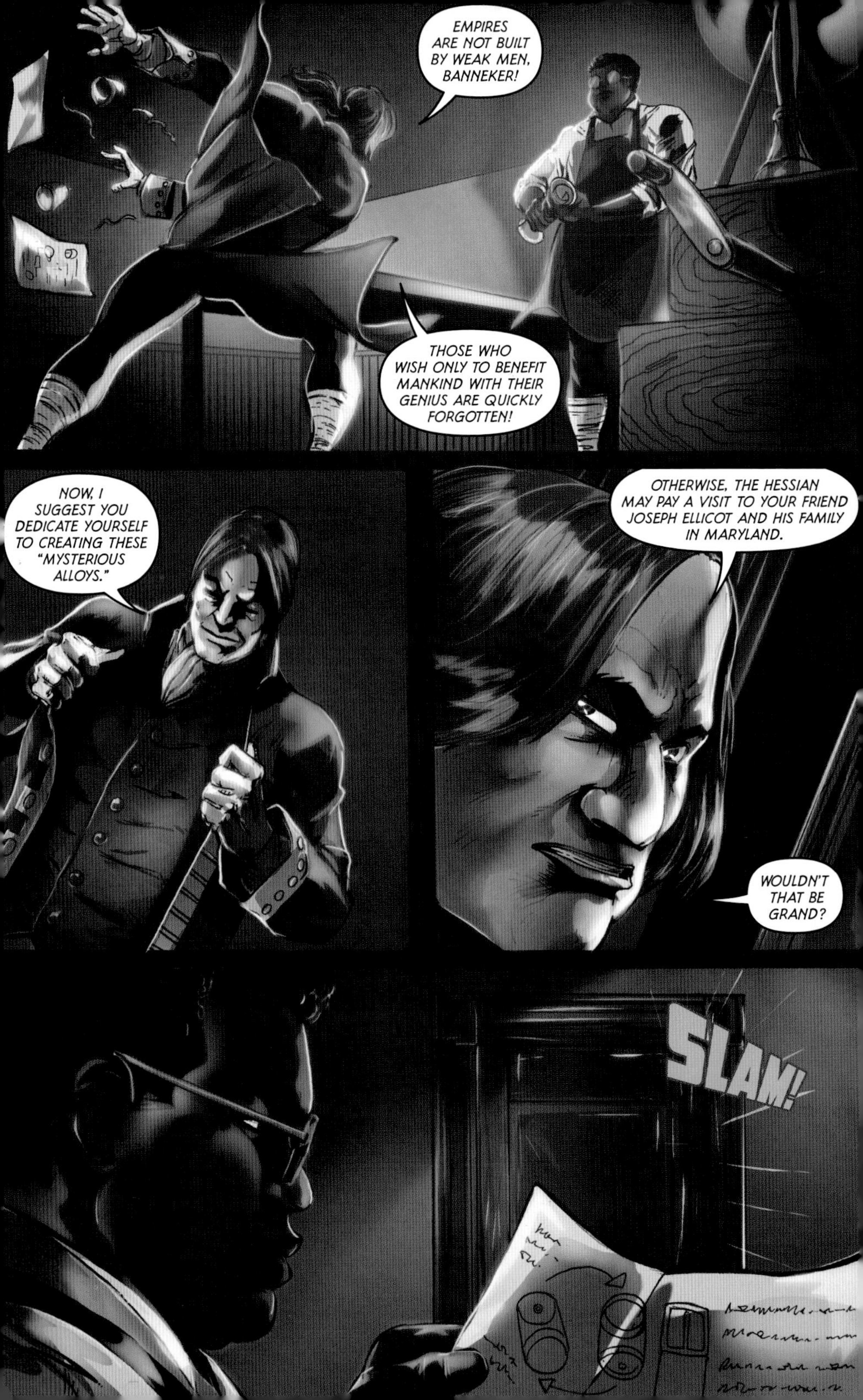
EMPIRES ARE NOT BUILT BY WEAK MEN, BANNEKER!
THOSE WHO WISH ONLY TO BENEFIT MANKIND WITH THEIR GENIUS ARE QUICKLY FORGOTTEN!
NOW, I SUGGEST YOU DEDICATE YOURSELF TO CREATING THESE "MYSTERIOUS ALLOYS."
OTHERWISE, THE HESSIAN MAY PAY A VISIT TO YOUR FRIEND JOSEPH ELLICOT AND HIS FAMILY IN MARYLAND.
WOULDN'T THAT BE GRAND?
SLAM!

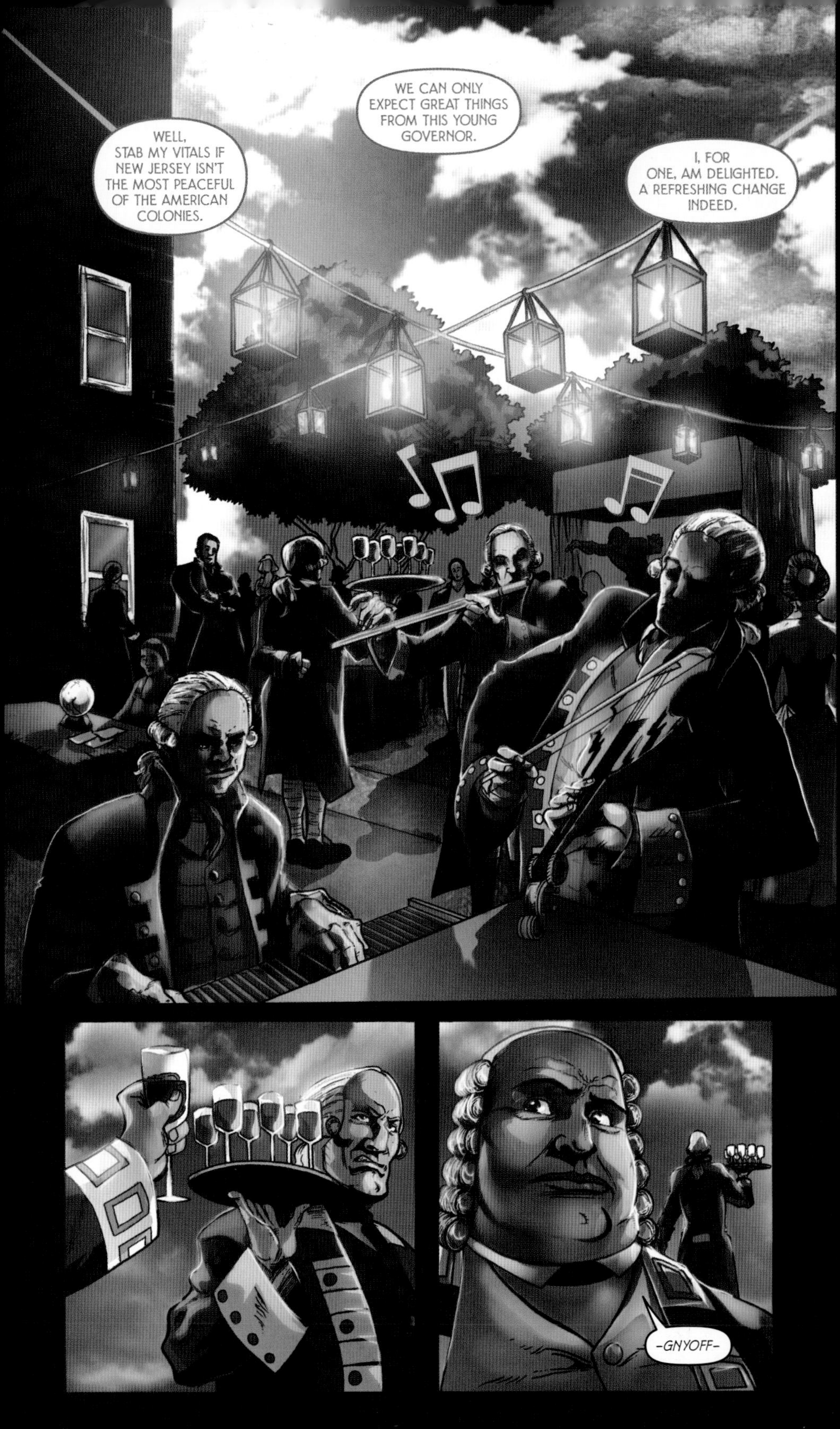
WELL, STAB MY VITALS IF NEW JERSEY ISN'T THE MOST PEACEFUL OF THE AMERICAN COLONIES.
WE CAN ONLY EXPECT GREAT THINGS FROM THIS YOUNG GOVERNOR.
I, FOR ONE, AM DELIGHTED. A REFRESHING CHANGE INDEED.
-GNYOFF-

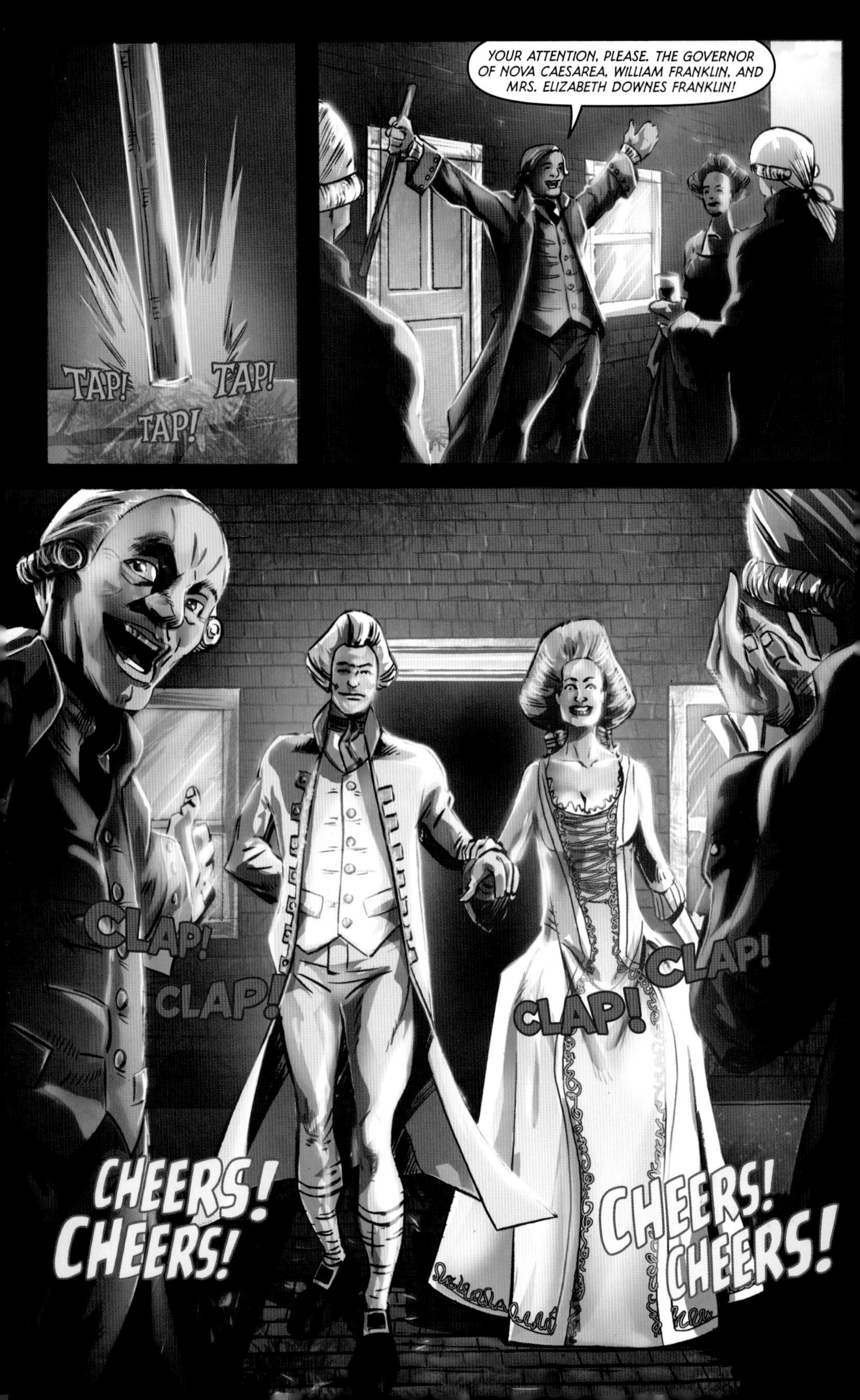
TAP!
TAP!
TAP!
YOUR ATTENTION, PLEASE. THE GOVERNOR OF NOVA CAESAREA, WILLIAM FRANKLIN, AND MRS. ELIZABETH DOWNES FRANKLIN!
CLAP!
CLAP!
CLAP!
CLAP!
CHEERS! CHEERS!
CHEERS! CHEERS!

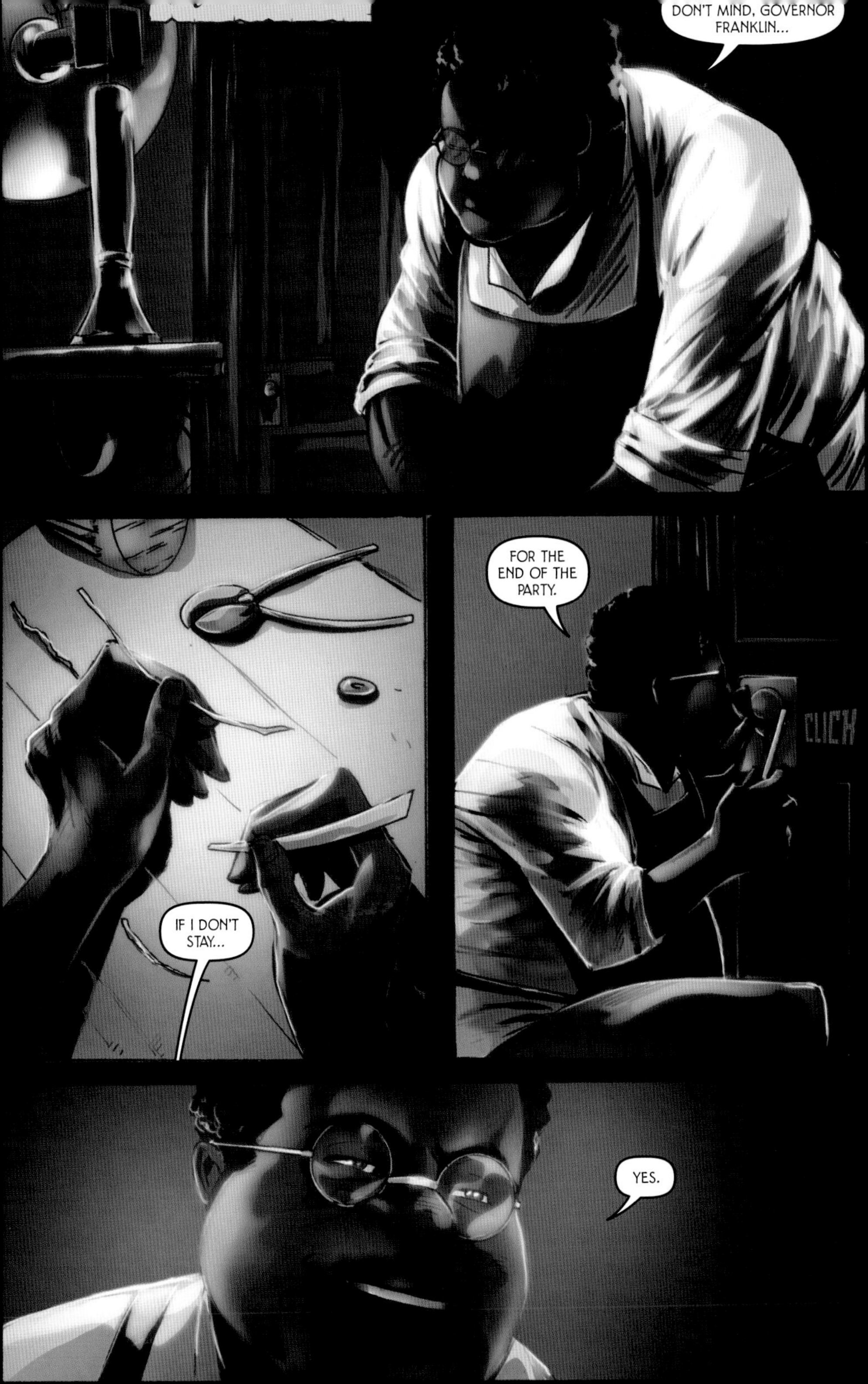
DON'T MIND, GOVERNOR FRANKLIN...
IF I DON'T STAY...
FOR THE END OF THE PARTY.
CLICK
YES.

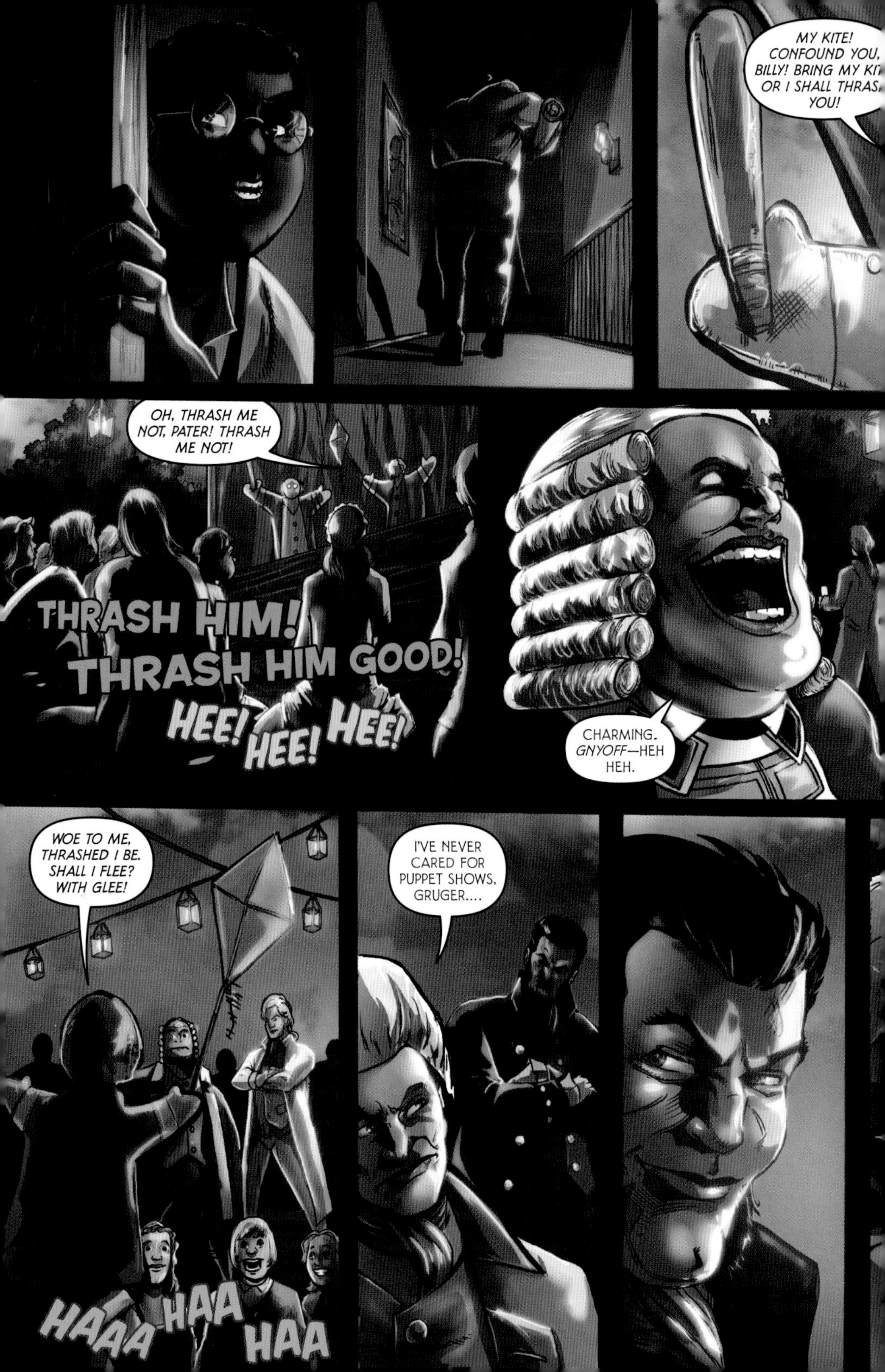
MY KITE! CONFOUND YOU, BILLY! BRING MY KIT OR I SHALL THRAS YOU!
OH, THRASH ME NOT, PATER! THRASH ME NOT!
THRASH HIM! THRASH HIM GOOD!
HEE! HEE! HEE!
CHARMING. GNYOFF—HEH HEH.
WOE TO ME, THRASHED I BE. SHALL I FLEE? WITH GLEE!
HAAA HAA HAA
I'VE NEVER CARED FOR PUPPET SHOWS, GRUGER....

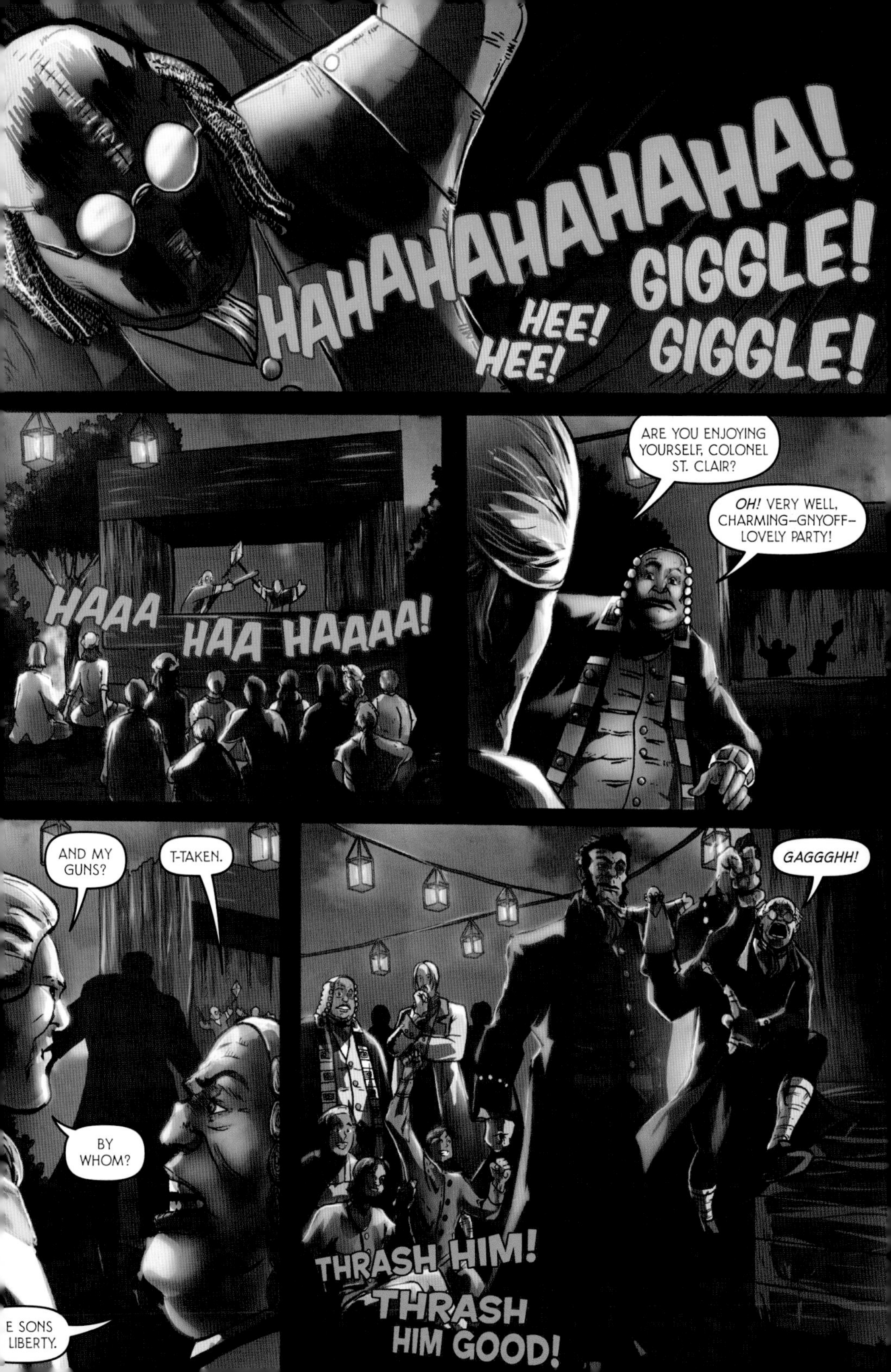
HAHAHAHAHAHAHA!
HEE! HEE!
GIGGLE! GIGGLE!
HAAA HAA HAAAAA!
ARE YOU ENJOYING YOURSELF, COLONEL ST. CLAIR?
OH! VERY WELL, CHARMING—GNYOFF—LOVELY PARTY!
AND MY GUNS?
T-TAKEN.
BY WHOM?
E SONS LIBERTY.
GAGGGHH!
THRASH HIM!
THRASH HIM GOOD!

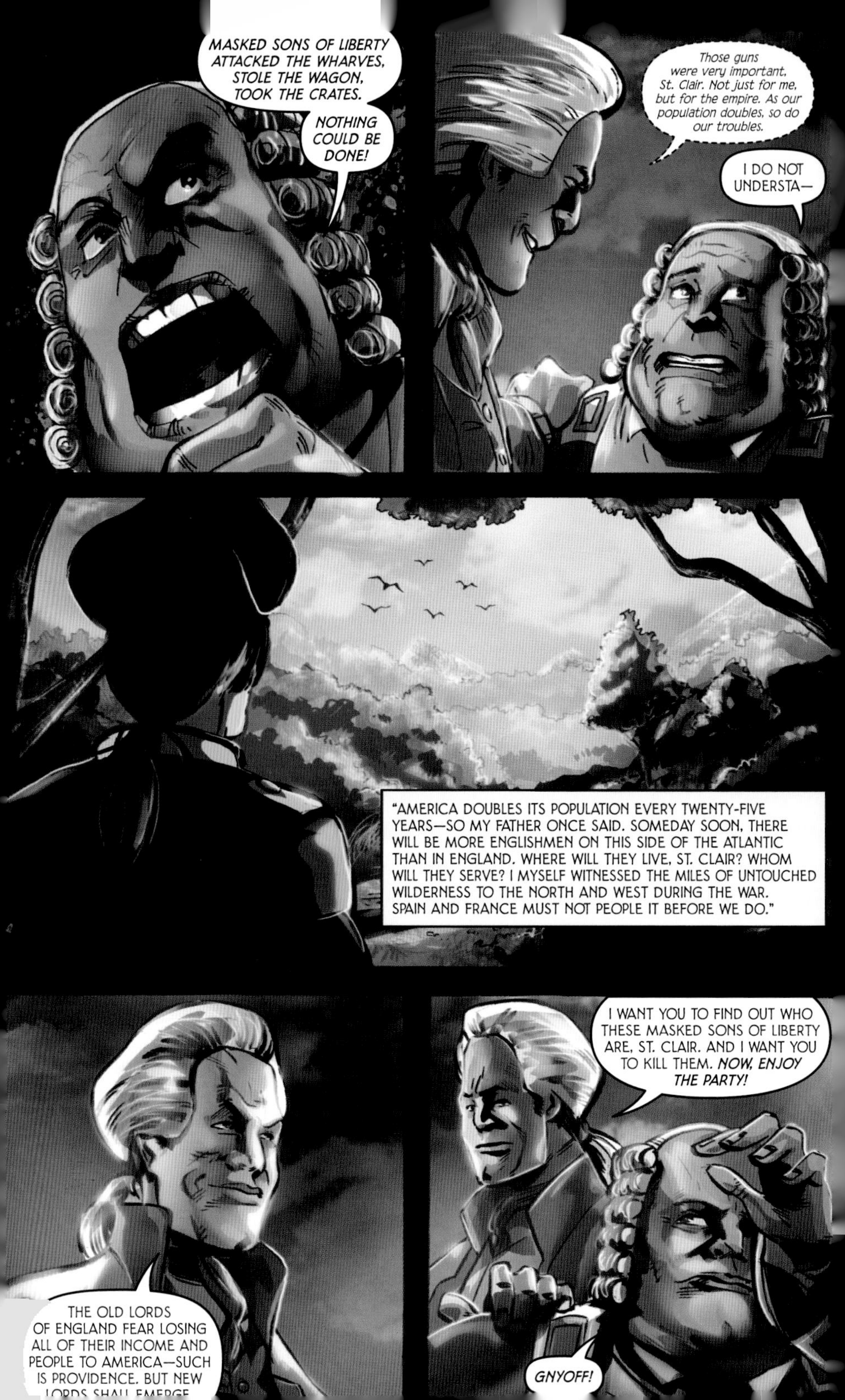
MASKED SONS OF LIBERTY ATTACKED THE WHARVES, STOLE THE WAGON, TOOK THE CRATES.
NOTHING COULD BE DONE!
Those guns were very important, St. Clair. Not just for me, but for the empire. As our population doubles, so do our troubles.
I DO NOT UNDERSTA—
"AMERICA DOUBLES ITS POPULATION EVERY TWENTY-FIVE YEARS—SO MY FATHER ONCE SAID. SOMEDAY SOON, THERE WILL BE MORE ENGLISHMEN ON THIS SIDE OF THE ATLANTIC THAN IN ENGLAND. WHERE WILL THEY LIVE, ST. CLAIR? WHOM WILL THEY SERVE? I MYSELF WITNESSED THE MILES OF UNTOUCHED WILDERNESS TO THE NORTH AND WEST DURING THE WAR. SPAIN AND FRANCE MUST NOT PEOPLE IT BEFORE WE DO."
THE OLD LORDS OF ENGLAND FEAR LOSING ALL OF THEIR INCOME AND PEOPLE TO AMERICA—SUCH IS PROVIDENCE. BUT NEW
I WANT YOU TO FIND OUT WHO THESE MASKED SONS OF LIBERTY ARE, ST. CLAIR. AND I WANT YOU TO KILL THEM. NOW, ENJOY THE PARTY!
GNYOFF!

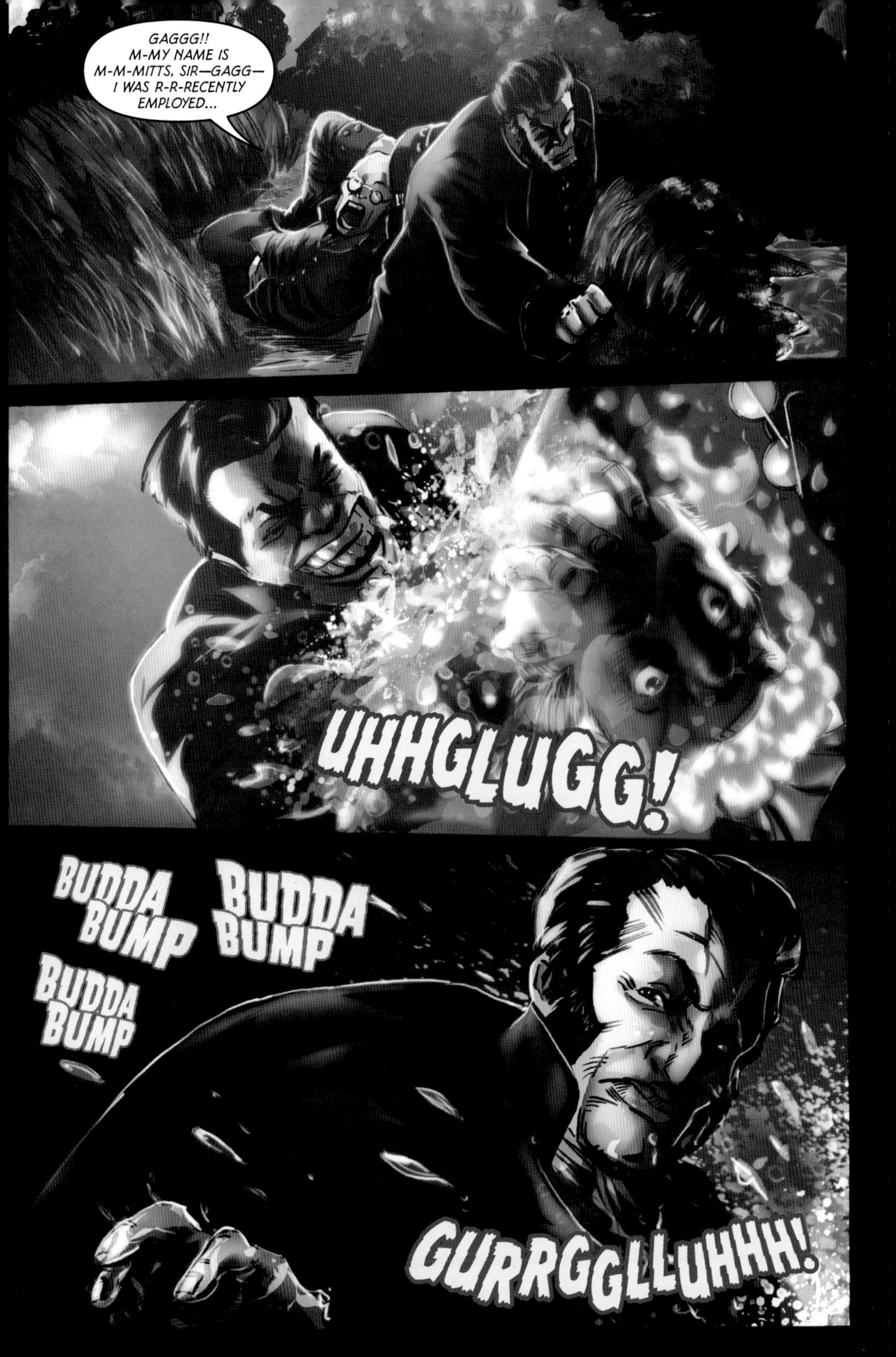
GAGGG!! M-MY NAME IS M-M-MITTS, SIR—GAGG— I WAS R-R-RECENTLY EMPLOYED...
UHHGLUGG!
BUDDA BUMP
BUDDA BUMP
BUDDA BUMP
GURRGGLLUHHH!

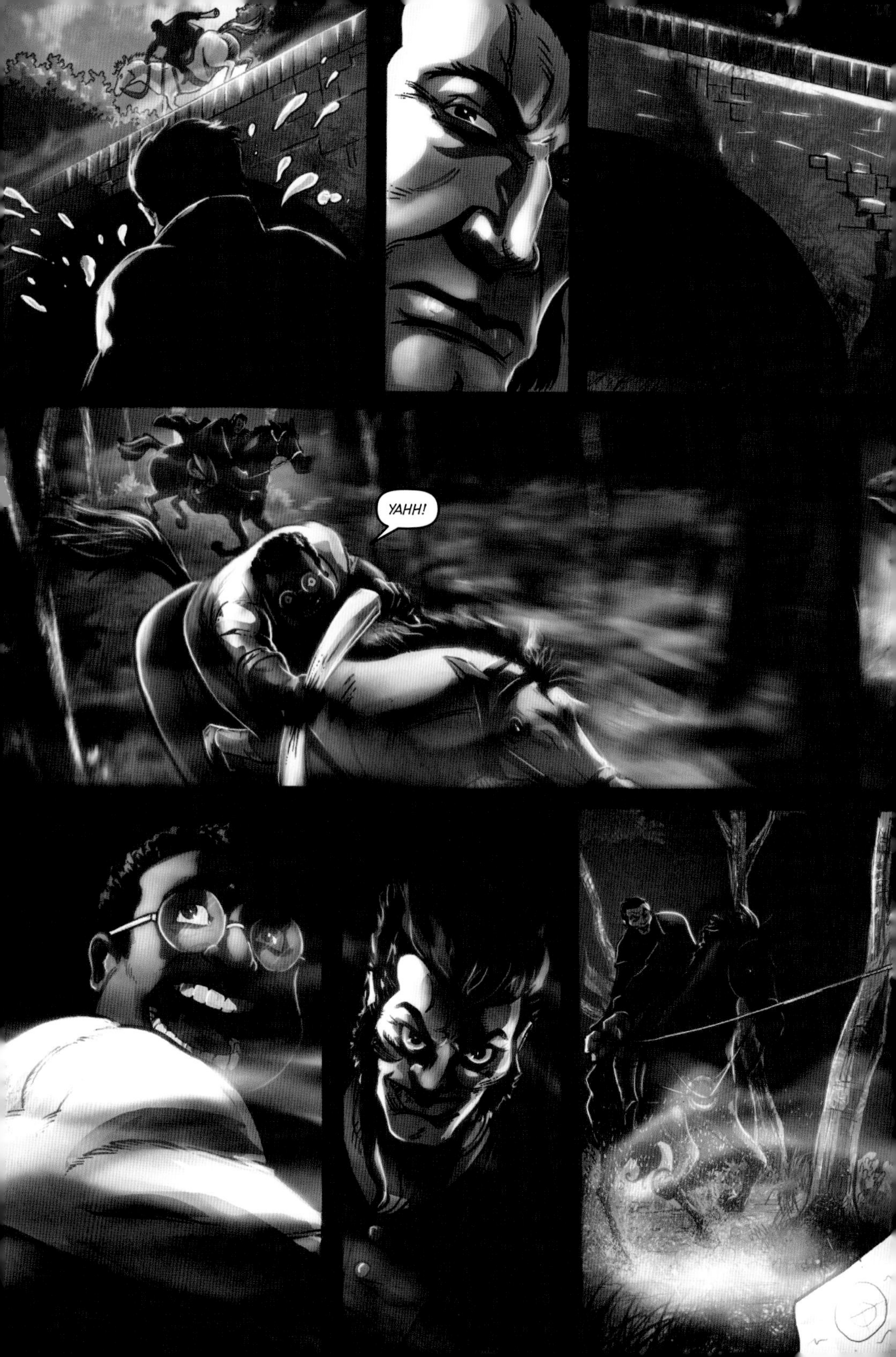
YAHH!

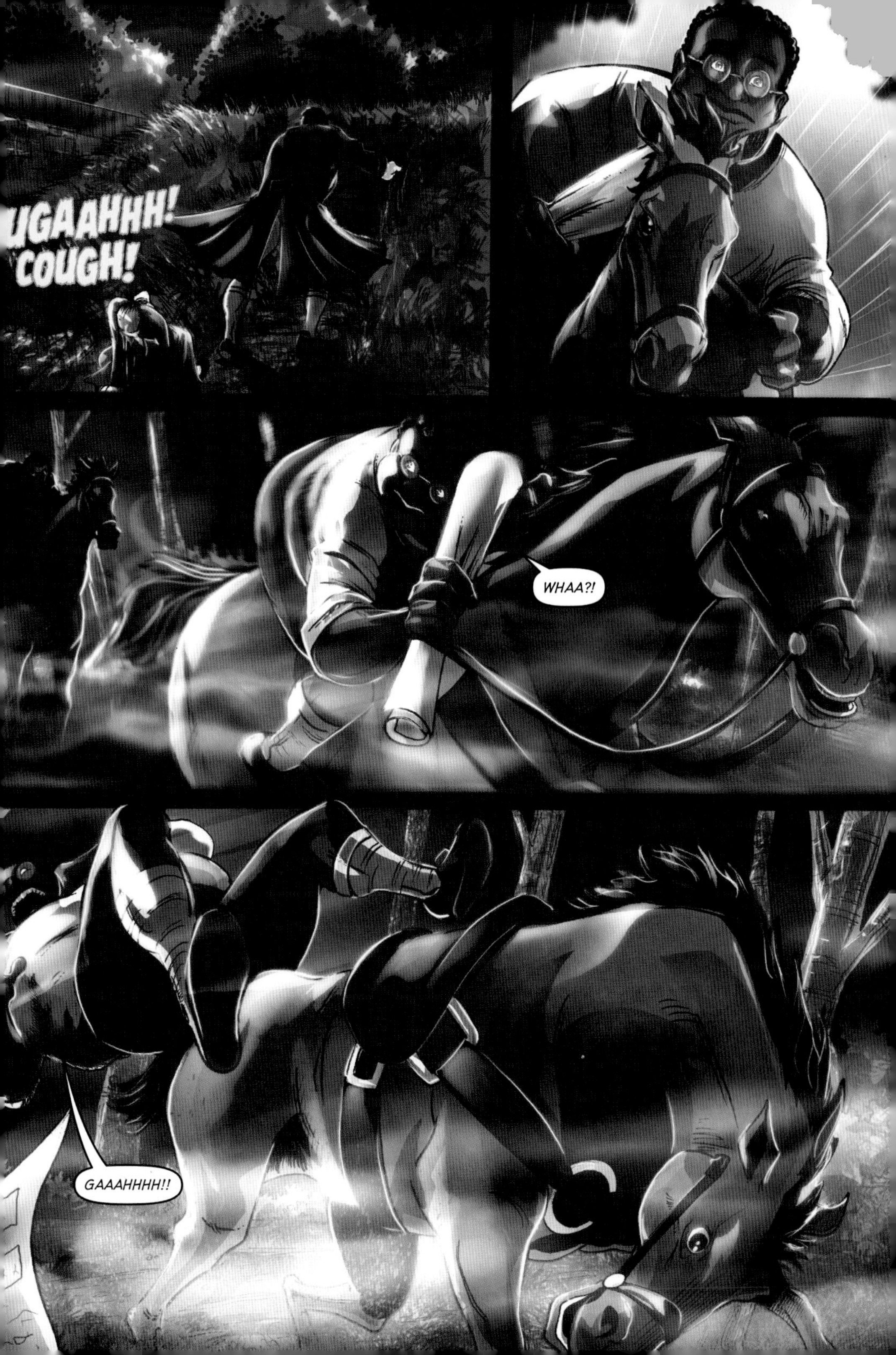
UGAAHHH! COUGH!
WHAA?!
GAAAHHHH!!

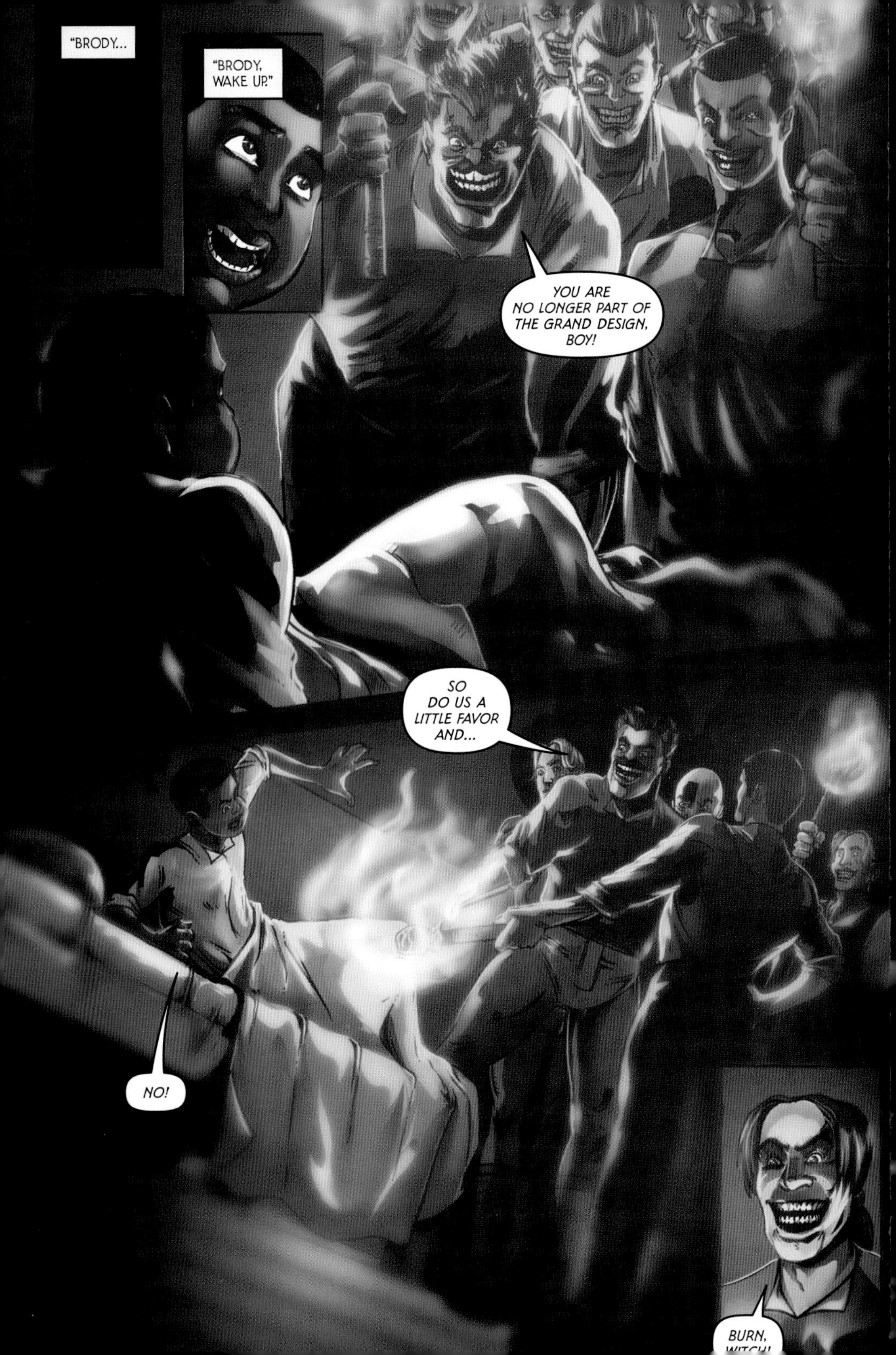
"BRODY...
"BRODY, WAKE UP."
YOU ARE NO LONGER PART OF THE GRAND DESIGN, BOY!
SO DO US A LITTLE FAVOR AND...
NO!
BURN,

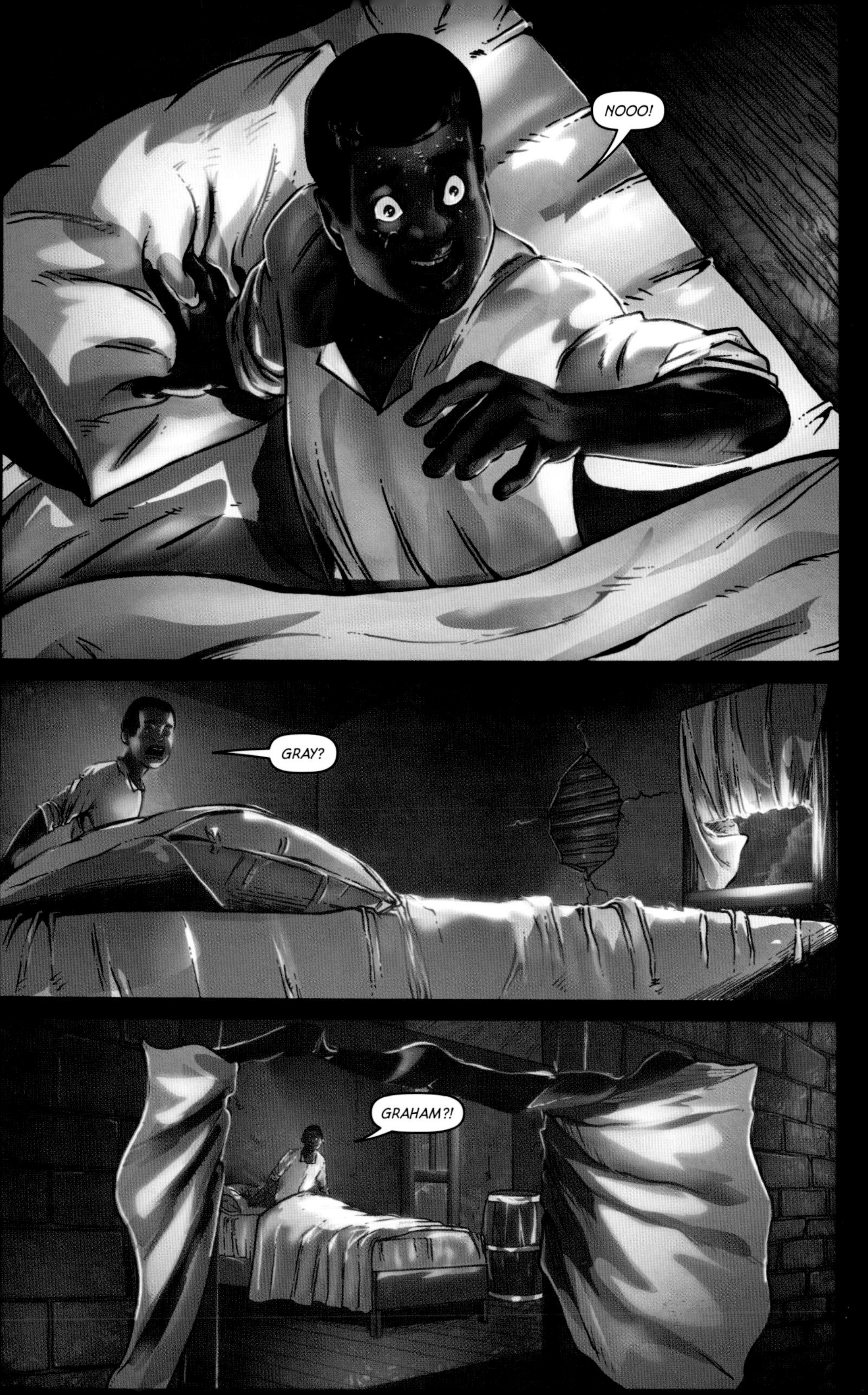
NOOO!
GRAY?
GRAHAM?!

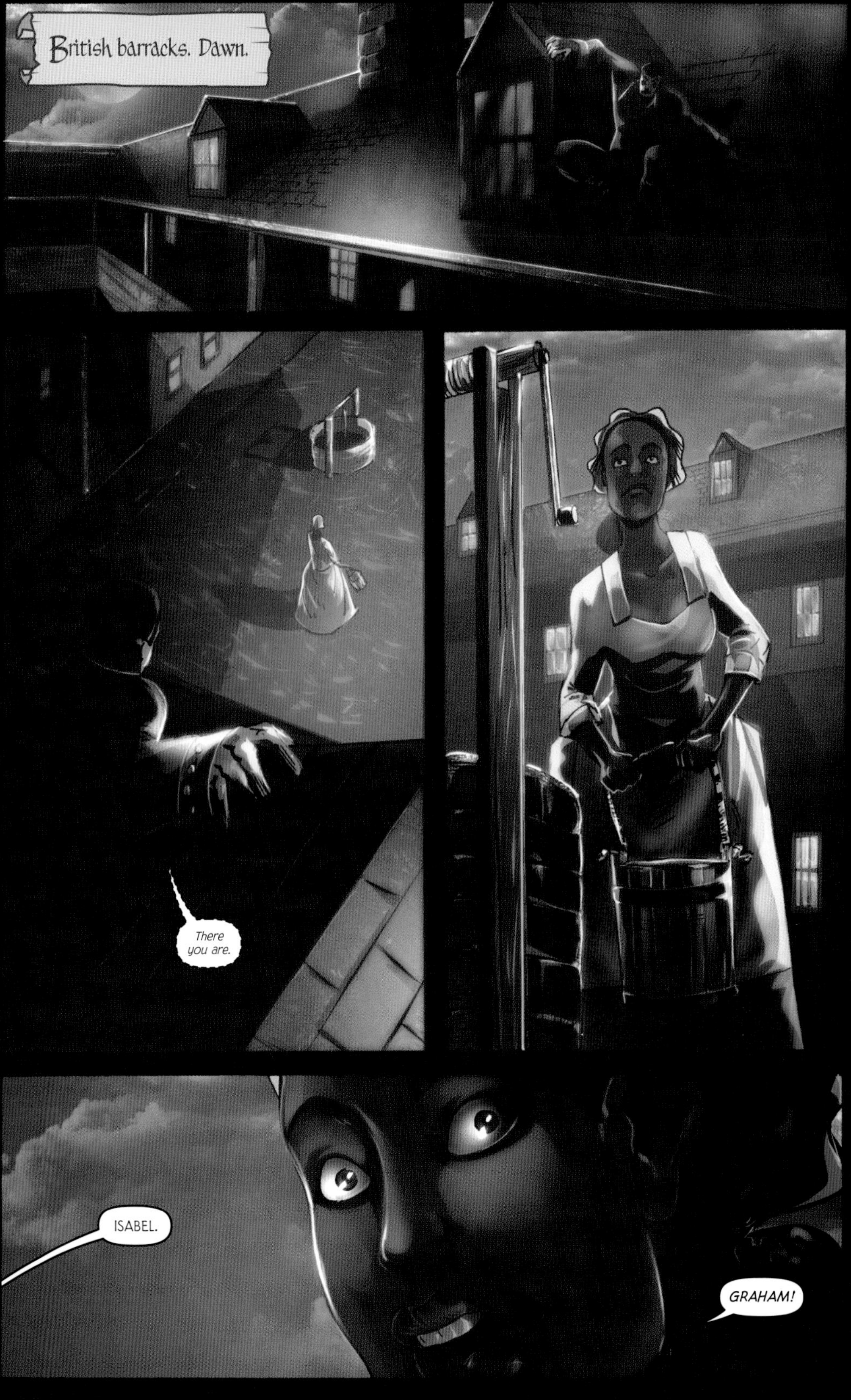
British barracks. Dawn.
There you are.
ISABEL.
GRAHAM!

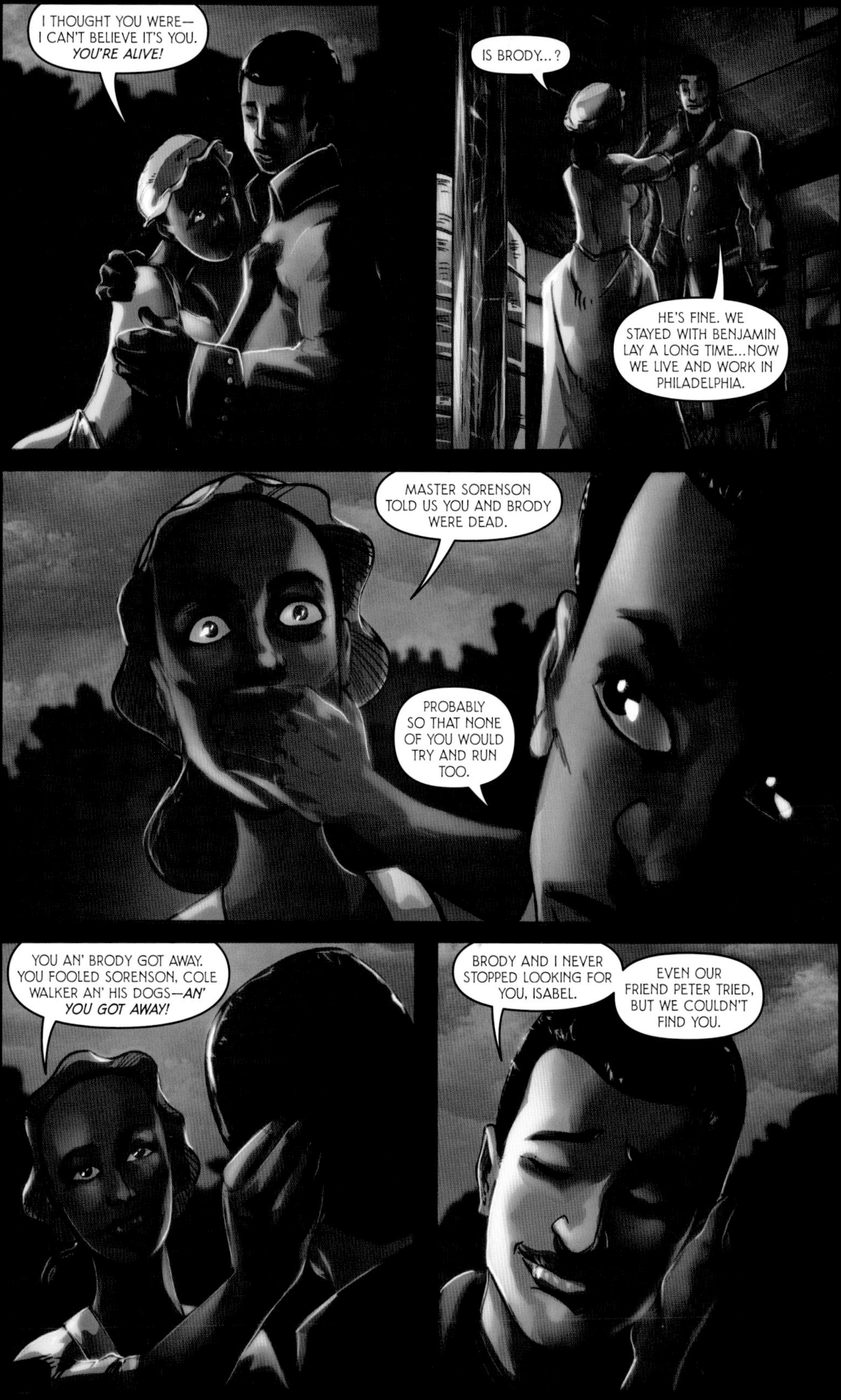

I THOUGHT YOU WERE— I CAN'T BELIEVE IT'S YOU. *YOU'RE ALIVE!*
IS BRODY...?
HE'S FINE. WE STAYED WITH BENJAMIN LAY A LONG TIME...NOW WE LIVE AND WORK IN PHILADELPHIA.
MASTER SORENSON TOLD US YOU AND BRODY WERE DEAD.
PROBABLY SO THAT NONE OF YOU WOULD TRY AND RUN TOO.
YOU AN' BRODY GOT AWAY. YOU FOOLED SORENSON, COLE WALKER AN' HIS DOGS—*AN' YOU GOT AWAY!*
BRODY AND I NEVER STOPPED LOOKING FOR YOU, ISABEL.
EVEN OUR FRIEND PETER TRIED, BUT WE COULDN'T FIND YOU.

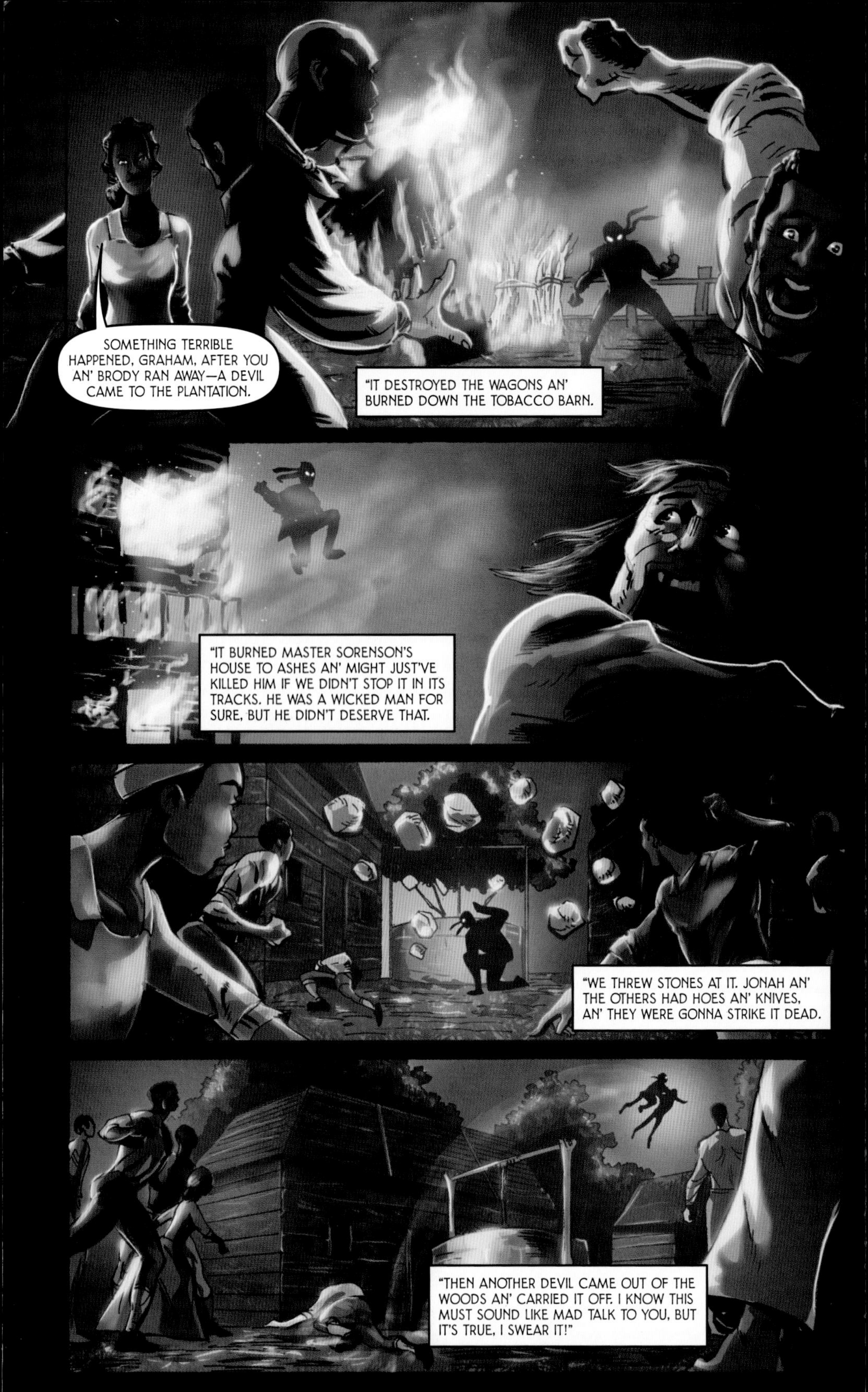
SOMETHING TERRIBLE HAPPENED, GRAHAM, AFTER YOU AN' BRODY RAN AWAY—A DEVIL CAME TO THE PLANTATION.
"IT DESTROYED THE WAGONS AN' BURNED DOWN THE TOBACCO BARN.
"IT BURNED MASTER SORENSON'S HOUSE TO ASHES AN' MIGHT JUST'VE KILLED HIM IF WE DIDN'T STOP IT IN ITS TRACKS. HE WAS A WICKED MAN FOR SURE, BUT HE DIDN'T DESERVE THAT.
"WE THREW STONES AT IT. JONAH AN' THE OTHERS HAD HOES AN' KNIVES, AN' THEY WERE GONNA STRIKE IT DEAD.
"THEN ANOTHER DEVIL CAME OUT OF THE WOODS AN' CARRIED IT OFF. I KNOW THIS MUST SOUND LIKE MAD TALK TO YOU, BUT IT'S TRUE, I SWEAR IT!"

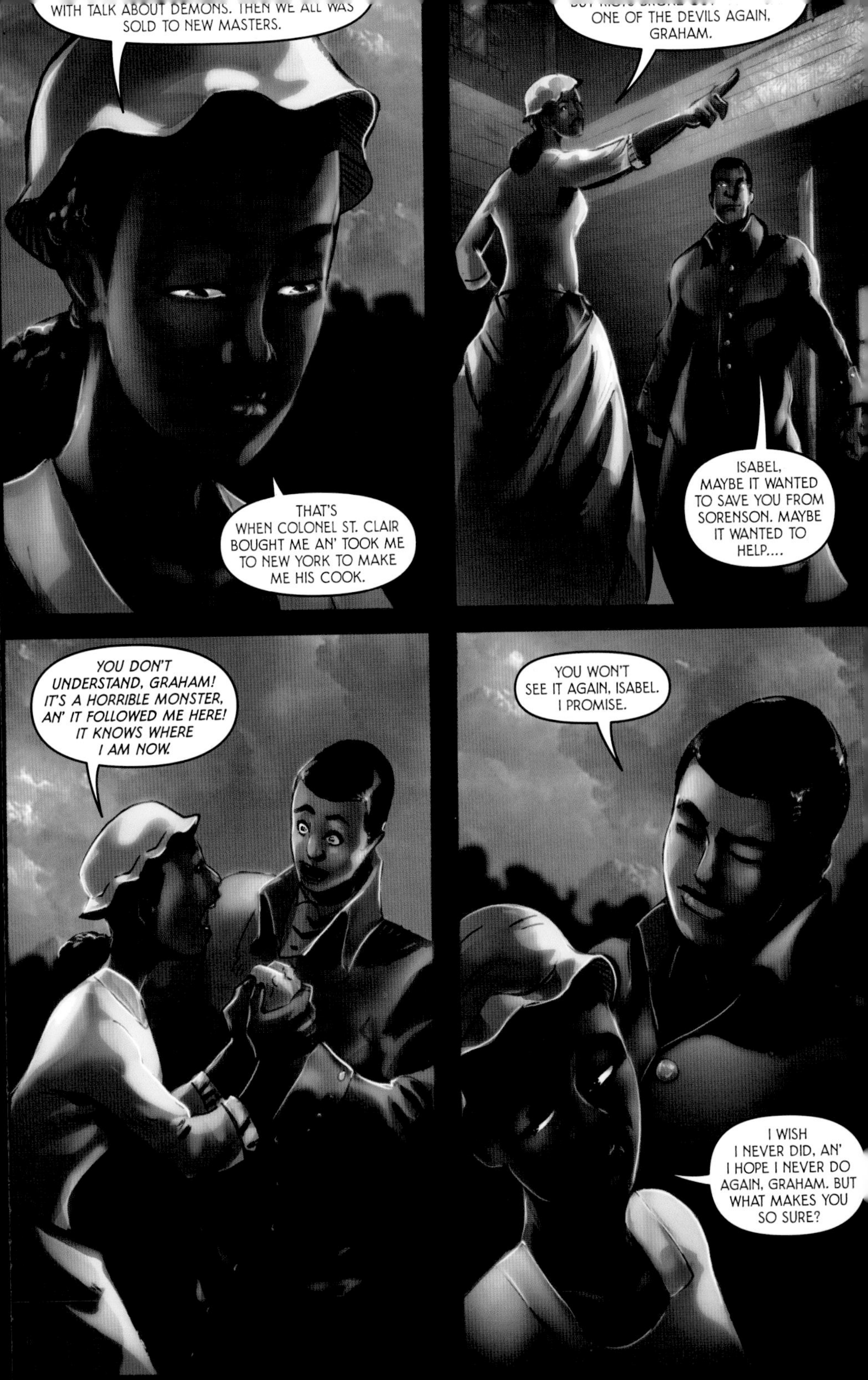
WITH TALK ABOUT DEMONS. THEN WE ALL WAS SOLD TO NEW MASTERS.
THAT'S WHEN COLONEL ST. CLAIR BOUGHT ME AN' TOOK ME TO NEW YORK TO MAKE ME HIS COOK.
ONE OF THE DEVILS AGAIN, GRAHAM.
ISABEL, MAYBE IT WANTED TO SAVE YOU FROM SORENSON. MAYBE IT WANTED TO HELP....
YOU DON'T UNDERSTAND, GRAHAM! IT'S A HORRIBLE MONSTER, AN' IT FOLLOWED ME HERE! IT KNOWS WHERE I AM NOW.
YOU WON'T SEE IT AGAIN, ISABEL. I PROMISE.
I WISH I NEVER DID, AN' I HOPE I NEVER DO AGAIN, GRAHAM. BUT WHAT MAKES YOU SO SURE?

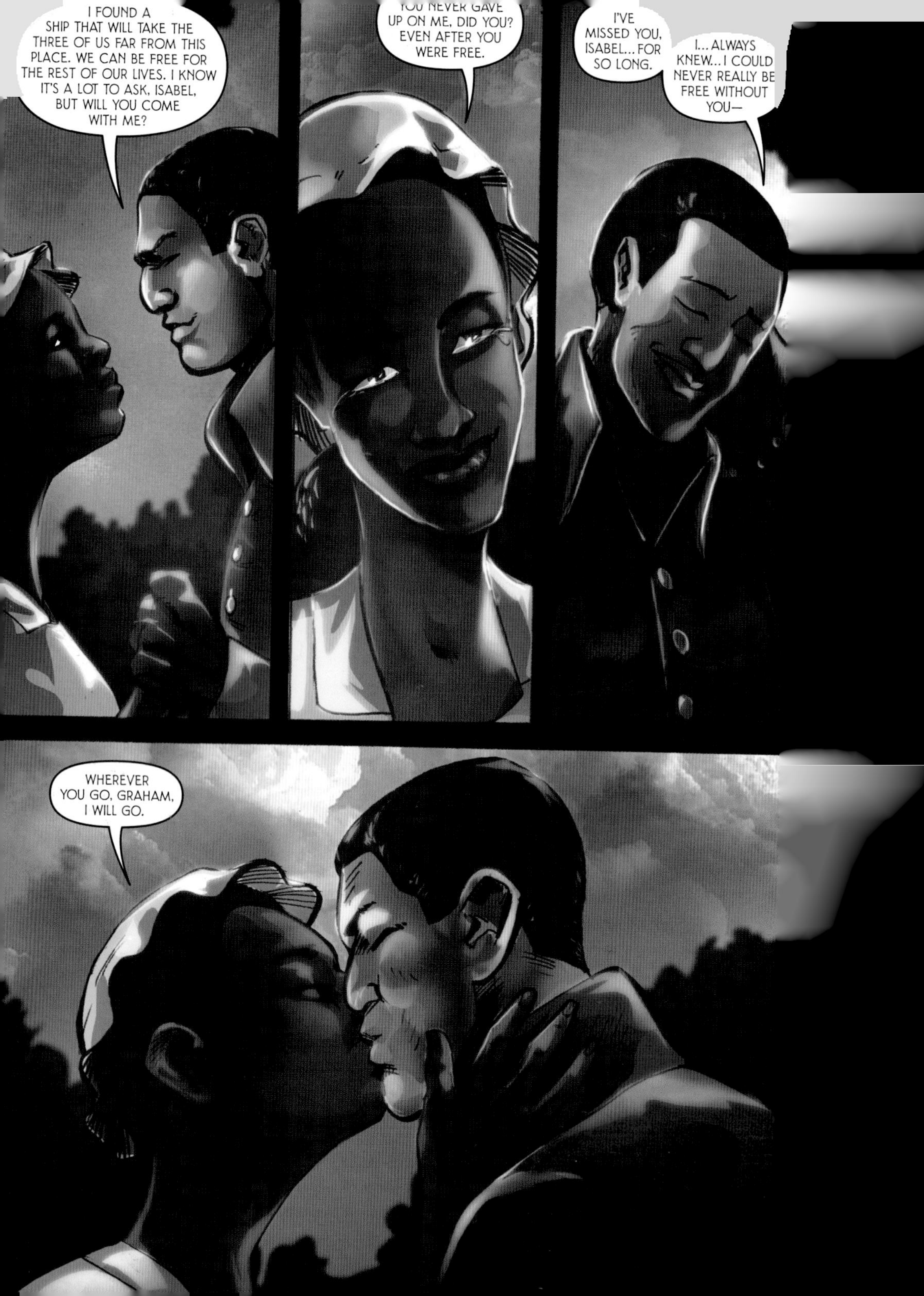
I FOUND A SHIP THAT WILL TAKE THE THREE OF US FAR FROM THIS PLACE. WE CAN BE FREE FOR THE REST OF OUR LIVES. I KNOW IT'S A LOT TO ASK, ISABEL, BUT WILL YOU COME WITH ME?
YOU NEVER GAVE UP ON ME, DID YOU? EVEN AFTER YOU WERE FREE.
I'VE MISSED YOU, ISABEL... FOR SO LONG.
I... ALWAYS KNEW... I COULD NEVER REALLY BE FREE WITHOUT YOU—
WHEREVER YOU GO, GRAHAM, I WILL GO.

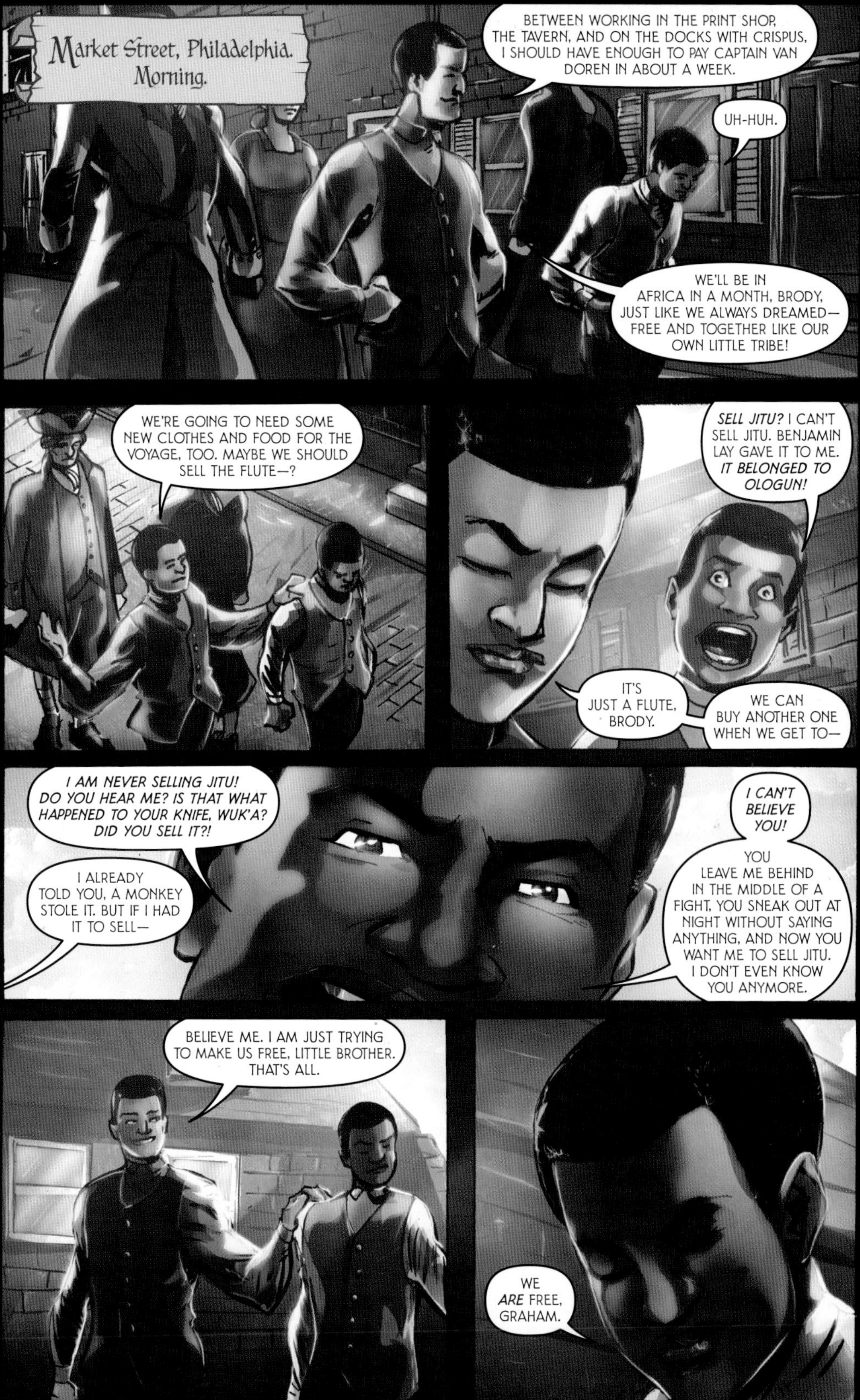
Market Street, Philadelphia. Morning.
BETWEEN WORKING IN THE PRINT SHOP, THE TAVERN, AND ON THE DOCKS WITH CRISPUS, I SHOULD HAVE ENOUGH TO PAY CAPTAIN VAN DOREN IN ABOUT A WEEK.
UH-HUH.
WE'LL BE IN AFRICA IN A MONTH, BRODY, JUST LIKE WE ALWAYS DREAMED—FREE AND TOGETHER LIKE OUR OWN LITTLE TRIBE!
WE'RE GOING TO NEED SOME NEW CLOTHES AND FOOD FOR THE VOYAGE, TOO. MAYBE WE SHOULD SELL THE FLUTE—?
SELL JITU? I CAN'T SELL JITU. BENJAMIN LAY GAVE IT TO ME. *IT BELONGED TO OLOGUN!*
IT'S JUST A FLUTE, BRODY.
WE CAN BUY ANOTHER ONE WHEN WE GET TO—
I AM NEVER SELLING JITU! DO YOU HEAR ME? IS THAT WHAT HAPPENED TO YOUR KNIFE, WUK'A? DID YOU SELL IT?!
I ALREADY TOLD YOU, A MONKEY STOLE IT. BUT IF I HAD IT TO SELL—
I CAN'T BELIEVE YOU!
YOU LEAVE ME BEHIND IN THE MIDDLE OF A FIGHT, YOU SNEAK OUT AT NIGHT WITHOUT SAYING ANYTHING, AND NOW YOU WANT ME TO SELL JITU. I DON'T EVEN KNOW YOU ANYMORE.
BELIEVE ME. I AM JUST TRYING TO MAKE US FREE, LITTLE BROTHER. THAT'S ALL.
WE *ARE* FREE, GRAHAM.

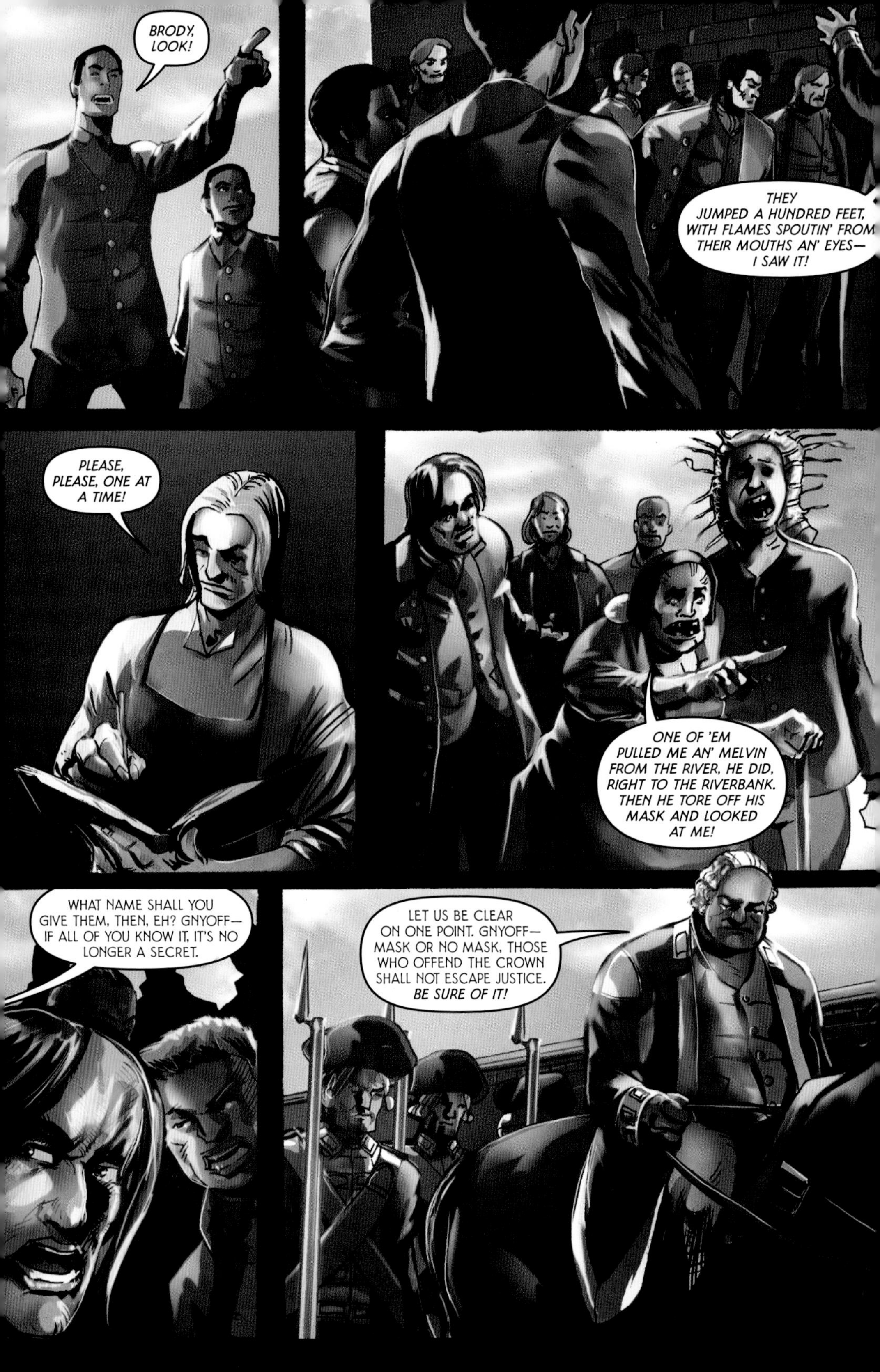
BRODY, LOOK!
THEY JUMPED A HUNDRED FEET, WITH FLAMES SPOUTIN' FROM THEIR MOUTHS AN' EYES— I SAW IT!
PLEASE, PLEASE, ONE AT A TIME!
ONE OF 'EM PULLED ME AN' MELVIN FROM THE RIVER, HE DID, RIGHT TO THE RIVERBANK. THEN HE TORE OFF HIS MASK AND LOOKED AT ME!
WHAT NAME SHALL YOU GIVE THEM, THEN, EH? GNYOFF— IF ALL OF YOU KNOW IT, IT'S NO LONGER A SECRET.
LET US BE CLEAR ON ONE POINT. GNYOFF— MASK OR NO MASK, THOSE WHO OFFEND THE CROWN SHALL NOT ESCAPE JUSTICE. BE SURE OF IT!

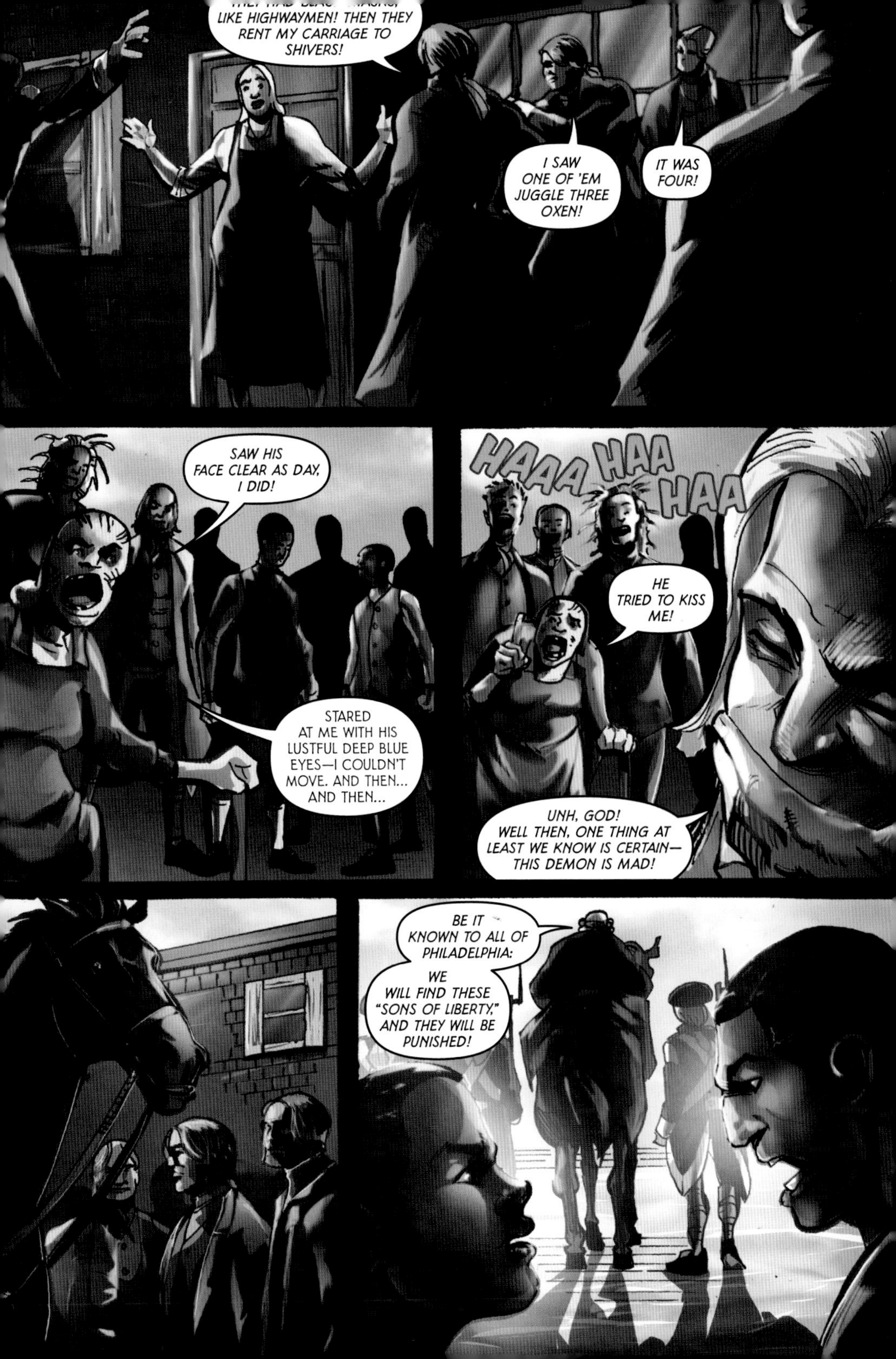
LIKE HIGHWAYMEN! THEN THEY RENT MY CARRIAGE TO SHIVERS!
I SAW ONE OF 'EM JUGGLE THREE OXEN!
IT WAS FOUR!
SAW HIS FACE CLEAR AS DAY, I DID!
STARED AT ME WITH HIS LUSTFUL DEEP BLUE EYES—I COULDN'T MOVE. AND THEN... AND THEN...
HAAA HAA HAA
HE TRIED TO KISS ME!
UNH, GOD! WELL THEN, ONE THING AT LEAST WE KNOW IS CERTAIN—THIS DEMON IS MAD!
BE IT KNOWN TO ALL OF PHILADELPHIA:
WE WILL FIND THESE "SONS OF LIBERTY," AND THEY WILL BE PUNISHED!

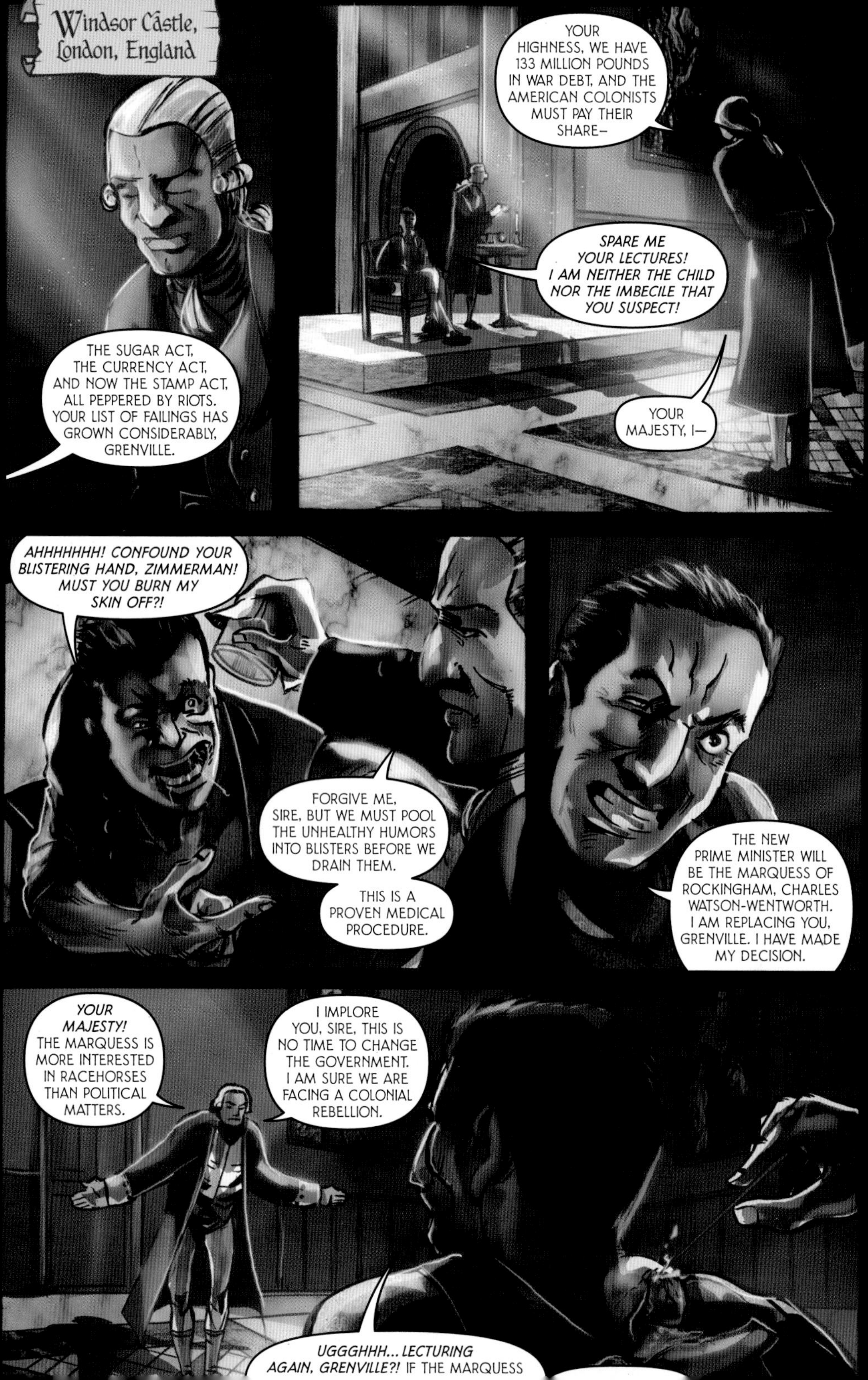
Windsor Castle, London, England
THE SUGAR ACT, THE CURRENCY ACT, AND NOW THE STAMP ACT, ALL PEPPERED BY RIOTS. YOUR LIST OF FAILINGS HAS GROWN CONSIDERABLY, GRENVILLE.
YOUR HIGHNESS, WE HAVE 133 MILLION POUNDS IN WAR DEBT, AND THE AMERICAN COLONISTS MUST PAY THEIR SHARE–
SPARE ME YOUR LECTURES! I AM NEITHER THE CHILD NOR THE IMBECILE THAT YOU SUSPECT!
YOUR MAJESTY, I—
AHHHHHHH! CONFOUND YOUR BLISTERING HAND, ZIMMERMAN! MUST YOU BURN MY SKIN OFF?!
FORGIVE ME, SIRE, BUT WE MUST POOL THE UNHEALTHY HUMORS INTO BLISTERS BEFORE WE DRAIN THEM.
THIS IS A PROVEN MEDICAL PROCEDURE.
THE NEW PRIME MINISTER WILL BE THE MARQUESS OF ROCKINGHAM, CHARLES WATSON-WENTWORTH. I AM REPLACING YOU, GRENVILLE. I HAVE MADE MY DECISION.
YOUR MAJESTY! THE MARQUESS IS MORE INTERESTED IN RACEHORSES THAN POLITICAL MATTERS.
I IMPLORE YOU, SIRE, THIS IS NO TIME TO CHANGE THE GOVERNMENT. I AM SURE WE ARE FACING A COLONIAL REBELLION.
UGGGHHH... LECTURING AGAIN, GRENVILLE?! IF THE MARQUESS

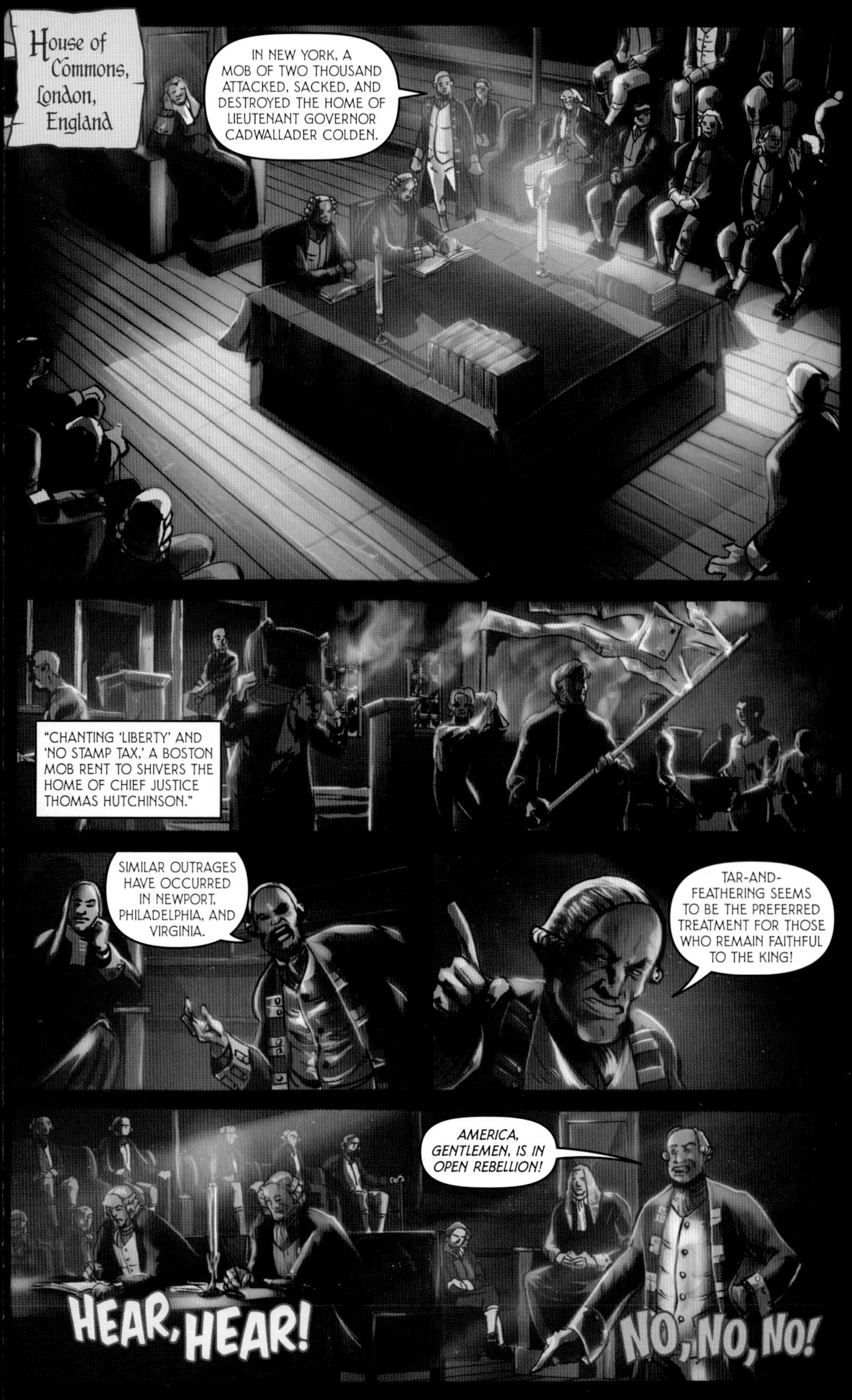
House of Commons, London, England
IN NEW YORK, A MOB OF TWO THOUSAND ATTACKED, SACKED, AND DESTROYED THE HOME OF LIEUTENANT GOVERNOR CADWALLADER COLDEN.
"CHANTING 'LIBERTY' AND 'NO STAMP TAX,' A BOSTON MOB RENT TO SHIVERS THE HOME OF CHIEF JUSTICE THOMAS HUTCHINSON."
SIMILAR OUTRAGES HAVE OCCURRED IN NEWPORT, PHILADELPHIA, AND VIRGINIA.
TAR-AND-FEATHERING SEEMS TO BE THE PREFERRED TREATMENT FOR THOSE WHO REMAIN FAITHFUL TO THE KING!
AMERICA, GENTLEMEN, IS IN OPEN REBELLION!
HEAR, HEAR!
NO, NO, NO!

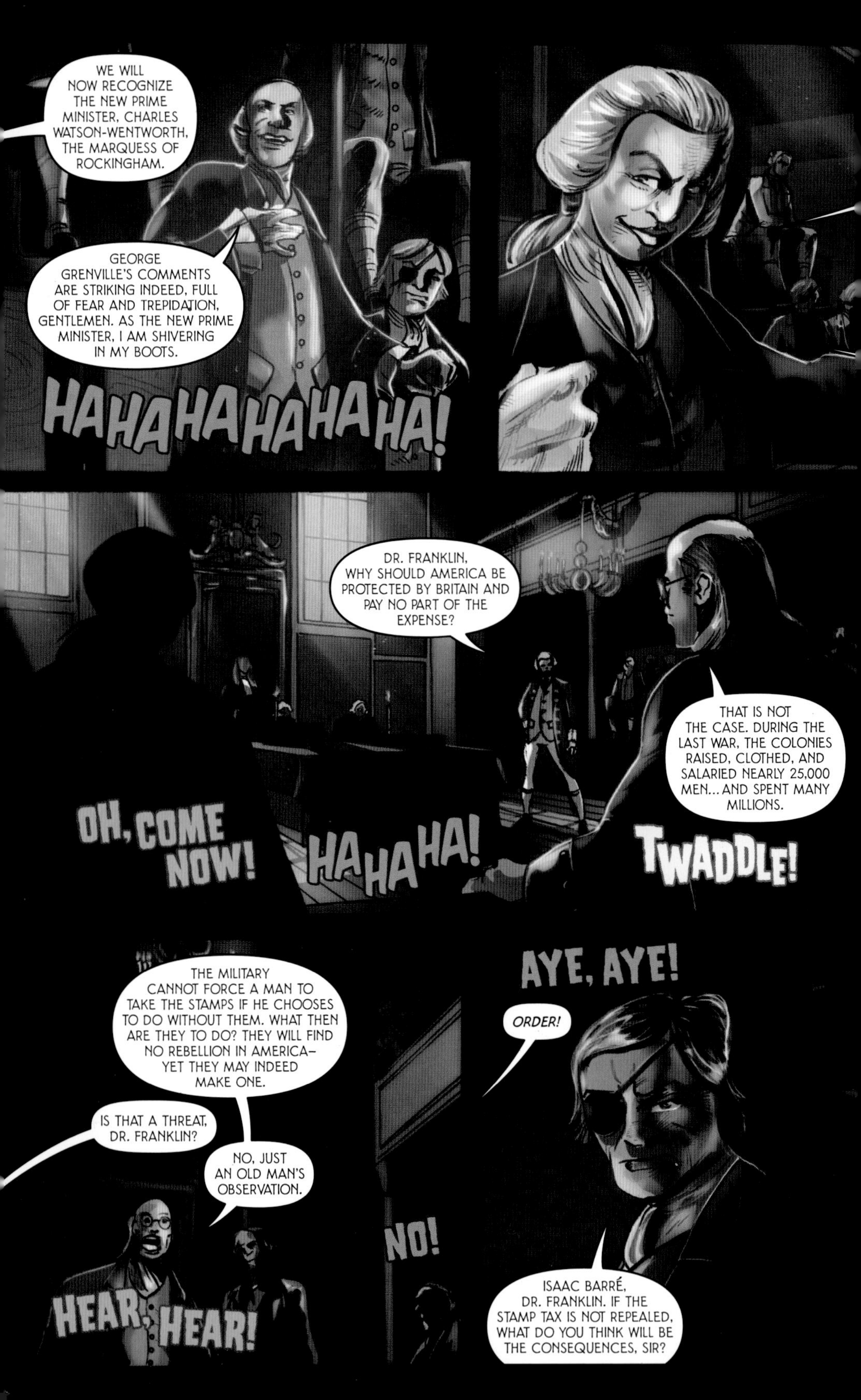
WE WILL NOW RECOGNIZE THE NEW PRIME MINISTER, CHARLES WATSON-WENTWORTH, THE MARQUESS OF ROCKINGHAM.
GEORGE GRENVILLE'S COMMENTS ARE STRIKING INDEED, FULL OF FEAR AND TREPIDATION, GENTLEMEN. AS THE NEW PRIME MINISTER, I AM SHIVERING IN MY BOOTS.
HAHAHAHAHAHAHA!
DR. FRANKLIN, WHY SHOULD AMERICA BE PROTECTED BY BRITAIN AND PAY NO PART OF THE EXPENSE?
THAT IS NOT THE CASE. DURING THE LAST WAR, THE COLONIES RAISED, CLOTHED, AND SALARIED NEARLY 25,000 MEN... AND SPENT MANY MILLIONS.
OH, COME NOW!
HAHAHA!
TWADDLE!
THE MILITARY CANNOT FORCE A MAN TO TAKE THE STAMPS IF HE CHOOSES TO DO WITHOUT THEM. WHAT THEN ARE THEY TO DO? THEY WILL FIND NO REBELLION IN AMERICA—YET THEY MAY INDEED MAKE ONE.
IS THAT A THREAT, DR. FRANKLIN?
NO, JUST AN OLD MAN'S OBSERVATION.
HEAR, HEAR!
NO!
AYE, AYE!
ORDER!
ISAAC BARRÉ, DR. FRANKLIN. IF THE STAMP TAX IS NOT REPEALED, WHAT DO YOU THINK WILL BE THE CONSEQUENCES, SIR?

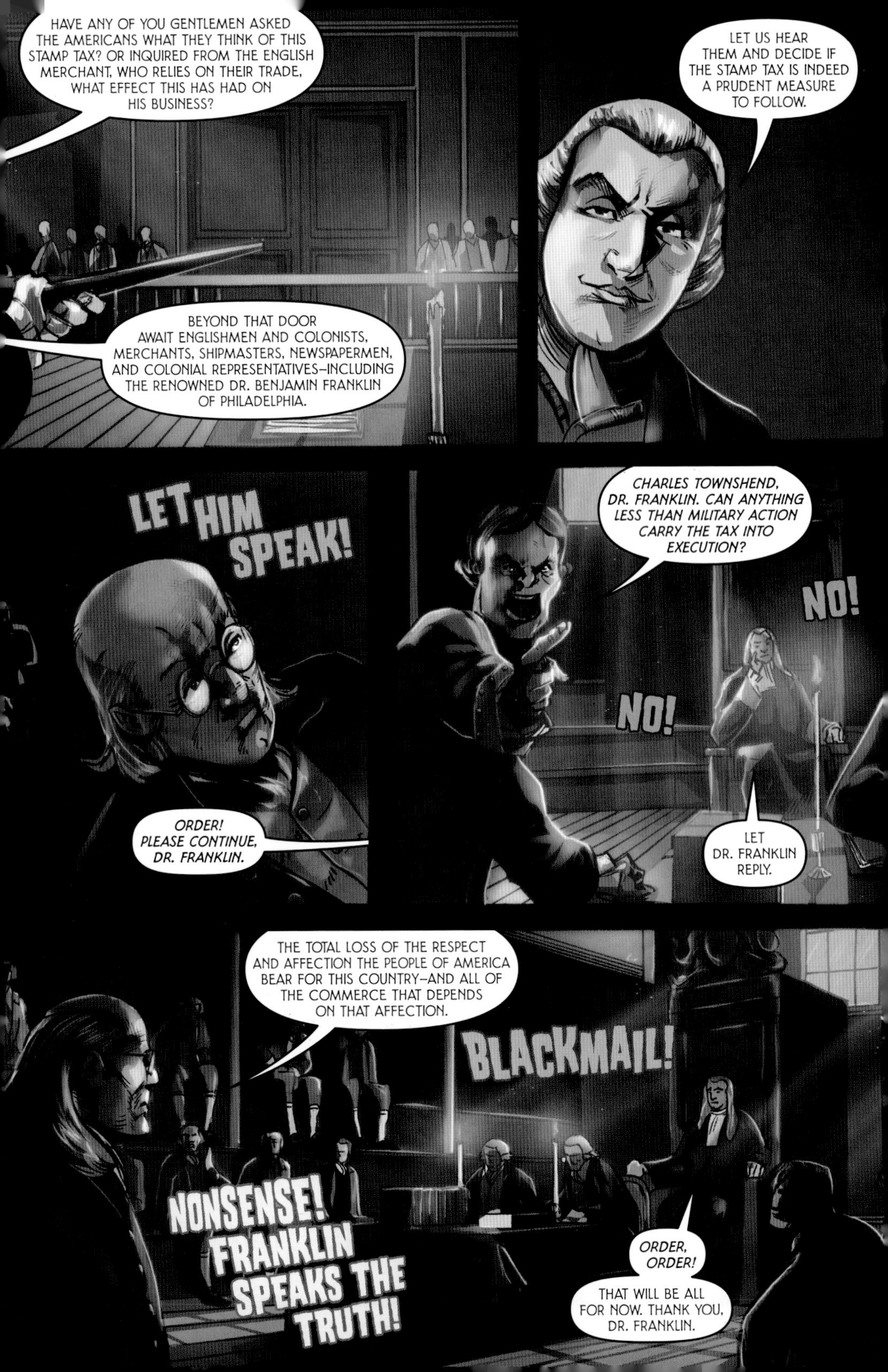
HAVE ANY OF YOU GENTLEMEN ASKED THE AMERICANS WHAT THEY THINK OF THIS STAMP TAX? OR INQUIRED FROM THE ENGLISH MERCHANT, WHO RELIES ON THEIR TRADE, WHAT EFFECT THIS HAS HAD ON HIS BUSINESS?
BEYOND THAT DOOR AWAIT ENGLISHMEN AND COLONISTS, MERCHANTS, SHIPMASTERS, NEWSPAPERMEN, AND COLONIAL REPRESENTATIVES—INCLUDING THE RENOWNED DR. BENJAMIN FRANKLIN OF PHILADELPHIA.
LET US HEAR THEM AND DECIDE IF THE STAMP TAX IS INDEED A PRUDENT MEASURE TO FOLLOW.
LET HIM SPEAK!
ORDER! PLEASE CONTINUE, DR. FRANKLIN.
CHARLES TOWNSHEND, DR. FRANKLIN. CAN ANYTHING LESS THAN MILITARY ACTION CARRY THE TAX INTO EXECUTION?
NO!
NO!
LET DR. FRANKLIN REPLY.
THE TOTAL LOSS OF THE RESPECT AND AFFECTION THE PEOPLE OF AMERICA BEAR FOR THIS COUNTRY—AND ALL OF THE COMMERCE THAT DEPENDS ON THAT AFFECTION.
BLACKMAIL!
NONSENSE! FRANKLIN SPEAKS THE TRUTH!
ORDER, ORDER!
THAT WILL BE ALL FOR NOW. THANK YOU, DR. FRANKLIN.

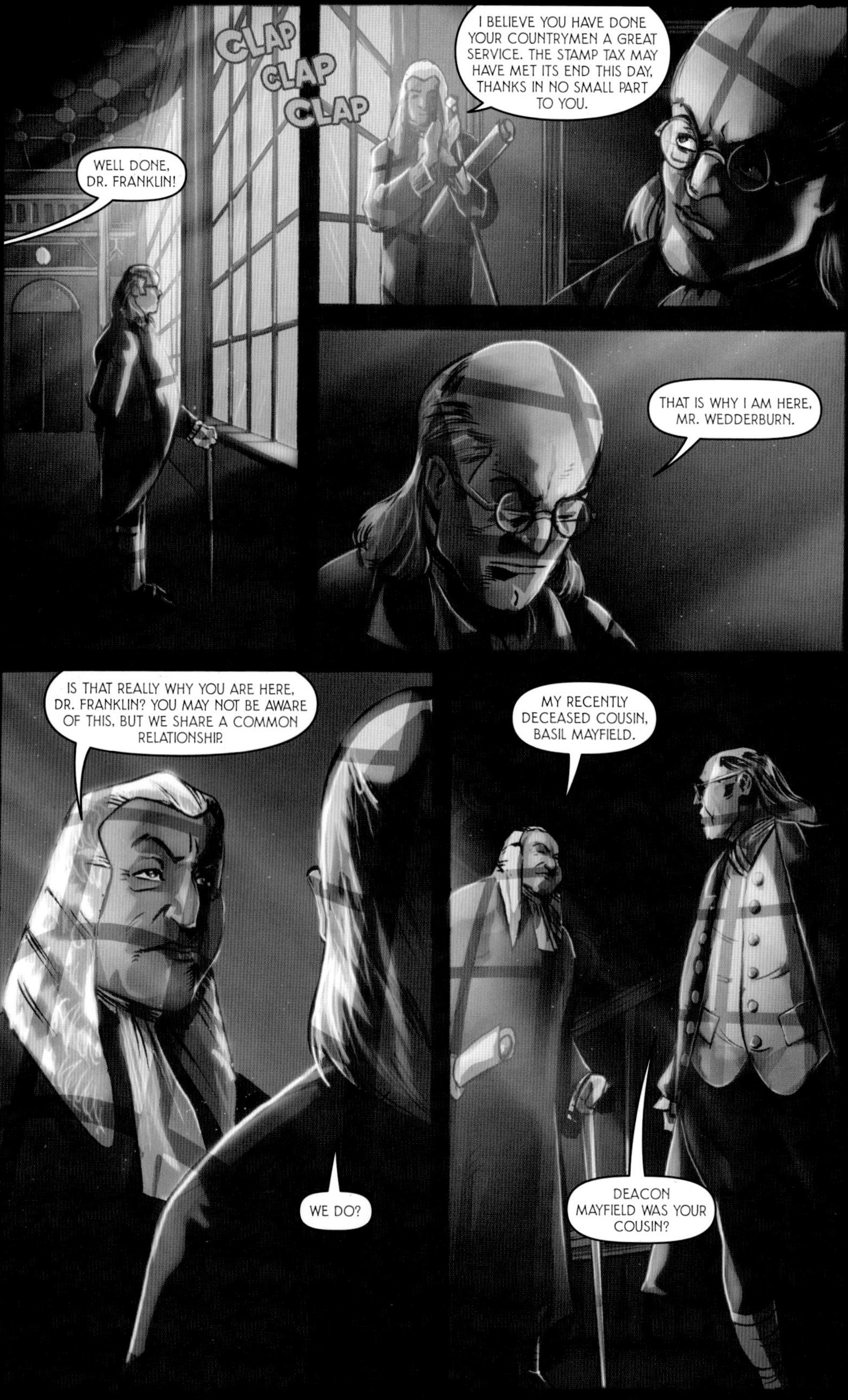
WELL DONE, DR. FRANKLIN!
CLAP CLAP CLAP
I BELIEVE YOU HAVE DONE YOUR COUNTRYMEN A GREAT SERVICE. THE STAMP TAX MAY HAVE MET ITS END THIS DAY, THANKS IN NO SMALL PART TO YOU.
THAT IS WHY I AM HERE, MR. WEDDERBURN.
IS THAT REALLY WHY YOU ARE HERE, DR. FRANKLIN? YOU MAY NOT BE AWARE OF THIS, BUT WE SHARE A COMMON RELATIONSHIP.
WE DO?
MY RECENTLY DECEASED COUSIN, BASIL MAYFIELD.
DEACON MAYFIELD WAS YOUR COUSIN?

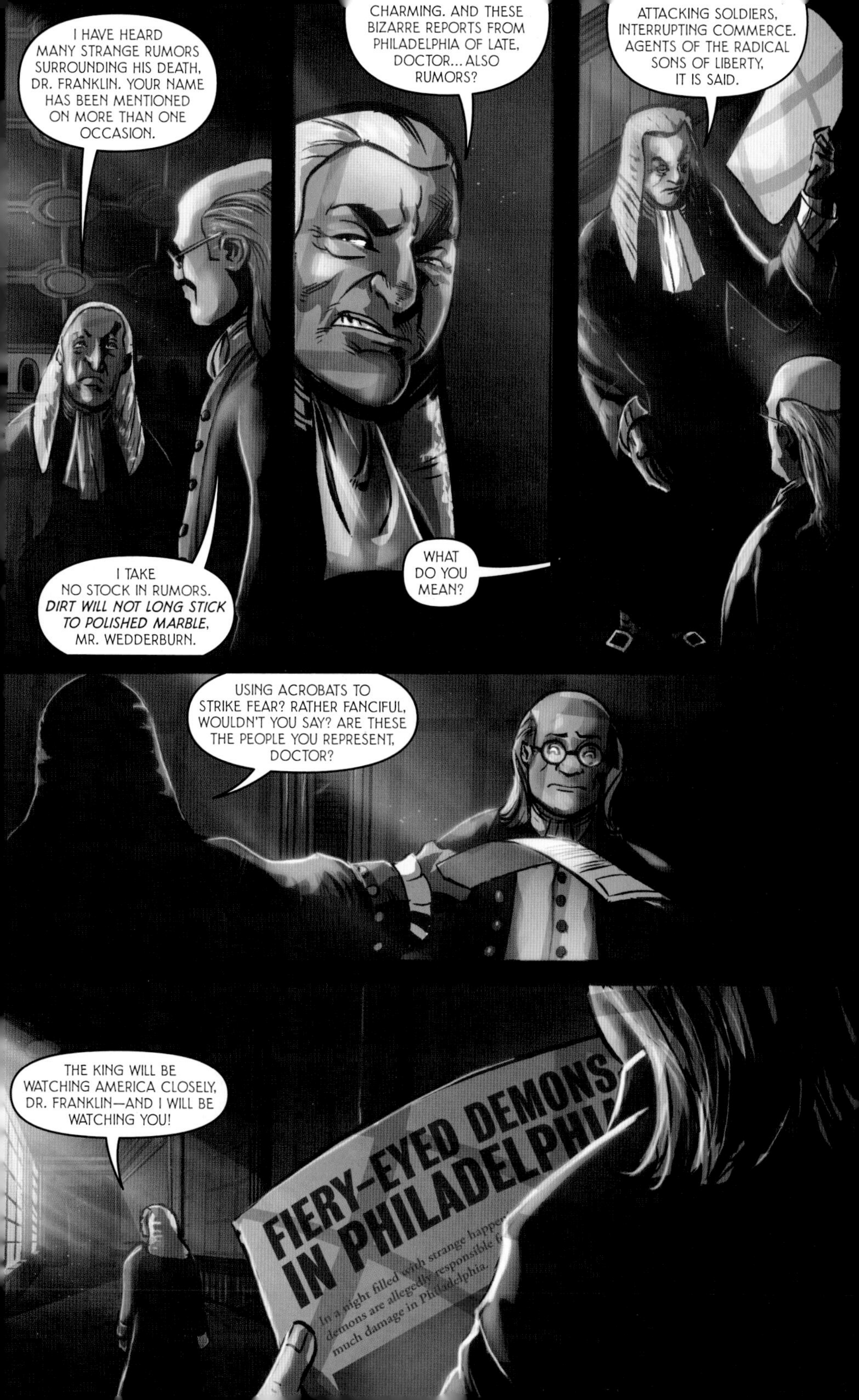
I HAVE HEARD MANY STRANGE RUMORS SURROUNDING HIS DEATH, DR. FRANKLIN. YOUR NAME HAS BEEN MENTIONED ON MORE THAN ONE OCCASION.
I TAKE NO STOCK IN RUMORS. *DIRT WILL NOT LONG STICK TO POLISHED MARBLE*, MR. WEDDERBURN.
CHARMING. AND THESE BIZARRE REPORTS FROM PHILADELPHIA OF LATE, DOCTOR... ALSO RUMORS?
WHAT DO YOU MEAN?
ATTACKING SOLDIERS, INTERRUPTING COMMERCE. AGENTS OF THE RADICAL SONS OF LIBERTY, IT IS SAID.
USING ACROBATS TO STRIKE FEAR? RATHER FANCIFUL, WOULDN'T YOU SAY? ARE THESE THE PEOPLE YOU REPRESENT, DOCTOR?
THE KING WILL BE WATCHING AMERICA CLOSELY, DR. FRANKLIN—AND I WILL BE WATCHING YOU!
FIERY-EYED DEMONS
IN PHILADELPHI

"I blame no one for this but myself. Too much time have I dedicated to bringing an end to the stamp act. I have been in a continual hurry from morning till night, informing, explaining, consulting, and disputing.

"I failed to find a cure for the two of you, as I promised. Now am I to believe that you are responsible for this?

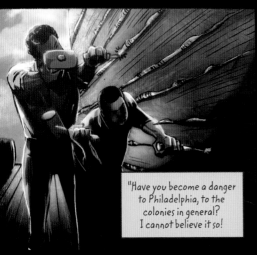

"Have you become a danger to Philadelphia, to the colonies in general? I cannot believe it so!

"Benjamin Lay and I swore to protect you as best we could, but what choice will I have if Philadelphia is threatened? Must I expose you to protect America?

"You must not use your powers again, no matter how certain you are that it is justified.

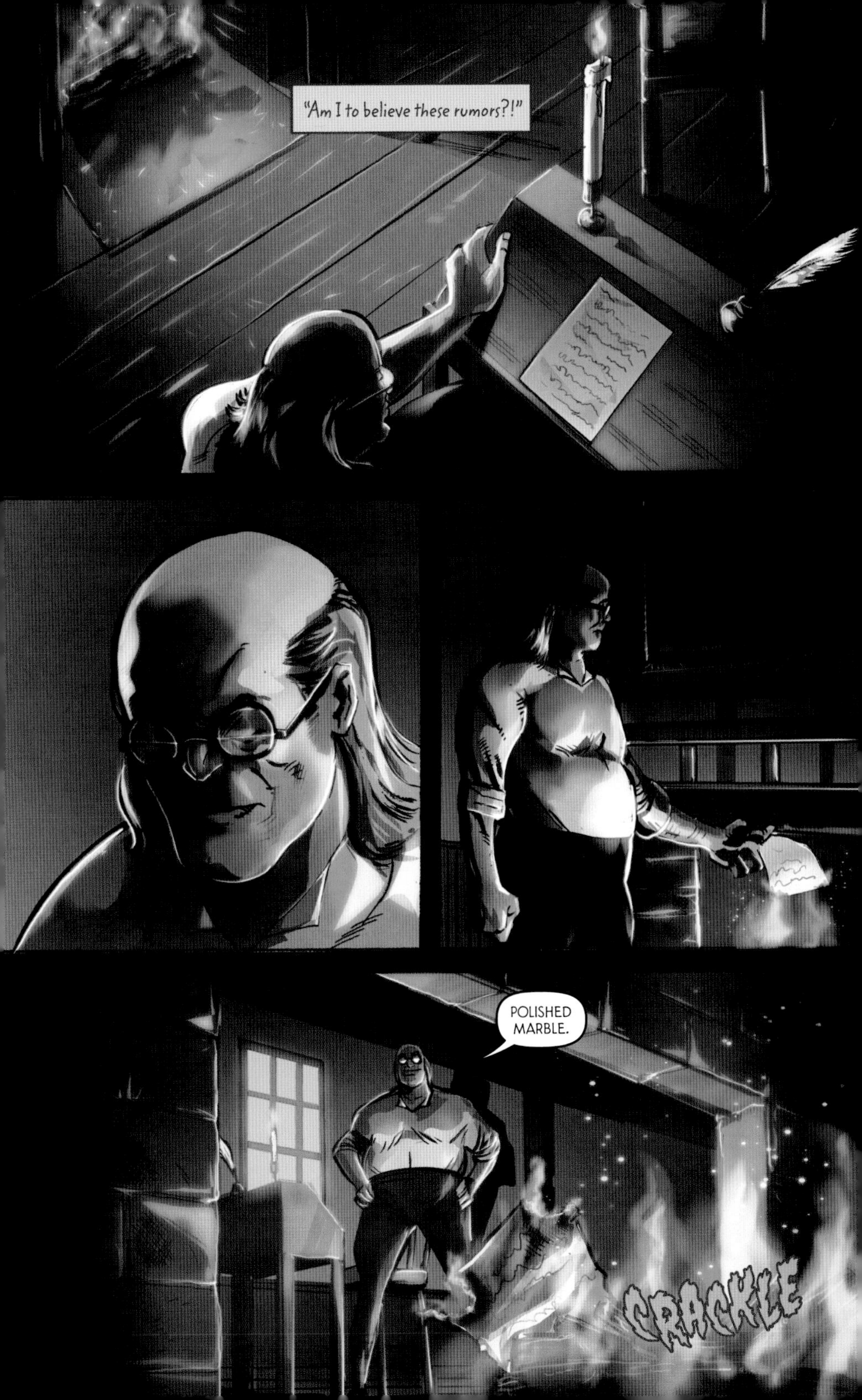
"Am I to believe these rumors?!"
POLISHED MARBLE.
CRACKLE

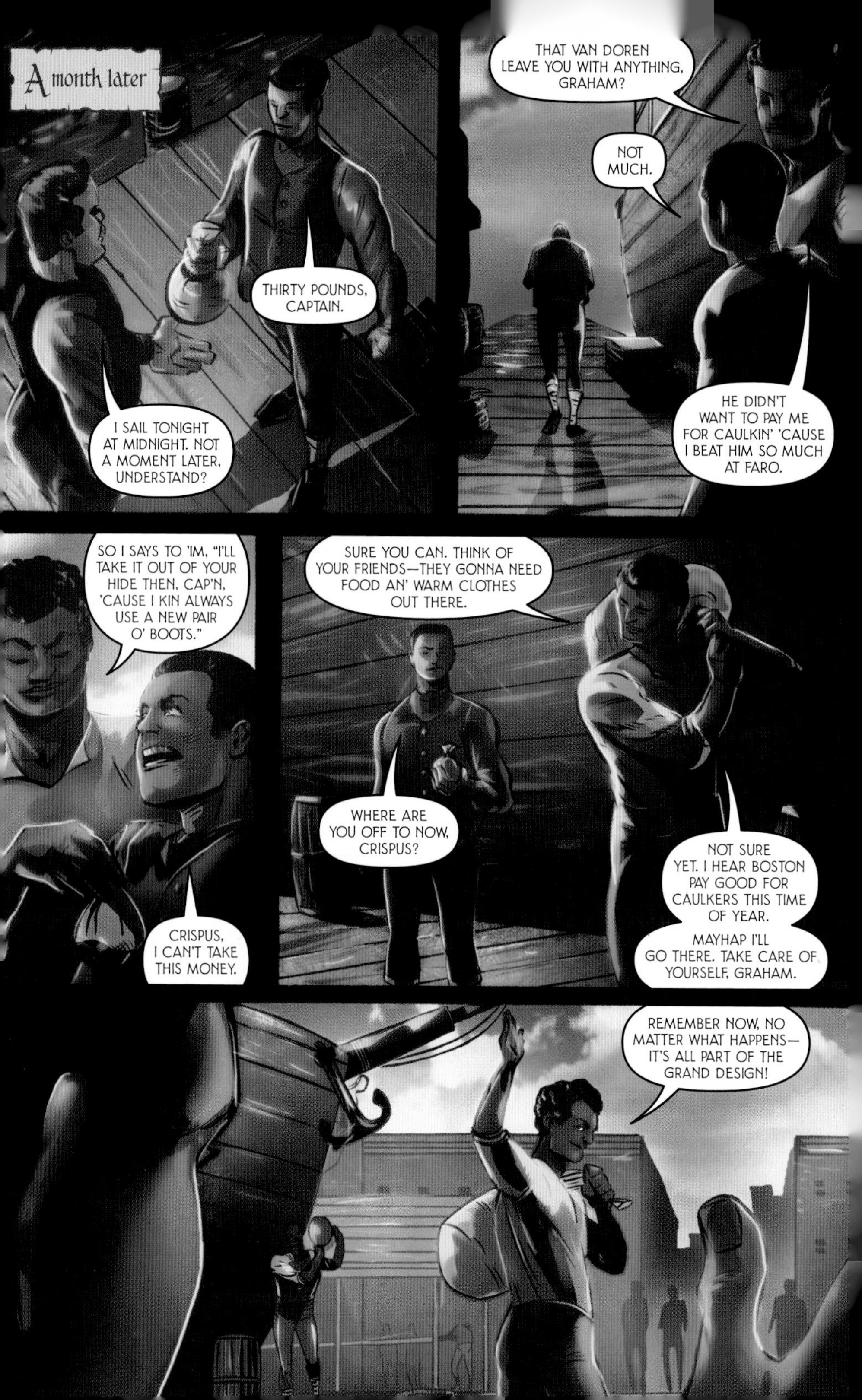
A month later
THIRTY POUNDS, CAPTAIN.
I SAIL TONIGHT AT MIDNIGHT. NOT A MOMENT LATER, UNDERSTAND?
THAT VAN DOREN LEAVE YOU WITH ANYTHING, GRAHAM?
NOT MUCH.
HE DIDN'T WANT TO PAY ME FOR CAULKIN' 'CAUSE I BEAT HIM SO MUCH AT FARO.
SO I SAYS TO 'IM, "I'LL TAKE IT OUT OF YOUR HIDE THEN, CAP'N, 'CAUSE I KIN ALWAYS USE A NEW PAIR O' BOOTS."
CRISPUS, I CAN'T TAKE THIS MONEY.
SURE YOU CAN. THINK OF YOUR FRIENDS—THEY GONNA NEED FOOD AN' WARM CLOTHES OUT THERE.
WHERE ARE YOU OFF TO NOW, CRISPUS?
NOT SURE YET. I HEAR BOSTON PAY GOOD FOR CAULKERS THIS TIME OF YEAR.
MAYHAP I'LL GO THERE. TAKE CARE OF YOURSELF, GRAHAM.
REMEMBER NOW, NO MATTER WHAT HAPPENS— IT'S ALL PART OF THE GRAND DESIGN!

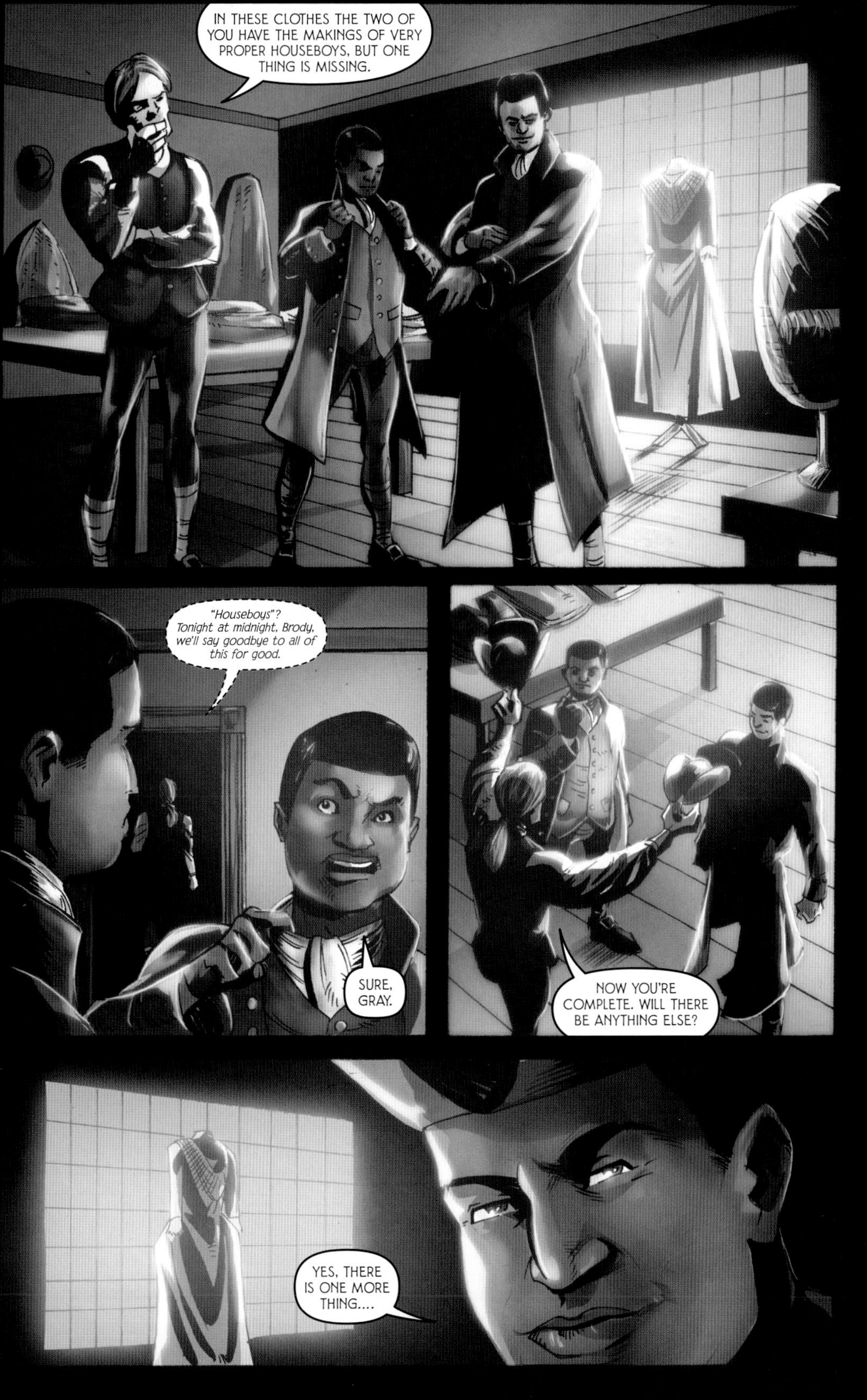
IN THESE CLOTHES THE TWO OF YOU HAVE THE MAKINGS OF VERY PROPER HOUSEBOYS, BUT ONE THING IS MISSING.
"Houseboys"? Tonight at midnight, Brody, we'll say goodbye to all of this for good.
SURE, GRAY.
NOW YOU'RE COMPLETE. WILL THERE BE ANYTHING ELSE?
YES, THERE IS ONE MORE THING....

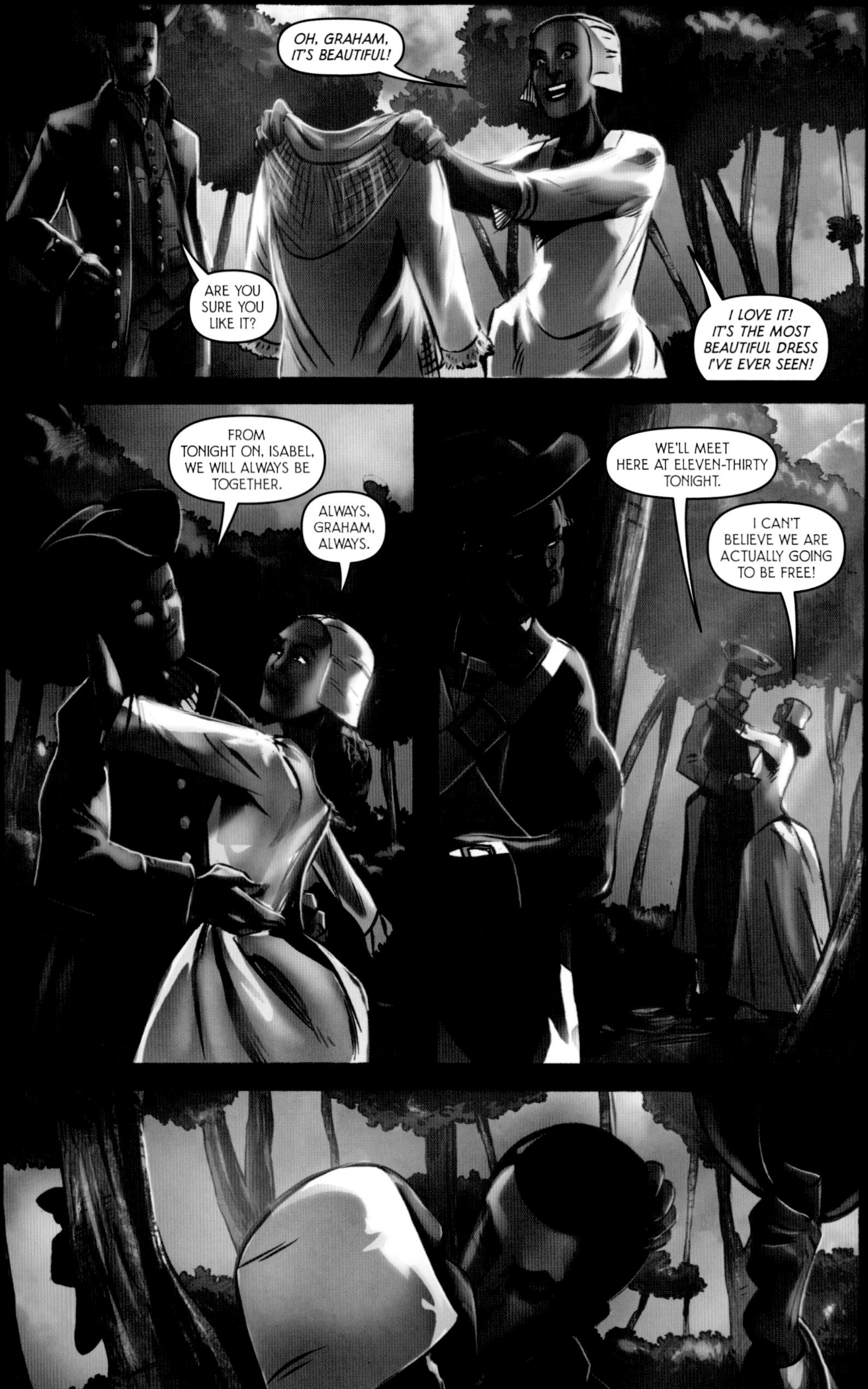

OH, GRAHAM, IT'S BEAUTIFUL!
ARE YOU SURE YOU LIKE IT?
I LOVE IT! IT'S THE MOST BEAUTIFUL DRESS I'VE EVER SEEN!
FROM TONIGHT ON, ISABEL, WE WILL ALWAYS BE TOGETHER.
ALWAYS, GRAHAM, ALWAYS.
WE'LL MEET HERE AT ELEVEN-THIRTY TONIGHT.
I CAN'T BELIEVE WE ARE ACTUALLY GOING TO BE FREE!

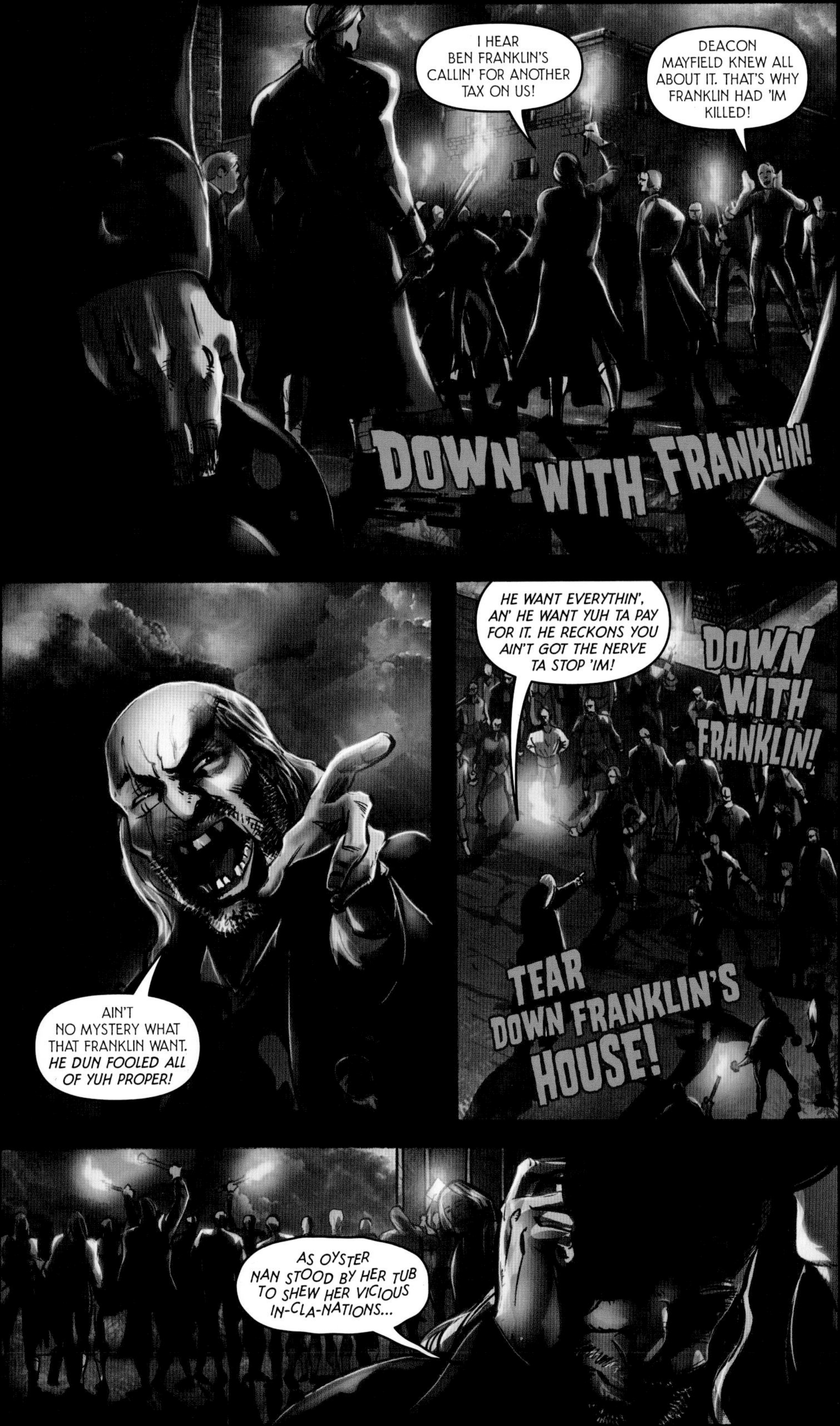
I HEAR BEN FRANKLIN'S CALLIN' FOR ANOTHER TAX ON US!
DEACON MAYFIELD KNEW ALL ABOUT IT. THAT'S WHY FRANKLIN HAD 'IM KILLED!
DOWN WITH FRANKLIN!
AIN'T NO MYSTERY WHAT THAT FRANKLIN WANT. *HE DUN FOOLED ALL OF YUH PROPER!*
HE WANT EVERYTHIN', AN' HE WANT YUH TA PAY FOR IT. HE RECKONS YOU AIN'T GOT THE NERVE TA STOP 'IM!
DOWN WITH FRANKLIN!
TEAR DOWN FRANKLIN'S HOUSE!
AS OYSTER NAN STOOD BY HER TUB TO SHEW HER VICIOUS IN-CLA-NATIONS...

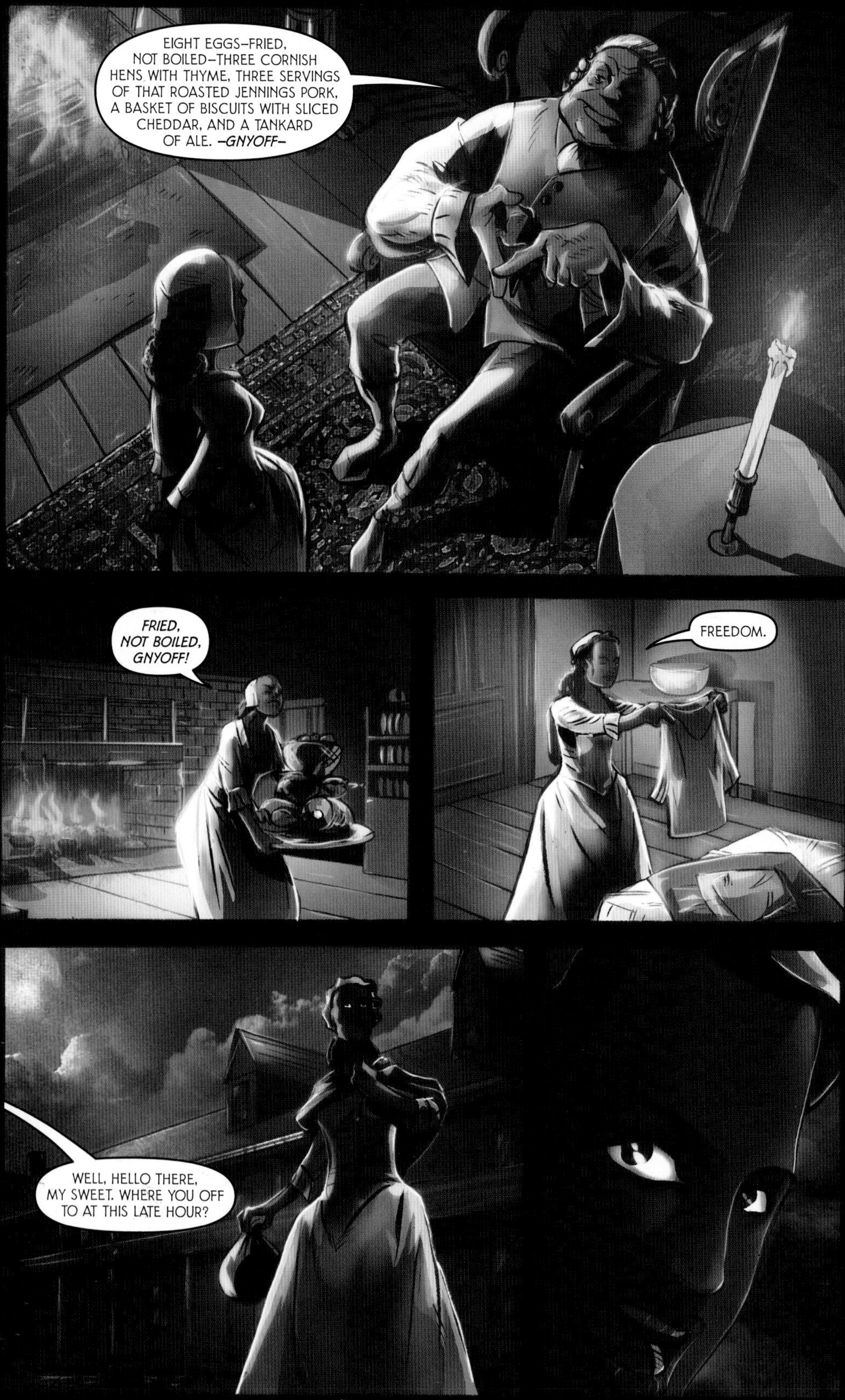
EIGHT EGGS–FRIED, NOT BOILED–THREE CORNISH HENS WITH THYME, THREE SERVINGS OF THAT ROASTED JENNINGS PORK, A BASKET OF BISCUITS WITH SLICED CHEDDAR, AND A TANKARD OF ALE. *–GNYOFF–*
FRIED, NOT BOILED, GNYOFF!
FREEDOM.
WELL, HELLO THERE, MY SWEET. WHERE YOU OFF TO AT THIS LATE HOUR?

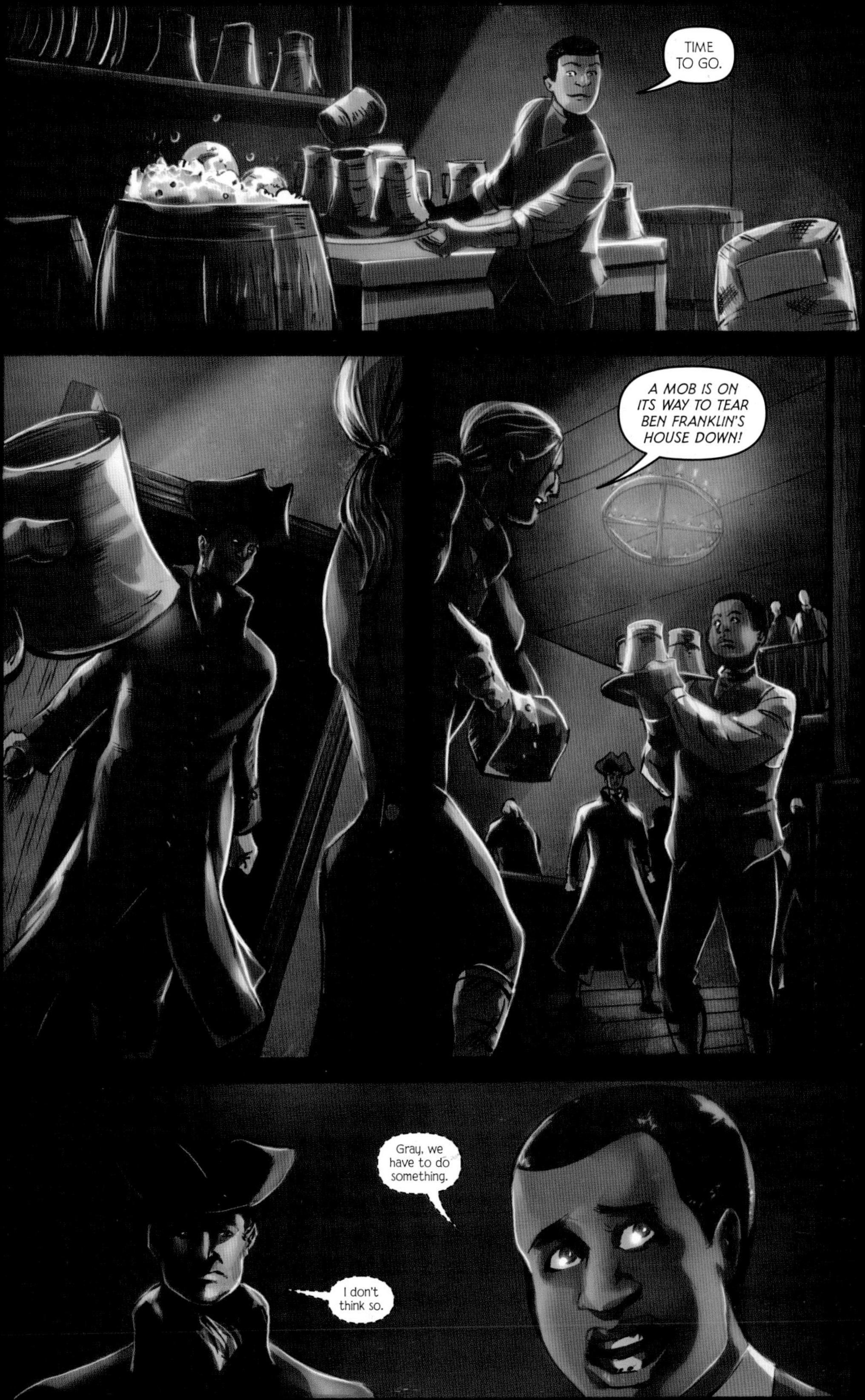
TIME TO GO.
A MOB IS ON ITS WAY TO TEAR BEN FRANKLIN'S HOUSE DOWN!
Gray, we have to do something.
I don't think so.

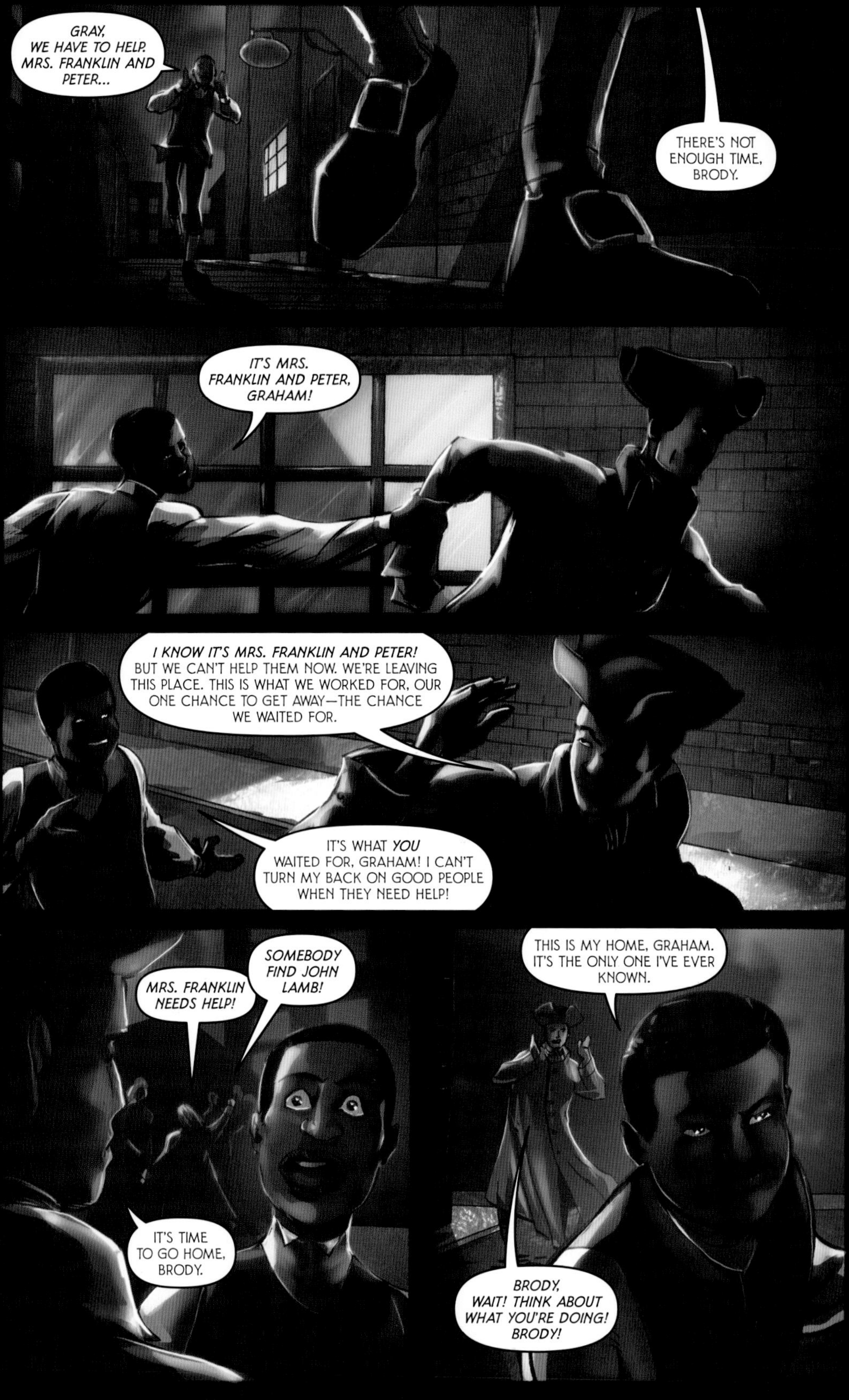
GRAY, WE HAVE TO HELP. MRS. FRANKLIN AND PETER...
THERE'S NOT ENOUGH TIME, BRODY.
IT'S MRS. FRANKLIN AND PETER, GRAHAM!
I KNOW IT'S MRS. FRANKLIN AND PETER! BUT WE CAN'T HELP THEM NOW. WE'RE LEAVING THIS PLACE. THIS IS WHAT WE WORKED FOR, OUR ONE CHANCE TO GET AWAY—THE CHANCE WE WAITED FOR.
IT'S WHAT YOU WAITED FOR, GRAHAM! I CAN'T TURN MY BACK ON GOOD PEOPLE WHEN THEY NEED HELP!
MRS. FRANKLIN NEEDS HELP!
SOMEBODY FIND JOHN LAMB!
IT'S TIME TO GO HOME, BRODY.
THIS IS MY HOME, GRAHAM. IT'S THE ONLY ONE I'VE EVER KNOWN.
BRODY, WAIT! THINK ABOUT WHAT YOU'RE DOING! BRODY!

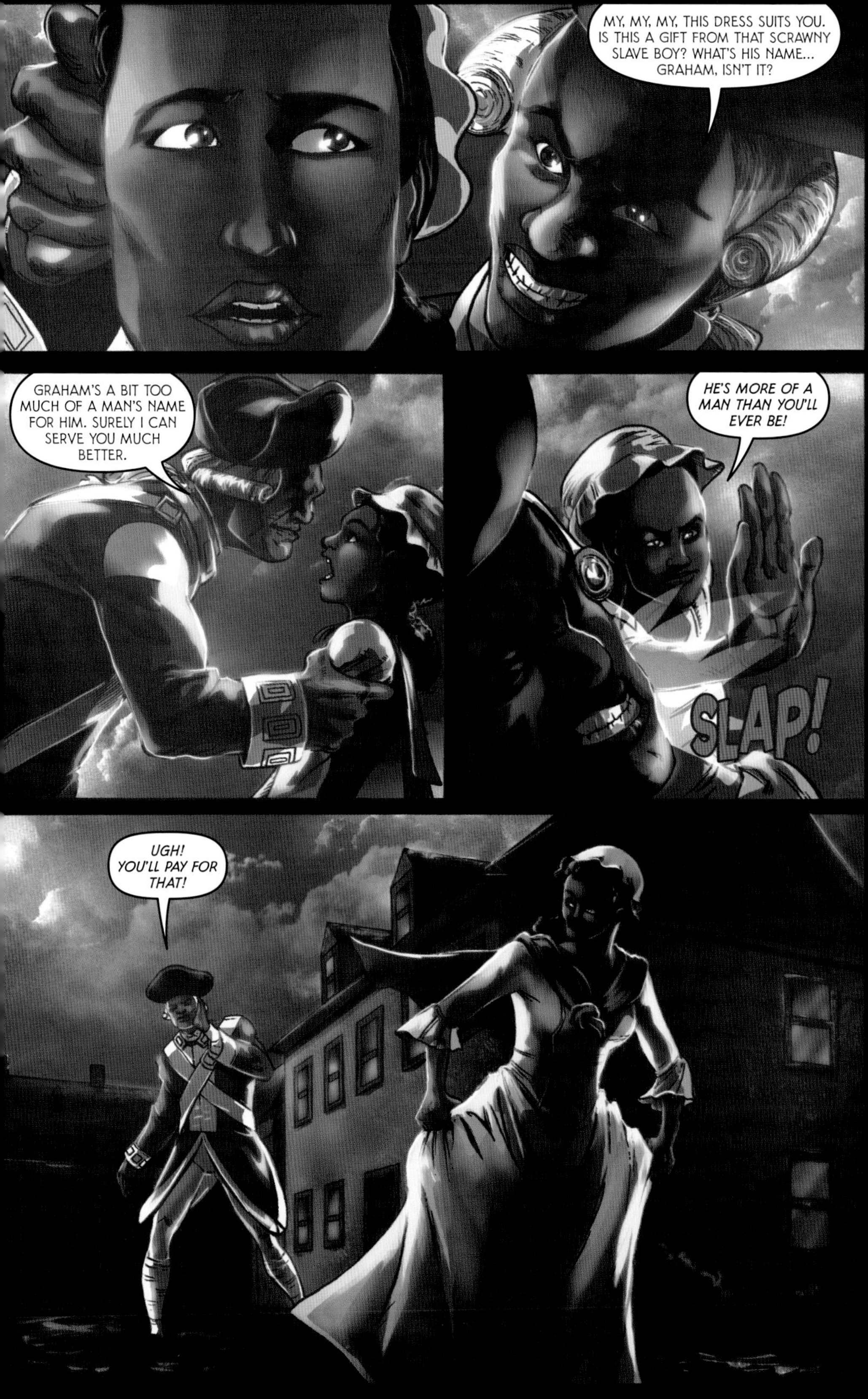
MY, MY, MY, THIS DRESS SUITS YOU. IS THIS A GIFT FROM THAT SCRAWNY SLAVE BOY? WHAT'S HIS NAME... GRAHAM, ISN'T IT?
GRAHAM'S A BIT TOO MUCH OF A MAN'S NAME FOR HIM. SURELY I CAN SERVE YOU MUCH BETTER.
HE'S MORE OF A MAN THAN YOU'LL EVER BE!
SLAP!
UGH! YOU'LL PAY FOR THAT!

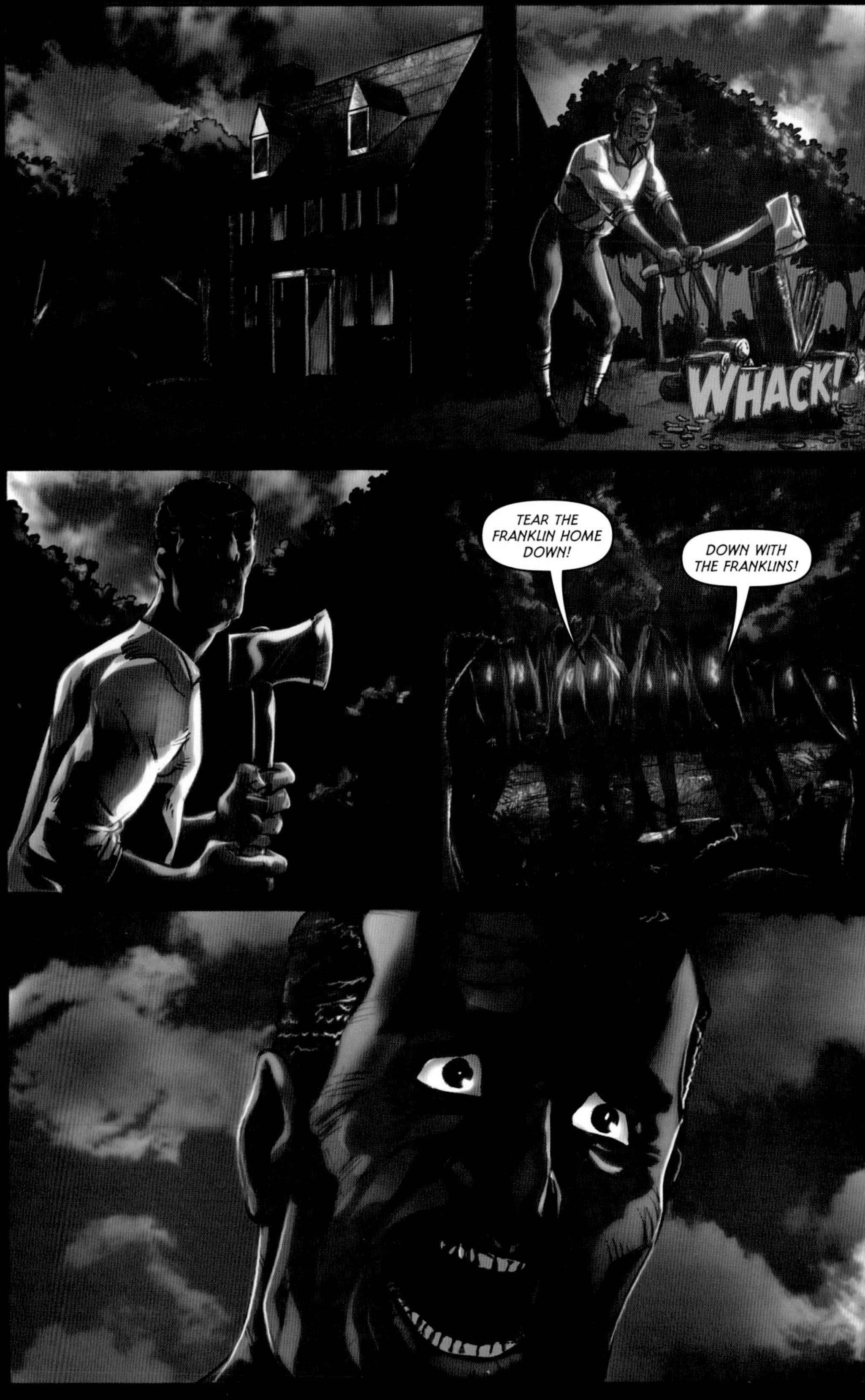
WHACK!
TEAR THE FRANKLIN HOME DOWN!
DOWN WITH THE FRANKLINS!

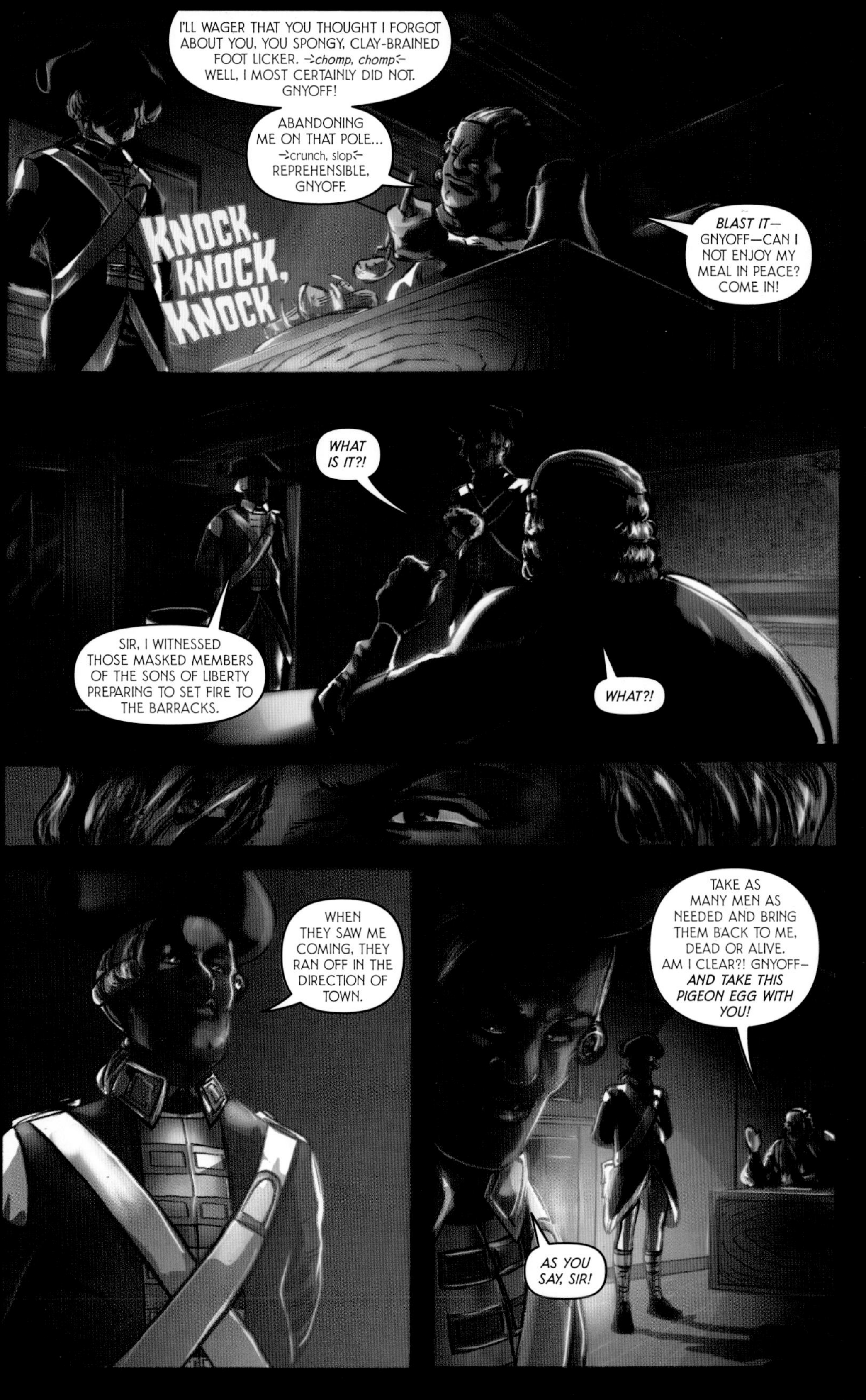
I'LL WAGER THAT YOU THOUGHT I FORGOT ABOUT YOU, YOU SPONGY, CLAY-BRAINED FOOT LICKER. ->chomp, chomp<- WELL, I MOST CERTAINLY DID NOT. GNYOFF!
ABANDONING ME ON THAT POLE... ->crunch, slop<- REPREHENSIBLE, GNYOFF.
KNOCK, KNOCK, KNOCK
BLAST IT— GNYOFF—CAN I NOT ENJOY MY MEAL IN PEACE? COME IN!
WHAT IS IT?!
SIR, I WITNESSED THOSE MASKED MEMBERS OF THE SONS OF LIBERTY PREPARING TO SET FIRE TO THE BARRACKS.
WHAT?!
WHEN THEY SAW ME COMING, THEY RAN OFF IN THE DIRECTION OF TOWN.
TAKE AS MANY MEN AS NEEDED AND BRING THEM BACK TO ME, DEAD OR ALIVE. AM I CLEAR?! GNYOFF— AND TAKE THIS PIGEON EGG WITH YOU!
AS YOU SAY, SIR!

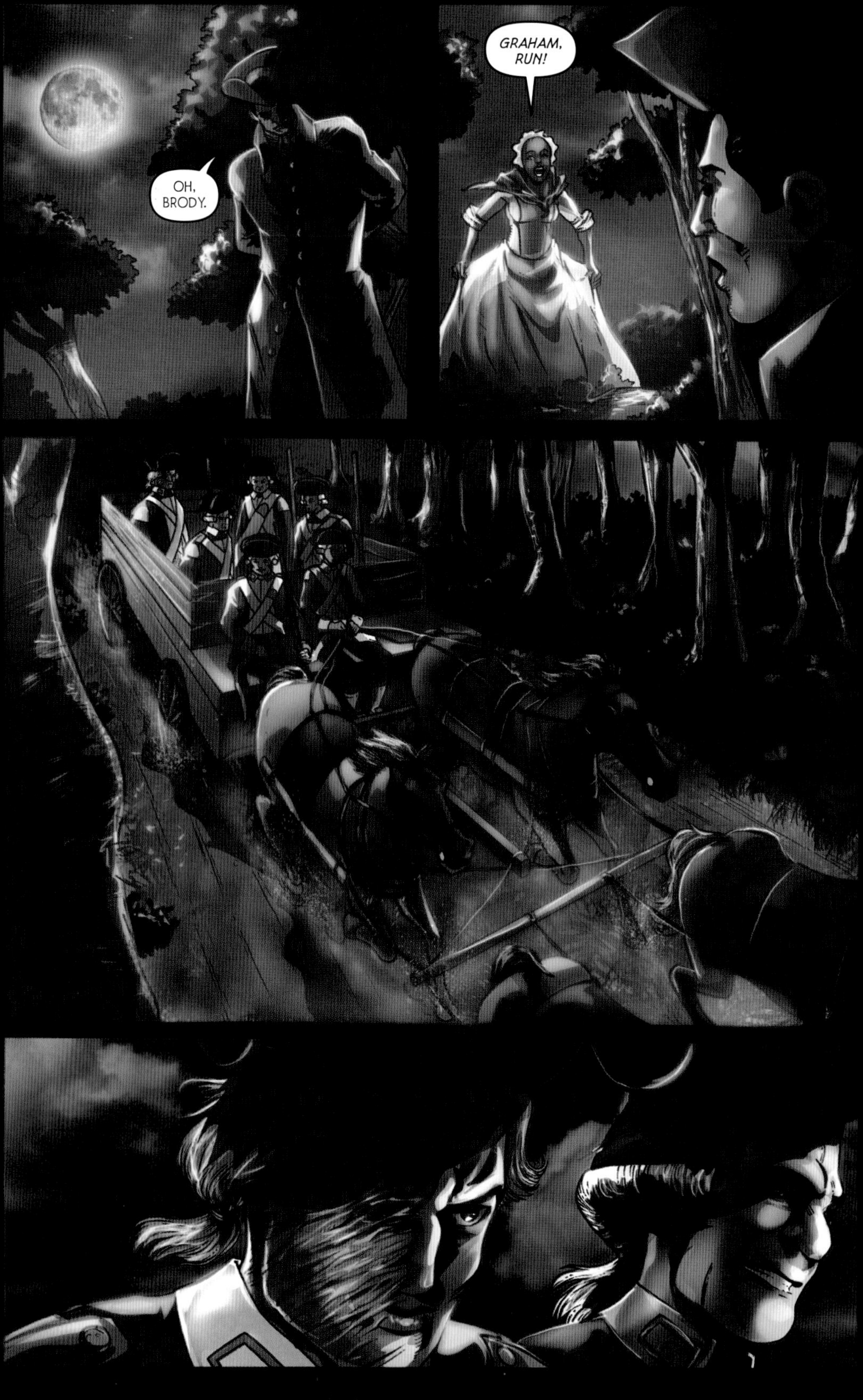
OH, BRODY.
GRAHAM, RUN!

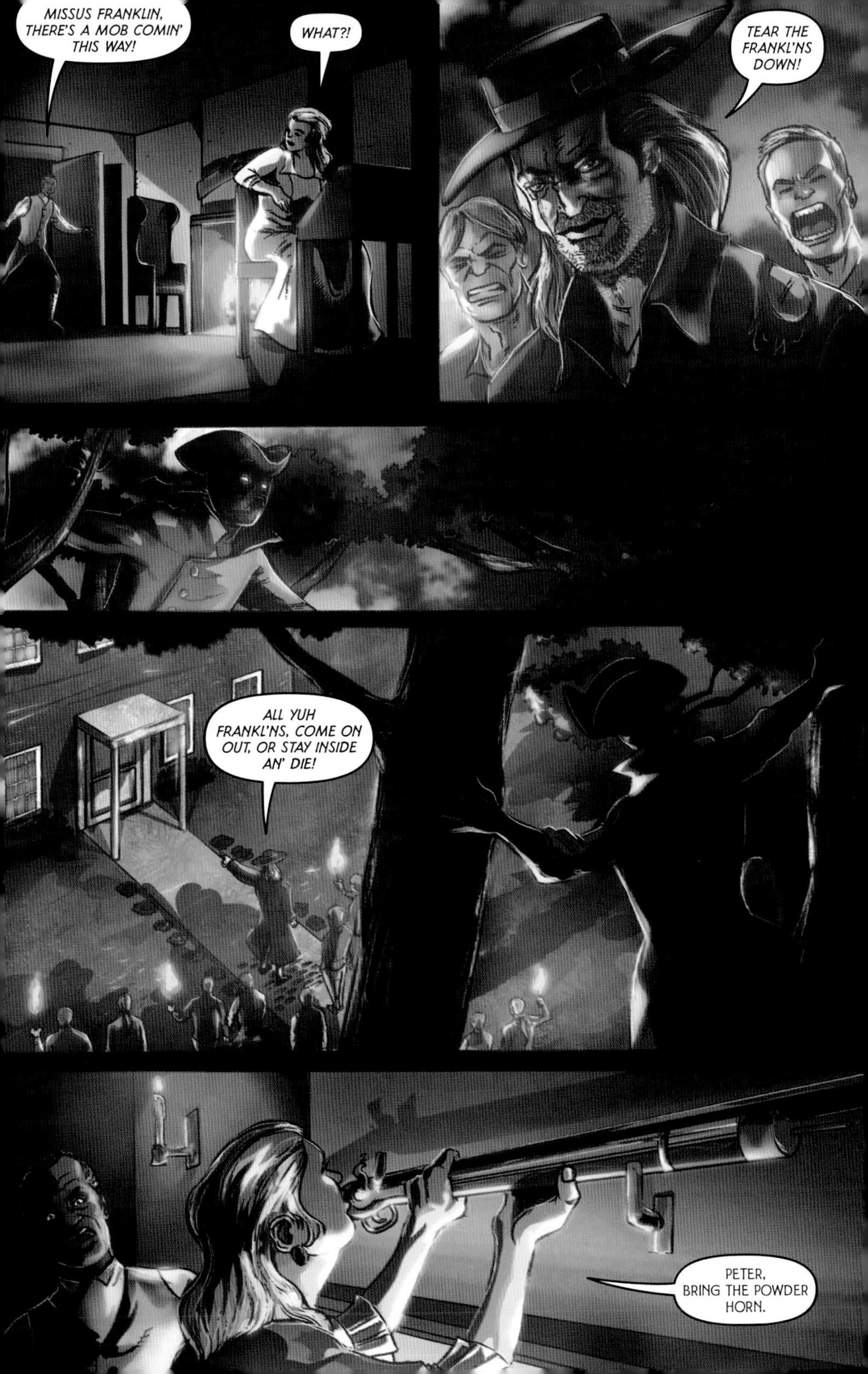
MISSUS FRANKLIN, THERE'S A MOB COMIN' THIS WAY!
WHAT?!
TEAR THE FRANKL'NS DOWN!
ALL YUH FRANKL'NS, COME ON OUT, OR STAY INSIDE AN' DIE!
PETER, BRING THE POWDER HORN.

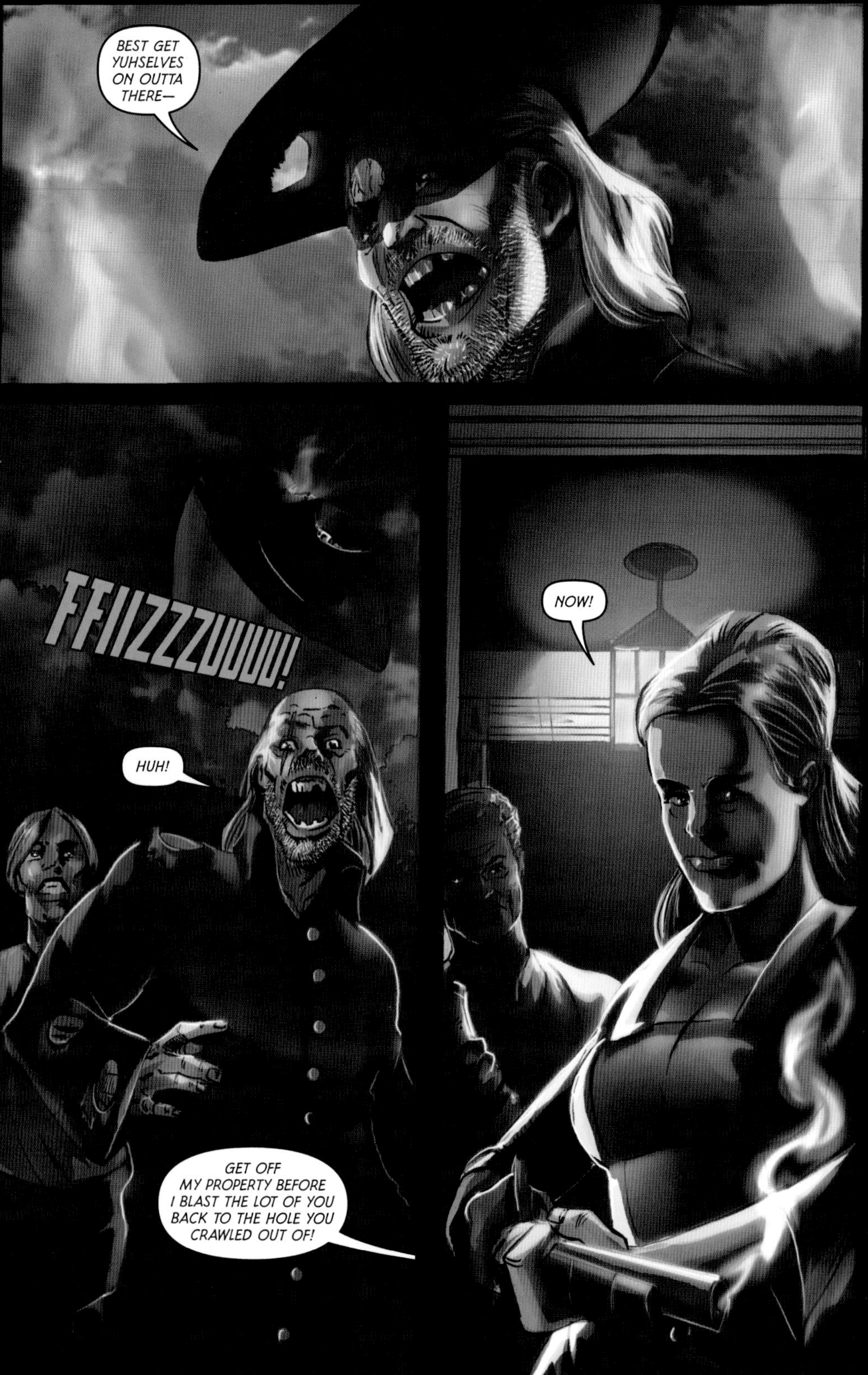
BEST GET YUHSELVES ON OUTTA THERE—
FFIIZZZUUUU!
HUH!
NOW!
GET OFF MY PROPERTY BEFORE I BLAST THE LOT OF YOU BACK TO THE HOLE YOU CRAWLED OUT OF!

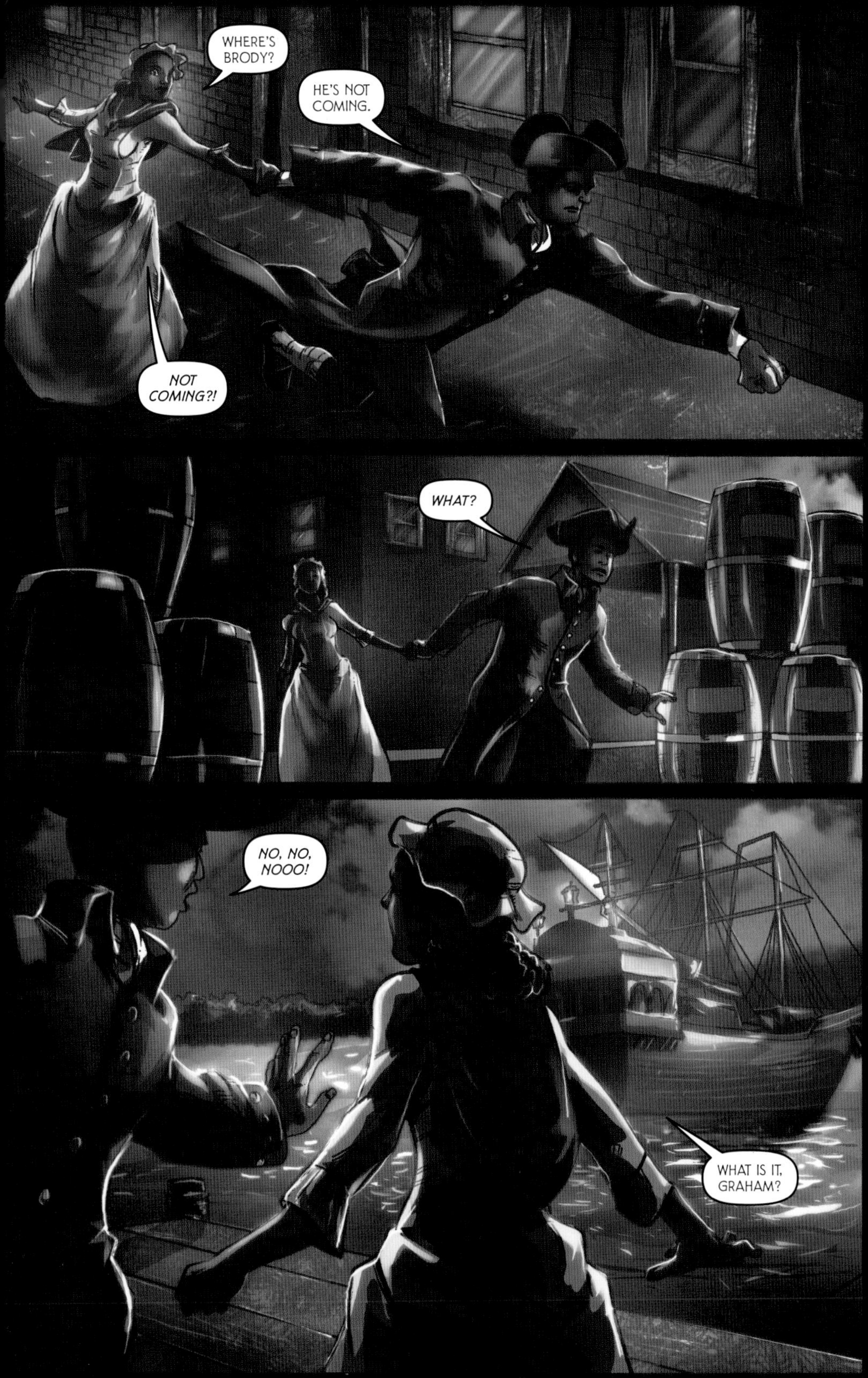
WHERE'S BRODY?
HE'S NOT COMING.
NOT COMING?!
WHAT?
NO, NO, NOOO!
WHAT IS IT, GRAHAM?

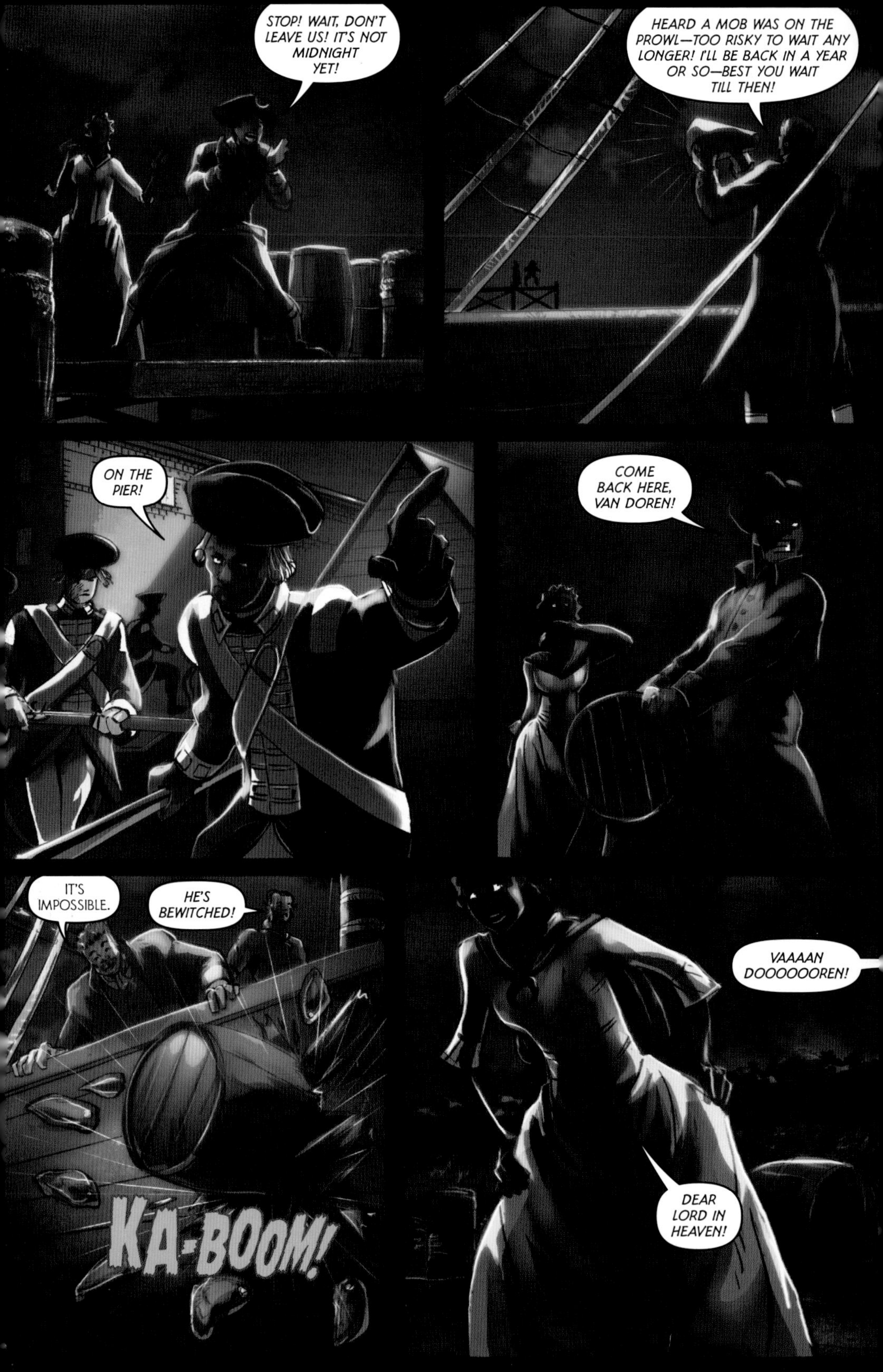
STOP! WAIT, DON'T LEAVE US! IT'S NOT MIDNIGHT YET!
HEARD A MOB WAS ON THE PROWL—TOO RISKY TO WAIT ANY LONGER! I'LL BE BACK IN A YEAR OR SO—BEST YOU WAIT TILL THEN!
ON THE PIER!
COME BACK HERE, VAN DOREN!
IT'S IMPOSSIBLE.
HE'S BEWITCHED!
KA-BOOM!
VAAAAN DOOOOOOREN!
DEAR LORD IN HEAVEN!

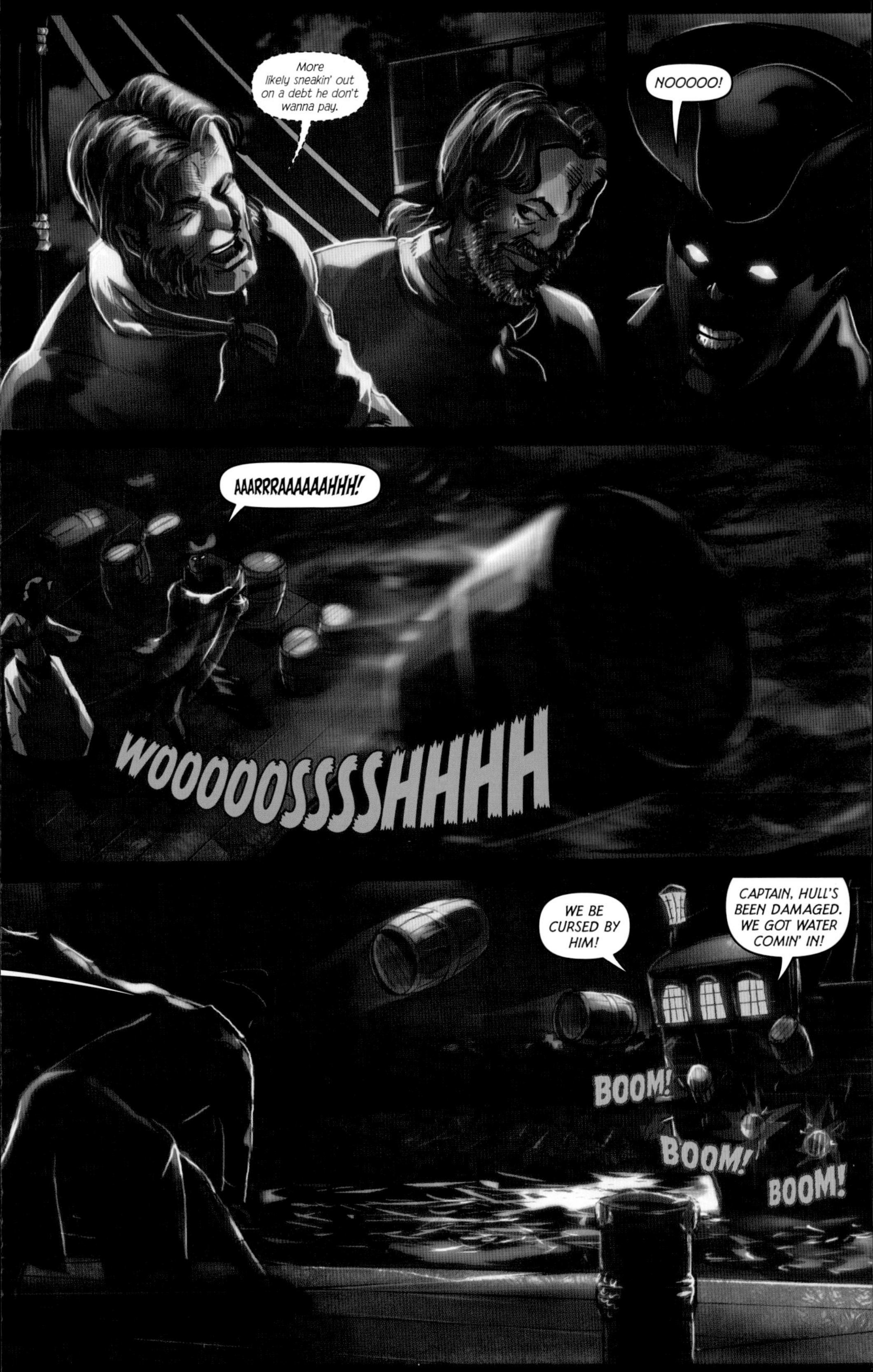
More likely sneakin' out on a debt he don't wanna pay.
NOOOOO!
AAARRRAAAAAAHHH!
WOOOOOOSSSSHHHH
WE BE CURSED BY HIM!
CAPTAIN, HULL'S BEEN DAMAGED. WE GOT WATER COMIN' IN!
BOOM!
BOOM!
BOOM!

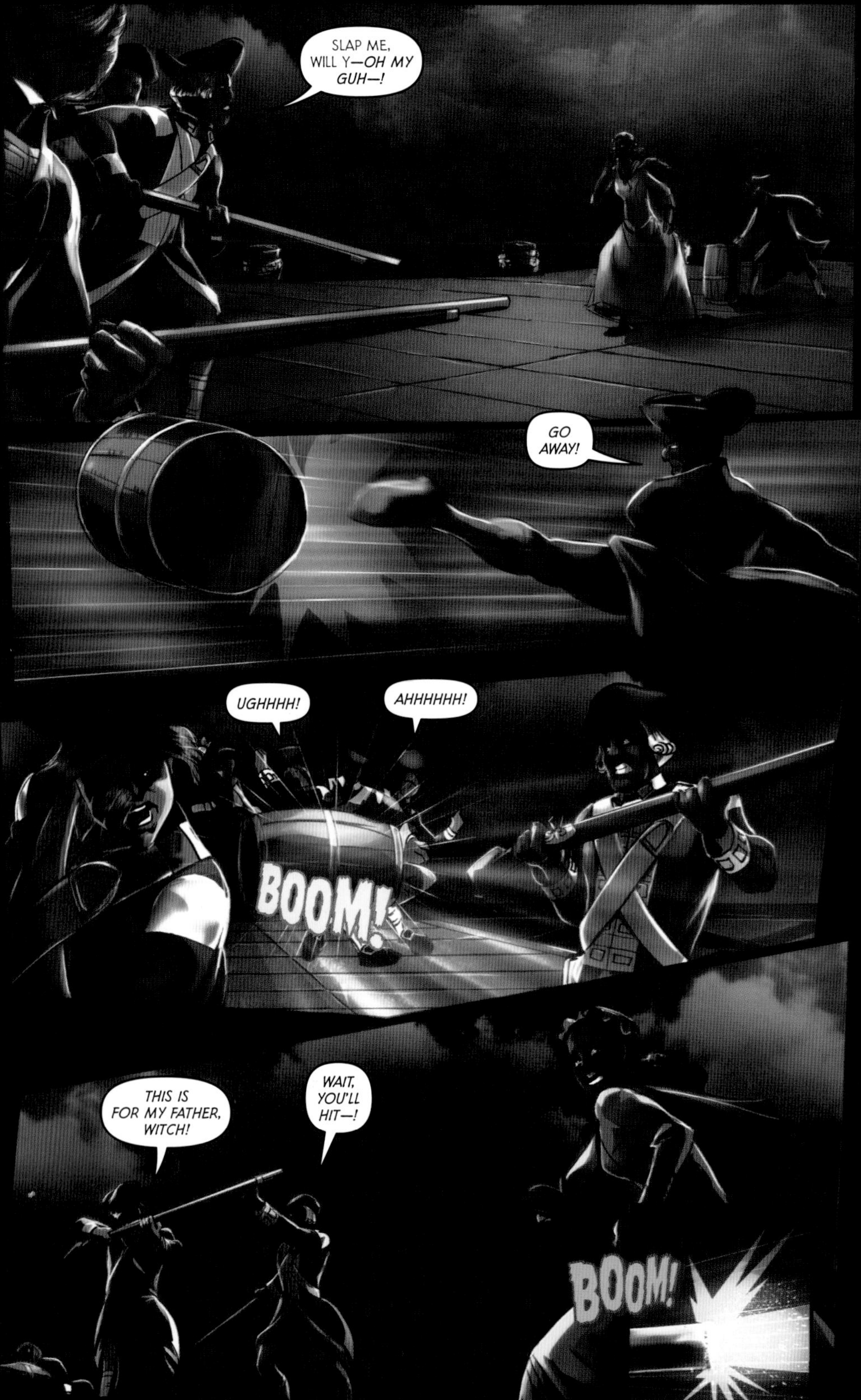
SLAP ME, WILL Y—OH MY GUH—!
GO AWAY!
UGHHHH!
AHHHHHH!
BOOM!
THIS IS FOR MY FATHER, WITCH!
WAIT, YOU'LL HIT—!
BOOM!

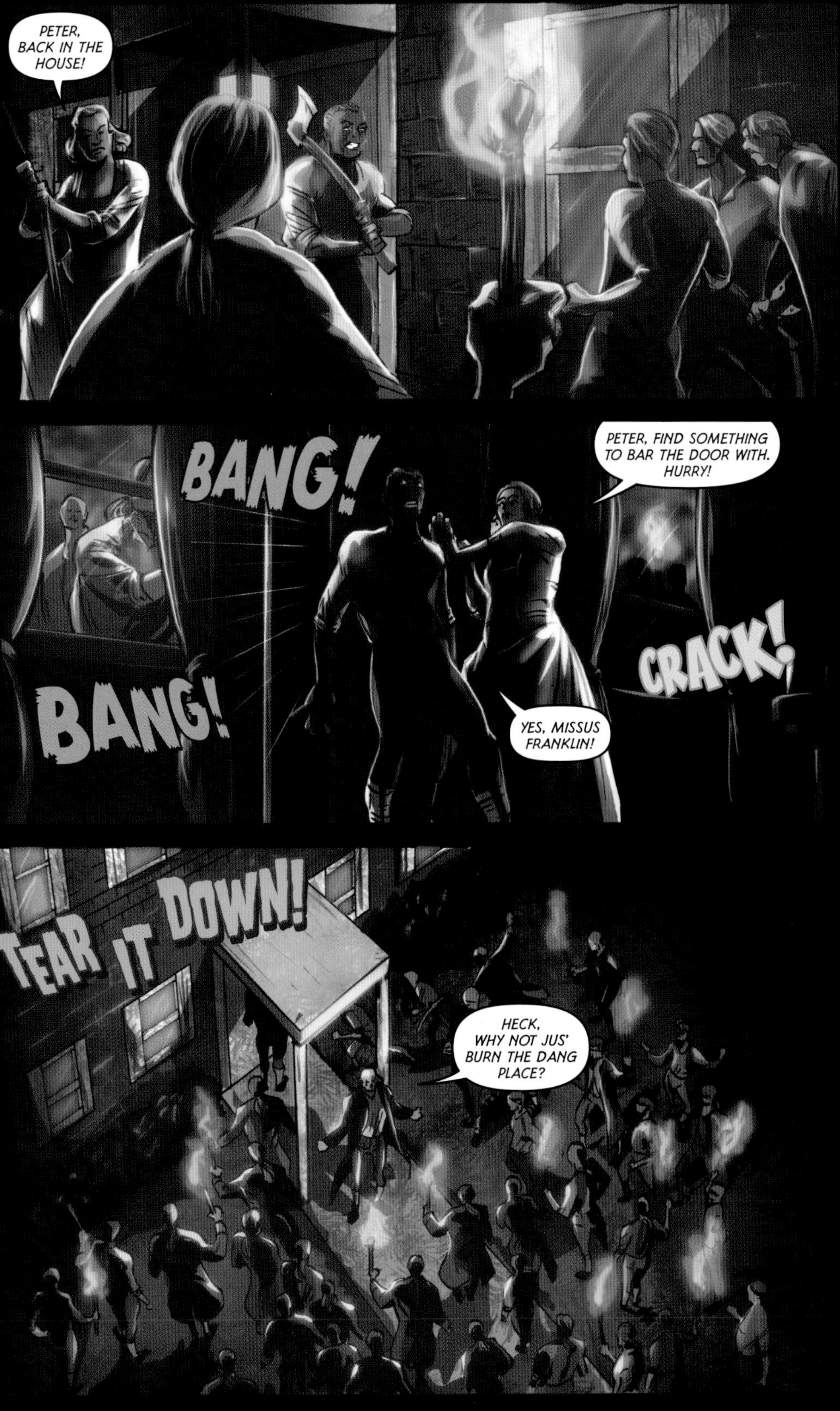
PETER, BACK IN THE HOUSE!
BANG!
PETER, FIND SOMETHING TO BAR THE DOOR WITH. HURRY!
BANG!
YES, MISSUS FRANKLIN!
CRACK!
TEAR IT DOWN!
HECK, WHY NOT JUS' BURN THE DANG PLACE?

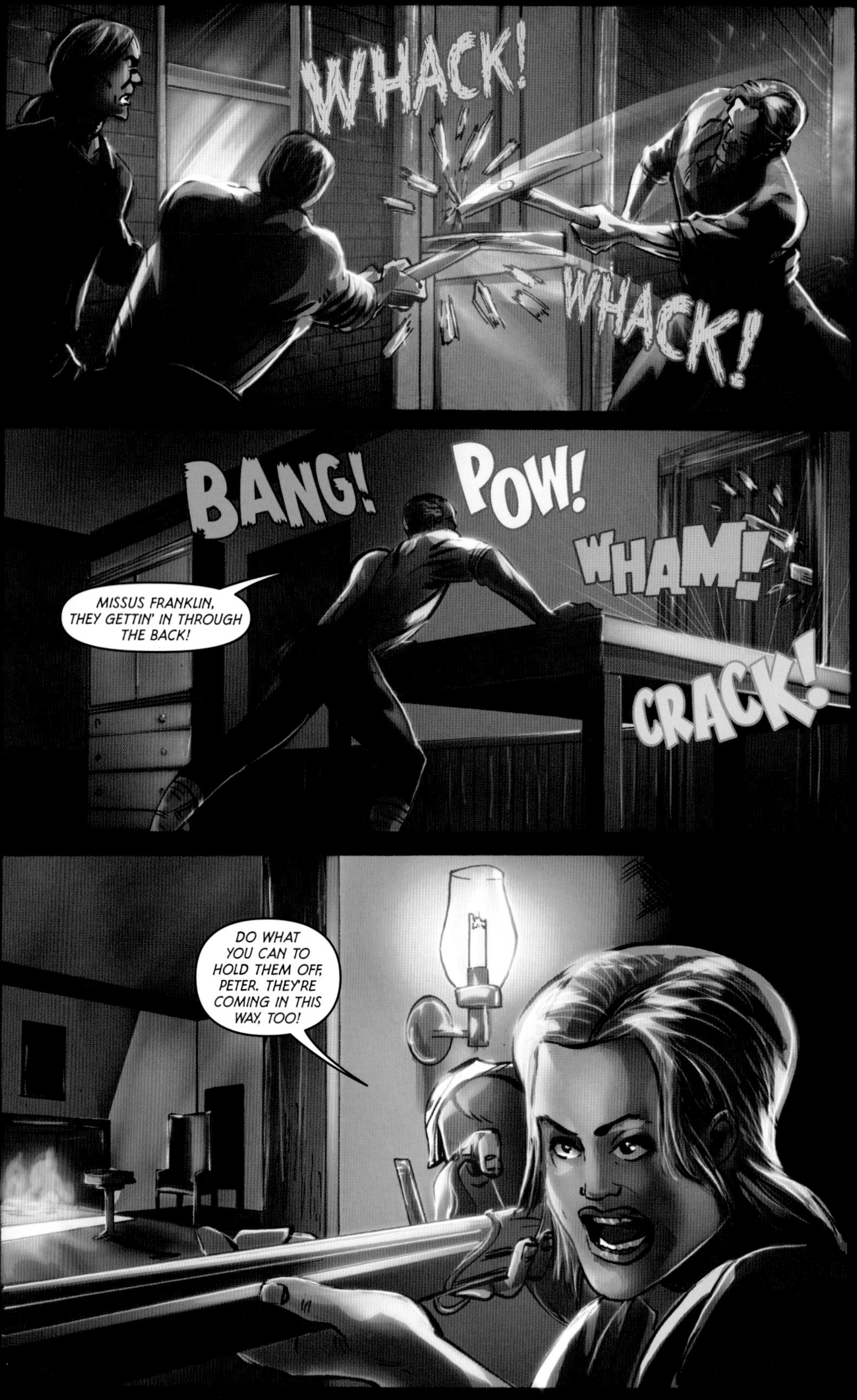
WHACK!
WHACK!
BANG!
POW!
WHAM!
MISSUS FRANKLIN, THEY GETTIN' IN THROUGH THE BACK!
CRACK!
DO WHAT YOU CAN TO HOLD THEM OFF, PETER. THEY'RE COMING IN THIS WAY, TOO!

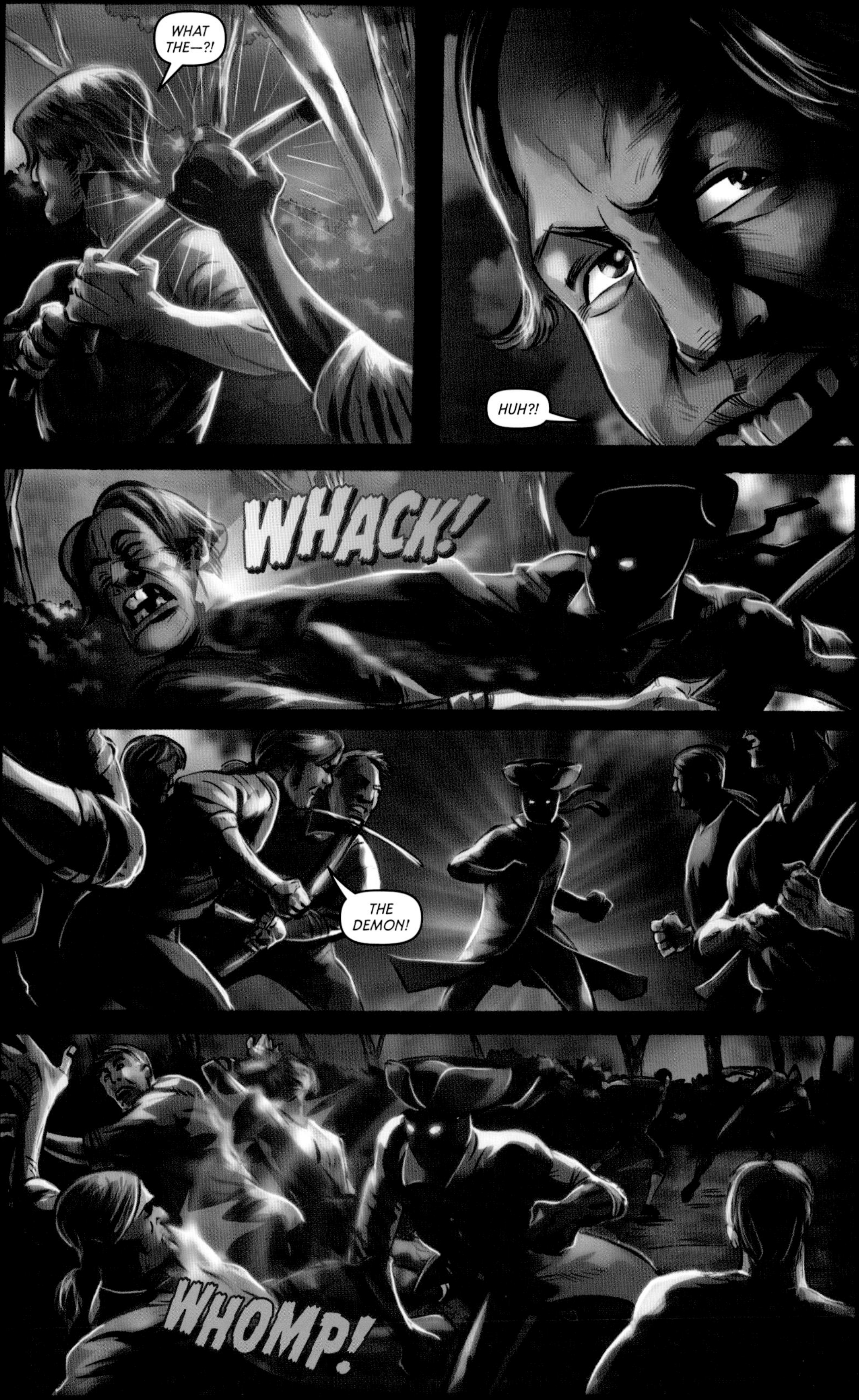
WHAT THE—?!
HUH?!
WHACK!
THE DEMON!
WHOMP!

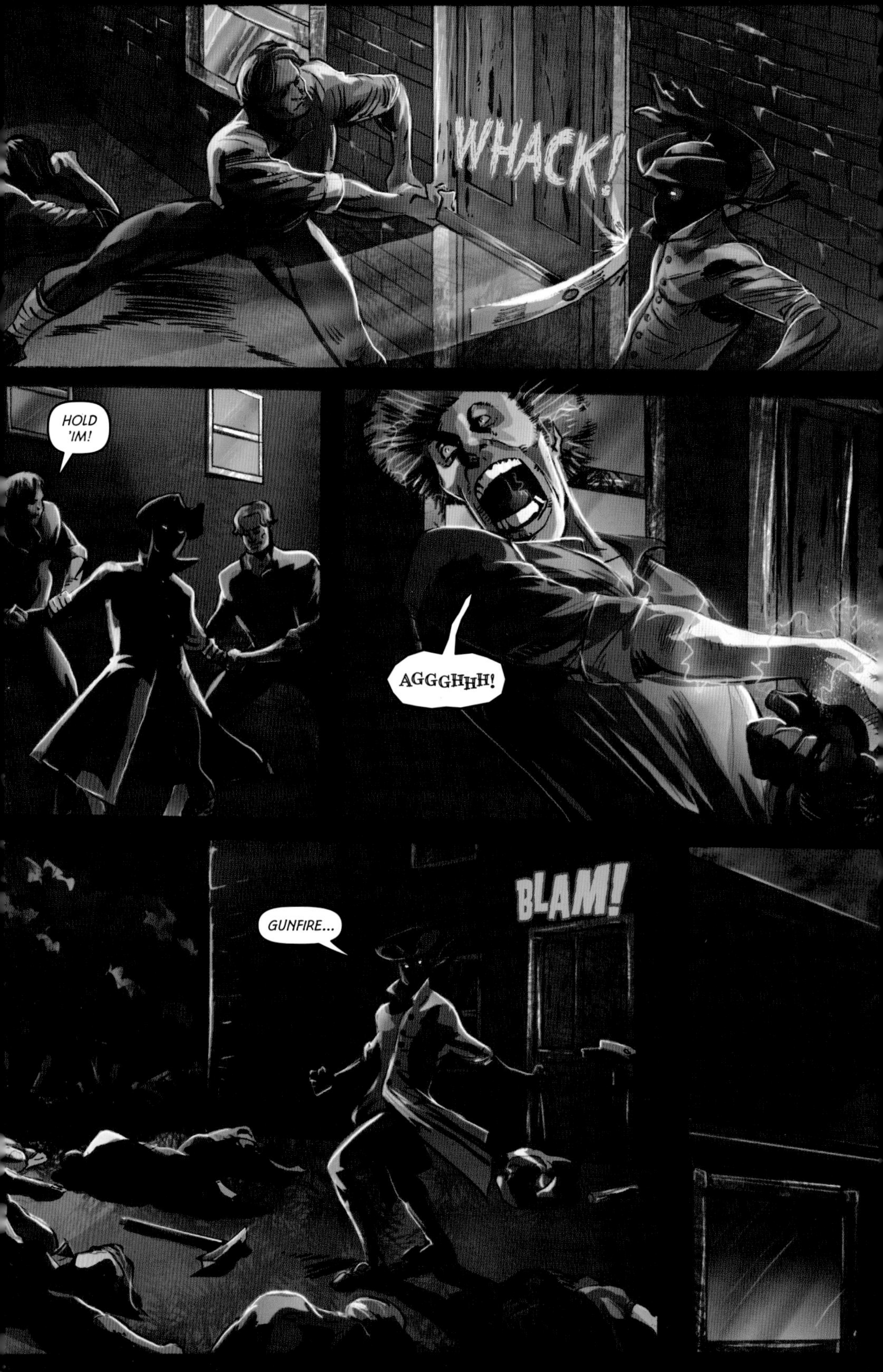
WHACK!
HOLD 'IM!
AGGGHHH!
GUNFIRE...
BLAM!

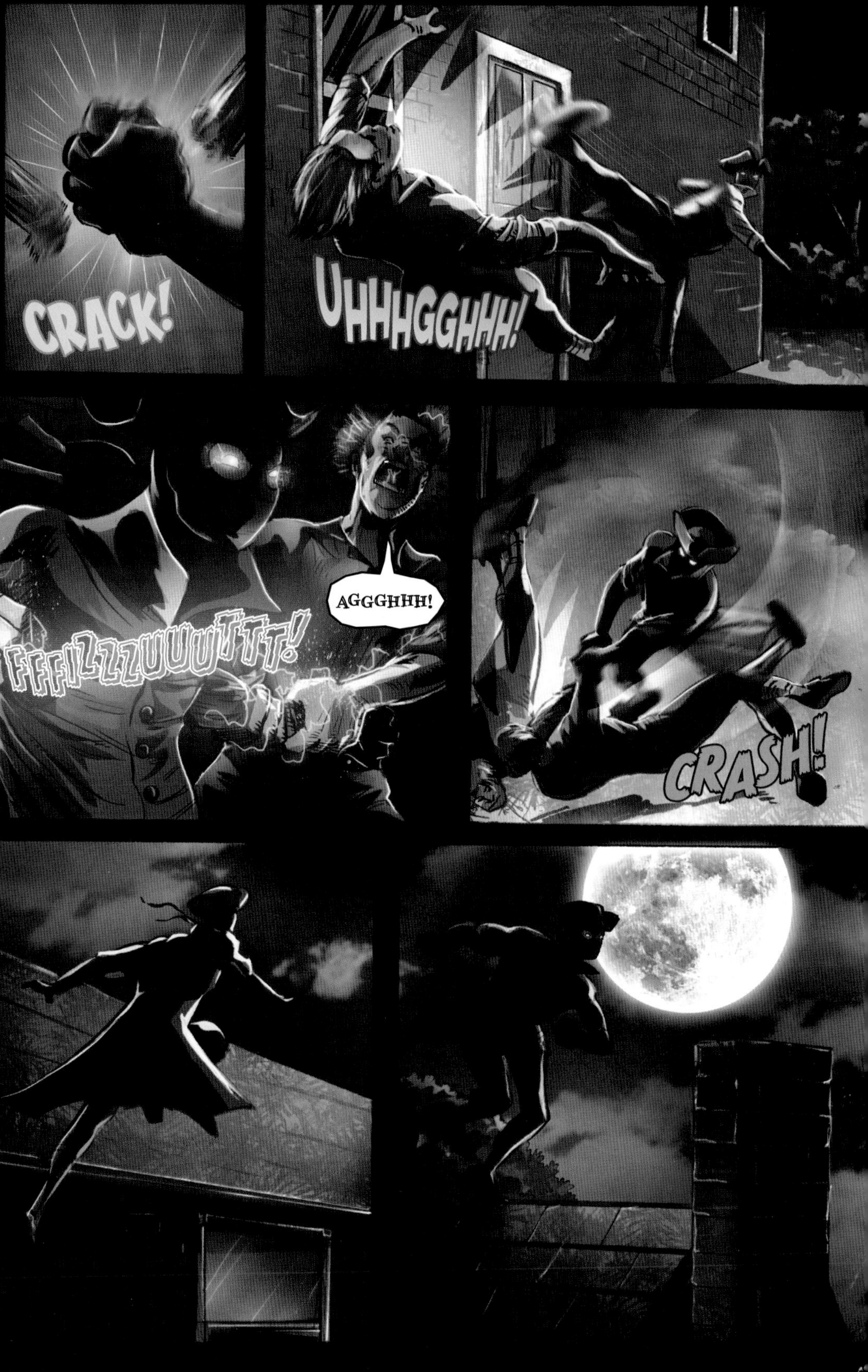
CRACK!
UHHHGGHHH!
AGGGHHH!
FFFIZZZZUUUTTT!
CRASH!

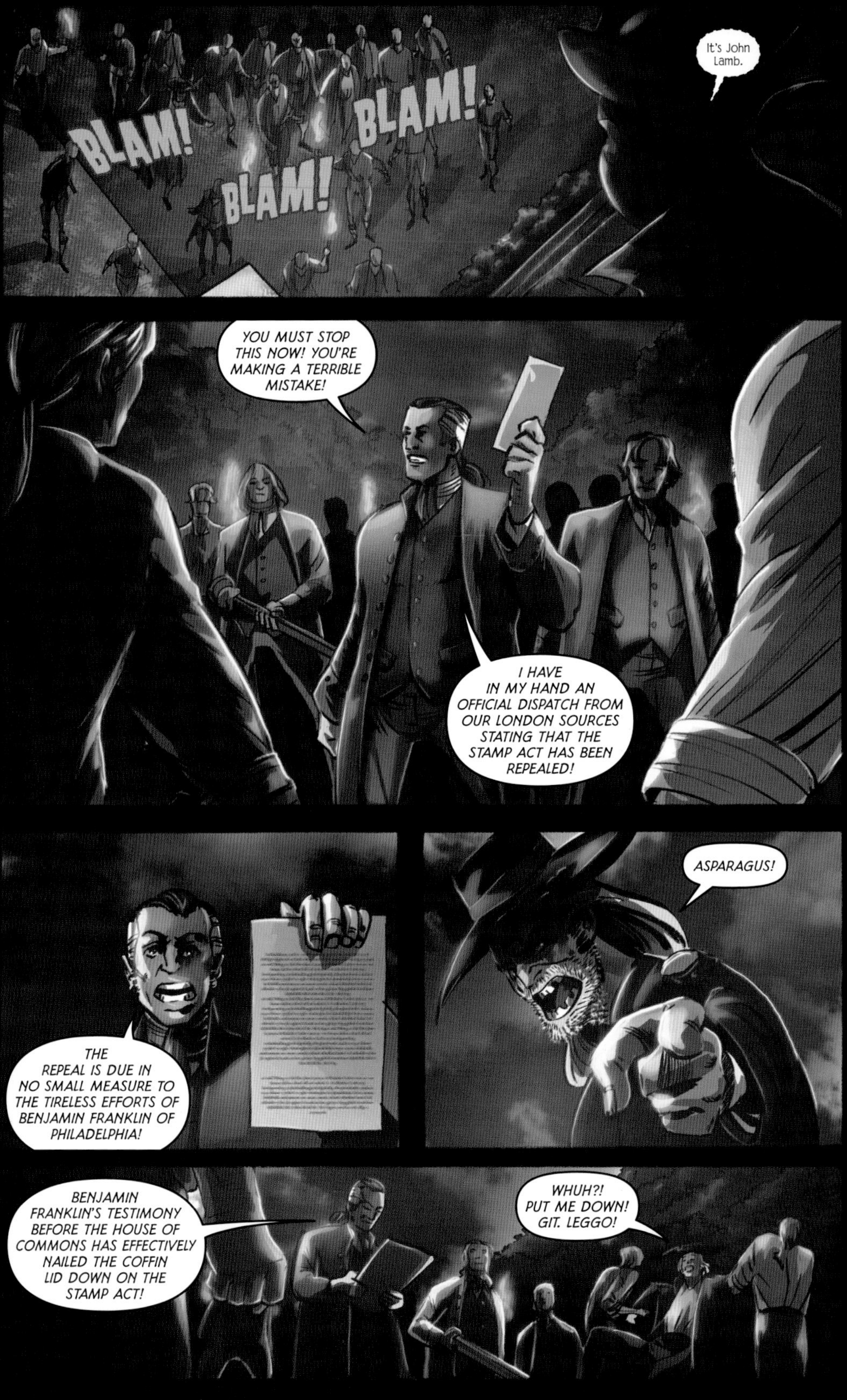
BLAM!
BLAM!
BLAM!
It's John Lamb.
YOU MUST STOP THIS NOW! YOU'RE MAKING A TERRIBLE MISTAKE!
I HAVE IN MY HAND AN OFFICIAL DISPATCH FROM OUR LONDON SOURCES STATING THAT THE STAMP ACT HAS BEEN REPEALED!
THE REPEAL IS DUE IN NO SMALL MEASURE TO THE TIRELESS EFFORTS OF BENJAMIN FRANKLIN OF PHILADELPHIA!
ASPARAGUS!
BENJAMIN FRANKLIN'S TESTIMONY BEFORE THE HOUSE OF COMMONS HAS EFFECTIVELY NAILED THE COFFIN LID DOWN ON THE STAMP ACT!
WHUH?! PUT ME DOWN! GIT. LEGGO!

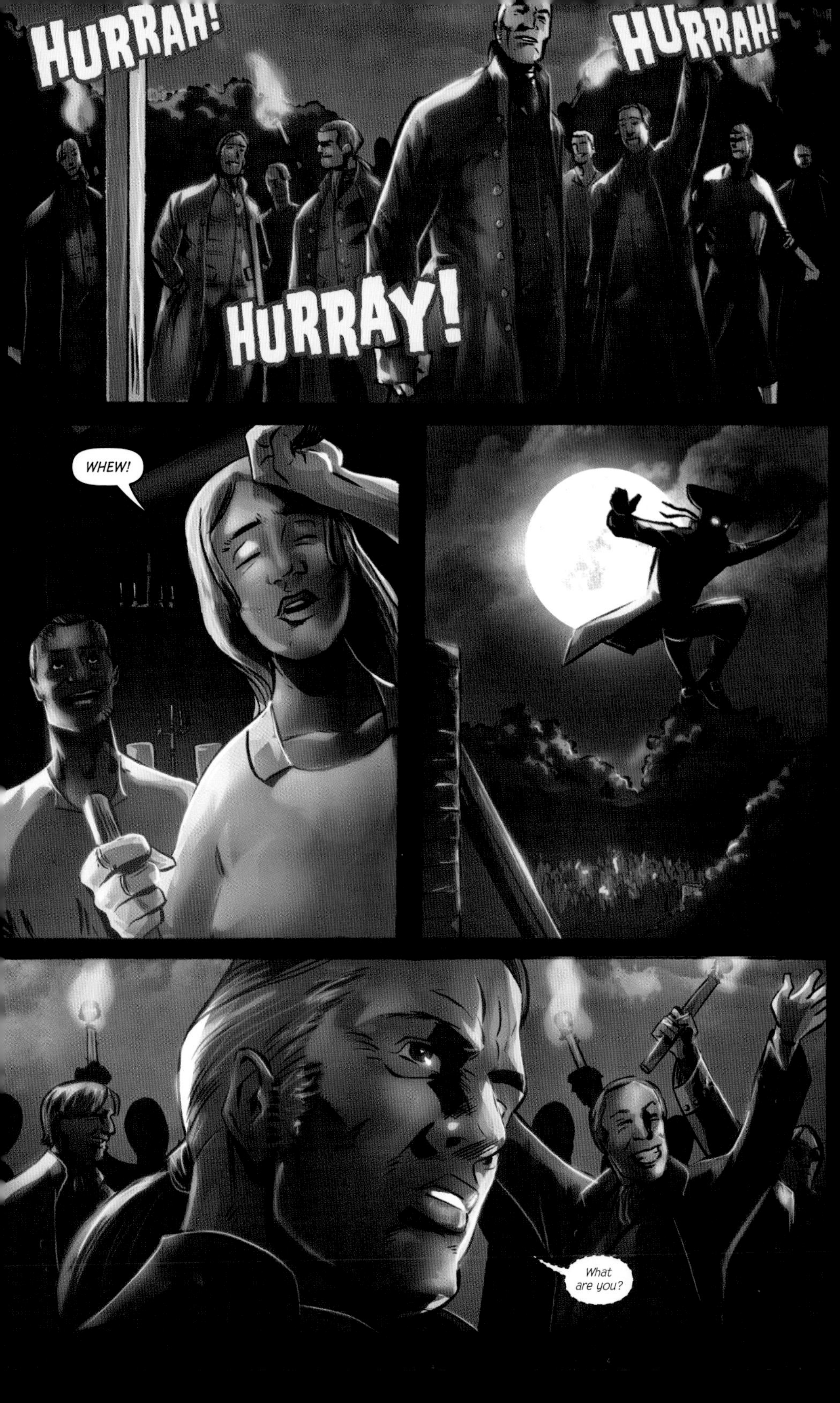
HURRAH!
HURRAH!
HURRAY!
WHEW!
What are you?

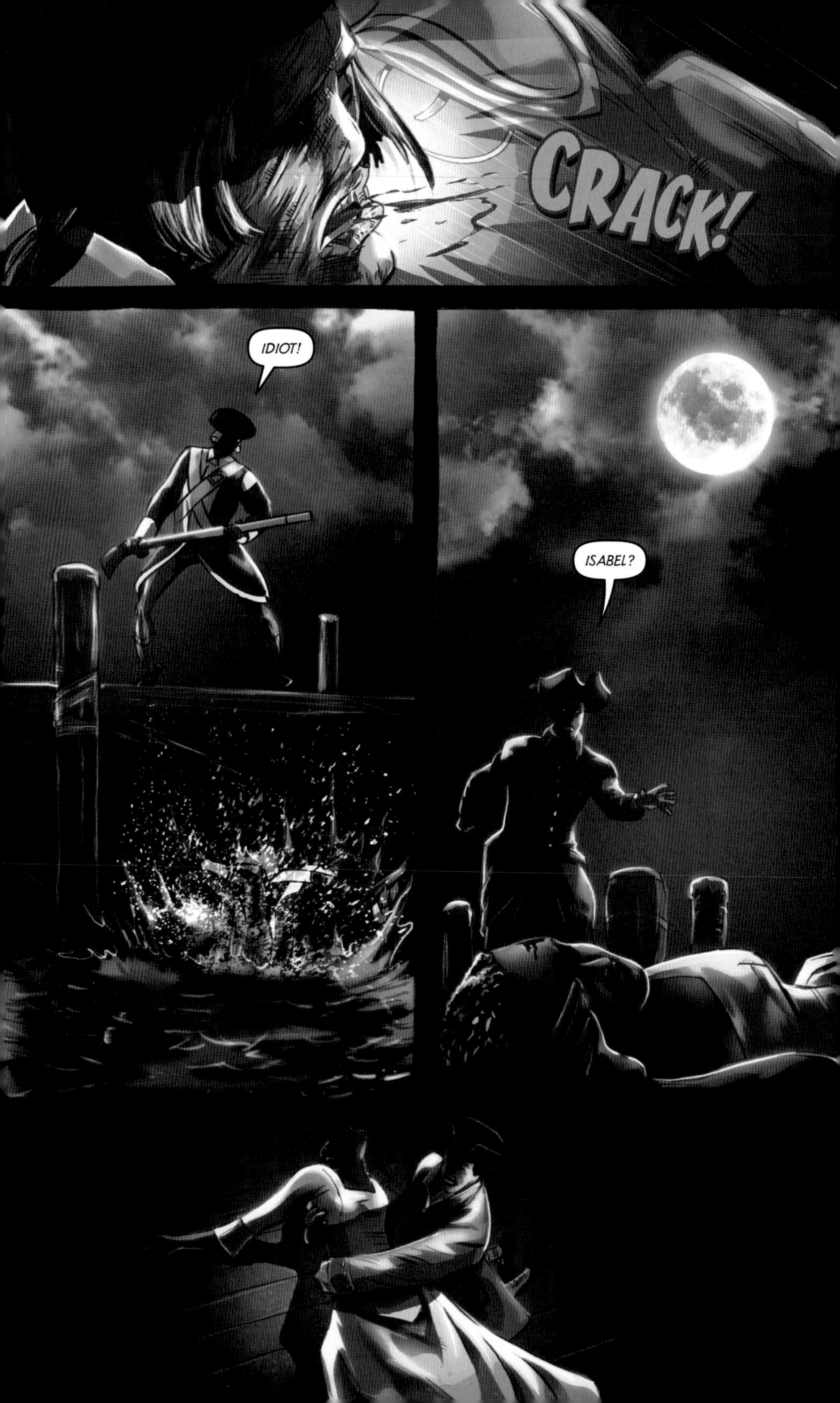
CRACK!
IDIOT!
ISABEL?

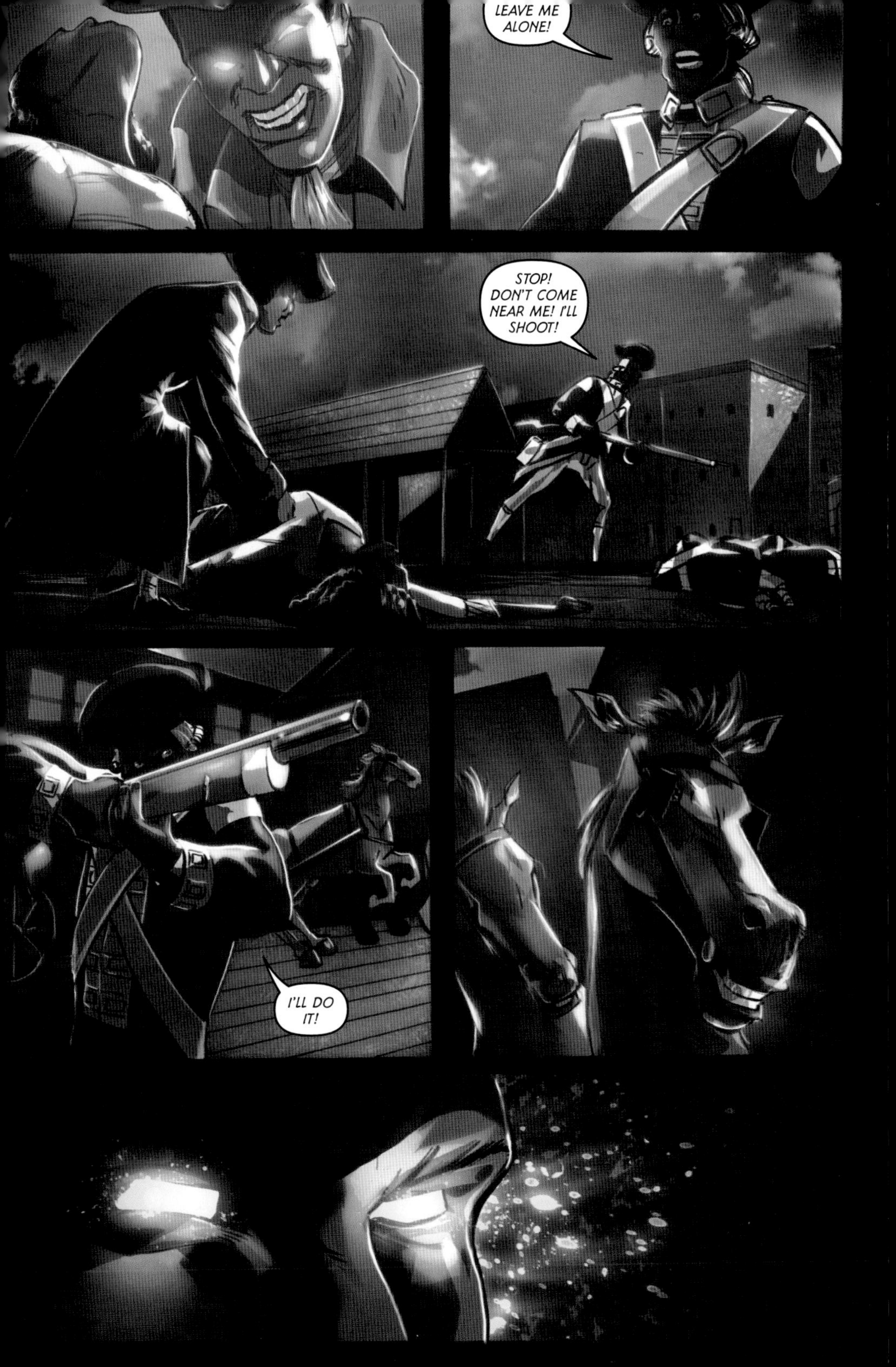
LEAVE ME ALONE!
STOP! DON'T COME NEAR ME! I'LL SHOOT!
I'LL DO IT!

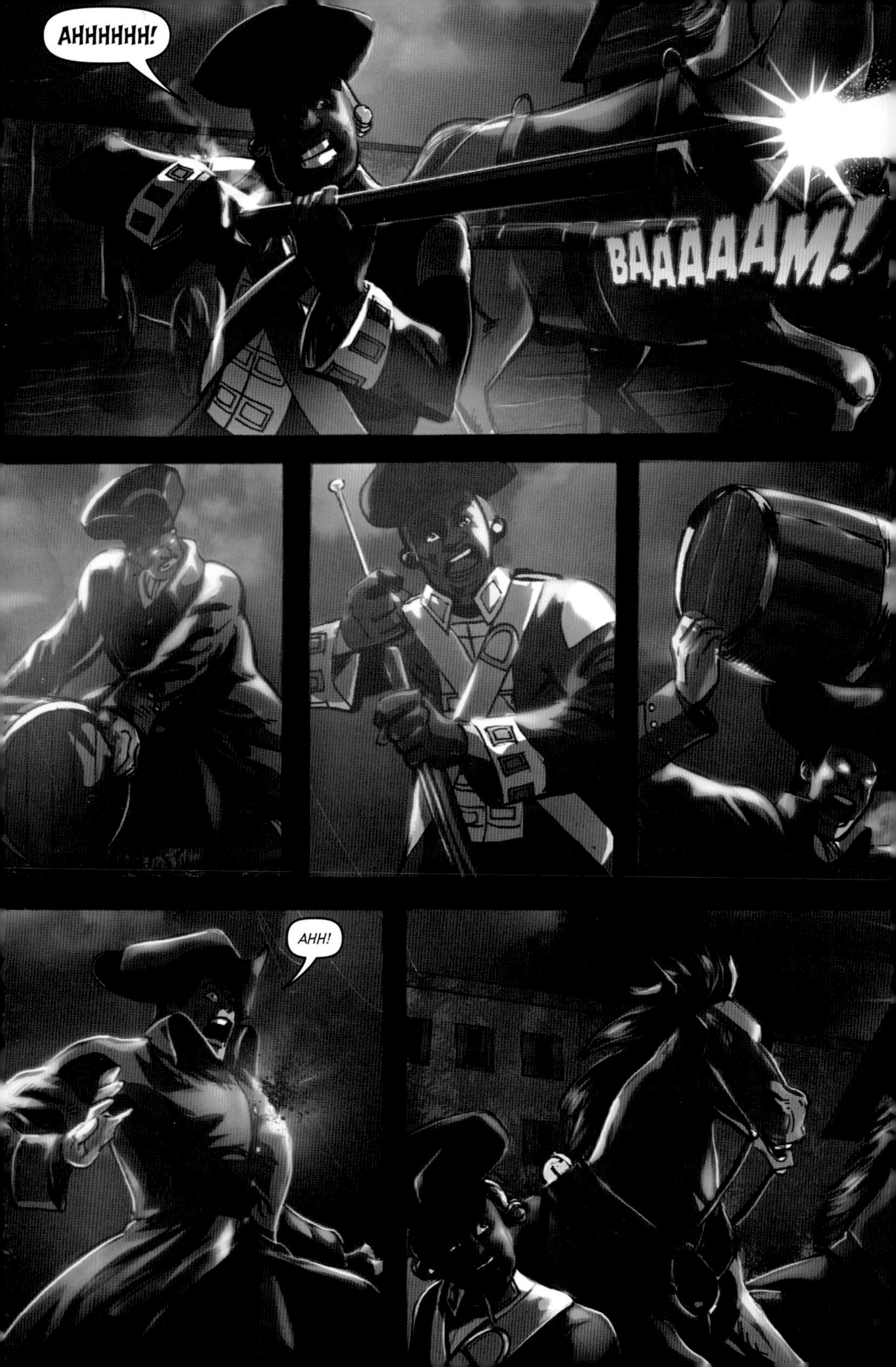
AHHHHHH!
BAAAAAM!
AHH!

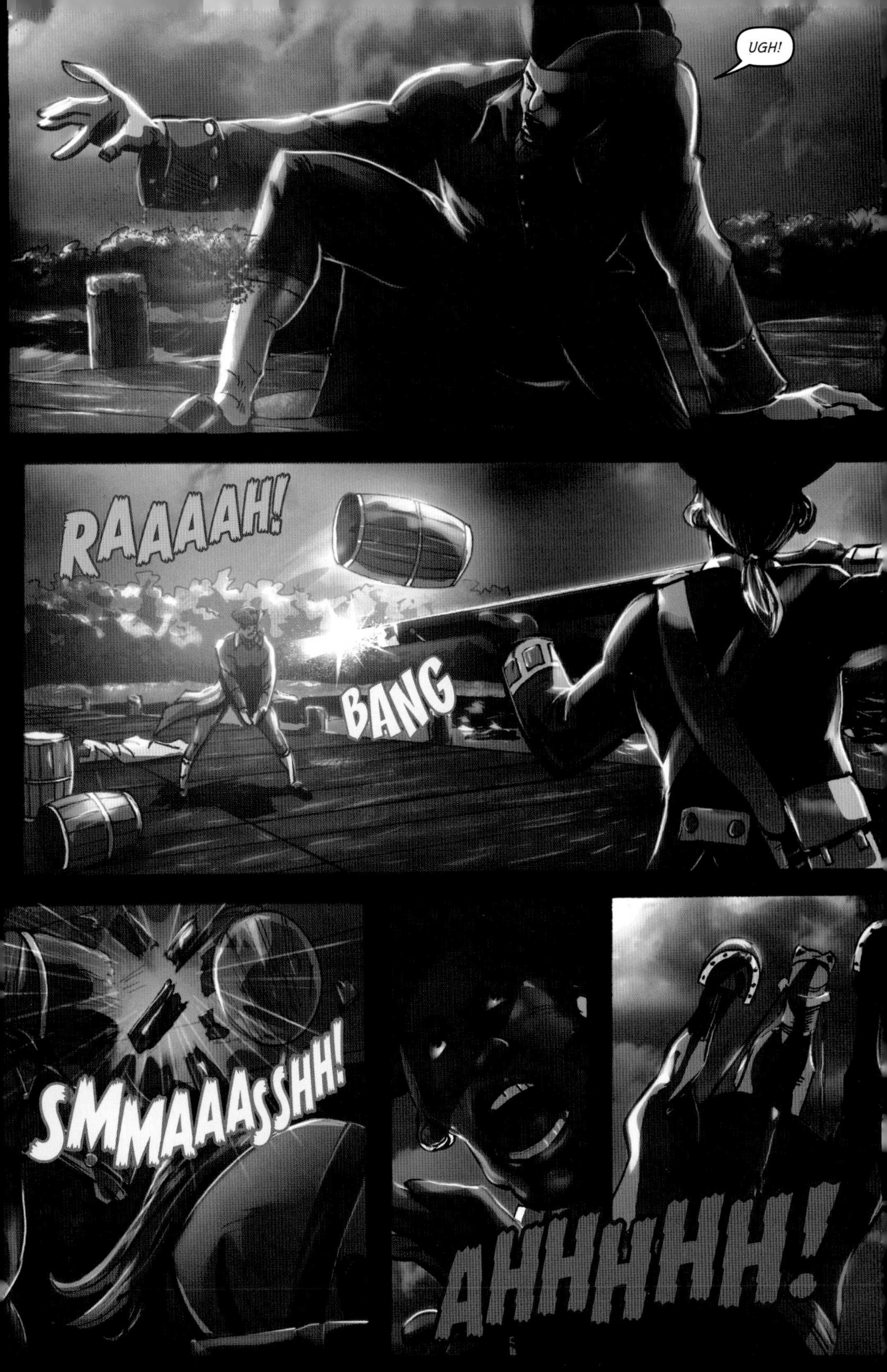
UGH!
RAAAAH!
BANG
SMMAAASSHH!
AHHHHHH!

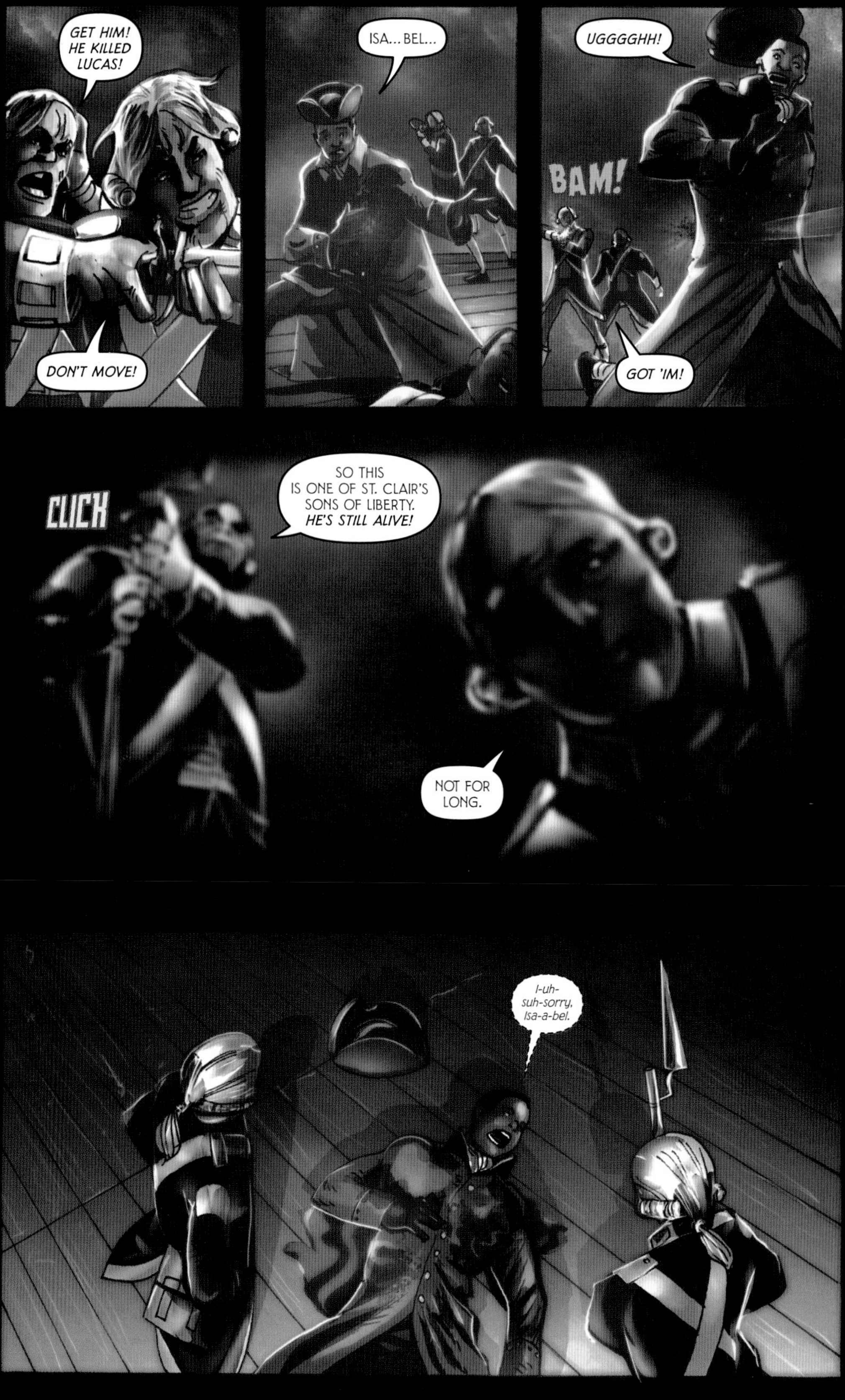
GET HIM! HE KILLED LUCAS!
DON'T MOVE!
ISA...BEL...
UGGGGHH!
BAM!
GOT 'IM!
CLICK
SO THIS IS ONE OF ST. CLAIR'S SONS OF LIBERTY. HE'S STILL ALIVE!
NOT FOR LONG.
I-uh-suh-sorry, Isa-a-bel.

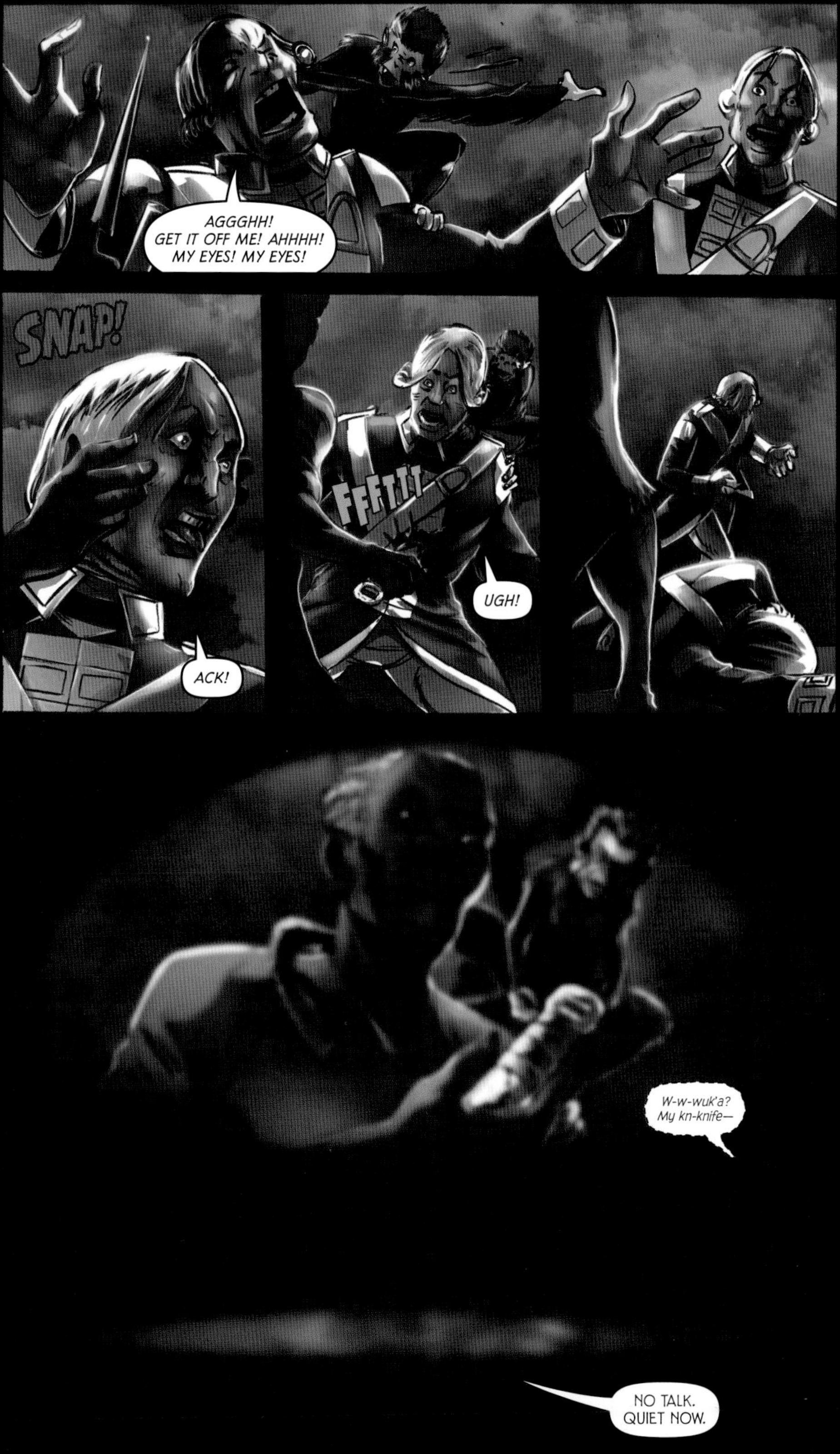
AGGGHH!
GET IT OFF ME! AHHHH!
MY EYES! MY EYES!
SNAP!
ACK!
FFFTTT
UGH!
W-w-wuk'a?
My kn-knife—
NO TALK.
QUIET NOW.

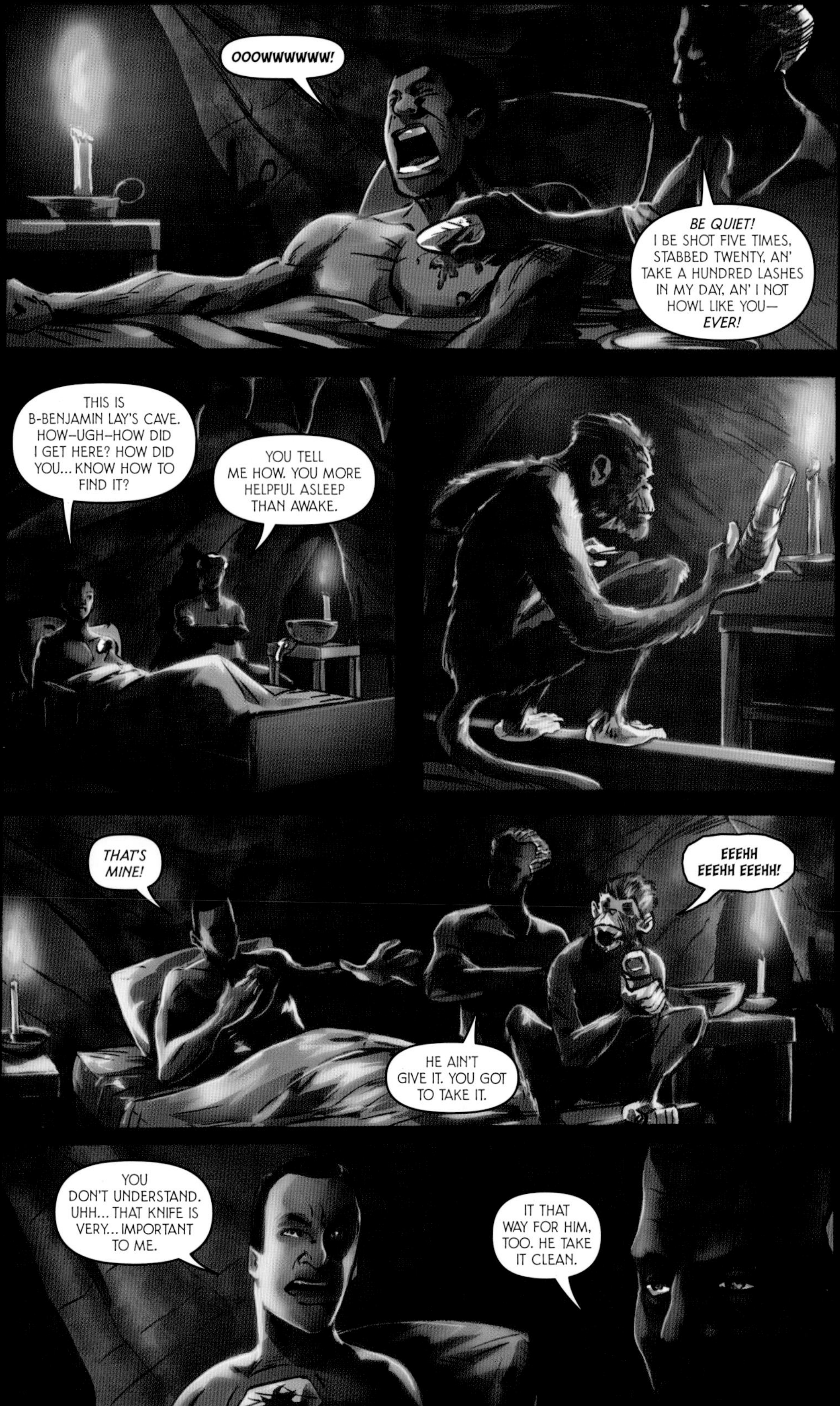
OOOWWWWWW!
BE QUIET! I BE SHOT FIVE TIMES, STABBED TWENTY, AN' TAKE A HUNDRED LASHES IN MY DAY, AN' I NOT HOWL LIKE YOU—EVER!
THIS IS B-BENJAMIN LAY'S CAVE. HOW—UGH—HOW DID I GET HERE? HOW DID YOU... KNOW HOW TO FIND IT?
YOU TELL ME HOW. YOU MORE HELPFUL ASLEEP THAN AWAKE.
THAT'S MINE!
EEEHH EEEHH EEEHH!
HE AIN'T GIVE IT. YOU GOT TO TAKE IT.
YOU DON'T UNDERSTAND. UHH... THAT KNIFE IS VERY... IMPORTANT TO ME.
IT THAT WAY FOR HIM, TOO. HE TAKE IT CLEAN.

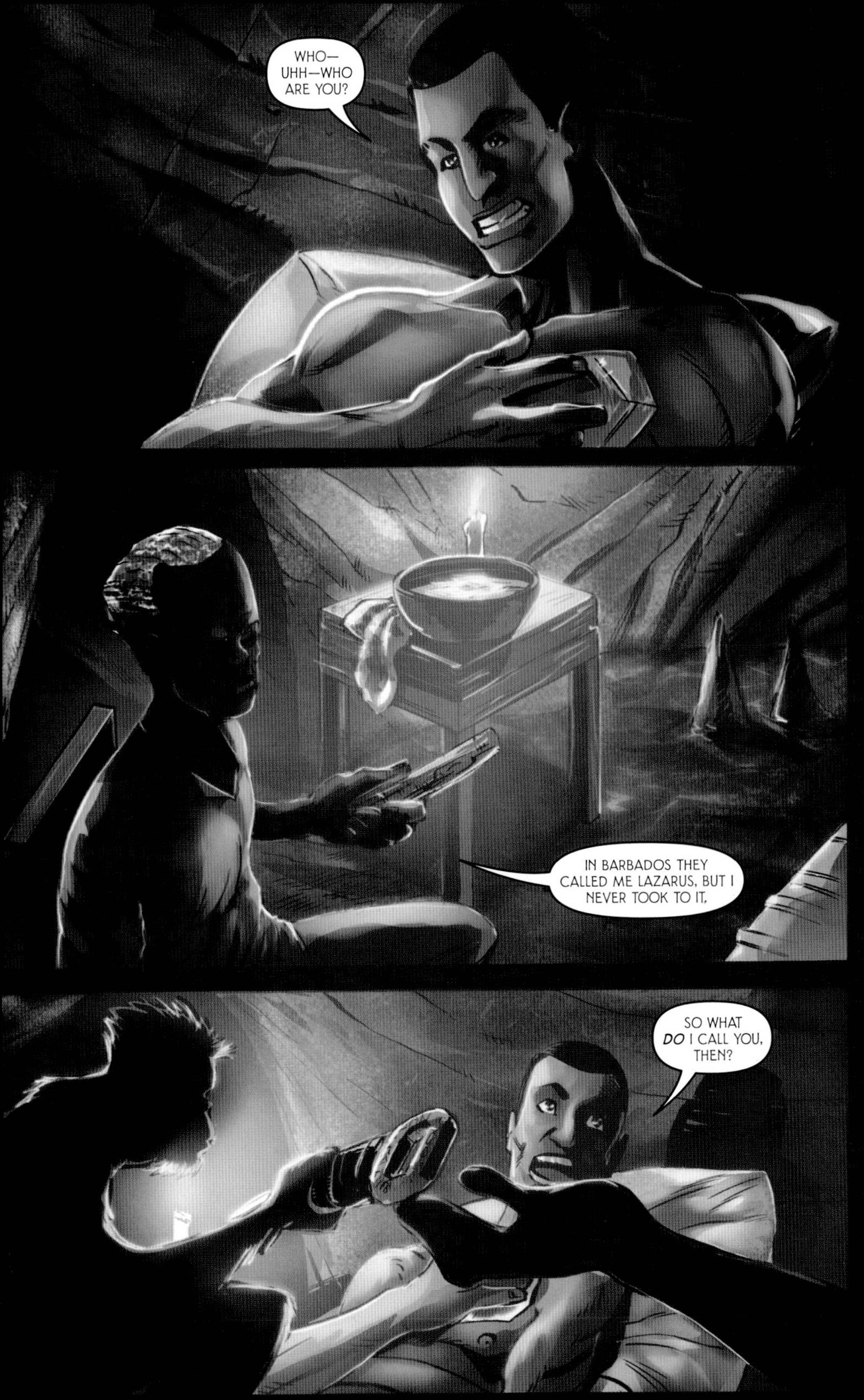
WHO—
UHH—WHO
ARE YOU?
IN BARBADOS THEY CALLED ME LAZARUS, BUT I NEVER TOOK TO IT.
SO WHAT *DO* I CALL YOU, THEN?

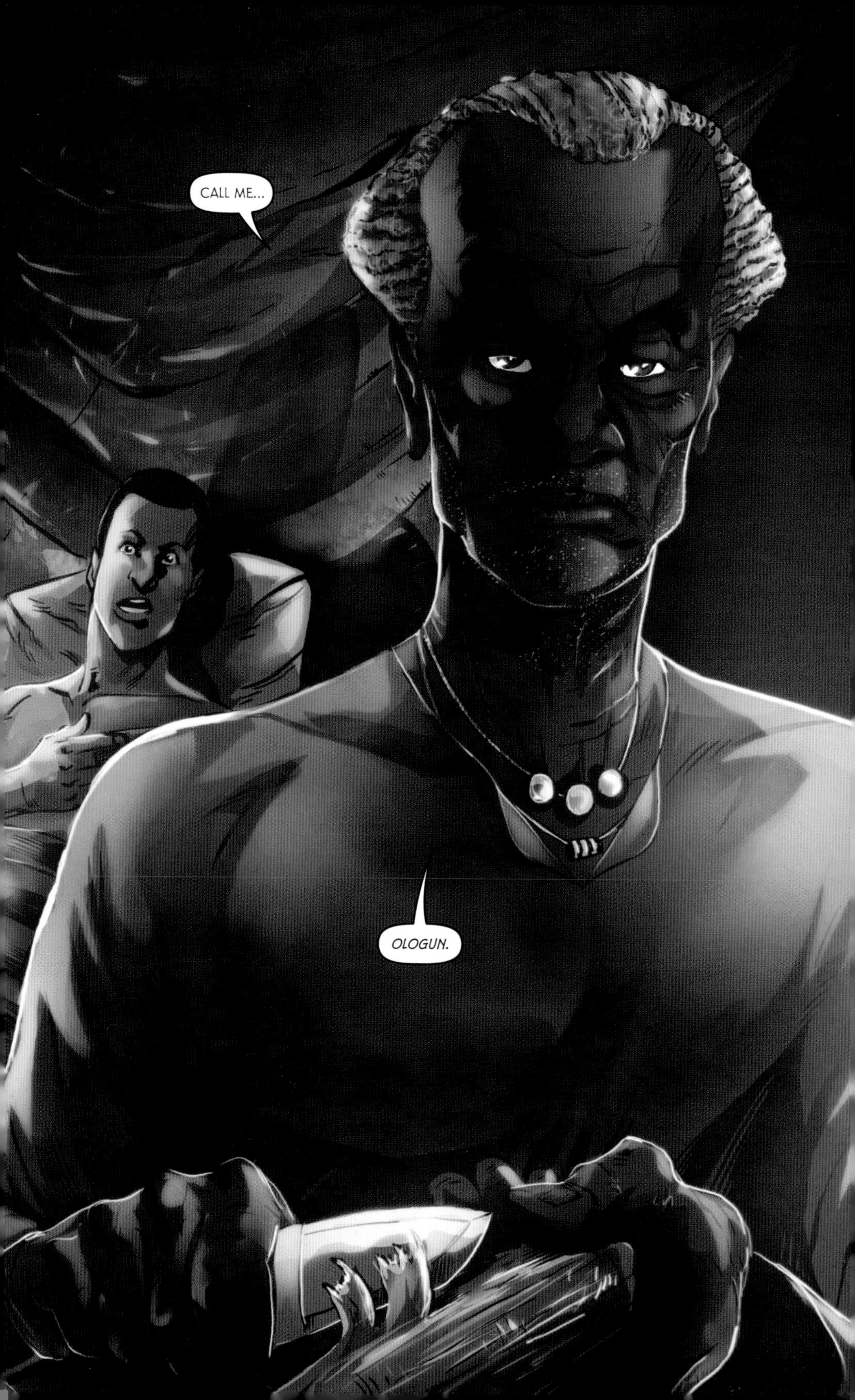
CALL ME...
OLOGUN.

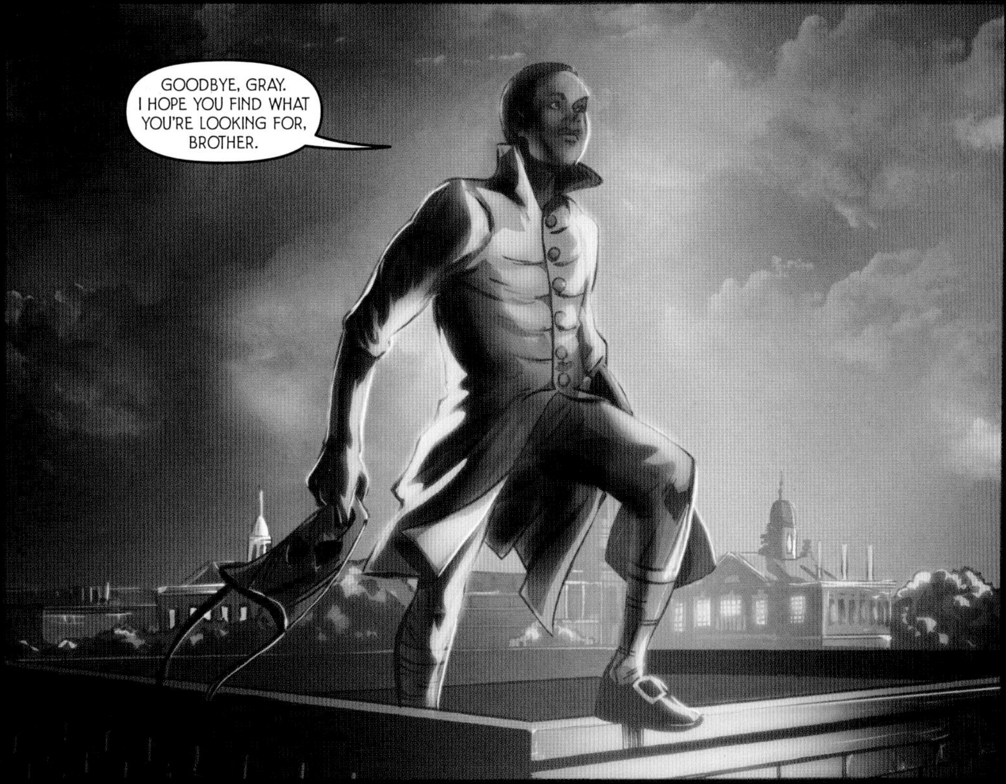
GOODBYE, GRAY. I HOPE YOU FIND WHAT YOU'RE LOOKING FOR, BROTHER.

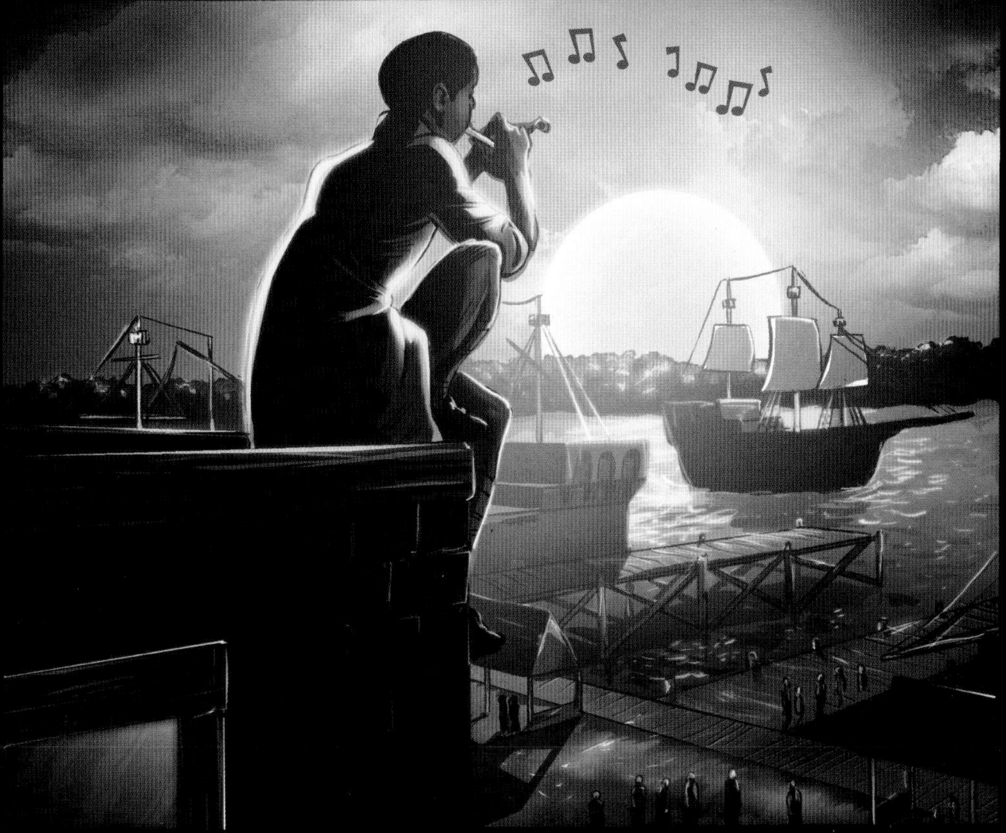

AUTHORS' NOTE

While some settings, characters, and events in this series are drawn from history, we have taken extensive liberties in the interest of crafting an exciting story. To learn more about the book's facts, fictions, and conjectures—and much more behind-the-scenes information—visit thesonsoflibertybooks.com.

ACKNOWLEDGMENTS

The Lagos brothers wish to thank the following for their support, hard work, friendship, and love over the years: Mr. Cal Hunter, Wes Reid, Jill Grinberg Literary Management, Steve Walker, Oren Kramek, Ryan Roman, Chris Dickey, Schuyler Hooke, Nick Eliopulos, Heather Palisi, Ellice Lee, and the Random House copyediting and production teams.

Dear friends: Neal and Rene Keeney, Christine Fullerton-Reid, Jason Michalski, Billy and Sue Horak, Neil Surgi of Bookland, Glen Ackerman, and Jefferson Lima Jr.

And our loved ones: Alexander's wife, Cristi Lee, and son, Attis Quinn; Joseph's wife, Laura, daughter, Sophie, and sons, Alex and Liam; Marisa and Mark Tucker; Carson Tucker; Jennifer and Cody Tackett; the Lagos family of Montevideo, Uruguay; and, most importantly, Mamá y Papá.

Steve Walker thanks his friends and family for their support, and Holly, who is my everything.

Oren Kramek dedicates his work on this book to his loved ones, family, and friends.